Lucy Mac
Goes Back Home

A Romantic Comedy
By
Julie Butterfield

For My Dad

Other books
by Julie Butterfield

Did I Mention I Won the Lottery?

Google Your Husband Back

Did I Mention I Was Getting Married?

Eve's Christmas

Agony Auntics

Isabelle Darby Cosy Village Mysteries:-

Deadly Whispers in Lower Dimblebrook

Wilful Changes – coming soon!

Chapter 1

'You want me to do what?'

Will's eyes were wide with alarm as he sat opposite Lucy at the kitchen table.

'Swap places, just for a while. On a temporary basis,' she added soothingly. 'Until you find the right job and we get back on our feet.'

'And by swapping places you mean …?'

'You stay at home and look after the children and I go back to work.'

Will's fingers drummed anxiously on the table. 'But what happens when I get another job?'

'Then we'll both have a job and we can decide what to do for the best.'

'For the best?'

'Yes. I can carry on working full time,' Lucy's stomach did a flip at the thought of returning to the workplace, picking up where she had left her highly trained reins. 'Or I could switch to part-time, maybe stop altogether and go back to being a full-time mother.' Her stomach settled a little. 'It's an opportunity we can't turn down,' she said firmly.

When Will had come home ashen faced a few weeks earlier and announced that the company he worked for had closed down unexpectedly, Lucy's eyes had been as big as Will's were now. Only that morning she had gasped at the size of the electricity bill and winced a little at the balance on their credit card. Then she had blithely dropped them both on the desk in the study, knowing that despite the amount owing, Will's latest career move and subsequent wage rise was more than enough to cover the payments.

'It's really good timing,' she insisted, trying to coax her husband onside. 'Oh, not the redundancy, but that Rob phoned when he did and asked if I wanted to go back to Simcock and Bright.'

Will looked uncertain. 'I suppose.'

'And he's desperate for me to go back as soon as possible. I'll be starting on Monday. You can look after the children and it means we still have a wage coming in while you find another job.' Her tone was upbeat, her mouth smiling despite the anxiety that was ripping through her chest.

When Rob had phoned the previous day, what Lucy had really wanted to say was, *'Are you mad? I can't possibly return to work. I'm a mother now. I have children to look after.'*

But she was right, it was an opportunity they couldn't turn down.

'So you want me to look after the children?' asked Will, the panic in his eyes starting to ease a little.

'Yes.'

'But just for a while, until I find another job?'

'That's right.' She nodded encouragingly.

'And then I stop looking after them and go back to work?'

'Of course! This is a short-term solution.'

Her throat was aching slightly from the light-hearted tone she'd adopted and the smile was starting to feel a little strained around the edges. She watched Will as he mulled over the suggestion. His deep blue eyes were thoughtful, his dark, almost black hair falling onto his forehead as he stared at the table. Lucy could practically see the cogs whirring.

'And you're alright about this?' he asked, his eyes meeting hers.

The smile stretched into a slightly manic grin. 'Of course I am!' she lied.

She remembered when she had announced her pregnancy to their friends and her naïve assurance that she would soon be back at work, that she wasn't meant to be a stay at home mum. She hadn't been able to envisage a life without the office and the adrenalin rush of signing up a new client. But that was before the arrival of Emily and the moment she held her daughter's tiny, soft body in her arms for the first time and looked into her eyes, she couldn't imagine leaving her for a moment, let alone so she could return to the cut and thrust world of marketing. But Rob's offer was too good to miss and they needed some help from somewhere to survive the crash of Will's company.

Will was still thinking.

'I always said I would go back to work,' reminded Lucy.

'I thought you'd gone off the idea. You seem happy at home.'

Oh, she was. Perfectly happy. She had no desire whatsoever to return to the office.

'Maybe I'll realise I've missed it and want to carry on working.'

The suggestion sounded ridiculous, even to Lucy's ears. She had made no pretence of wanting to return to her job over the last four years. She loved every minute she spent with her babies, even when she was complaining about how tiring it was looking after two small children.

Will looked at her doubtfully. 'Really?'

'Maybe. At least it will give me a chance to find out. And if I think it was a mistake, when you get another job I'll leave.'

It sounded simple and Lucy relaxed a little. Maybe it would only be for a few weeks. She would be back home looking after her children in no time at all. Will was watching her and she gave him a confident smile, trying to convince them both it was a good idea and with a small shrug of his shoulders he nodded.

'Okay. Sounds like a plan.'

He left the table to flick on the kettle, whistling softly and Lucy stared at his back.

'You're okay with the idea?' She realised she had been secretly hoping he would say absolutely not, that they could cope without a wage for a little while and Lucy's place was at home, with their children.

'Sure. Why not?' He reached up to pull down the biscuit tin from where Lucy kept it, just out of her reach to avoid accidental biscuit moments. She had to pull out the small stool to reach the tin, which gave her a few extra seconds to consider the consequences of the casual addition of a biscuit to her cup of tea and her waistline. There was a small mark on the floor made by the constant sliding of the stool from its home to the biscuit cupboard.

'Well, it's not easy looking after two small children. I thought you might be worried about taking it on board full time.'

Will put her favourite mug on the table along with the biscuit tin. He clearly didn't understand the rule of only taking the number you had deemed acceptable. Leaving the tin within easy reach meant more biscuits could be nibbled without going through the thought process once more.

'Yeah, but it's not the same as a real job is it?'

He turned his back, reaching for his mug and Lucy stared open-mouthed. 'Not a real job?'

'Oh, I know it's hard, they run you ragged, you're on your feet all day and it's really tiring,' Will said hastily. 'What I mean is, it's not quite the same as going into the office on a daily basis, the pressure, the stress, dealing with targets and all sorts of problems you weren't expecting. Staying at home looking after children has got to be easier.'

Lucy dunked her biscuit in her tea and gazed at him thoughtfully. 'You think so?'

'Yes. It can't be as difficult as going to work, can it?'

He suddenly looked less sure of himself and for a moment Lucy almost told him. Told him about the relentless grind, the sheer impossibility of getting two seconds to yourself in a day which was full of nothing but pressure, targets and problems. Maybe she should tell him about the planning needed to get two small children up and fed and dressed in time to take Emily to nursery school and get Harry back in the house before he had a complete meltdown because it was one minute past his allocated nap time. The cleaning and washing she had to fit in before it was time to collect Emily and then provide a lunch acceptable to them both, which was akin to brokering peace in the Middle East, followed by more cleaning and washing plus shopping and preparing the evening meal and every other job that needed to be done in between. The longing to be able to go to the bathroom completely by herself and shut out the rest of the world, without having Harry scratching at the door and chattering away and Emily peering underneath the gap asking if she had finished. The almost overwhelming need to have an occasional five minutes of complete and utter peace and solitude. Of course, the result of her hard work was that when Will arrived home his children were bathed, content and happy to cuddle him on the settee in adorable, sleepy mode, while Lucy escaped to the kitchen, holding onto the kitchen work surface for support and drinking wine straight from the bottle.

'It's not the same as going to work,' she eventually answered, having discarded the truth as an option.

'It could be fun actually,' Will said, nodding his head positively.

'Fun! You think so?'

'Absolutely! And it will give me a chance to get to know them a little bit better. I regret not getting home until their bedtime during the week.'

Lucy sipped her tea. 'You'll certainly be able to spend lots of time together,' she agreed.

'Quality time.'

'Mm.'

'It's actually a great idea Lucy. It solves a problem and I think I might enjoy it.'

Lucy took a bite of her biscuit. She really ought to warn him, give him some idea about just how difficult he was going to find this.

'It's all about organisation you see,' he carried on. 'You need to treat it like a job, know what's expected, map out your day, allow a little contingency time for emergencies and stick to the plan.' He grinned, looking pleased with himself. 'I'm not saying you're disorganised,' he added generously. 'I just think that a more business-like approach could make it a lot easier.'

Or there again, maybe she would just let him find out for himself she decided, taking more biscuits and lining them up on the table. When she had been a high-flying marketing account manager in the heart of Leeds, she'd rarely had time for lunch and if she did it would be a quick meeting over sushi and a skinny latte. Everyone was obsessed with their weight or their cholesterol level or trying out a new diet that only allowed them to eat solids every other Thursday. It had been easy to keep her slender figure in shape. Now there was the constant temptation of biscuits and cakes and left-over fish fingers and Lucy's day had become one long struggle against the comfort offered by food. She would probably lose a stone in her first week back at work. She may be terrified at the thought of returning to an office where the occupants hadn't spent the last four years changing dirty nappies and singing nursery rhymes long after the children had gone to bed, but it would undoubtedly be good for her waistline.

'You're probably right,' she said, working her way through the biscuits. 'I've probably been doing it all wrong.'

Will gave her a wary look but Lucy was engrossed in her biscuits. Had he been a tad insensitive he wondered?

'You do a wonderful job,' he said. 'A really wonderful job.'

'But you think you might do better?'

'No! Not better! Definitely not better!' He clearly had been insensitive. 'Not at all. I didn't mean that. Just, differently.'

'It's okay.' Lucy's fingers were sliding back towards the biscuit tin. 'You think you can be more organised and maybe you can.'

Will winced. 'I didn't mean …'

'No, really it's okay. I'm going back to work and you'll be in charge of the children for a while so let's hope that you're right and it's all just about organisation,' and with another handful of biscuits, Lucy left the kitchen, smiling despite a rather frosty look in her eyes.

Will chewed on his lip. He had a feeling he may have said the wrong thing. He hated the thought of Lucy going back to work if she didn't want to, even temporarily. But it was a definite solution to their crisis. And he was undoubtedly getting the better deal. Lucy would be leaving the house each day to fight her way through the morning commute and spend the day dealing with difficult clients and unreasonable demands. He would be staying at home and looking after his children. And despite what Lucy may say, he didn't think that sounded very hard at all.

Chapter 2

Leaving Will to entertain Emily and Harry, it would be good practice after all, Lucy disappeared upstairs where she sank onto the end of the bed, nibbling on her nails. She'd decided it wasn't a good idea to let Will know that the very idea of returning to work left her feeling nauseous, or that her breathing became difficult at the thought of walking back into the office she had left four years earlier.

Lucy Mathers, Account Manager, had loved her job. Ruthless and determined, she had sailed into meetings in her power suits and sky-high shoes and relished the confrontation and her ability to overcome every obstacle and get a signature on the bottom line. She had been tough, uncompromising and able to negotiate any deal. But that was a lifetime ago, when Lucy had been a very different person.

Now she was Lucy Mathers, housewife and mother. She spent her days looking after small children and cleaning. The thought of going head to head in a debate over funding and resource allocation made her feel quite dizzy and remembering how single-minded and determined she used to be left her limp with exhaustion. She wasn't capable of going back to Simcock and Bright. What on earth had possessed her to even suggest such a ludicrous thing? These days she couldn't even persuade Emily to eat her crusts, how could she expect to talk round a recalcitrant client?

Her stomach was a knot of anxiety and there was a loud humming in her ears, which she suspected might be her brain going into overdrive before she realised it was Alice ringing on the mobile which was clutched in Lucy's rather sweaty hand.

'You're coming back to work?'

'Yes. Will is going to look after the children until he finds a new job. I start on Monday.'

Lucy held the phone away from her ear as a deafening squeal came down the line.

'Oh my God, that's fantastic! Amazing! I'm so happy. Are you excited?'

'Yes.'

'Really excited?'

'Really.'

'That's wonderful news, Lucy!'

'Yes. Wonderful.'

There was a pause.

'What's wrong?'

'What do you mean?'

'I mean what's wrong? You're not excited, not at all. I know you very well Lucy Mathers. I've known you for a long, long time and that is not your excited voice. So, what's wrong?'

Lucy caught sight of herself in the large oak framed mirror on the wall. She looked pale. And frightened.

'What if I can't do it anymore?' she whispered.

'Do what?'

'You know, the job,'

'What on earth are you talking about? Why wouldn't you be able to do it?'

Because, thought Lucy, she'd spent the last four years being a mother. She had devoted herself to bringing up two adorable children and that didn't need a killer instinct, a ruthless edge and a nose for a good deal. It needed love and endless patience. If she were to write a new CV today, her key skills would be that she knew all the words to every song in Frozen, could change a nappy with only one hand and that she always had a packet of baby wipes in her pocket, ready to deal with any emergency.

'I don't know. I've been out of the office for so long, maybe it's not as easy as it sounds coming back and picking up as though the last four years hadn't happened.'

'But you were the best. That's why Rob wants you back, because you were the golden girl of the whole operation. You don't stop being good at your job because you've had children.'

Lucy sighed down the phone. 'Don't you?'

'Don't you want to come back?' Alice's voice was gentle and for a moment Lucy felt the sting of tears in her eyes.

'No. Yes. Sort of.'

'What did Will say?'

'He thinks it's a good idea and it will be easy looking after the kids full time.'

Alice snorted. 'He's in for a rude awakening!'

'He said it's all about organisation and time management.' Lucy smiled. 'It's almost worth going back to work to watch him discover just how hard it is looking after two small children.'

'Have you told him you're worried about coming back?'

Lucy sighed again. 'No,' she said reluctantly.

'Why not?'

Because he would be devastated if he knew how worried she was. Because he was already devastated at losing his job and being in a position where Lucy had to consider returning to work. Because she had seen him looking through the credit card statement a few nights earlier with a worried crease knitting his eyebrows together. Because when he had taken his new job with its wonderful salary, she had been the one who had insisted that they finally redo the kitchen, which formed a large part of the credit card balance that was now giving them both sleepless nights. Because she loved him.

'He's already worried enough about finding another job. I don't want him worried about me as well.'

'Maybe he'll get another job really quickly and you can change your mind about coming back,' suggested Alice.

'I don't think so, jobs are few and far between in his field. We don't want to move house so that means finding a job close by, which is even more difficult.'

'What is it he does again? Something to do with bodies?'

Lucy laughed. 'Forensic accountant. No bodies.'

'Right,' Alice sounded vague. 'Well, I'm sure he'll get a job soon. But stop worrying. Everyone is really looking forward to you coming back and you'll soon be back in the swing of it all. I'll be here to help you and Rob is so excited. You can do it, Lucy, really you can.'

Could she, wondered Lucy as they said goodbye. Could she clear the baby mush from her brain and pick up where she had left off?

Dropping the phone back onto the bed she knelt down in front of the wardrobe, digging deep until her fingers found the edges of the shoe box. Pulling it free she sat back down and slipped off the lid to gaze inside. They were still there, waiting for her. She had placed them carefully and lovingly in the box when Emily was three days old and Lucy had found them on the floor of the spare room, buried beneath the chaos of her last day of work which had turned into her first day of motherhood. Wrapping them in tissue, she had whispered that she would be back for them one day. Her glorious, appallingly expensive, bright red Christian Louboutin shoes. The first time she had slipped them on she knew they had to be hers. Even in the sale she had baulked at the price, but she had still bought them. They had been on her feet the day she signed up McCarthy and McCarthy, the single most lucrative account her company had ever won. They had travelled to London with her when she had sailed in to rescue a dispirited Riddlington & Co who were about to defect to a competitor. She had even squeezed them onto her swollen and protesting feet the day she had delivered her final presentation, which had resulted in a new multi-million-pound account for Simcock and Bright. 9 months pregnant, her stomach so large she had to sit a foot away from the board room table and unable to stand upright for more than 30 seconds in the ridiculously high shoes, she had kept the negotiations going even as she had felt her waters break in her large, executive black leather chair. Only when agreement was reached and contracts signed, had she leant forward and asked Alice in a calm voice to phone for a taxi and get hold of Will as quickly as possible.

Rob had been dining out on the story ever since. When he'd had one too many glasses of wine, he would tell all and sundry that Lucy Mathers was the consummate professional, not even childbirth had stopped her from closing the deal. He had told Lucy that her job would be waiting for her when she decided to return, that there would always be a desk for her at Simcock and Bright. In reality, someone called Sarah was sitting at Lucy's desk within hours of Lucy giving birth, albeit not in Lucy's chair which was still drying out. Sarah had been followed by Craig, neither of whom appeared to have the qualities that Rob was looking for.

Then six months ago Grant Cassidy had arrived and Rob had been looking very pleased with himself ever since. 'Got that edge that you used to have darling,' he'd told Lucy. 'He's at the top of his game, just like you used to be,' he had said happily. 'No account he can't close, just like you in the old days.'

And that was when her crisis of confidence had arrived. Because Lucy wasn't at the top of her game anymore. She had no edge, that had remained in the office when she'd departed in the direction of the maternity wing. These days all she really wanted was to spend the day with her children. The work may be harder, the days much longer, but as she hugged their warm little bodies at the end of the day and watched them drift off to sleep, the rewards were far greater and gave Lucy a bigger thrill than her work ever had.

Rob may have taken a liking to Grant but Alice was not a fan. 'Arrogant, misogynistic bastard,' she had reported. 'Thinks he's God's gift, to marketing and to women. Swans around the office in his fancy suits and silk ties. Can't stand the man. You need to come back and put him in his place, Lucy. And quickly, before his head gets too big to fit through the door.'

Maybe his sharp suits and silk ties were the equivalent of her beautiful shoes, thought Lucy. Did he fasten his jacket each morning and give a silent salute to the mirror because he looked the part?

'Is he good at his job?' she'd asked Alice a few weeks earlier as they sat in their favourite restaurant having a catch up with Alice taking out her anger on a bottle of wine.

'Well he's okay I suppose,' had been the reluctant reply. 'Bit like you used to be. Can be very persuasive and all the clients love him.'

There was that word, *used* to be. Lucy was now very definitely in the past tense.

'Rob seems to rate him,' mused Lucy.

'All Rob cares about is the bottom line. He loves anybody who signs up new accounts.'

'Well that is sort of the point,' Lucy had said waving over the waiter to supply more wine. She had taken too long emptying her glass and Alice had demolished the bottle.

'Yes. I know,' Alice had said crossly. 'But there are ways and means and I don't like his ways at all. Just because he's good looking he thinks everybody should do whatever he wants.'

'He's good looking?'

'Well, if you like that sort of thing.'

'What sort of thing?'

Lucy had asked curiously.

'Smooth and smarmy. Hair always combed and tie always straight.'

They sounded like good qualities to Lucy but she didn't argue.

'And his eyes!' slurred Alice.

'What's wrong with them?'

'Nothing. They just look at you, you know. All blue and … like blue eyes.'

'I thought you liked men with blue eyes?'

'I do. But his are, well really blue.'

Lucy waited for more of an explanation but Alice just topped up her glass again.

'So, what are his ways? The ones you don't like?'

'He gets everything he asks for!'

'If he's signing up new clients, Rob will be happy to let him have what he wants. It's the way Rob operates,' Lucy had suggested reasonably.

'Well, I don't like the way he goes about it. Even when he does smile.'

'Smile?'

'Yeah. He does have a nice smile,' Alice had admitted. 'Well quite nice. If I didn't hate him, I might like his smile. And his eyes. If they weren't so blue, I might like them as well. A little bit.'

Lucy was beginning to suspect that Alice didn't hold Grant Cassidy in quite the contempt she claimed but as Alice worked her way to the bottom of the second bottle, her explanations became harder to follow and Lucy ended the evening none the wiser about Grant's ways and means. But he had achieved a monumental status in Lucy's eyes. He was the one who had taken her position. He was now at the top of the food chain at Simcock and Bright, the one with the silk ties that declared his status in the office. Last year, when the Christmas party had gotten underway and the wine had started to flow, according to Alice it was Grant that had been the subject of Rob's tales of daring deeds and clients won with single-minded determination. He was Lucy's nemesis, the one she would be compared to when she returned. What would they say, she wondered?

'Oh that's Lucy, she used to be as good as Grant but she left to have babies and now … well it's never the same when they come back to work is it?'

And now she would have to go back to work and face Grant, with his silk ties, ridiculously blue eyes and beautifully combed hair and try and remember what had made her so very good at her job. She needed to become the Lucy she had once been.

Sliding the shoes out of the box, she laid them reverently on the floor before pulling off her woolly socks and wriggling her toes in anticipation. Her foot disappeared into the shiny red leather, stopping halfway down. Frowning she slipped the shoe off and checked to see if she had left some tissue tucked into the toe. Nothing. Putting the shoe back on the floor she pushed a little harder, squeezing her toes together and grunting until her foot was finally forced in. She gasped in pain. Oh my God, she thought, it was like a scene from Cinderella, and she must be one of the ugly sisters because this was far from the perfect fit. Since leaving work she had worn nothing more glamourous than a patent leather loafer. The majority of her day was spent in socks and trainers, or her slippers that looked like little rabbits and came past her ankle. Not exactly Louboutins but far more practical. Forcing the other foot in, Lucy stood up, swaying as she perched atop the four-inch heel. She felt slightly nauseous as she gazed down at the floor. Her toes were crammed uncomfortably together and walking was agony. What on earth had happened to her feet, she wondered in horror? They seemed to have grown half a size. Did pregnancy do that? Was this a side effect no-one admitted to, sudden and catastrophic growth of the feet? Wincing in pain, Lucy walked around the bedroom a few times, gasping in agony at every step. Good grief, she'd worn these on the very day she gave birth, when her stomach had reached everything five minutes before she had. Why would they let her down now? Unable to take the pain any longer she sank on the bed, pulling them off as her toes exploded outwards in relief.

This was not a good sign. Maybe it wasn't just the Louboutins that were no longer a good fit, maybe Lucy simply wasn't ready to return to work. What if her killer instinct had left along with her ability to wear stilettos? The panic returned. Her breathing was coming in short, painful bursts and her heart was drumming against her ribs. She couldn't do this; she would have to tell Will that she had made a mistake even suggesting she should go back to work. She would explain that her shoes didn't fit her any more, he would understand.

But then she thought of the credit card bill, the electricity bill, the mortgage payments and sundry other envelopes piled high on the desk and she closed her eyes. With a groan, she put her shoebox away. She may not be wearing her Louboutins on Monday when she returned to Simcock and Bright but return she must.

Chapter 3

On Monday morning, the alarm shrieked out its wake-up call and Lucy's eyes flew open as she threw out her hand to stop the noise. Today was the day. Today, Lucy Mathers was going back to work and with her stomach a knot of anxiety she lay staring at the ceiling, her hand still clutching the clock as Will remained unmoving beside her. She wondered if she could pretend that she hadn't heard its shrill demand. She would explain to Will that they had both slept through the alarm and she had missed her opportunity. Of course, she couldn't turn up late, not on her first day. It was a shame but there it was, she would have to forget about going back to Simcock and Bright.

Will stirred, mumbling something and Lucy could hear the sound of the children waking up ready to start their day. The weekend had been spent preparing for this moment. Going through her wardrobe, she had been shocked by the sheer volume of outfits where the zip no longer made its way to the top before becoming embedded in the soft rolls of Lucy's stomach. She had discarded the Louboutins, there was no way she could spend an entire day in those heels, not just yet and much to Will's amusement she had spent most of Sunday walking around the house in shoes rather than trainers, trying to get used to being a few inches taller. She'd gazed longingly at the biscuit tin but left it out of reach in the hope that she might lose half a stone before Monday morning and she had spent much of the day shaking with fear, which she had told an anxious Will was simply the excitement of returning to a job she had loved.

Train timetables had been produced and pored over and Lucy had finally settled on the 8:08 from Horsforth which would get her into Leeds at 8:24, leaving ample time for the 10-minute walk to the Simcock and Bright office in Park Square. But she had spent the night caught in a dream where the train was late, or even worse just didn't appear and she was forced to run from the station arriving with sweat dripping from her nose and everyone staring at their watches and tutting in disapproval. Perhaps, she thought as she lay in bed, she should catch the earlier train but that would get her into Leeds just after 8:00 and would look desperately early. It also meant that she would need to leave the house in the next 30 minutes and there was still so much to do.

Taking a deep breath, Lucy closed her eyes again. 'You can do this,' she muttered to herself. 'You can do this,' and then threw back the covers with such energy that Will gave a little yelp and sat upright in bed.

'What's happening, what's wrong, what …?'

'The children are awake,' advised Lucy who was already throwing on her dressing gown and heading for the bathroom.

'What?'

'Come on Will,' she said brightly. 'It's Monday, back to work day – remember,' and she shot off in the direction of the shower before she gave in to Harry's increasingly loud demands and made herself late by cuddling his warm little body and breathing in his delicious baby smell.

A good hot shower later, her hair washed and fragrant and her hands shaking slightly, Lucy got dressed. Despite her abstinence from the biscuit tin she didn't appear to have lost any weight over the weekend but breathing in deeply and grunting a great deal, she managed to fasten a teal coloured skirt before slipping on an ivory silk blouse, not tucked in to show off the enviable waist she'd once had, but left to hang over the waistband and hopefully hide the muffin top that was wobbling alarmingly. The matching jacket was long enough to hide the slight wrinkles where her skirt stretched tightly over her bottom, clinging to her every curve, and she slipped her feet into a pair of black heels, hoping the couple of extra inches would give the impression of a willowy figure. She turned to the mirror, the shoes didn't seem to have made any discernible difference, although they pinched Lucy's toes and pulling a face at her reflection, she grabbed her bag and wobbled down the stairs. She really couldn't believe she had worn shoes this high every day of her working life. She felt like a new born giraffe swaying in the breeze as she negotiated the steps.

In the kitchen Will still looked half asleep as he struggled with breakfast.

'I put everything out last night,' Lucy said. 'Look.'

On the surface was a selection of cereals complete with Post-it notes advising Will which was Emily's favourite followed by her second favourite, which she might choose depending on the mood of the day. Harry's favourite was also listed together with an explanation that sometimes he said cornflakes but he didn't actually like cornflakes, he meant porridge which he couldn't say very well and had taken to describing as cornflakes. Both children were sitting at the table looking mutinous at the plate of toast Will had placed in front of them.

'I thought they liked toast?' Will asked, baffled as he examined the mountain of cereal boxes.

'No. You like toast. They like cereal.'

'But Harry loves toast. I know he does because I've seen him eat toast fingers!'

'He likes toast fingers in the afternoon but not a slice of toast in the morning,' shouted Lucy from the utility room where she was hurling clothes into the washing machine. She put on a washing cycle every morning to avoid the laundry basket exploding from overuse. If the weather co-operated, she hung it out to dry after taking Emily to nursery and putting Harry down for a nap and if not, she had to remember to drag it out of the washer and throw it into the tumble dryer.

Dashing back into the kitchen she took Will by the hand and led him upstairs into Emily's bedroom.

'These are Emily's clothes for the day,' she explained. 'And Harry's are on the top of his drawers.'

Will rubbed his eyes. He was used to being up and out of the house before the children got dressed during the week and on a weekend, their squirming little bodies would climb into bed with Lucy and Will for a cuddle before Lucy led them out of the bedroom with promises of games and stories, leaving Will to catch up on some much needed sleep. She had come to realise that Will had no idea how the children came to be dressed and ready for their day each morning.

He was staring at the pile of clothes.

'Do you understand?' Lucy asked loudly and slowly. 'These are the children's clothes, the clothes you are going to place on our children.'

'I get it! I know how to dress children.' He pulled his arm away from Lucy's tight grasp. 'Stop worrying. I can manage. It's not like I've never been left alone with them before.'

Lucy grimaced. Will had looked after the children on many occasions, when Lucy decided on an afternoon in Leeds by herself or met friends for a meal and a drink. There had even once been an entire weekend when Lucy had joined a handful of friends at a spa. She had arrived home to find both Harry and Emily happy, fed and comfortable as they lay on the settee in Will's arms watching TV as their father slept. They were wearing the same clothes Lucy had dressed them in the morning she'd left, Harry had chocolate smeared in his baby curls and Emily had a hole in her woollen tights that she had made larger by stuffing toys inside and using as an impromptu storage space until she could hardly walk for the huge collection of random objects that stuck to one side of her leg like a hideous growth.

'I know,' Lucy said soothingly. 'I'm just making sure you know where everything is.'

Will stopped scowling and swept her into his arms planting a kiss on her mouth. 'Stop worrying about me and just concentrate on yourself,' he demanded. 'Are you ready?'

Of course she was ready, thought Lucy. She'd had everything sorted and laid out since Saturday evening. Her bag had been emptied of toddler paraphernalia such as the odd sock, baby wipes, a rather crusty bib, Harry's favourite book and Emily's crayons. Before the arrival of her children, Lucy's bag had been a shrine to lipsticks and perfume along with scented tissues and always a spare pair of tights and it gave her a small thrill to look inside now and see that she had gone full circle.

Everything was ready, everything except for Lucy herself and the nerves in her stomach were literally ricocheting against her sides.

'Ready as I'll ever be,' she answered nervously and Will drew her back for another kiss, a gentle, lingering kiss. 'You'll smash it Lucy. I know you will.'

Refusing to let herself cry, it would mean another five minutes with the mascara and Lucy was getting perilously close to departure time, she sniffed and nodded, blinking rapidly to disperse the tears.

'Thank you, but you will remember the clothes won't you Will?' she added anxiously as he groaned and turned her back in the direction of the staircase.

'I've written down the times for nursery,' she said over her shoulder as she tottered unsteadily down the steps, hanging onto the handrail. 'Don't be late because you'll get a black mark and if you get too many black marks during the term, they may not let Emily back.'

'What! It's a nursey school not a military academy! They can't do that.'

'It's one of the most oversubscribed nursery schools in the area and they have a waiting list a mile long. They can do what they like, so please don't be late.'

Back in the kitchen Lucy dropped a kiss on Harry's head, clenching her fists against the sudden longing to sweep him into her arms and forget about the whole silly business of going back to work. She should stay at home with her babies. She should be dashing to nursery, anxious about getting a black mark, jogging back home before Harry started voicing his disapproval. She should be washing and cleaning and shopping and complaining about how tired she was as she played with Emily and pretended for the thousandth time to be Olaf as Emily danced around the room in her Elsa costume. Whatever was she thinking? Going back to work was a ridiculous idea. She couldn't do it. Panic filled her and she caught her breath but Will was there, reaching out to grab her hand and squeeze it gently.

'You can do it Lucy.'

Breathing deeply, Lucy nodded, trying to be as confident as Will. 'Of course,' she said brightly. 'Of course I can.'

'Do you want me to run you to the station?'

'No. You haven't got time and I need to get used to walking there.' Although the idea of walking anywhere in her shoes made Lucy's toes cry out in alarm.

'I've got plenty of time,' said Will easily. 'It's your first day. Let me drive you.'

'You need to get the children washed and dressed and get Emily to nursery. You haven't really got that much time.' Lucy looked at the clock anxiously. 'Do you want me to get Emily ready, she takes so long putting everything in her bag. I can get started and …'

'I have it all under control Lucy darling. Stop worrying.'

Lucy looked round the kitchen at the discarded cereal packets, at Harry's sweet face covered in butter and the toast in his hair. Emily had upended the small backpack she took to nursery and was inspecting the contents and Lucy could see one of her daughter's shoes by the door which made her worry about the location of the other shoe. Will didn't seem to understand the time it took to remove the detritus of breakfast and get them ready for the day ahead.

'Are you sure you can do this Will?' she blurted out anxiously. 'Do you think you can cope?'

Will grabbed a flannel, aiming it at Harry's bobbing face. 'Yes! I'm looking after two children, *my* children. It's a bit insulting that you think I can't cope,' he sniffed, managing to wipe half of Harry's face before losing his grip and letting the toddler shoot under the kitchen table.

'But …'

'But nothing. I have been listening Luce, I've written down everything we need to do today, I know where we need to be and what time. I've even put it all on a spreadsheet and set alarms on my phone so I don't forget anything.'

'A spreadsheet?'

'Yes. I told you, I'm treating this like a job. I've allocated timings for everything. It's all organised.' He looked pleased with himself as he looked round to see where Harry had disappeared to.

'Right. Well if you're sure,' said Lucy doubtfully.

'Absolutely sure.'

'Okay. I've made some lunch and put it in the fridge. Harry can be really fussy and Emily is usually good but she has a thing about green at the moment and she doesn't like anything green on her plate.'

'Green? Nothing green?'

'Nothing. But don't worry it won't last because last week it was orange, which is lucky because that only really covered carrots and butternut squash. We had a week where it was brown and that was tricky because I always give her brown bread.'

Lucy was gathering her handbag, checking she had her phone in its depths and an umbrella to hand. She winced at the pain already spreading across her feet and gave herself an anxious look in the mirror. The teal outfit suited her glossy chestnut hair and her soft pink lipstick was still in place. Staring in the mirror she decided she looked okay. Her jacket was doing a fine job of hiding the straining waistband, the shoes, however painful, emphasised her slim calves and the makeup carefully applied that morning did a good job of concealing the dark shadows under her hazel eyes. She looked ready for work, all she had to do now was remember everything that she'd pushed to the back of her overwrought brain over the last four years and walk back into the office ready to show them all that Lucy Mathers was back and raring to go.

'Who knows, she might already be over the green thing,' she said brightly. 'But you might want to put it on your spreadsheet.'

She bent down and wrapped her arms around Emily's tiny body. 'Goodbye my darling. Be good for daddy and I'll see you tonight.'

Watching out for the smears of butter on the floor she knelt down and peered under the table. 'Harry, mummy is going to work, have you got a kiss for me.' A small red fire engine came flying out. 'Oh, your favourite truck! Thank you, Harry, thank you.'

Standing up, she felt panic begin to descend again. She had to get out soon or she simply wouldn't make it. 'Goodbye Will,' she said huskily, leaning over to kiss him as he pulled Harry from under the table.

'Good luck,' he whispered back, their eyes meeting. 'Have a wonderful day and don't give us a second thought. I have it covered.'

Lucy walked to the kitchen door, pausing to look back at her family, Harry now firmly ensconced in Will's arms and Emily happily colouring in at the kitchen table. Feeling the tears pricking at her eyes again she lifted her hand waving manically to distract herself.

'Bye everyone, see you all later,' and closing the door she stepped out into the cold February air and set off to work.

Chapter 4

By the time Lucy had walked the 15-minute journey to the local train station, her feet were on fire. She had adopted a slightly rolling gait to try and keep the pressure off her toes as much as possible but she couldn't help the occasional whimper from escaping.

Grabbing a coffee from the small deli opposite the station, she made her way to the platform and anxiously scanned the information board. Her train was only 3 minutes late and she let out a puff of relieved air. The platform seats were all taken but she leant against a stone pillar which allowed her to take the pressure from one grateful foot at a time. Sipping her latte, she caught sight of herself reflected in the station house window. Despite her somewhat peculiar stance, she looked every inch a successful business woman. Her beloved camel trench coat had been retrieved from the spare room and protected her from the sharp February air. Her chestnut hair sat on her shoulders, glossy and neat, her handbag was slung over her shoulder, one hand held her coffee and the other the soft brown leather briefcase that Will had bought her years earlier, when she had been promoted. Even the shoes looked okay, they gave no hint of the screaming pain inside. She looked the part, although if anyone had been able to see past the soft wool coat, they would have seen Lucy's heart leaping around her chest in nervous anticipation.

The train arrived, thundering down the track and she managed to slip onto a recently vacated seat for which her toes thanked her profusely. The journey seemed to take no time at all to a quaking Lucy and a little over 20 minutes later, she quickly remembered the art of blindly ignoring everyone around her as she pushed and shoved her way through the ticket barrier and was standing outside the Queens Hotel in the centre of Leeds, waiting to cross the busy road. For a moment the nerves eased. She had stood in this very spot almost every day for so many years, it was almost as though no time at all had passed and she was Lucy Mathers, Marketing Account Manager, full of confidence and courage. The wind bit her face and she suspected her nose was glowing red with the cold, but she couldn't help a small smile from escaping. The buzz of the city was all around her; the traffic whizzing by, the faint thunder of trains in the background and the heaving mass of commuters to every side of her, waiting to swarm across the road and then disperse on their own personal rat run. She remembered it all so clearly.

The lights flickered to red and the reluctant traffic stopped. Lucy squared her shoulders and surged forward, it was every commuter for themselves and it didn't pay to be polite. Another 10 minutes' walk and she was standing outside Simcock and Bright. Located just off Park Square, an unexpected patch of green amid the hustle and bustle of Leeds city centre, the office stood amidst a neat row of Georgian buildings. How many times had she walked through those doors she wondered? Thousands upon thousands. She had loved her job and every morning as she'd turned the last corner and seen the Simcock and Bright door almost within touching distance, there had been a spring in her step. This morning the door seemed gigantic and threatening and her feet were dragging as she drew closer.

'Lucy! Lucy!'

It was Alice, running towards her, breathless and red faced having sprinted the last few yards, her blonde bob far from smooth and her blue eyes sparkling with excitement.

'Oh my God Lucy! I can't believe you're here. I know you always said you'd come back to work but it seems to have been so long. Don't you think? But you're here now and I'm so pleased! Are you excited?'

Laughing Lucy hugged her friend tightly. 'I don't think I'm as excited as you seem to be!'

'Sorry. I'm babbling, aren't I? It's just that it hasn't been the same since you left!'

The anxiety came thundering back. 'It will take me some time to get used to it all again Alice, I ....'

'Stop worrying! It will all come flooding back. Nothing has changed! Now come on, Susie has got a pass ready for you.'

'A pass? A pass for what?'

'The door. Oh, I forgot, that has changed. We all have passes now so no-one can walk in off the street. Security.' Alice shrugged. 'It's a pain because if you forget your pass you have to press the buzzer and ask to be let in. Susie just opens the door for you but Leena is really difficult about it. Makes you sign a form to say you've forgotten your pass and then she makes a great song and dance about making sure you hand back your temporary one at the end of the day.'

'Leena?'

'The other receptionist. Didn't I tell you Claire left? Sorry, another small change. Well Claire left and Leena arrived.'

Lucy watched as Alice swiped her pass against a black box to the side of the door. The door sprang open and they negotiated their way around the huge palm trees now cunningly placed to block a street view of the reception area.

'The trees?' asked Lucy as she unhooked a palm frond from her hair.

'Gives a more welcome first impression and privacy to clients standing in reception. Or so Rob says. You'll soon learn how to side step them. '

Alice reached out and helped Lucy untangle herself from the tree. 'Come on, everyone is dying to see you.'

It was as though Lucy has stepped into a time tunnel. Alice was right, inside nothing seemed to have changed. A pale wooden staircase swept up to the next floor and large windows along the front and back of the building flooded the space with daylight. Alice led the way upstairs where the extensive use of glass to make individual offices made the whole floor seem bright and airy. Rob's office was immediately to the right, with a view of the street on one side and a view of the staircase on the other. He was in the perfect position to see everyone who arrived at Simcock and Bright and as he saw Lucy appear at the top of the staircase, he emerged from his office smiling widely to envelop her in a bearhug.

'Lucy Mathers is back!' he shouted to the office, 'She's finally come back.'

There was a muted round of applause and Lucy looked around to say thank you before realising that most of the faces were complete strangers. But Rob was pulling her into his office pushing Lucy into the seat in front of his desk before throwing himself back into his own oversized chair and grinning in delight.

'It's been a long time Lucy, but I knew you'd be back one day. You were too good to stay at home and play mummy.'

Lucy bit her tongue. Rob and his wife had four children although it was well known in the office that he had a tendency to forget their names, left their entire upbringing to his wife and had never changed a nappy in his life.

'Bet you've been chomping at the bit to get back into the office, haven't you?' he demanded. 'Probably couldn't wait until the little blighters were at school.'

'At school? Harry is only two. He's a long way from school yet! Emily's just started nursery in the mornings.'

'Really?' Rob looked vague. 'What age do they start school then? Well, it doesn't matter. Now they're at er... nursey or wherever, it means you can come back!'

When Rob had made one of his regular phone calls demanding that she return to the bosom of Simcock and Bright, Lucy had ever so casually mentioned that this time she could take him up on his offer because Will was between jobs and able to look after the children. Delighted that she had agreed to return, Rob hadn't bothered asking any more questions and arranged for Lucy to start the following Monday.

'Yes, well, the timing was right,' agreed Lucy.

'Fantastic! You know that Dawlish has gone?'

Peter Dawlish had been at Simcock and Bright even longer than Rob and although he had never set the world on fire, he had been an integral part of the team, until he announced that he was following his long-time dream to relocate to Canada and was doing so the following month.

'Yes, Alice told me …'

'And then of course we lost Graham.' Rob shook his head sadly, a deep sigh lifting his wide frame. 'That was a sad moment.'

'Lost? Oh dear. You mean Graham …'

'Yes.'

Alice kept her friend up to speed with everything that happened, births, marriages, all manner of comings and goings. She was surprised that Alice hadn't mentioned a death in the office.

'I didn't realise ….'

'Went to work for the competition. Calm as you like, just told me he was going.'

'Competition? He's not dead?'

'Dead?' Rob looked startled. 'He's died?'

'No! I just thought you meant that …'

'Might as well be. Left without a minute's notice,' sniffed Rob

'So, you're a bit short staffed at the moment?' Lucy asked, changing the subject hastily.

'We certainly are. We have several new accounts in the pipeline plus we have accounts coming up for renewal and we've heard on the grapevine that one of them is looking around. It's McCarthy & McCarthy.'

'No! But I signed them up. They were delighted with everything we did for them. What's gone wrong?'

'Not really sure,' said Rob darkly, 'but we really don't want to lose them, they're one of our most profitable clients.'

Lucy nodded thoughtfully. They'd been a tough company to bring on board but she'd worked night and day to find the detail that would swing the contract her way and the whole company had celebrated for two days non-stop when she'd finally obtained their signature on the bottom of the contract.

'So that's why you need me back?' she said, her confidence suddenly taking a few steps up the ladder.

'Absolutely!' boomed Rob.

'Right,' said Lucy. She remembered Mr McCarthy senior. A grumpy, belligerent Yorkshire man who was a mean negotiator with an eagle eye. She had soon come to accept that there was no room for delicacy in their discussions and she had been every bit as direct and brusque as he was. She'd faced him, chin high and eyes narrowed, countering every objection he'd raised and answering every question he'd thrown at her, both of them relishing the combat. He'd finally accepted the deal she'd presented, sending her a small wink as he'd lifted his pen and signed and Lucy had been unable to stop grinning back.

She took a deep breath. It was a big ask, after a four-year break to come straight back in at the deep end and negotiate with Mr McCarthy. But she'd done it once.

'Well, I'm flattered,' she said with a smile.

'You were always the one I could rely on Lucy. Shame about the babies really, you were at the top of your game.'

Lucy's smile became a little fixed. She didn't think it was a shame about her babies at all. And she was fairly sure Will didn't feel that way.

'But at least you've got over it now,' Rob carried on, waving his hand as though Lucy had recovered from a particularly nasty bug of some kind. 'And it's back to work!'

'I wanted my babies Rob,' she said firmly.

He looked at her blankly.

'You have a family,' she reminded him.

He looked a little surprised. 'Yes. Well I suppose it has to be done.'

She knew she was wasting her time. 'But I'm back now,' and feeling on safer ground Rob beamed and nodded.

'Indeed you are!'

'So, you want me to help with the McCarthy situation?'

Lucy's head was already filling with questions and ideas. The first thing she needed to do was look at the original contract and the aims agreed. Then she would examine the performance over the last few years and see why McCarthy would be unhappy with Simcock and Bright.

'That's right. Can't emphasise how important this is,' Rob was shuffling papers in front of him, usually a sign that his interest was waning.

'Okay,' said Lucy brightly. 'Well the sooner I get started the better.' She stood up, wincing at the explosion of pain in her feet.

'That's the attitude! That's why you were at the top of your game!'

Past tense.

'Okay, then I'll get settled and ....'

'Excellent! Absolutely excellent! I'll let Grant know.'

'Grant?'

'He'll be so relieved.'

'Er, why?'

'He's heard all about you of course. You're something of a legend here you know.'

'Yes, you keep telling me. Grant? Is Grant going to be helping …?'

'A chip of the old block is that man. Just like you used to be.'

More past tense.

'Right. Well I haven't met him yet but you say he's going to be helping ....'

'But of course, he can't do everything, can he?'

'I don't suppose anyone can,' agreed Lucy. 'What exactly is he …'

'That's why it will be such a relief to him that you've come back. You can get on with all the other bits and pieces while he concentrates on rescuing McCarthy & McCarthy and signing up the new clients.'

Lucy sat back down with a bump.

'Grant is working with Mr McCarthy?'

'Yes, it's his account now, of course.'

'Of course.' Only minutes earlier Lucy had been worried about taking on such an important task on her first day back. So why was she now feeling as though she'd had something important taken away from her?

'But he desperately needs someone to pick up the slack.'

'And that's why you wanted me to come back? To deal with the bits and pieces,' stated Lucy quietly.

'That's it! You have the experience; we don't need to spend weeks training you. You can take over all the other jobs that Grant has and leave him free to deal with the important stuff.'

Because he's at the top of his game, thought Lucy. Whereas she just used to be the best. Before the baby thing came to blight her path.

'Lucy?'

'Yes, sorry, just thinking. I'm going to do all the jobs that Grant hasn't got time for, right?'

'Got it!'

Lucy stood back up, wobbling slightly in her heels and gripping the edge of the desk for support. 'Then I'd better get on with it,' she said, earning a beam from Rob.

'That's the attitude! Let's get you settled.'

Walking out of his office they took a few steps down the hall as Rob continued to shout across the office at a few late comers, drawing everybody's attention to the fact that Lucy had returned. Her head already aching a little, Lucy stopped outside her office. 'I'll need to get up to date with the office systems again Rob,' she started to say, her hand resting on the door handle. 'Before I start working on any cases.'

'Of course, I'll get Alice to help you. In fact, she can show you to your office now. Alice, over here!'

'Oh, but I …' Lucy turned to stare into the office that had been hers for eight years, ever since she had been promoted to account manager. It looked much the same, except that the desk was a lot neater than Lucy had ever kept it and her chair seemed to be occupied. She could see the top of a blond head leaning back against the black leather, one hand resting on the desk, its fingers drumming impatiently, the occupant facing the window. The chair suddenly swivelled around and the man it contained looked directly at Lucy standing in the corridor. For a moment their eyes met, then his gaze dropped to her hand resting on the door handle before drifting back up to her confused face peering through the glass. He stared for a moment, his lips tilted in amusement before he slowly turned his chair back to face the window, leaving only the top of his blond head on view once more.

'Plenty of time to meet Grant later, let Alice show you to your office. We've managed to squeeze you in down the corridor, only one free at the moment I'm afraid. Grant's using a second office as a base of operations for all the new clients he's trying to get on board and the McCarthy deal of course. But maybe when he's finished, we might be able to persuade him to let you have it eh,' and with another beaming smile, Rob disappeared back to his office leaving Lucy staring at the back of the head occupying her chair.

Chapter 5

The door closed on Lucy's retreating figure and for a moment Will felt a moment of blind panic. He looked around to find both children watching him with interest. They may be too young to understand the economic disaster the Mather's household was facing, but they knew that their mother had left for the day and daddy was now in charge, which was not the normal state of affairs.

Will took a deep breath. Only a few weeks before he had led a team of highly intelligent and focused accountants. He had a reputation for being calm in the face of adversity, always ready with a solution and quick to react. He may be standing in his kitchen and not the board room, but surely he could cope in the same organised way with his new circumstances. All he had to do was look after his children for a few weeks. The main thing was that Lucy felt comfortable going to work each morning, he didn't want her worrying about what may be happening at home as well as trying to catch up on everything that had happened in the office over the last four years.

His laptop was perched on the breakfast bar with its carefully organised and colour coded to-do list. Lucy had run through the children's day and it hadn't sounded too complicated. He would treat this like any other task he had taken on board over the years. He would plan and execute it exactly as if he were in the office, calm efficiency was the order of the day.

Taking another deep breath and squaring his shoulders, Will glanced at the clock and saw that he was already a few minutes behind his schedule. He needed to get on with it, after all this was his new role. And the first job was getting his children dressed and ready for the day and not be late delivering Emily.

'Okay guys. Time to get dressed. Then we can take Emily to nursery,' he announced brightly before shepherding both children upstairs where he grabbed Emily's clothes and spread them across her bed.

'Right Emily,' he said in a brisk tone. 'You first. Here are your clothes.'

'Daddy, I don't want to wear my yellow socks today, I want to wear my pink socks.'

Will looked at the small pile of clothes Lucy had prepared for Emily, including a pair of yellow socks. He looked down at Emily's hopeful face. 'I don't suppose it matters what colour they are, does it?' he murmured. 'Does Mummy let you choose which socks you wear?'

'Oh yes,' answered Emily seriously. 'Always.'

'Okay, do you know where your pink socks are?' He looked around the bedroom. Perhaps her socks would be in one of the drawers of the chest painted a soft cream and decorated with unicorns.

'I do,' Emily nodded her head.

'Then can you put them on and get dressed as quickly as possible so we can get you to nursery?'

'Yes daddy.'

'Do you need me to help you?'

'No daddy. I can do it.'

Relieved at his daughter's obvious organisation, Will scooped Harry into his arms. 'Okay, then you get dressed Emily and I'll sort Harry out,' and leaving Emily to get herself ready, he carried the squirming toddler into his bedroom where he spent the next 10 minutes trying to pin him down long enough to dress him in the clothes that Lucy had left out. Slightly breathless and with a growing sense of time flying by, Will went to check on Emily's progress.

Her bedroom was empty and thankful that his daughter was already dressed and ready, Will went downstairs in search of her.

'Emily? Where are you, sweetheart?'

'Here Daddy, I'm just getting my pink socks ready.'

Following the sound of her voice, Will poked his head around the door of the utility room only to gasp in horror. Emily had dragged in a kitchen chair and was standing at the sink which was full to the top with water and an explosion of bubbles, her arms disappearing into the water as she washed a pair of bedraggled pink socks.

'Emily! What are you doing?'

Leaping forward, Will lifted her down from the chair and peered through the mountain of bubbles to find the plug.

'I'm washing my pink socks. You said I could wear them.'

'But I didn't realise they needed washing! Are these your only pink socks?'

Will recovered the dripping items and squeezed them over the sink. His shirt sleeves were now wet and Emily's hair was covered in stray bubbles. She was still dressed in her pyjamas, which were sodden.

'No but they're my favourite ones and you said I could wear them.' Emily's face took on a slightly mutinous look. 'They just need a wash and then Mummy gets them dry really quickly by putting them in there.' She pointed to the tumble dryer, crossing her chubby little arms across her body as she prepared for an argument.

'But not quickly enough for you to wear them to nursery,' said Will, taking a desperate look at his watch. 'We need to leave in a few minutes and the socks won't be dry in time.'

'Mummy always says they'll be ready in a jiffy,' Emily insisted sternly.

'Yes darling, but we don't have a jiffy. We need to get you dressed now and take you to nursery.'

'You said I could wear them.' Emily was scowling and despite Will trying to move her gently in the direction of the door, she stood firm in the middle of the utility room. 'You said I could wear my pink socks.'

'I didn't realise they weren't ready though.'

'You said I could wear my pink socks,' she reiterated crossly.

'But they're wet!' Will pulled a hand through his untidy hair. 'We'll be late if we wait for them to be dry. We need to get you dressed sweetheart, quick as we can.'

His daughter stayed unmoving in the centre of the room, her eyes resting on the dripping pink socks. She gave her father a long assessing stare that left Will feeling that this was a pivotal moment. He tried to meet his daughters gaze with authority even as he quaked inside. She was four, he reminded himself, he dealt with difficult clients every day, he was an excellent negotiator.

'I'll wash and dry them while you're at nursery,' suggested Will. 'Then you can put them on when you come home. But we haven't got time right now Emily, you'll have to put on the yellow socks.'

An alarm sounded on his phone and he winced.

'We'll be late Emily,' he begged, trying not to let the desperation show in his voice. 'It will have to be the yellow socks, we need to get you dressed.'

For a moment he thought his pleas were falling on deaf ears as Emily gave him a stern look.

'As soon as I come home?'

'The very minute.'

'Okay.'

Picking her up, Will sprinted up the stairs two at a time and dressed Emily in 30 seconds flat, complete with yellow socks. He could hear another alarm sounding on his mobile. He tried to remember what was on his spreadsheet. That could be the alarm telling him that they should be dressed and ready to leave. Or was it warning him that if he hadn't already left, he was now late?

'Good girl Emily,' he shouted encouragingly, 'come on!' and tucking her under his arm he flew back down the stairs.

'Right, shoes, coats, bag and we're off.'

Harry was nowhere to be seen and Will peered under the kitchen table, grabbing hold of him by the trousers and pulling him out to push his arms into his coat. 'Emily, what are you doing?'

'I'm looking for my hair slide.'

The contents of her bag were now spread across the kitchen floor and with a whimper, Will started pushing everything back into the small duffel bag Emily took to nursery.

'No daddy, I need my hair slide.' Pulling the contents back out, Emily gave him a cross look as she sorted through the small pile of objects she took with her each day.

'Hair slide? What does it look like?' asked Will frantically. Lucy hadn't mentioned anything about a hair slide.

'It has a pink bow and I want to wear it today.' Emily's hand reached out. 'Here it is,' she said happily, pulling it from the hair of a small doll.

'Good! Good! Right let's get it in your hair.' Will shoved it onto the side of Emily's head but she pulled it out and handed it back to him gravely.

'Wrong side daddy.'

'Sorry, sorry. Okay.' Clipping it on the opposite side Will pushed everything back into the bag.

'Mummy brushes my hair before she puts my slide in,' she told her father helpfully.

Will looked at her silky hair, dishevelled and sticking up wildly on one side with a hair slide hanging at a jaunty angle from the other side.

'No need this morning, it looks lovely,' he said brightly, making a mental note to brush it before Lucy got home that night. 'We need to go Emily. Shoes, where are your shoes?'

Still sitting on the floor, Emily produced one shoe from under her bag.

'Here we are daddy.'

'And the other one?'

Concentrating on pulling on her shoe, Emily didn't answer and Will looked around a kitchen that was already starting to look like a war zone.

'Have you got the other shoe, Emily? Do you know where it is?' he asked urgently.

An alarm sounded and in irritation, Will grabbed at his mobile phone to silence it.

'Emily, do you know where your other shoe is?'

The first shoe now fastened, Emily looked around the kitchen.

'Hmm, must be here somewhere,' she said thoughtfully.

'Yes, but where sweetheart? Where is it?'

It took 5 minutes of searching before Will finally found it wedged behind the door to the hallway. Sweat had started to roll down his nose and he was finding it increasingly difficult to keep his tone low and moderate for the sake of his children.

'Harry no!' he groaned as he turned around to see that his son, bored with the wait, had struggled out of his coat, leaving the arms inside out and the hood still wrapped around his head. Will tried to push Harry's chubby arms back in but the sleeves were twisted and he had to stop, take the coat off altogether and start again, all the time looking nervously at the clock ticking away relentlessly.

'Let's go,' he yelled with the coat finally back in place. Grabbing at Emily's bag with Harry tucked under one arm and his mobile phone shrieking at him, Will finally managed to get both children out of the door. A final glance at the clock told him he was 10 minutes late, there was no way he would be able to get Emily to nursery on time. It was the first task of his first day and he had failed and shaking his head at the impossibility that was making two children move as fast as he needed them to, he slammed the door, already rehearsing his apologies to the nursery and his confession to Lucy.

Chapter 6

Lucy followed a chattering Alice to the very end of the corridor and a small office that had been squeezed in with a shoe horn. It had no window and barely enough room for a desk, let alone Lucy.

'Didn't this used to be the records room?' asked Lucy in horror.

'Yes. But Grant said that he needed the records room to be more accessible, he wanted the filing system to be organic and have a flow that wasn't possible in such a small space. Graham had left so we moved the files into his office.'

'And Grant needs a spare office because he's so busy?'

'He calls it the task force room,' answered Alice pulling a face. 'He has everything laid out on the desk and a white board on the wall with the task of the day. No-one is allowed to move anything without his permission.'

'And this is the only office space left?'

'Sorry,' mumbled Alice looking around the tiny room. 'I should have warned you. It is a bit small.'

'Small? It doesn't even have a window!'

Alice hung her head. 'I know.'

Lucy looked round for somewhere to hang her coat. There was a hook on the back of the door which would have to do, although her coat now blocked out what little light came through the glass panel. Squeezing behind the desk she sank onto the chair and slipped off her shoes. Going back into heels would have to be a gradual thing, she decided. A little like training for a marathon, she would have to work up to a full day.

The room was ridiculously small. Directly opposite was a much larger room, not the size of Lucy's old office but an acceptable space with a large window that looked onto the street below. It was full of filing cabinets and boxes which appeared to have been dumped in the middle of the room.

'And is the filing system flowing as it should?' she demanded.

'Well, it isn't actually in place yet. Grant said it needed careful thought and the first step was to put all the files in there.'

Lucy's eyes narrowed.

'When?'

'When?' echoed Alice.

'When did he arrange to have all the files moved in there?'

'Oh, er, last week. Came swanning in one morning and announced that we needed to update the system and he'd been researching a more …'

'An organic system with flow, yes I get it. Is Grant the office manager as well now?'

'Er no, that's still Hannah. But Grant told Rob it would help make things run smoother and Rob told Hannah it sounded like a good idea and Hannah said okay, she'd give it a go.' Alice sighed. 'It's not easy arguing with Grant, he always seems to get his own way.'

'I bet he does,' muttered Lucy. She knew the situation well. She had once been that person, the one in the big office next to Rob, allowed a free reign as long as she continued to sign up bigger and better clients. But now it appeared she'd been brought back as a glorified assistant for Grant and all her privileges had long since been redistributed. Lucy reminded herself that this was a short-term solution. She just needed Rob to continue to employ her until Will found another job and then she could apologise and say she had found it all too much and she was leaving, this time for good. She took a deep breath; she didn't need a big office and she certainly didn't need the pressure of being the best performing account manager. She didn't need to match Grant in the performance stakes, she just needed a job.

Despite Alice's assurances that nothing had changed, Lucy found that in fact, just about everything had. Alice guided her through several new systems and Lucy spent the next hour with her head reeling as she tried to get to grips with the new layout.

There was nowhere for Alice to sit so she spent most of the morning dashing up and down the corridor and it was whilst Lucy was alone in her tiny office that the phone began to ring. Seeing Rob's name flash, Lucy grabbed the receiver.

'Hi Rob. What can I do for you?' she asked, trying to sound bright and positive.

A beeping noise answered her and frowning at the phone she pressed a button that said call.

'Hi Rob.'

Nothing. Swearing under her breath Lucy pressed a couple more buttons at random shouting 'hello' after each one. The beeping noise changed tone, became a little angrier, more insistent and Lucy continued bashing at numbers and symbols.'

Hello! Rob? Hello!'

'Hello Lucy.'

At last! Except that the beeping noise continued and the voice seemed to be very close. She looked up to see Rob standing in the doorway.

'Having trouble?'

'No! Well yes.' Lucy glared at the phone and replaced the receiver.

'Everything okay?' he asked, looking a little uncertain.

'Of course! Wonderful.' She gave him a confident smile. She couldn't afford for Rob to think he had made a mistake offering Lucy her job back. 'Just getting used to the office again, that all.'

Rob nodded. 'I understand. Grant has just told me off for expecting too much of you.'

Lucy stiffened. 'Too much? In what way?'

'Well he's had experience of this sort of thing in the past …'

'What sort of thing?' interrupted Lucy.

'Oh, well, er you know, coming back to work after having a baby.'

'Really? Grant had a baby?'

'What? Oh, er, funny. No, he's just been there, you know in the workplace. Anyway, he said I mustn't ask too much of you, take it slowly that sort of thing.'

Lucy struggled to keep the smile on her face.

'I don't think that's going to be necessary,' she said firmly. 'I'll soon pick things back up.'

Rob gave a relieved grin. 'That's what I said! I told him you'd soon be giving him a run for his money.'

'And what did he say?' she asked casually.

'He can't wait!' laughed Rob. 'Thinks it will be great when there's two of you both fighting to be the best!'

Oh, I bet he does, thought Lucy, laughing along somewhat grimly as Rob tried to turn around and leave her office, a tricky task for a portly man.

When Alice came back, she showed Lucy which buttons to press to answer a call and they spent the next few hours poring over all the new systems as Lucy asked question after question and wondered if it had always been this complicated. Every time the door opened Lucy's coat would jump off the hook and throw itself onto the floor until Alice picked it up and took it outside to hang it in the small cloakroom area.

Checking her watch, Lucy wondered if Will had collected Emily from nursery on time and if he had remembered to walk back via the small park where Lucy always let them have five minutes on the swings before going home for lunch. Perhaps she should ring and see how they were doing. Her hand reached out to the phone and then paused. Or perhaps he would think that she was checking up on him. Maybe he was best left to get on with his day. She checked her mobile, there were no missed calls or texts so he hadn't called for help. Maybe she would phone her friend Fran and ask if she had seen Will at nursery when she'd picked up Zach. No! that was even worse. Fran knew Will was on child duty, she would be keeping her eye on him and would have let her know if she thought there was a problem.

They would probably be having lunch now, she decided. Harry would be in his high chair throwing banana around and Emily would be picking at any tiny piece of crust left on her bread and laying them in a neat line on the table. Lucy suddenly felt a surge of longing. If only she was at home, faced with clearing the kitchen after lunch, getting the washing dried, having to read The Hungry Caterpillar to Harry for the hundredth time and helping Emily to line up her cuddly toys in the very strict order that she demanded. She could be sat on the settee with them both in her arms, able to smell their hair, feel their rounded bodies close to hers. Her eyes pricked with tears. It would get easier, she told herself firmly. It had to get easier.

'So sorry I haven't introduced myself earlier,' interrupted a deep voice. 'You must remember what it's like, I haven't found a minute to call my own this morning.'

In the doorway stood a tall man with a flat stomach that spoke of careful eating and wide shoulders that indicated time in the gym. His blonde hair was immaculately combed, his chin smooth and stubble free. His suit looked handmade and fitted like a glove, his silk tie was perfectly knotted and his leather shoes were polished to a brilliant shine. He had very blue eyes which were fixed on Lucy and a hand was extended in her direction.

'Grant Cassidy,' he said smoothly, his handshake firm. 'And you, of course, are Lucy Mathers.'

Hitching up a trouser leg, he perched himself on the corner of Lucy's desk. It was the only place to sit in the tiny space.

'So good to meet you, I have of course heard all about you.' He smiled, showing even white teeth and laugh lines that crinkled the corner of his eyes. 'In fact, I nearly didn't take the job because of you. Rob spent so much time telling me how wonderful you were I was worried I wouldn't be able to live up to your memory.' He smiled again, the white teeth flashing. 'Fortunately, I decided to risk it.'

Lucy saw Alice approach the door, catch sight of Grant and turn on her heel to disappear again.

'It's nice to meet you at last,' she offered, making sure she smiled. 'Alice has told me all about you.'

'How wonderful that we'll both be working for Simcock and Bright,' continued Grant, 'I was thrilled when Rob told me you were coming back.'

Meeting the blue stare, Lucy decided that he didn't look overly thrilled. In fact, she was fairly sure that was a tiny hint of amusement on the curved lips.

'That was always the plan,' she said.

'Oh? I understood that you'd had to come back because your husband lost his job?'

Lucy's smile froze as she looked up at the charming, smiling man on her desk. 'Did you?' she asked stiffly. 'You must have misunderstood. You really can't afford to listen to office gossip you know. First lesson at Simcock and Bright.'

'Office gossip?' he mused. 'No, I think it was Rob who told me.'

Holding his eyes, Lucy forced a chuckle, leaning forward in her chair. 'Oh dear, you don't know Rob very well do you? I'm afraid he's the worst gossip of them all! Always getting the wrong end of the story. Still,' she sent him a kind smile,' when you've been here longer you'll get to know his little ways. Don't forget I've had ten years to get used to him!'

Neither let their smile slip as their eyes did battle. Underneath the table Lucy was clenching her fists so hard her nails were digging into her skin.

'I see,' Grant said finally. 'Then I must have misunderstood.'

'It happens,' shrugged Lucy.

He stood up, smoothing down his jacket and Lucy saw him sneak a quick glance at his reflection in the glass door pane.

'Well lovely to finally meet you Lucy,' he offered. 'And now I must get on, so much to do, you understand. Especially with McCarthy & McCarthy.' He sighed, his eyebrows knitting together with worry. 'I really need to get to the bottom of why they're so unhappy. That's the problem when promises are made to new clients to get them onboard. Assurances are given that can't be kept. The clients invariably become deeply dissatisfied and decide to leave.'

'McCarthy & McCarthy were very happy when I signed them up. Nothing unreasonable was agreed!'

'Well, I'm sure I can find a solution,' said Grant and with a nod, he left the tiny office, his departure spoilt somewhat by the narrowness of the door and the proximity of Lucy's desk which needed careful negotiating.

Waiting until she heard his office door open and close, Lucy let out an explosion of pent up air.

'The bastard,' she hissed as Alice appeared in her doorway. 'The absolute bastard! How dare he imply it's my fault McCarthy & McCarthy are unhappy! How dare he say Will is unemployed and I had to come back to work!'

'But I thought Will had been made redundant and that's why you've come back?' asked Alice.

'Of course it is, but he shouldn't say it! That's just rude.'

Looking a little confused Alice nodded. 'I told you he was awful!'

'As if he knows Rob better than I do. He's only been here two minutes,' scoffed Lucy. 'Trying to make out they're big buddies.'

'I had heard they get on really well, they meet up quite a lot outside of work.'

'And sticking me in this pokey little office. I know his game. New filing system! What a load of rubbish, he's just trying to undermine me, using stupid jargon like fluid filing to get his own way!'

'He's always introducing new ideas,' complained Alice. 'He made us change the way we recorded the sales figures. It took ages to get to grips with the new system. Although,' she added thoughtfully, 'it does seem to work better.'

Lucy paused in her rant to glare at her friend and Alice started shaking her head.

'But nobody likes him,' she reiterated. 'Everyone thinks he's arrogant even if they think he's good looking. And everybody hates the way he insists on things being done exactly as he wants them. Okay, most of his ideas are good, but' she added hastily at the look in Lucy's eye, 'we still hate him.'

Lucy glowered. 'Does anybody know why McCarthy & McCarthy are unhappy?'

Alice shook her head. 'Just that they've been heard to say they'll be looking for a new agency. Rob is desperate to keep them.'

'I wish Rob would let me look after them,' said Lucy thoughtfully. 'I'm sure I could get old Mr McCarthy to stay.

'Grant had only been here a few weeks when he was given all the best accounts. It was part of the reason Graham left, he was fed up with playing second fiddle.'

'I can't say I blame him,' said Lucy darkly. 'And I have the feeling I'm going to feel exactly the same. Working with Grant Cassidy is not going to be easy.'

Chapter 7

It was a long morning. Lucy's mind constantly wandered to her family as she tried to bring herself up to date. The office which had seemed so familiar when she'd arrived that morning, challenged her at every turn. Every cupboard she opened, every file she looked at seemed to hold something new and by early afternoon she was clutching her head, wishing for the hundredth time she had never made the ridiculous suggestion that she should return to work. Head down, thoughts of Grant Cassidy's smug face spurring her on, she said little apart from the occasional question she would direct at Alice. Seeing her friend cast a quick look at her watch, Lucy apologised.

'God I'm sorry Alice. I bet you're starving.'

'Well I wouldn't mind some lunch.'

Sitting up straight, Lucy rubbed the small of her back. She could do with a breath of fresh air, a break from the mountain of information in front of her and a ham and pickle sandwich. And maybe a bag of crisps and a custard slice. But she could also do without forcing her shoes back on her feet.

'Why don't you go get us both a sandwich while I finish off looking through these lists then we can eat in here.' Lucy looked round doubtfully, 'Or in the kitchen and you can bring me up to date on some of the gossip.' Despite what she had told Grant, Lucy had always found office gossip very useful for keeping abreast of what was happening.

'Okay,' agreed Alice happily. 'Although we're not eating sandwiches this month.'

'No sandwiches,' asked Lucy distractedly, already back to reading the file in front of her.

'No. We've gone carb free. Having a detox every now and then is really important, especially when the weather is cold and your immune system might be low,' instructed Alice.

'Okay, well whatever you normally have, that'll be great,' and once again absorbed in her work Lucy pushed some money in Alice's direction and sat back in her chair.

'What is that?' she asked in horror 15 minutes later.

'A protein lunch smoothie. They're all the rage now.'

Lucy stared at the slimy green drink Alice had produced in a see-through cup and a straw with an end that formed into a small spoon. '

'You'll need to use the spoon as you drink,' advised Alice, 'or all the good bits get left at the bottom.'

'There are good bits in here?' asked Lucy doubtfully.

'Seaweed, which can be a bit stringy and sometimes gets stuck in the straw. And some of the pieces sink. Although I like it when there are bits left at the bottom, it's like an extra snack.

'Bits of what?'

Well, sprout and bean shoots, that sort of thing.'

Lucy felt her stomach heave in protest. 'And you actually drink this?'

Alice nodded. 'Lots of us do. It's really good for you,' and taking the top from her container she slurped some of the foul-smelling liquid and pulled a satisfied face despite the green gloop that was now draped across her chin.

'So, no sandwiches at all?' asked Lucy faintly, unwilling to even take the lid from her drink.

'No.'

'Well what about the organic wrap shop that did those amazing salmon and cream cheese things.'

'It's a juice bar now.'

'Okay,' Lucy was getting desperate. 'Well what about the waist watchers sandwich shop, nothing more than 350 calories?'

'Sandwiches just aren't popular anymore. It's an organic vegan health food shop.'

Lucy watched in horror as her friend took another slurp of green sludge. How could sandwiches become unpopular? She was fairly sure Will still managed to find a sandwich every day. Or maybe she was even more out of touch than she'd realised and he was slurping on green protein shakes. It would explain why he was always so hungry. She would have to check with him when she returned home, which couldn't be soon enough, she decided.

'We get a Friday special every week,' said Alice.

Lucy felt a little more optimistic. 'And what's that? A carvery? A pizza? A Chinese!'

'A loaded shot,' answered Alice, now digging in her spoon to collect trailing fronds of something unrecognisable from the bottom of her cup.

Lucy closed her eyes briefly, hardly daring to ask. 'What's the shot loaded with?'

'Avocado.'

Lucy nodded. Okay, that wasn't too bad. She was quite partial to avocado.

'Mixed with olive oil to aid digestion, pickled jelly fish to cleanse the colon and a little fermented liquorice to open up your sinuses.'

'Are you mad?' whispered Lucy. 'Why would you put any of that in your mouth.'

'Because it's good for you,' said Alice in surprise. 'You knock it back in one, it's like having a huge shot of vitamins. You used to be a fan of healthy eating Lucy, I'm surprised you don't want to try the power shake.'

The drink was perched on the furthest edge of her desk, Lucy's face a very similar colour to the contents. There was a time when she would have joined in with gusto. But these days she was more of a £3.50 meal deal kind of a girl. And the snack would most definitely be crisps and not fruit.

'I er, I think I'll give it a miss thanks Alice.' Surely there was somewhere left in Leeds that did old fashioned carb laden sandwiches. 'Suddenly I'm not very hungry.'

Shortly after lunch Grant loomed in the doorway again, a couple of files held aloft. 'Lucy, would you mind taking these off my hands?' he asked in his deep, smooth voice. 'Rob and I are out for lunch and I need them checking for this afternoon.'

Lucy wondered where they were going and if it sold real food. The sort you had to chew rather than slurp.

'What do you need?'

'Nothing too taxing,' the white teeth flashed. 'Just a little proof reading really. It's two of the latest clients I've brought onboard and I just need to read over their contracts before we get them signed.'

He dropped the files in front of Lucy, 'Rob's suggestion, he said you wouldn't mind helping out.'

'Proof reading? Why haven't you passed it to someone in the main office?'

'Is that what you used to do?' asked Grant. 'Interesting. I like to do the final checks myself. Make absolutely sure everything is as it should be. But you know how busy I am and Rob said he was sure you'd be able to pick it up, he's very confident in your abilities.'

Grant's voice suggested that he had no such confidence as he continued. 'It's so flattering isn't it, having someone believe in you as much as Rob does. Let's hope it all works out.' Another flash of white teeth. 'Anyway, must dash. We have a table booked. I see you've joined in the latest office fad.'

They both looked at the foul green shake still on Lucy's desk as Grant laughed. 'I'm afraid I can't bring myself to drink them, no matter how good they're meant to be for you. Give me pasta or a good steak any day. I'll take the consequences.'

He stood up, patting his washboard flat stomach and fastening his jacket slowly so Lucy had ample opportunity for admiration. Lucy's own stomach growled loudly.

'I'll be back at 3:00, appreciate it if you could get this finished for then, if it's not too much for you on your first day back of course,' and he was gone, another insincere smile in Lucy's direction, another sneaky peek at himself in the glass panel of the door and he was walking down the corridor, humming happily.

Lucy sat for a moment. She could put the files back on Grant's desk and tell him to do his own proof reading. She could take them out into the main office where there would be no end of people willing to take on the job. She could put the files on Rob's desk and tell him she was leaving.

She thought of Will's desperate face when he broke the news of his redundancy and gave a sigh. Or she could just do what Grant wanted and spend the next hour or so reading through the files.

When Alice appeared with yet another coffee a few minutes later, she found Lucy poring over the two contracts, her lips set in a straight line and her face like thunder. Peering over Lucy's shoulders she read the names on the files.

'Oh those are Grant's latest conquests.'

'They're good clients,' Lucy admitted begrudgingly. 'He did well.'

'And doesn't he know it,' sighed Alice. 'Why are you proof reading them?'

'Because Grant is too busy,' she ground out. 'And apparently that's what I do now. Anything Grant wants to throw my way.'

At 2:00 Grant appeared in the doorway, Rob standing directly behind him.

'Had chance to finish those files Lucy?'

'You said 3:00.'

'Did I? Don't worry if you haven't had time. Maybe you need ….'

'They're finished.' Lucy dropped the files on the edge of the desk, watching Grant's face closely.

'Excellent,' shouted Rob from the corridor where he was peering in. 'Excellent work Lucy!'

'Yes, excellent,' murmured Grant. 'Thank you,'

He turned, waiting for Rob to move out of the way so he could leave the office.

'The dates didn't match up by the way.'

Grant stopped. 'Dates?'

'Yes, on the contract page, the dates were all a little askew.'

'I see. Well good job you noticed.'

Lucy smiled. 'It is, isn't it.'

'Well done Lucy,' shouted Rob, still trying to look around Grant's broad shoulders into her office. 'You always had an eagle eye for detail.'

'In that case, I do have a few more – if you don't mind? I can understand if you've had enough, first day back and everything.'

'That's okay. Just leave them on my desk.'

Grant's eyebrows rose slightly. 'As long as you're happy taking on these jobs for me. I don't want you to feel …'

'I'm happy Grant. Quite happy. Just put them on my desk,' and nodding, Grant followed Rob down the corridor.

Within five minutes Lucy's desk was covered in folders. Looking anxious, Alice appeared in the doorway. 'Shall I help?' she asked. 'There are so many. I can't really understand why he needs all these checking. Some of them are quite old contracts,' she mused flicking through them. 'You'll never got through them all today.'

'Oh won't I,' said Lucy grimly. 'Won't I just.'

She worked non-stop, reading through every file, looking for any mistake no matter how small and using her yellow highlighter viciously whenever she found so much as a missing comma. With interest, she noted the clients Grant had brought on board over the last few weeks and months, the type of business he tended to close, the size of the average account he was bringing to Simcock and Bright. He was good, she admitted to herself. No wonder Rob was happy to let him have free reign in the office. His revenue stream was impressive. Could she match it? There was a funny squirming feeling in the pit of Lucy's stomach. Did she want to? If this job was only going to be for a short while, did she need the hassle of taking on Grant Cassidy?

Alice appeared in the doorway, more files on her hands, her cheeks pink with mortification.

'Er, these are two files Grant asked me to give you,' she said dropping them on Lucy's desk and retreating to the door.

'Why?' Lucy looked at them with interest, not recognising either name.

'Well, he, er, he said that they needed following up and could you, er, give them a ring.'

'Okay.' Watching Alice hopping from one foot to the other Lucy opened the first file. 'What needs following up?'

'Er, a courtesy call to remind them about payment.'

Lucy's hand stopped flicking through the papers.

'What.'

'A payment reminder call,' whispered Alice.

'And why wouldn't this go to accounts. Don't they still chase payment?'

'Yes.'

'So why aren't they chasing these payments?'

Alice was twisting her fingers around, nibbling on her lip so firmly it was starting to bleed.

'Because Grant said you needed practice. It would help you to get back into the swing of things to do a few little errands like this.'

'I see.'

Very calmly Lucy closed the folders.

'He asked you specifically to give them to me?'

'Yes,' whispered Alice.

'Thank you, Alice.'

'I'm so sorry! I didn't want to take them, I said they should go to accounts and that you already knew what you were doing and didn't need to be treated like a complete newcomer but he …'

'Don't worry about it!' assured Lucy standing up and straightening her skirt. Was it her imagination or was it already a little looser around the waist? She slipped on her shoes hardly feeling the pain beneath the rage that was coursing through her veins and picking up both files she walked towards the door, which meant Alice had to walk backwards into the corridor.

'What are you going to do?' bleated Alice in concern 'Shall I take the files? I can give them back to Grant, Lucy where are you going?'

Ignoring her, Lucy walked down the corridor, taking the time to smile and wave at the occupants of the main office as she sailed past. Up the staircase and on the next floor was the accounts department and pausing in the doorway she looked around to see who she knew. Most of the faces were unfamiliar but there were a couple that she recognised and with a determined smile she walked into the room shouting a cheery hello to them all.

'Lucy my darling, I heard that you were back!' A large woman with a mane of frizzy ginger hair grabbed her firmly and enveloped her in a huge hug. 'What a sight for sore eyes you are! Decided to come back to civilisation eh? Everybody expected you to come back long before this. We didn't think you'd be able to stay away for long! Had bets that you'd be stir crazy after a few weeks and desperate to be back in the office.'

Good grief, thought Lucy. Had nobody believed she might have been happy to stay at home and look after her children?

'Well, good to be back, Kathy,' she said insincerely, extricating herself from the hug and trying to look as though she was delighted to be back in the fold.

'So, who has taken over from Martha?' she asked innocently.' 'I just need a couple of payments chasing.'

'I can take them for you.' A figure appeared at her side, a tall man with light brown hair and grey eyes who looked vaguely familiar.

He held out his hand. 'Simon. We met at Rob's birthday bash.'

'Oh of course. Sorry, so many new faces today,' apologised Lucy. 'Well thank you for dealing with them,' and she turned back towards the stairs.

'I did wonder why Grant wanted them back?'

Lucy stopped and turned back to Simon who was looking down at the files with a frown.

'Grant took them back?'

'Yes, they were on my desk but Grant came looking for them. Said something about you starting at the bottom again and wanting lots of practice.'

'As if Lucy needs to start at the bottom,' scoffed Kathy, peering at the files. 'Doesn't he know how long she did this job?'

Simon was staring at Lucy intently. 'He asked me to send all his reminders to you from now on, it did seem an odd request.'

'No!' snapped Lucy, then smiled apologetically. 'Sorry, I think there's been a slight misunderstanding. I don't need to any reminders how the accounting system works.'

He nodded thoughtfully. 'No more accounts reminders?'

'No more account reminders.'

Tilting his head to one side slightly, he gave Lucy a sympathetic look. 'Grant giving you a hard time?'

'Nothing I can't handle,' she replied stiffly.

He didn't look convinced but nodded his head encouragingly. 'I'm sure you can. And if there's anything I can help you with, just let me know.'

Lucy felt a sudden prick of tears. She was sure she had never been this emotional in her previous working life but any suggestion of kindness at the moment could reduce her to a blubbering wreck.

'Thank you,' she managed with a sniff.

Walking back down the steps she paused in the corridor, watching Grant as he sat opposite Rob's desk. They were laughing about something Grant was saying, his hands raised in the air as he spoke.

Straightening her shoulders, Lucy opened Rob's door, giving him a big smile. Instinctively he smiled back as she knew he would. Lucy had spent years appearing in his office, sometimes to seek advice, sometimes to moan and complain, other times to deliver great news and seek approval. She may have been absent for a while but she had spoken the truth to Grant earlier. She knew Rob very well.

'Lucy!' boomed Rob. 'All going well?'

Lucy perched herself on the edge of Rob's desk as she had a hundred times before. 'Of course!' she said brightly.

'Wonderful! Bet you're glad to be back aren't you?'

Glad? Oh Lucy was anything but glad. Right now she would give heaven and earth to be at home coping with tetchy toddlers, dirty nappies, piles of laundry and a sink full of washing.

'Couldn't be happier,' insisted Lucy.

Grant was watching the display with a small smile. 'Trying to catch up with all the changes?' he asked sympathetically.

Lucy saw Rob's smile disappear as he looked at Lucy anxiously.

'It's not a problem,' she waved her hand in the air. 'The fundamentals are the same.' Apart from the changed telephone system, the new computer system, the thousand and one passwords she had been forced to write down discreetly in the back of her diary because she couldn't seem to commit any of them to memory, the change to the way information was recorded – even the pens had been relocated!

'It would seem I remember the systems better than Grant does actually,' she laughed.

At Rob's frown she carried on. 'Grant wanted me to chase up a payment,' she said. 'Oh, don't worry, I've taken the files back upstairs. After all,' another laugh, 'you haven't brought me back into the office to work for accounts have you?'

Grant's smile remained fixed in place as Lucy turned back to Rob. 'Unless that is what you wanted? Did I get the wrong end of the stick and …?'

'Good God of course not! Grant what were you thinking? I've told you how good Lucy is, you don't need to give her silly little jobs like that. She's an account manager!'

Shaking his head Grant let a puzzled frown join his eyebrows. 'No idea how that happened,' he said carelessly. 'I've got much more important jobs lined up for Lucy.'

'Probably just a misunderstanding,' offered Lucy.

'Indeed. Was there anything else? It's just that Rob and I were in the middle of discussing something important.' The smooth voice dropped a tone. 'Oh goodness, that sounded so rude! I do apologise, it's just that …'

But Lucy was already on her feet, waving away his apology. 'Please carry on. By the way all the files you passed over are checked and back on your desk Grant. A little word of advice,' she sent him an encouraging smile, 'from someone who did this job for a long, long time. Don't let them pile up like that. If you find any mistakes after the contracts have been exchanged it can be a real disaster,' and with a last bright smile at Rob she walked out of the office, keeping her back straight and refusing to limp despite the pain in her toes.

Chapter 8

Leaving on the dot was a new concept for Lucy. She had always been the last in the office, unable to tear herself away until she had dotted every 'i' and crossed every 't'. And then it was often straight to the local wine bar where she would meet Will or a handful of friends. Of course, that was all pre-baby. These days she couldn't remember the last time she had been in a wine bar at 5:00 let alone knocking back the cocktails at the end of the day. And Lucy didn't care whether it was good form or not to leave bang on time on her first day back in the office, she had an ache inside her that wouldn't be fulfilled by anything but holding her children close.

Squeezing her shoes back on, she picked up her bag and closed the door on her broom cupboard of an office. Rescuing her coat she flung her arms round Alice, thanking her for her help and set off for the stairs. She could see Rob, still in his office where he would probably stay until there was no possibility of his children being awake when he arrived home and Grant, in what Lucy still thought of as her office, sitting in her chair. Refusing to look in his direction she heard him call out her name loudly.

She turned, as did everyone else including Rob. 'Had a good first day back?' Grant shouted from his desk. She realised that contrary to the rest of the day when his door had remained tightly shut, it was now open wide so everything he said could be heard by the rest of the office.

'Yes, thank you,' she said stiffly, her eyes on Rob who was looking at his watch and frowning.

'A lot to take in after such a long break,' Grant suggested sympathetically.

'Not really.' Lucy turned around and kept on walking.

'Shame you need to go so early. I was just about to come and talk to you about a couple of cases. But I understand, you have a family to get back to. More important than anything that's happening here eh?'

Lucy stopped. She was now in line with Rob's office and Grant had left his desk to stand in his doorway and address her retreating back. She saw Rob sit up a little straighter, listening to the conversation.

'Perhaps you need a little help with your time management,' she shouted back brightly, turning to face Grant. 'Well known fact Grant, if you can't do the job in the allocated hours, you're doing something wrong. If you're not too overwhelmed tomorrow, perhaps we can schedule a meeting?'

She saw Rob grin and Alice execute a discreet fist pump from the corner of the office and with a cheery wave she shouted, 'Goodnight everybody, goodnight Rob,' and walked with her head held high towards the staircase and her escape route.

It was dark and cold outside but Lucy's anger warmed her cheeks as she hurried towards the station. Well at least she knew what she was up against. Grant Cassidy was not at all delighted she had returned to the fold of Simcock and Bright. He had no intention of helping her settle in or welcome her back to her role. In fact, Lucy had a very real suspicion he would make life as difficult as he could for her and seeing a train arriving, she pushed her way down the platform, eager to put as much space between herself and the office as possible.

Arriving at her stop she almost cried at the thought of the walk home. She had decided that paying to park her car every day was an unnecessary cost when the station was only a 15-minute walk from home. The short journey was something she wouldn't have thought twice about in years gone by. But that of course was before, when, as everyone had been at pains to remind her throughout the day, Lucy had been good at her job, at the top of her game and not some clapped out mother who had thrown away her career for babies. The new Lucy, it seemed, wasn't quite up to scratch.

Casting a longing eye at the taxis at the entrance to the station, Lucy wrapped her coat tightly round herself, ignored the pains in her feet and trudged home, her lovely, warm home where her children would be waiting for her, clean, happy and ready for a cuddle on the settee and where Lucy would be able to forgot all about the trauma of her day and return to the very important business of motherhood.

Will was asleep. He had fallen onto the settee to catch his breath before he took the children upstairs for their bath and the next thing he knew there was the sound of the door opening and Emily squealing in delight that mummy was home. Jumping to his feet he immediately looked around for Harry. He had spent a good part of the day looking for Harry who it appeared liked nothing more than to sit under the kitchen table, behind the settee, in the wardrobe – anywhere out of sight basically, which had left Will dashing round the house in a high state of panic. For once the toddler was sitting in the centre of the room, jamming toys into his mouth and drooling happily.

Rubbing his eyes blearily, he scooped up his son and went into the kitchen. Lucy was standing in the doorway, a cold waft of air still surrounding her. Putting Harry on the floor, Will reached out and gathered her into his arms and for a long blissful moment they remained there, leaning on each other, soaking in the warmth and strength of the other's body. Lucy closed her eyes. She needed to tell Will that she couldn't do this, that she wasn't ready for a return to the office. She wanted to stay where she was and simply not move.

'Hard day?' he whispered in her ear.

'So, so hard,' groaned Lucy. 'You?'

Will gave a deep sigh and Lucy opened her eyes, peering over his shoulder as she stared at her kitchen. Her beloved island unit was almost unrecognisable under the chaos of the day. Dirty plates formed a small leaning tower, remnants of banana skins, biscuit wrappers and half eaten sandwiches covered the black sparkly surface together with one of Harry's shoes, what looked like a plant from the front garden, plucked from its home and wilting as it lay in a small pile of soil surrounded by dozens of coffee mugs, many still full of coffee.

The highchair Harry used was in the corner, covered in handprints of dried food, smears of jam and small peaks of congealed, unidentified mush decorated with beans. The floor was littered with shoes and coats that hadn't quite made the short journey to the coat cupboard and the sink was piled high with yet more plates and cups, plus a pair of pink socks drying over the tap and what looked like Emily's pyjamas which had been left to dry on the draining board.

Her eyes swept the scene slowly, finally coming to rest back on Will whose head was drooping in shame. His hair stood up at every conceivable angle, one sleeve of his jumper was covered in something sticky and his face looked ragged with exhaustion.

'It was a bit more difficult than I was expecting,' he admitted, risking a quick glance at Lucy. 'They never stop!'

Lucy unfastened her coat and slipped off her shoes.

'Well, that's children for you.'

'I just didn't seem to have enough time to do anything.' He looked round the kitchen, his shoulders slumping in despair. 'I thought I'd clean up after lunch but then Harry went missing …'

'Missing!' Lucy's hand shot to her mouth. 'You lost him?'

'No! Well yes, I mean he was in the house but I couldn't find him anywhere.'

Lucy looked relieved. 'Probably in the wardrobe,' she said, throwing her coat over the back of a chair. Actually, the walk to the coat cupboard did seem a long way.

'He was in ….. how did you know?'

Lucy shrugged. 'He likes to sit in the wardrobe after lunch, he takes his cars in there and has a car chase round your shoes. Sometimes he falls asleep.'

Will shook his head. How could he not know that about his own son?

'Well, I found him eventually and then Emily said that you took them to the park in the afternoon.'

Lucy swung round to look at her daughter, who was sitting at the kitchen table with her colouring book.

'No, we go to the park on the way home from nursery.'

'I told him that mummy,' lisped Emily carrying on with her colouring. 'But he didn't listen.'

'Well we didn't have time, I wanted to get home and get on with lunch. And Emily said that if you missed the park on the way home you go back in the afternoon.'

Lucy turned back to her daughter who returned her gaze solemnly.

'Emily, that's not what happens. Why did you tell Daddy that?'

Emily placed her crayon on the table and gave her father a long look from her deep blue eyes, before turning back to Lucy.

'I got a black mark this morning,' she said. 'We were late.'

Lucy's gaze returned to Will.

'What! But I told you to make sure you were on time. How come you were late?'

Will frowned at Emily. 'Well er, Emily couldn't find the hair slide she wanted and I couldn't find one of her shoes and …'

'He told me not to tell you.'

Lucy's gaze was swivelling from Will to Emily.

'Will!'

'I'm sorry! I'm sorry!'

'For what? Getting a black mark or encouraging Emily not to let me know?'

'Both. All of it. Everything,' groaned Will.

He wrapped his arms back round her and buried his head in her hair.

'I didn't appreciate how long it all took. It's impossible keeping on top of everything there is to do,' he muttered.

Lucy was still taking in the state of the kitchen over his shoulder. 'So I see.'

'But you knew it would be, didn't you?'

He lifted his head to look into Lucy's eyes.

'Maybe,' she shrugged.

'And you decided to let me find out for myself.'

There was a tiny twitch at the corner of Lucy's mouth.

'What happened to your timetable?'

'Didn't have time to read it,' admitted Will.

'And the alarms you set on your mobile?'

'There were so many going off at the same time, didn't have a clue what they were for.'

'Tired?'

'Oh yes,' he groaned.

'What's for dinner?'

He took a step back and stared at her blankly. 'Dinner?'

'Yes. Our dinner.'

'Do I have to make dinner as well?' he asked in shock.

Lucy pushed him away, the small smile disappearing. 'Yes! Didn't you come home to a cooked meal every night?'

'Yes, of course. I just didn't think,' Will pushed a hand through his already wild hair. 'But how do you find the time to cook as well as everything else?' he asked in genuine confusion.

'It's all about time management,' replied Lucy starting to scoop the contents of the sink into the dishwasher. 'You organise your time and have a contingency plan for when things don't go well.'

Recognising his own words, Will hung his head again. 'Okay. Right, must try harder eh?'

He was peeping at her from underneath his eyelashes and Lucy couldn't help but grin.

'A lot harder. And you can start by giving these two a bath while I clear this mess. And order a takeaway.'

Will moved across the kitchen to slip his arms around her waist as she stood at the sink.

'And then we'll open a bottle of wine and you can tell me all about your first day back at work,' he whispered in her ear. 'I want to hear all about it.'

What seemed like hours later the children were in bed asleep, the kitchen was sparkling again and Will and Lucy were curled up on the settee.

'But surely you didn't really want the hassle of renegotiating McCarthy & McCarthy on your first day back at work?'

'No,' agreed Lucy.

'Just do what Rob wants, look after the smaller clients and get used to being back in the office,' Will suggested reasonably.

'Yes.'

'And if Grant wants to do all the work himself let him.'

'Right.'

'No point making life any harder for yourself. Hopefully I'll get a new job soon. You might only be there a few weeks.'

Lucy nodded. Because Will was right. She just needed to do what was asked of her and let Grant suffer the torment of McCarthy & McCarthy. Why was that such a difficult concept for her to come to terms with?

'It was so strange being back. On the surface nothing had changed but underneath, everything was different.'

'Good different?'

'I don't know. Just different. I remembered how much I used to love working there. What a thrill I got every time I signed up a new client or did a presentation.'

Will sighed. 'You don't want to take the easy route, do you?'

Lucy nodded then shook her head.

'I don't know,' she wailed.

'You want to give Grant Cassidy a run for his money?'

'Maybe.'

'Even though you could just do what you've been asked, help Grant out and let him do all the work, all the worrying?'

Lucy fell silent. When Rob had mentioned the McCarthy deal she had started to shake inside, petrified of picking up such a high-profile case so soon. But moments later when he announced that Grant would be dealing with the negotiations, she had felt unreasonably bereft. Maybe, she thought, that was why she was finding it difficult. She may not have enjoyed the return to work, but she refused to let Grant Cassidy suggest that she could no longer cope with the job she had once owned

'He's in my office,' she blurted out. 'I know it's his office now, I left. But it hurts to see him there, he even has my chair. I nearly gave birth in that chair.'

Will raised his eyebrows. 'You feel attached to the chair?'

'Yes. Oh, I know it sounds a bit odd.'

'Not at all,' denied a grinning Will. 'That chair is like one of our children.'

She poked him in the ribs. 'Okay, I get it. I'm being over emotional about an office chair. Very funny.'

'Take it back.'

'What?'

'If it means that much to you, take it back.'

'The chair?'

'Yes. The chair.'

'I can't do that.'

'Why not. The old Lucy would have done exactly that. She would have gone into Rob's office and told him she wanted the chair and she was taking it back.'

Lucy sat up. 'And what would Rob have done?' she asked, caught up in the story.

'Rob would have said okay.'

'He would?' whispered Lucy.

'He would. Because you've told me a thousand times that Rob isn't interested in the details. He doesn't care who sits on what chair. He's only interested in results. And if having the chair gets the results, he would say take the chair.'

Lucy nibbled on her lip thoughtfully. Will was right. That's how she had dealt with Rob during her time at Simcock and Bright. She had told Rob what she was going to do, what she needed and Rob, disinterested, would say okay, just get the job done.

'Grant said he wanted a fluid filing system,' she murmured, almost to herself.

'And Rob probably just said okay and never gave it a second thought,' said Will yawning.

'He said he needed a second office so he could sign up the new clients and save McCarthy & McCarthy.'

'Didn't you tell Rob that you were taking Alice as your PA so you could sign up McCarthy & McCarthy?'

Lucy nodded. She had walked into Rob's office one morning and told him that she needed her own full time assistant and she was taking Alice out of the general office. And Rob hadn't even looked up from the papers on his desk as he said, 'Whatever, just get them signed up'. She had invented the tactics Grant Cassidy was using. She swirled the wine in her glass, her mind dancing. Could she take back the chair? Did she still have the fight somewhere deep inside her?

'Although personally I think you should take things as easy as you can.'

'That would be sensible,' murmured Lucy.

'But I know what you're like,' he grumbled. 'I bet you want to show him you're still up to the job.'

'Rob?'

'Grant. Rob doesn't need convincing.'

'Mm. Maybe.'

'Come on,' said Will, yawning some more. He pulled her up from the settee and her thoughts. 'Take me to bed but please understand, there is no way you're having your wicked way with me tonight! I've been looking after the children all day and I am exhausted!'

Chapter 9

Falling out of bed with a groan, Lucy jumped in the shower, dressed and then headed to the kitchen. Finding the washing from the previous morning still in the washing machine, she threw it in the tumble dryer. Rifling through the freezer she took out some chicken and put it out to defrost, next to an onion, some mushrooms and half a bottle of red wine, Will would have to work out the rest himself. She threw together some lunch for Emily and Harry, making a selection of sandwiches, colour co-ordinated and crust free and stuck a Post-it note onto their favourite yoghurts in the fridge. She laid out a selection of fruit with more Post-it notes telling Will who liked what and then collected the small bag Emily took to nursery and put it on the kitchen table before placing Emily and Harry's shoes by the door. Dashing back upstairs and finding the children were now in bed with Will, she laid out a clean selection of clothes in their rooms and diving under Harry's bed she pulled out all the toys that he usually stashed there each night before going to sleep. He would want them later in the day and Will would have no idea where they were hidden.

Leaving Will to start the morning struggle of getting two children downstairs, she ignored Harrys' loud protests at not being allowed to wear his superman cape for breakfast and ran back downstairs to stick a note on the front of the fridge reminding Will that Tuesday was a mums and tots morning for Harry and that under no circumstances was he to be late dropping Emily at nursery school. She also emphasised that park visits were made on the way home, baths were to be taken one hour after tea and that both children should be ready for their final story and bed by the time she came home. She had spent a considerable amount of time cleaning the kitchen the previous night, established that the plant had been courtesy of Emily who had decided they should get mummy some flowers to welcome her home and tidied away all the toys that Harry had left sprinkled across the floor. But she had no intention of having a repeat tonight.

She took out a small chicken pie she had made and frozen ready for the children and left another note telling Will to serve it with peas and broccoli for Harry and carrots for Emily if she was still anti green. Going through the mental list in her head she grabbed the children's coats and left them by their shoes and then ran back up the stairs and into her bedroom. She'd dug out a wool shift dress which skimmed her hips and mercifully did not require anything fastening around her waist, although she would swear that it had already gone down a size after a day refusing to partake of the vile green smoothie and surviving on coffee alone. Taking a deep breath, she slipped on a pair of black patent shoes and felt her toes concertina together in protest. But the pain wasn't as bad as the previous day, maybe her feet were reluctantly starting to recall what to do when the heels came into sight.

She took a little more time with her makeup, deliberately opting for a red lipstick instead of the softer pink she had sported the day before. Red lipstick and sky-high heels, that had been the Lucy of old and maybe she needed to channel some of that energy her way now. Running back down the stairs she found both children eating their breakfast and a clearly nervous Will chewing his thumbnail and drawing up a timed to do list.

Grabbing her coat and bag, already out of breath, Lucy kissed both children.

'Don't forget to take the washing out,' she reminded.

'Washing?'

'Yes, I've put some more in but you need to get it dry.'

Will scanned his carefully timed list. 'Well,' he said dubiously, 'I might able to fit it in after lunch.'

'It takes five minutes,' snapped Lucy. 'You open the washing machine door, take out the contents and hang them on the line or put them in the tumble dryer!'

Reluctantly Will squeezed in a line saying washing.

'Argh!' she slapped her hand against her forehead. 'I forgot, it's my turn to take a cake to mums and tots.'

Will's eyes grew wide. 'I can't make a cake,' he yelled in panic pointing a finger accusingly at his spreadsheet. 'I haven't got time to make a cake! I don't know how to make a cake! I can't …'

'Relax!'

Lucy was busy texting, her thumbs flying over the keys even as she was checking the time. She had to leave in the next 2 minutes or she would be jogging to the station. 'I'm going to let Fran know I forgot and see if she can pick up my turn. She can grab one from the shop.'

Will's shoulders relaxed. 'Oh, so I don't actually have to make a cake?'

'Yes. Absolutely. But exceptions are allowed and you taking over from me and then having to ask Fran to take over the cake rota is an acceptable exception.'

Will was looking confused but relieved as Lucy threw her phone back in her bag and blew him a kiss. 'I'm off, and don't be late dropping Emily at nursery,' she shouted. 'And remember to take the washing out. And make some dinner!' and she was gone, leaving Will staring anxiously at the retreating figure and Emily and Harry staring at their father.

Arriving in the centre of Leeds with plenty of time to spare, Lucy made a slight detour before finding herself at the door of Simcock and Bright. She paused and took a deep breath. Then with her chin held high, she waved her pass at the black box and went inside.

'Morning Rob,' she sang brightly as she walked into his office and placed a coffee on his desk. 'Skinny Latte with an extra shot of expresso and a hint of vanilla.'

She sank into one of the chairs next to his desk and crossed her legs. It took a little more effort that she had expected, her stomach interfered with the move and her legs weren't used to being flung in the air with such gusto of late.

'Morning Grant,' she offered in a friendly way.

'Lucy you star, you remembered!' shouted Rob.

'Been together too long to forget,' she answered, taking a peep at Grant's profile.

'So, how did it go yesterday?' asked Rob leaning back in his chair.

Lucy smiled easily. 'Great! Straight back into the swing of it all,' she lied.

'Really,' asked Grant, concern lacing his voice. 'Four years is a long time. You mustn't be afraid to ask for help you know Lucy. We all understand it's a big move coming back to work after so long.'

Rob's head swung back to Lucy. 'Is it too much,' he asked anxiously. 'Am I expecting the impossible?'

Lucy fought the desire to throw her own coffee straight into Grant Cassidy's face. Instead she gave a carefree laugh.

'Don't be silly. Don't forget how long I worked here,' she scoffed looking at Grant. 'It will take more than a short break to make me forget how to do the job.'

Smoothing down one already smooth trouser leg and picking away a non-existent piece of fluff, Grant leant forward with a sympathetic look on his face. 'Well you're very brave Lucy. My sister went back to work after having a baby and she found it impossible to pick it all back up. She said motherhood had left her quite a different person.'

Lucy's lips thinned a little as she watched him smile suavely in her direction. She doubted he even had a sister. Maybe she would find out. Expose him as a siblingless liar.

'Well everyone's different,' she said smoothly, standing up. 'Rob asked me back because he knows what kind of worker I am.' Rob was fiddling with the papers on his desk. Lucy knew he'd come to the end of his interest span but she was reluctant to allow Grant to stay in the office dropping hints that Lucy had nothing but post baby mush between her ears and was struggling to cope.

'How about we go over the files you wanted to show me yesterday? We don't want to get to the end of the day and find you've run out of time again do we?' she added playfully.

'Oh I don't think …'

'Excellent idea you two. Good luck,' and dismissed, Grant had no option but to stand up and follow Lucy out of the door as Rob turned his attention back to his laptop.

'Oh, what am I saying!' declared Lucy as they set off down the corridor. 'I've just remembered I have a conference call booked; I need to get my papers together.'

'Conference call? Who with?' asked Grant in surprise. 'You only came back yesterday, who are you talking to?'

'I know!' said Lucy with a breathless giggle. 'You'd think everyone would have forgotten me but amazingly some of the clients have heard that I'm back and want to catch up.'

Grant stared at her in amazement. 'Which clients? Who's heard you're back?'

'Ah look at the time! So much to do. Sorry about the meeting Grant but we'll catch up later. I'm sure I'll have half an hour free this afternoon,' and with an apologetic shrug, Lucy strode down the corridor and slid into her tiny office, shutting the door firmly behind her as he stomped into his own office and slammed the door.

Chapter 10

Five minutes later Alice arrived in Lucy's tiny office to find her chewing the end of her pen and staring at the wall. Slipping her coffee onto the desk she disappeared to return seconds later with a small fold-up plastic chair which she slotted at the end of the desk.

'Now I can spend time in here helping you,' she said brightly.

'On a plastic chair!'

'Better than nothing.' Alice was a definite glass half full person.

When she'd been in her large office, now occupied by Grant, Alice had sat on the opposite side of Lucy's desk whenever she was needed. Space hadn't been a problem, in fact, Lucy could have accommodated half the bodies in the main office and still had plenty of room.

She sipped at her coffee. 'Will said I should take the chair back.'

'But I've only just found it!'

'Not your chair, my chair.'

'Your chair? Which ….?'

'Okay Grant's chair.'

Alice screwed up her nose. 'You want Grant's chair? Well, we could swap it. He probably wouldn't notice. But,' she looked around doubtfully. 'I don't think it would actually fit in here. Not if you want to keep the desk?'

'I don't actually want his chair. It's a metaphor.'

'Oh! A metaphor.' There was a small pause. 'What for?'

'You know, being the person I was, taking back control of my life.'

'And the chair …?'

'Represents all those things.'

'Right. So how are we going to get the chair back? Metaphorically of course.'

'I don't know,' admitted Lucy with a sigh. 'I need to come up with a plan.'

They sat in silence for a moment, Alice staring round for inspiration and Lucy slumped over her desk.

'So sorry to intrude.' The smooth voice entered the room followed by a well-groomed head as Grant peered round the door. There wasn't room for a third person and looking around the squashed space Grant stayed in the corridor. 'Just wondered if you had started your conference call yet?'

Sitting up a little straighter, Lucy threw a casual glance at her watch. 'Any minute now? Can I help you?'

'No, no. It's nothing. Just making sure you're okay. We have a new system for conference calls, I persuaded Rob to upgrade last month. Alice, have you set Lucy up with a password and access code? Who is the call with by the way? Perhaps I can help?'

Lucy sat very still, her hand playing idly across the pile of files on her desk as Alice, her back to Grant, met her eyes.

'Just doing exactly that,' said Alice. 'In fact, I need to get a move on or we'll be late for the call. My fault,' she gave a little laugh, 'so excited to see Lucy back.' Pushing her chair back, which left Grant taking a hasty step backwards, she grabbed the door. 'Sorry Grant, you'll have to speak to Lucy later, must get on with the call,' and in one smooth movement, she closed the door in his face.

Lucy could see his shadow hovering in the corridor briefly before he turned and disappeared, no doubt straight into Rob's office.

'Er, conference call?' asked Alice hazily.

'No conference call. I just needed to get rid of him this morning.'

Silence fell again and Lucy went back to chewing the end of her pen.

'You don't seem very happy to be back,' Alice said eventually, looking disappointed. 'I thought it would be like old times and somehow it's … different.'

Lucy gave a big sigh. The job which had consumed her every moment had disappeared into the ether with the arrival of Emily. Lucy remembered sitting in the hospital, gazing in awe at the small person in her arms and wondering how she could ever have thought anything else was important. And then Harry came along and her life became solely about looking after her children. It was a 24-hour job and she soon forgot the bliss of time spent alone. She barely remembered what it was like to luxuriate in the shower in the morning, to curl up and read, to pop out to the shops on impulse and not have to fill the car to the rafters with baby paraphernalia. It was a life so totally removed from anything she had experienced before and one which had filled her with more happiness and satisfaction than she had ever dreamed possible.

Maybe she would never have made the decision to return to work if things had been different. But until Will found something, she needed this job. She may be planning to run back home as quickly as she could and resume the mantle of motherhood the minute Will was employed again, but for now, she was at Simcock and Bright, the place she had spent many happy years and she was not going to let Grant Cassidy spoil whatever time she had here.

Sitting up straight, her eyes glinting, she looked at a despondent Alice slouched in a fold-up chair opposite her.

'No,' she said loudly.

'Er, no you didn't want to come back?' hazarded Alice.

'No. I mean yes, I didn't really want to come back but that's beside the point. I'm here now. But what I mean is - No, I will not let Grant Cassidy treat me like this.' She looked around the pokey office. 'I will not sit in this ridiculous office and be given menial tasks to do.' She slammed her hand on her desk which made it rock slightly and Alice snatched at her cup of coffee before it disgorged itself over the files.

'I am an account manager and I will be treated as such. If I am staying here then things have to be different!'

Jumping to her feet in excitement and tripping over her plastic chair, Alice leapt upwards punching the air. 'Yes!'

'Rob asked me back because I was good at my job,' announced Lucy. She paused, that was still a small sticking point. She had serious doubts about whether her brain was up to the task. Would she be able to pick it up again after all this time?

She moved on hastily. 'I left to have a baby. People look at me like I'm a different person but I haven't changed.' Actually, thought Lucy, she was very different. It was amazing how suddenly becoming a mother changed the priorities in your life.

'I haven't changed much,' she qualified. 'But I should be treated the same as anyone else. I should be treated the same as Grant!'

Another air punch from Alice whose cheeks were now pink with excitement.

'Absolutely!' she yelped. 'So what are you going to do?'

Lucy stopped. She hadn't gotten that far. 'Well, I need to get out of this office for a start,' she said thoughtfully. 'It's a bit of an insult. They wouldn't have put anyone else in here.'

'Agreed!'

'It doesn't matter that I left to start a family. When I'm in the office I'm Lucy Mathers, Account Manager, that's what counts.'

'Oh, you're so right.'

'I need to remind them how good I was … am,' asserted Lucy, her heart giving a little skip as she crossed her fingers hopefully. 'And make them forget that I've had four years away. The fact that I have babies,' her voice choked a little as a vision of Emily and Harry flashed into her head, 'is neither here nor there. In the office I'm not a mother ….'

Her phone was ringing and she saw Will's name flash up on the screen.

She pressed accept. 'Everything okay?'

'I'm lost,' groaned Will. 'So lost!'

'Oh Will!' Sinking back into her chair, she saw Alice creep out of the office and close the door quietly behind her. His voice sounded so desperate, she really hadn't given enough thought to how this was affecting him. 'It will be okay,' she said soothingly. 'Everything is going to be okay.'

'No, it won't. I don't know where I'm going. I have no idea which direction to go in.'

Lucy closed her eyes. Will's face had been grey with worry when he had told her about his firm closing down and although he had remained determinedly upbeat, that had been for Lucy's sake and she knew he was worried about finding another job. And now she was expecting him to become a stay at home father out of the blue.

'It will be okay,' she said gently. 'I believe in you Will, I know that you'll get back on your feet and find another job. This is all just temporary and I know ….'

'I'm lost!' shouted Will. 'I am actually lost. I can't find the bloody parent and toddler group, I've been running up and down the same few streets for the last 20 minutes. I have no idea where it is.'

Lucy stared at the phone. 'What on earth are you talking about?'

'I've never been. You told me that you took Harry there and you told me I had to take him there but it wasn't until I set off that I realised I didn't actually know where there was. You once pointed it out when we were driving by but I was expecting a big sign and there's nothing.' He was panting and Lucy could tell he was running, she could hear the pushchair bouncing along the pavement as Harry chuckled.

'Why didn't you ask me this morning?' she snapped, scanning her phone for the address.

'Why didn't you tell me this morning!' he yelled.

'Because I didn't know that you'd never been. What kind of father never goes to parent and toddler group?'

'The sort who goes to work! You just left a note saying I had to take Harry. No address.'

'Not disturbing anything am I Lucy?' Grant's head appeared around the door. 'No conference call in progress?'

'I had a train to catch! I can't carry on doing everything in the house as well as work.'

'You don't have to do everything in the house. But you do need to tell me where I need to take the children!'

'Is this your conference call Lucy? Shall I come back later?'

'I'm texting you the address,' Lucy said in a huff. 'Stick the postcode in Google for directions.'

'Thank you,' growled Will stiffly.

'Have you got it?'

'Sorry got …'

'I'm not talking to you Grant.'

'Yes. It's literally two minutes around the corner.'

'Do you need more information?'

'What about?'

'I'm not talking to you Grant!'

'No. I've found it.'

'Will ….' but the call had ended and the screen was now blank.

'Problems?' asked Grant sympathetically. 'Always tricky when the children are still young isn't it? It's not easy to turn off and concentrate on work.'

Lucy threw the phone down on the desk and took a deep breath. 'Not in the slightest. No problem. What can I do for you Grant?'

'Well, we don't seem to have much luck getting together to discuss the cases I need you to take on board.'

'I don't think a discussion is actually necessary,' announced Lucy, sitting back and crossing her legs. The corner of the desk caught her knee and made her eyes water. She thought longingly of her lovely big office and equally huge chair.

'I know what I'm doing Grant, that's why Rob asked me back.' She crossed her fingers, making a silent but heartfelt wish that Will would get a new job soon and she could announce she had changed her mind and was reverting to the joys of being a stay at home mother. 'So I think I should just take over the cases and do my own thing with them.'

Grant let his eyebrows meet in a rather disbelieving arc. 'You think you can cope?'

'Cope? Of course I can. Why ever not?'

Grant gave a small moue, his immaculately clad shoulders raising an inch. 'I just don't want you to be under any stress ….'

'No stress Grant. None at all. I'm ready to get started, bring it on.'

Chapter 11

Will arrived at the playgroup red faced and panting. He parked the buggy in the entrance hall with a mountain of similar ones and scooped Harry into his arms before following the noise drifting down the corridor, pushing open the door to the room he presumed held the toddler group.

The room was occupied by a large semi-circle of women, all sitting with their backs to the door and as Will stepped in the room, the thrum of conversation stopped, each woman falling silent as they turned around to stare at the late arrival. For a moment he was paralysed with indecision. One foot slid backwards. He could be out of the room, indeed the building in less than 30 seconds. He didn't have to put himself through this, he really didn't.

'Will! You made it.'

It was Fran, who he knew from the occasional BBQ and general get together and who had leapt into the fray and taken over his cake making duties.

'Hello Fran,' he said in a voice that emerged as a terrified squeak. She had seen his foot and its discreet backwards movement and leaving the circle she came to stand in front of him.

'It's okay,' she whispered, taking a firm hold of his arm to stop any more reversing, 'really, they don't bite.'

Keeping a grip on his arm, she turned to face the rest of the group.

'This is Will everybody, Harry's dad and Lucy's husband. Lucy has gone back to work temporarily and Will has taken over child minding duties until he starts a new job.'

Will gave her a grateful glance. She could have said, 'This is Will. He hasn't got a job so his wife's been forced back to work and the reason he's late is because he didn't even know where the toddler group was.'

There's no point introducing everybody, you won't remember all their names,' added Fran with a friendly smile. 'Come and join us,' and with a little push against his back he was in the room.

'Hello everybody,' he said in a voice that was still an octave or two higher than normal. 'Nice to meet you all.'

The room was full of small children. Some were laid on the floor, prone and biddable whilst others were crawling, rolling, shuffling and lurching around, mother's hands shooting out constantly to stop them from disappearing under tables, crashing into walls and colliding into other toddlers. Stepping carefully towards to the only empty seat, in the middle of the group, he sank into a chair, clutching Harry against his chest like a safety vest.

'How are you finding it then Will?' asked one figure who had a sleeping baby over one shoulder and a hand securely fastened around the jumper of another child who was wriggling determinedly at her feet.

'Oh er, okay.'

'Really?'

The chatter stopped for a moment and Will looked round at a sea of disbelieving faces.

'Well, not exactly okay,' he admitted. 'There's a lot more to it than I was expecting.'

The faces relaxed slightly.

'In fact, it's really hard,' he blurted out honestly. 'I think I preferred going to work for 10 hours a day.'

There was a collective murmur of approval, suddenly everybody looked a little friendlier.

'My husband did if for 2 weeks when I was in hospital,' announced one woman cheerfully. 'He cried when I came home and now every morning he brings me a cup of tea in bed, he says it's probably the last hot drink I'll get until he comes home.'

The women laughed.

'My old man said looking after kids was an easy job, so I booked a week away with my mother and my sister-in-law and left him to it. When I came back he apologised and made me promise never to go anywhere without him again!'

More laughter and Will smiled. Were they being sympathetic or just telling him how demanding the job was and how rubbish he was likely to be, he wondered?

The woman sitting next to Fran leaned forwards. 'It's a backbreaking job,' she said softly. 'But most men seem to think it's the simplest thing in the world and we have it easy, staying at home with a baby or two while they go off to work every morning. It's nice to hear a man admit it's difficult.'

Will grimaced. 'To be honest, I can't wait to get back to work. A difficult day in the office is nothing compared to looking after my two.'

There was a collective nod of approval and suddenly the atmospheres seemed much more inclusive. Will had a feeling he may have passed a test of some sort as the interest in him waned and chatter filled the room again. Harry slid to the floor and made for the toybox and Will tried to relax a little.

'What job did you do?' asked a voice from the chair next to him.

He turned around. The voice belonged to an attractive young woman with short golden hair and round, pale blue eyes.

'Forensic accountant,' he said. 'That's someone who …'

'I know,' said the voice with a smile.' My sister used to date a forensic accountant many years ago. My name's Jen.' She held out her hand and with a smile Will took it in his own. It wasn't often anyone had the faintest idea what his job entailed.

'I think you're very brave, not just taking on childcare but coming here.'

'It wasn't really an option,' admitted Will. 'Lucy left me a full list of where the children went and when I had to take them. We agreed that for the next few weeks I would take her place, so here I am!'

Jen smiled. 'Still, you deserve credit. We can be a little judgemental,' she said, the blue eyes twinkling. 'The best thing you could have done was admit you were finding it hard, otherwise you may have found yourself coping with the tea rota next week and collecting the subscriptions.'

'I should have made the cake today,' Will admitted in a low voice. 'I'm afraid it will be a shop bought one and it's entirely my fault.'

Jen giggled, holding one hand in front of her mouth and whispering. 'Mine are always shop bought. I just take them out of the packaging and then bash them about a bit so they don't look too perfect.'

Will grinned. At least the expectation of perfection was limited.

An hour later, a cup of cold tea on the table and an uneaten piece of cake on his plate, he retrieved Harry for the umpteenth time and sat back on his chair with a groan. The only place the children couldn't go was into the small kitchen, or out of the room into the corridor. Those were the two places Harry seemed determined to head off to and Will's back was aching from constantly scooping him up and returning him to the group. Jen cast him a sympathetic look as he returned to the inner circle. Her own little boy was sitting happily at her feet chewing on a rubber ring which he seemed to be enjoying enormously.

'Teething,' supplied Jen and Will nodded knowingly as though he understood why that would make Alfie want to chew on what looked like a dog toy. He made a mental note to ask Lucy how she stopped Harry from disappearing constantly, or maybe that was why she always had backache on a Tuesday evening and was even more exhausted than usual

A slightly older woman, neatly dressed in comfy trousers and a jumper stood up and clapped her hands. Will thought she looked like the type to have immaculately behaved children. If she told them to sit still and not go into the kitchen, they probably did exactly that.

'Okay ladies – and gentleman,' she added with a smile in his direction. 'I hope you've all had chance to get a cup of tea because now …'

Will sighed in relief. Thank God it was time to go home. He still had to collect Emily from nursery, go to the park and get lunch over with and he was already exhausted.

'Song time!'

His head jerked upwards. Song time? Lucy hadn't mentioned anything about songs.

The music started, the group of mothers abandoned their chairs and sat on the floor and like the call of the Pied Piper, the children magically returned, crawling over toys and each other as they sought out their mother's knee.

Reluctantly Will slithered onto the floor. At 6' 4" his legs were ridiculously long and they stuck out into the circle, causing several small bodies to fall over them as he desperately tried to tuck them inwards. Harry reappeared, plonking himself on Will's knee and clapping his hands enthusiastically as music suddenly filled the room.

Will recognised the tune, frantically racking his brains to remember the words as around him the mothers launched into 'The wheels on the bus' with children either singing along or watching with gummy smiles and enthusiastically waving hands. Highly embarrassed, Will tried to join in, both Emily and Harry had been singing it loudly the evening before as they sat in the bath. Will had been curled up on the bathroom floor at the time wondering if he could squeeze 40 winks while his children splashed happily in 2 inches of bubble filled water.

Jen laughed as she saw him struggle.

'Don't worry, you'll soon pick up the words,' she whispered in between verses. 'We always start with this one.'

Start with, thought Will in anguish. There were more songs coming? He'd rather hoped this was a one off.

'Do you sing every week?'

'Of course. Song is important for children. Wait until we start dancing.'

'Dancing!' gasped Will. 'I have to dance?'

Then he saw the twinkle in Jen's eye and his shoulders slumped in relief.

'You're teasing me.'

'No dancing,' she confirmed.

Grimacing at the pain in his legs, Will tried to join in, although his slightly out of tune voice mumbling words he didn't really know was painful to his own ears let alone anyone else's. He saw Jen watching him and he blushed.

'Never been much of a singer,' he muttered self-consciously.

'But you're trying,' said Jen seriously. 'And believe me, that's more than a lot of fathers would do.'

Will shrugged. He was doing this for Lucy as much as for the children. 'I need to do my share,' he said adamantly. 'Lucy has gone back to work, the least I can do is come to toddler group.'

Jen smiled at him, her pale eyes crinkling at the corners. 'Well I think you're doing wonderfully,' she congratulated, 'you should be proud of yourself.'

Will shrugged his shoulders and looked round at the group. He didn't feel very proud of himself. Only a few weeks ago his day would have been spent gazing at expenditure declarations as he argued about reasonable business expenses. He would have meeting after high flying meeting with a constant round of presentations, discussions and appraisals. Now he was sitting on the floor surrounded by small children and singing songs, worrying about the cake he would have to bake in a few weeks and hoping it didn't rain before he brought in the washing.

He closed his eyes and ignoring the sudden increase in noise level as they hit the last verse, he sent a small prayer winging upwards. Please oh please let him find a job soon. He really couldn't wait to get up at some ungodly hour and have to sit in traffic all the way into Leeds before working a long exhausting day. It sounded like absolute bliss!

Chapter 12

Lucy was slumped in her chair. Will was right, all she had to do was keep her head down, accept the work that Grant threw her way for a few weeks and then leave. She could stay in her tiny office, check Grant's files, make his phone calls and get paid. Why was she making it so much more difficult?

Pushing back her chair, only to remember that it was already wedged in against the wall she was flung forward against the desk where she caught her tights on a drawer front and watched a huge ladder spring unchecked along her thigh to disappear under the hem of her dress.

Howling in frustration she picked up a stapler to throw at the door only to see Grant's outline with a nervous Alice bobbing around behind him.

'Lucy, I have a meeting with a prospective client if you want to join me,' he said. 'I told Rob you would probably want to wait a little longer before …'

'No! I don't need to wait. I'll be there.'

Grant nodded. '15 minutes, in the large meeting room,' he instructed and he was gone, leaving Lucy with a smile on her face and Alice grinning.

'I told you it wouldn't take long before you were back in the swing of it all,' whispered Alice, peering down the corridor to make sure Grant had gone. 'I think Rob has told him to stop treating you like a trainee and give you some proper work to do.'

'About time,' grunted Lucy with feeling. She stood up, pulling her skirt down to hide the ladder now running rampant up her leg. She really needed to get her drawers stocked with spare pairs. Or just get a bigger office where she didn't have to compete with the desk for space.

Checking her lipstick and dragging a brush through her hair, she grabbed a pen and paper and turned to Alice.

'How do I look?' she asked nervously.

'Like an account manager with Simcock and Bright,' giggled Alice. 'You look wonderful. Go show Grant Cassidy how it's done.'

Although Grant had said 15 minutes, by the time Lucy walked down the corridor the visitors were already in the meeting room and the door had been firmly shut. When Lucy opened it and walked in, everybody stopped to stare at her from a meeting which had obviously already started

'Ah Lucy. Glad you could join us,' said Grant solicitously.

The room was dominated by a large oval table which was surrounded by men in grey suits, all sitting in wide, comfortable chairs, briefcases set neatly by their feet and pens in hand. The only seat available was a small office chair abandoned in the corner of the room and aware of every eye watching her, Lucy walked over and dragged it over to the table. Looking around for the widest space available, she realised that the large, executive chairs had been set wide enough apart to stop any more being added. No-one moved and she was left pushing her chair as close to the table as she could, which still left her sitting on the margins of the group and a good foot below the level of everyone else. The desk was too far away for Lucy to rest her notepad on so she left it on her knee and sat back, her cheeks pink with colour and meeting the interested gazes of the gathered suits with a challenging stare.

'Sorry about the delay,' apologised Grant smoothly once Lucy was finally seated. 'Let's get started shall we. And now Lucy has joined us, coffee anybody?'

A murmur of voices answered with various requests and with a smile Grant turned to Lucy.

'Did you get all that Lucy?'

Looking up from her pad where she had written the date and was trying to remember if Grant had mentioned the name of the client, Lucy stared round at the sea of faces.

'What?'

'The coffees,' there was a slightest suggestion of a sigh as Grant maintained a pleasant smile. 'Did you manage to get down what everybody wanted?'

'You want me to arrange the coffees?'

She detected a couple of sympathetic glances sent in Grant's direction whilst the rest of the gathering looked down at the table, obviously feeling slightly awkward in the presence of someone as dim-witted as Lucy appeared to be.

Grant wrinkled his nose a little, grimacing in apology at the group.

'Er, yes please,' he said in an encouraging tone. 'If you can manage?'

Lucy stared at him. She looked around at the visitors in their large leather chairs and Grant sitting at the head of the table and slowly she stood up, her little typist chair swivelling as she pushed it backwards.

'You want me to organise the coffees?'

'I do. Yes. Please.'

Without saying anything she walked out of the door, leaving it ajar behind her. Pausing for a moment in the corridor as she tried to control the thudding of her heart, she heard Grant speak softly to the occupants of the room.

'Just back after having a family,' he offered. A wave of understanding 'aahs' swept the room. 'Just trying to get her back into the swing of things,' he continued. 'Equal opportunities and all that sort of thing.' There were several understanding grunts.

Lucy turned to stare back into the room. Grant was shrugging his shoulders, making his feelings clear on women who insisted on returning to work after having babies. She caught his eye but his expression didn't change and he simply stared until she turned away and walked back into the main office.

A couple of minutes later Lucy returned. Pushing the door open she strode in with her head held high. Behind her was Luke, the office trainee, pushing a board room chair in front of him like a shopping trolley and behind him followed Alice and June carrying trays holding coffee pots, cups, milk jugs and a selection of biscuits.

Lucy smiled serenely at the gathering. 'I'm so sorry,' she offered. 'I left it to Grant to organise the refreshments and the seating and …'

She shrugged expressively and gave a wry smile. Their attention was all on Lucy now and they shuffled in their seats, clicking their pens and watching as she tilted her head to one side and let her eyes sweep across the group

A few of them dared a little peep in Grant's direction as Lucy gave him a teasing look. 'Grant may be good at his job,' a slight raise of one perfectly plucked eyebrow and a little twist of her lips gave the impression that she wasn't entirely convinced by this statement. 'But organising the office for a meeting is not his forte!'

The grey suits were all sitting a little straighter now, the whiff of conflict making them nervous and their pen clicking went up a level until it sounded like a backing track. Their eyes swivelled between Lucy, who was calmly directing the coffee and Grant, who sat stiff and unmoving in his seat. Alice and June laid the trays on the side table and Lucy thanked them and waved them out of the room.

'Please everybody, help yourself,' she said graciously waving a hand in the direction of the trays.

Warily, the suits stood up to help themselves to a coffee and a biscuit and as the chairs emptied, Lucy caught Luke's eyes and nodded to the end of the table opposite Grant. In a matter of seconds they had moved several of the chairs slightly sideways and slotted in an additional seat for Lucy.

By the time the group were back at the table, Lucy was amongst them, her eyes meeting Grant's in a long hard stare across the table. His lips were pressed tightly together and he made no move to take a cup of coffee, watching Lucy as she sat back in her large chair and set her pen and pad down in front of her, claiming her space.

'Thank you,' murmured one of the group and Lucy gave him such a wide smile that a chorus of 'thank you' followed, each one getting his own welcoming smile.

'Shall we press on?' demanded Grant, 'We're running a little late now,' his eyes pinned on Lucy as though to make the point that the tardiness was entirely her fault.

'Don't worry,' smiled Lucy. 'I'm sure everybody understands,' she added, ignoring the look Grant threw at her.

'Will you take the notes please Lucy,' he snapped as he opened the folder in front of him.

Lucy gave a little pout. 'Forgotten to arrange for one of the admin staff to attend? Don't worry, I'll help,' and sending a smile winging round the table, she settled into her seat with a little wiggle, flipped open her notebook and picked up a pencil, facing the group who to a man were now looking in her direction rather than Grant's.

'I'll try not to go too fast,' Grant offered, the smooth tone returning. He looked round at the room. 'Lucy only came back to work yesterday after a long break. It will take her a little bit of time to get up to speed.'

Lucy's pencil snapped, half of it flying across the table to rest in front of Grant. Ignoring it, Lucy calmly produced another one.

'Grant started at Simcock and Bright in my absence,' she said. 'This will be my first opportunity to see him in action, check he's managing okay.' She gave them all a confidential smile. 'It's taken Rob quite some time to find someone to fill the gap I left. We're hoping Grant will now be a permanent fixture at Simcock and Bright, even though I've returned.'

Almost as one, every man at the table looked at her, a row of eyebrows winging upwards as they reassessed the young woman sitting in their midst.

'Lucy is having one of her little jokes of course,' drawled Grant as all eyes swung away from Lucy in his direction. 'She was famed for her sense of humour when she worked here before, four years ago. That's when she left to start her family. As we all know a lot can happen in four years. But she's back now so let's hope she decides to stay.'

'Why wouldn't I?' challenged Lucy, bringing the eyes back in her direction.

'You may decide it's just too much for you.'

'Doubtful. I can cope Grant. Don't forget I did this job for a long time.'

'But that was some time ago. And so much has changed since then.'

'It's not that long ago, and nothing major has changed.'

'Well I'm here for one thing. That's a fairly major change.'

'But not a very important one, not in the scheme of things.'

Really? Someone taking over your job, being in the position you used to be.'

'For now.'

'Permanently,' snapped Grant.

The two were glaring at each other as the eyes in the room followed their exchange like a rather heated tennis rally, before one of them cleared his throat a little nervously and Grant visibly tried to regain control, shaking his head and returning to the matter in hand.

The meeting was over within an hour. Lucy had to congratulate Grant on his recovery and his presentation which was efficient, interesting and to the point. He had stopped several times to ask Lucy if she was managing to keep up and she had smiled sweetly on each occasion and said she was fine and eventually the meeting ended. She and Grant stood at the top of the stairs, saying goodbye and thank you to the visitors until there was just the two of them left. Turning to Grant, Lucy let the smile drop from her face and despite the difference in their height, she drew herself up tall so she could stare into his eyes.

'I am an account manager at Simcock and Bright,' she said through clenched teeth. 'I am your equal.'

Grant didn't move and out of the corner of her eye she saw Rob approach.

'Enjoy your first meeting back at Simcock and Bright?' he shouted cheerily.

'Wonderful,' Lucy said through gritted teeth. 'Great to be involved again.'

She saw Grant give her a searching look which she ignored. She would fight her own office battles; she wouldn't resort to telling tales.

'Lucy was very helpful,' Grant said in a conciliatory tone and earning a beam from Rob.

'Told you she was good! Just give her a chance.'

'Indeed,' murmured Grant.

'On our way out to lunch,' boomed Rob cheerfully. 'Just checking you'll be okay for a couple of hours.'

Okay? She had been okay for the 10 long years she had worked at Simcock and Bright. Why would today be any exception.

'Of course.' She smiled although it involved a great deal of effort. 'Going anywhere special?'

'Meeting one of the new clients Grant is trying to bring on board. You know, the big one,' said Rob winking. 'Spot of lunch and a long chat about expectations. You know what it's like.'

Of course she knew what it was like. Hadn't she done it herself on many occasions

'Why don't I come with you,' she suggested impulsively. It had to be better than sitting here drinking green gloop.

Rob raised his eyebrows approvingly. 'That's the way Lucy! Always wanting to get your teeth into whatever's going on. I don't see why you couldn't come, your chance to show Grant how it's done eh?' and he gave a loud laugh, turning to the man standing behind him.

'Fantastic idea,' said Grant smoothly. 'Unfortunately, just not possible with today's clients.'

Lucy waited, her smile fixed in place.

'The meeting is at the Oakley club. That's a gentleman only club I'm afraid Lucy…'

'I'm aware of the Oakley club, thank you,' snapped Lucy. 'Although I'm surprised that you're having a meeting there,' she said to Rob. 'I would have thought that gives out all the wrong messages. And excludes any female members of the negotiating team. You may lose the clients simply because you didn't allow some of them to attend the meeting.'

Rob's smile disappeared as he turned to Grant. 'She has a point actually …'

'Don't worry,' interrupted Grant in a reassuring tone. 'I checked out all the names on the list they provided. No women involved.'

Except of course, Lucy and he had just made sure she would be excluded from joining them.

'Right. That's okay then. Sorry Lucy, maybe next time,' and the issue already forgotten, Rob gave her a wide smile and headed back down the corridor with Grant following respectfully.

Their voices disappeared down the staircase, and Lucy stood quite still until she heard the front door close with a slight thump. Turning on her heel she walked into her office, kicking the waste paper bin only to yelp as it hit one of the table legs and bounced back to hit her on the shin.

'How did it go?' asked Alice appearing in the doorway and having to sidestep the bouncing bin. 'I heard one of them say how charming you were as they were leaving. What did Grant say?'

Lucy threw herself into her chair and sat back as far as she could without hitting her head on the wall. She kicked the bin again, this time making sure she aimed it through the legs of the desk where there was no possibility of a counter attack.

'It was okay in the end,' she said dispiritedly. 'I took the notes which gave me a chance to listen to Grant pontificate.'

'Was it unbearable?'

'No. Not really. In fact he's quite good,' said Lucy reluctantly.

'And it's a start isn't it?'

'A start?'

'You know, getting your own clients and being a proper account manager again.'

'Being invited into a meeting to organise the coffee and take notes? Hardly,' snorted Lucy. 'While I'm following him around and being his assistant, I'll never get my own clients. And without my own accounts to manage I'm not really an account manager, am I?'

Alice looked a little uncertain. 'It will just take a little bit more time.'

'Or a miracle,' groaned Lucy.

There was a small silence as Lucy stared morosely around and Alice tried to think of something encouraging to offer

'And look at this office. Rob wouldn't dream of asking anybody new to the company to work in the filing room. Why is it okay to shove me in here?'

Alice chewed at her fingernails in distress. 'I did try and stop them. I reminded Rob that you were coming back and now wasn't the time to move all the files but Grant said that after everything he'd heard about you, he knew you wouldn't care how big your office was, you would be able to do a fantastic job even if you were sitting in the car park.'

Lucy groaned, dropping her head into her hands. 'And that's the genius of the man,' she admitted. 'Not once has he said he doesn't think I can't do the job. That I could argue with.' She shook her head in reluctant admiration. 'He's playing Rob quite superbly.'

She stared round the office again, which didn't take long. 'Who have they gone to see?'

'Haydock Sportswear. Grant has had several meetings with them but he doesn't seem to be getting anywhere. They won't commit to anything.'

Standing up suddenly, Lucy slid from behind her desk.

'Do you want a coffee?' asked Alice, moving to one side so Lucy could get out of the door. 'Or lunch? Those two will be gone for hours, we could go get a bite?'

Lucy had grabbed a salad from the deli by the train station. She hadn't wanted to risk another encounter with one of the vile green protein shakes.

'A coffee would be lovely thank you Alice,' said Lucy as she stood up and walked out of her office. She peered down the corridor but all was quiet, Rob and Grant would be half way to the Oakley Club by now. It only took her two strides to reach Grant's second office and opening the door she stepped inside.

'What are you doing! No one is supposed to go in there. Grant said he has everything exactly how he needs it and no-one must touch anything. Lucy! Oh please stop, you shouldn't be doing that!'

Alice was waving her arms around in agitation in the doorway but Lucy wasn't listening. She was walking around the large desk, trailing her fingers along the small neat piles of files and reading the sloping script that covered the white board on one wall.

'Lucy!' said Alice urgently. 'Please come out of there.'

'Relax. I won't move anything but I want to see what's happening.'

Alice remained in the doorway, pulling at the ends of her hair. 'I don't think it's a good idea at all …'

'Then don't come in. How about that coffee you promised? Just leave it in the doorway and then you can say you never entered.' Lucy couldn't help grinning, it was like being a child and sneaking into a forbidden room at school. 'Stop worrying Alice. I'm just looking.'

When the coffee arrived a few minutes later, Lucy was engrossed in the files. She was reading the notes about Haydock Sportswear, the client Grant was taking to lunch and she could see why he was having trouble getting them to agree to anything other than a casual chat. They had every marketing agency in the country fighting for their business. And to Lucy's experienced eye it wouldn't result in a great deal of profit for Simcock and Bright. Their list of requirements was extensive, the competition was strong. It was often the smaller clients who ended up bringing the best results.

She placed the folder carefully back in place and moved over to the white board where a list of potential new clients occupied a central column. Normally the client list would be allocated to those with the free time and the expertise. Lucy had always been given the top clients because she was good at her job. Grant was obviously now taking his pick. Because he was also good at his job and more importantly, because he hadn't spent the last four years looking after children.

Lucy ran her eye over the list, smiling when she came across one name in particular, Blooming Lovely. She looked at the small pile of orange folders on the corner of the desk. Orange meant potential, and she flicked through them until she came to a very thin folder with Blooming Lovely printed on the front. Sitting in the large office chair, she groaned in delight at both the room and support it offered her and with Alice's cup of coffee at her elbow, Lucy started to read through everything that Simcock and Bright knew about Blooming Lovely.

Chapter 13

Lucy sat in Grant's spare office for the next few hours. She relaxed in the large comfortable chair and let the weak winter sun shine on her face. Glimpses of green could be seen outside and the sky, although a washed out blue, was clearly visible. Alice had slowly overcome her horror at Lucy's occupation of the office and she had crept in several times to place a cup of hot coffee at Lucy's elbow and take away the cold cup that had been forgotten as Lucy scoured through the files and lost herself in thought.

These were the sort of clients she should be working with. This was why Rob had asked her to come back to the fold, not to be a glorified personal assistant for Grant. Her fingers itched to gather up the files and take control. She was used to sharing accounts. There had been plenty of account managers at Simcock and Bright and they would all work together. Lucy always achieved the best results, she was considered the most talented and she had her pick of the top accounts, just as Grant had now. She didn't expect Rob to instantly give Lucy the most important customers, but she couldn't sit in her poky little office checking Grant's work, proofreading, chasing mundane queries. How could she prove to herself and Rob that she was still the Lucy Mathers of old if she couldn't get her hands on some of these clients?

She heard the boom of Rob's voice from halfway up the staircase closely followed by Alice's anguished face appearing at the doorway and sliding her shoes back on, Lucy slipped out of the office and across the corridor into her own. She had been careful to place everything back exactly where she had found it and the room looked serene, untouched. But she had copied every sheet of paper that lay inside the folder marked Blooming

Lovely and there was now a nondescript grey folder sitting in her top drawer.

She heard a slightly drunken Rob demanding coffee and she looked up to catch Grant surreptitiously checking if she were still sitting in her office. Giving him a bright smile she waited until the office had returned to its normal calm state and checked her watch. In five minutes Rob would have finished his coffee and be sitting in his chair feeling magnanimous and maybe a little sleepy. In 10 minutes he would be open to any suggestion she made if it sounded remotely feasible. In 30 minutes he would begin to feel tetchy, the intake of alcohol at lunchtime didn't really agree with him although he would never admit that. In an hour he would want to call it a day and go home but he would have to weigh up the advantage of a snooze on his settee with the possibility of being called upon to perform some fatherly duties. He may be asked to peel some potatoes or even worse help with some homework. Children, as far as Rob was concerned, were there to love unconditionally, from afar. Hands on parenting was something that filled him with horror. If he stayed in the office he would be grumpy and looking for someone to find fault with.

Lucy kept a careful eye on her watch and 12 minutes later, she checked her lipstick, straightened her skirt and walked down the corridor into Rob's office. As she expected Grant was sitting in the chair opposite and whilst Rob had slightly flushed cheeks and glazed eyes, Grant looked as sharp as ever.

'Lucy!' shouted Rob effusively. 'Come and join us. What a shame you couldn't come to lunch,' he added giving Grant a slightly reproachful look.

Taking the chair next to Grant, Lucy gave Rob a big smile. 'Couldn't be helped,' she said generously. 'How did it go?'

She turned slightly in her seat, giving Grant a supportive smile. 'Did you have better luck today? Any sign that they might be taking us seriously?'

She saw his shoulders stiffen and his head whip round in her direction but before he could speak Rob had already answered.

'Not really,' he said with a sigh. 'They're happy to talk but won't commit to us taking part in a pitch.'

Grant's eyes narrowed. 'It's just a matter of time,' he said easily. 'Nothing we can't overcome.'

'Bit disheartening though?' offered Lucy. 'So many meetings and still no commitment. After all, when do you stop? There's only so many expensive lunches, theatre tickets, golf invites and the like that you can justify before you have to make the decision to pull back.'

For once the smooth smile was absent from Grant's face as Rob slammed his hand on the table.

'She's right,' he shouted. 'That's my Lucy, always looking at the bottom line. She has a lot of experience in these things you know Grant.' He leant forwards, tapping the side of his nose, 'You should listen to her, she knows what she's talking about.'

Smiling sweetly, Lucy sat back in her chair.

'I don't think we're at that position yet,' said Grant stiffly. 'I will get us this contract Rob, I know a thing or two about the business myself you know.' He gave a short laugh that sounded anything but happy and Lucy nodded.

'Of course you do,' she said soothingly. 'It's just a little unusual for a company to take so long before they even agree that we can pitch.'

Rob cast an admonishing glance over the table at Grant's stony face. 'She's right!'

Lucy continued. 'But if I can help, well, you know where I am.'

'She might have some ideas. She was always the best at getting the clients on board.' Rob looked across the table affectionately. 'How's it going then Lucy? Everything alright?'

Lucy had a quick glance at her watch. She had 9 minutes left.

Sighing, she took her time answering, crossing her legs and nibbling delicately on her bottom lip.

'Lucy?'

'Sorry Rob but, well, if you must know I think I've made a mistake.'

She could feel the elation in the air. She saw the slight jerk of Grant's knee and could feel the palpable relief flowing from him. The smooth smile was back in place.

'What? Lucy! What do you mean?' Rob was sitting up straight, staring at Lucy in shock.

Lucy gave another small sigh and let a little knot of worry play along her eyebrows. Grant turned a concerned face in her direction but not before she'd seen the blaze of triumph in his eyes.

'I don't think it's going to work out Rob. I hadn't understood why you wanted me back.'

'Why? Because you were the best account manager we'd ever had! Why else would I have been pestering you for the last four years to come back?'

'Well that's why I thought you wanted me to come back, to carry on, keep doing the same job.'

'I do!' Rob's face was twisted in confusion. 'What are you talking about?'

'It's just,' Lucy cleared her throat delicately, 'it's just that you appear to have brought me back to be an assistant. Grant,' she paused and gave him a wide, appreciative smile, 'is doing such a wonderful job and of course he's busy. But surely that means you need another account manager, not someone to check files and chase up details. Anyone in the office could do that. You could take on a trainee and save yourself a lot of money Rob.'

Grant's smile was beginning to slip, his hands resting stiffly on his knee, his tense shoulders unmoving.

'No,' she said decisively. 'You don't need me in this role. I think we both made a mistake.'

Rob's mouth was hanging open. He stared at Lucy before he pressed his hands flat across his desk.

'No! You can't leave! I don't want an assistant or an office worker. I want you, Lucy Mathers!'

Lucy raised her eyebrows. 'Really?' she asked doubtfully.

'Of course! I need your skills, your touch with the clients.' He suddenly caught sight of Grant sitting silently next to Lucy.'

'I need both of you. What a team we would have, eh? You can't go Lucy,' he pleaded.

'I see,' said Lucy slowly. 'So, you do want me to be an account manager again?'

Rob nodded fervently.

'You want me signing up new clients, opening new accounts, making sure Simcock and Bright is everybody's first choice?'

Rob continued to nod solemnly and there was a small noise from Grant as he cleared his throat.

'And of course, to help Grant as much as possible win new clients and keep McCarthy & McCarthy,' added Lucy.

'Of course,' answered Rob.

'Okay, I understand.'

'Will you stay?' Rob asked hopefully.

Lucy took a peep at Grant's face which was immobile and devoid of expression as he stared at Rob's desk.

'Well I suppose now we both know what you want from me …'

'Wonderful,' shouted Rob. 'Wonderful. Phew. I'm glad we've cleared that up. Don't want Lucy leaving before she's even got started, do we Grant?'

'Of course not. Absolutely not.' Grant turned to give Lucy a smile, reluctant admiration in his eyes. 'Perish the thought!'

Lucy accepted their accolades modestly.

'So,' she said brightly to Rob. 'I better get on with it hadn't I? Of course,' she added generously. 'I'll carry on helping Grant with anything he needs.'

He nodded stiffly in response.

'But I'm thinking, it's time to start getting some of these new clients on board.'

'So soon?' asked Grant gently. 'You don't think you need a little bit longer …'

'If she says she's ready,' interrupted Rob. 'Then she's ready.'

'So I was hoping,' continued Lucy, ignoring them both, 'that I could take on Blooming Lovely.'

Grant's head swivelled in her direction and his eyes bored into her. She could see the emotions playing across his face, he knew she'd been in his office.

'Of course it's not a big case, I'll leave those to Grant for now,' she laughed, earning an approving nod from Rob. 'But it sounds as though he'll have his hands full with Haydock Sportswear.'

Rob nodded again.

'But I was thinking it would help if I took over this smaller client, to see what I can do with them.'

'Excellent idea Lucy,' said Rob enthusiastically. 'Absolutely excellent idea, don't you think Grant?'

Grant was still staring at Lucy although she kept her eyes firmly on Rob's face.

'Yes, I suppose. Where did you come across Blooming Lovely? I hadn't realised that I'd given you the file?'

'It's a new client isn't it?' asked Lucy vaguely. 'I thought we were in the running for the business?'

'Yes, but where did you come across their file? I thought …'

'Does it matter,' shouted Rob, waving his arms around in irritation.

Lucy looked at her watch. 30 minutes had passed. Rob would now be feeling the effects of the wine and brandy he had consumed over lunchtime. He was entering his tetchy phase.

She stood up without answering Grant, smiling happily at Rob.

'I'll get started,' she announced efficiently. 'We don't want to waste any more time.'

Rob nodded, he was a great believer in getting on with things, especially as his attention span was so short.

She could see Grant was torn. Did he follow Lucy and interrogate her about where she learned about Blooming Lovely or did he stay and try and influence Rob?

Lucy headed out of the door, closing it firmly behind her and as she set off down the corridor she could see that Grant was still sitting opposite Rob, straightening his tie as no doubt he searched for the right words to tell Rob that Lucy wasn't up to the job, that she wasn't ready to take on a new client. He was wasting his time, she thought with a grin. Rob had made his decision and already lost interest. He would be bad tempered and short with Grant now if he tried to push the subject. She had won, she had her first potential new client since her return to Simcock and Bright. Now she just had to hope and pray that she was as good as everybody seemed to think she was.

Chapter 14

Back in her office, Lucy shut the door behind her and tried desperately not to scream out with glee. She peered up the corridor to see if Grant was in sight then despite the pain in her feet, executed a quick little jig of delight.

Alice's face appeared at the door, pink and anxious.

'What happened? Does Grant know you've been in his office? Does Rob know? Are you okay?'

Lucy grinned happily. 'Grant suspects, Rob doesn't care and I've got a chance of a new client!'

'What? Fantastic!'

'Blooming Lovely. It's a florist about to open a superstore in Leeds. No-one has had a floral superstore before, it will be interesting to see what we can do for them.' Lucy's eyes took on a faraway look. 'Who goes to a floral superstore? What are they looking for?' she mused.

'I've no idea but what did Grant say?'

Lucy dragged herself back. 'About what?'

'About you going into his office?' squealed Alice.

'Oh, he can't prove anything,' shrugged Lucy. 'Besides, he shouldn't have all the new cases in there. Rob used to keep them and dole them out.'

'Was he angry?'

'Rob?'

'No Grant.'

'Probably.' Lucy remembered the burning look he'd cast her way when she'd mentioned Blooming Lovely. 'Yes, he was angry,' she decided with a grin.

'His eyes go much darker when he's angry,' Alice said thoughtfully. 'And the tips of his ears go ever so slightly pink.'

Lucy stared at her friend.

'He was really cross when Graham went to work for the competition and I noticed then how pink his ears were.'

'You seem to have spent a lot of time studying Grant Cassidy. I thought you didn't like him?'

'I don't! Nobody likes him.'

Alice had gone rather pink herself.

'But you've noticed that his eyes go darker and his ears turn pink?'

Alice flushed deeper. 'Noticing things about your working colleagues doesn't mean you like them,' she said defensively. 'I just take note of what he's doing so I can… so I can…'

'Yes?'

'So I can tell you!'

'Right. And it doesn't mean that you fancy him something rotten?'

'No! I've told you, I don't like him.'

Lucy gave her friend a grin. 'Liking someone and fancying them isn't the same thing at all Alice.'

'Well I don't,' said Alice huffily. 'I don't do either of those things. I mean I don't like him or fancy him.'

Lucy relented. 'If you say so. Now, I've already done a little bit of research on Blooming Lovely but I need to get every scrap of information I can on this company and I would appreciate your help so let's get cracking. Oh and whatever happens, keep Grant out of my office for the rest of the afternoon,' and forgetting about her friend's possible crush, Lucy pulled out the Blooming Lovely file from her drawer and took great pride in transferring it to a bright orange pending customer file with her name in large letters in the bottom right hand corner.

It wasn't easy avoiding a conversation with Grant. His face loomed in her doorway several times but she'd already begun to recognise the sound of his door opening and his footsteps on the corridor and she was invariably on the phone speaking loudly whenever he appeared. Waving him away apologetically, she mouthed 'later' several times until eventually she heard him walking angrily in the opposite direction and Alice appeared to tell her he had left the office for an appointment. Lucy slipped into his second office and watched him striding down the pavement, his blond hair seemingly immune to the effects of the wind, before disappearing from view and then she spent the rest of the afternoon at the large desk, stretching out her legs and browsing through every piece of information Alice brought her about Blooming Lovely and their new floral superstore.

***

Will heard the front door open and close and knew that Lucy was back home. The children had finished their baths and were wrapped up warm and snuggly in their pyjamas and waiting for their night time story. Harry had dropped his towel in the bath and although Will had squeezed it as much as possible it was still soaking wet. Emily had watched Will take it out of the bath with a sigh and then somehow her tights had also fallen in the water and although Will gave her a searching look, she had smiled back prettily and told him it had been an accident. He had taken the soaking items into the utility room and was just considering what to do with them when he heard Lucy return home.

He was exhausted. His back ached, his head ached. His knees were sore from crawling round the floor, his spirit was defeated and he really wanted to go to bed. But he had managed most of the items on his to do list and survived the day. There was even a half-prepared meal sitting on the hob, if he could stay awake long enough to eat anything. Walking into the kitchen, his heart constricted at the sight of his wife, hair a little curly from the damp air outside, dark shadows under her eyes and looking every bit as tired as he felt.

'Good day?' he asked gently, wrapping his arms around her as she struggled out of her coat.

'Actually, not bad.'

'Take back the chair?'

Lucy giggled. 'Not quite, but it's certainly moving a little nearer!'

She took a quick peek round the kitchen. It was far from spotless but nowhere near the shambles of the previous night. She picked up one of Harry's toy cars, carefully placed for her to stand on in her bare feet.

'And you?'

Will nodded, trying to look positive. 'Okay,' he said injecting a bright note he didn't really feel.

'Toddler group?'

'Well we got there in the end.' They both looked a little shame faced at the memory of their altercation earlier that morning. 'It was okay.'

Lucy nodded, looking guilty. 'I suppose it's not easy being the only man there,' she admitted. 'If you want to give it a miss while you're at home …'

'No,' interjected Will firmly. 'If it's what would normally happen then I'll carry on going.'

Lucy nodded, too weary to argue.

'I got my first potential client today.'

Will looked up from the sink in surprise. 'Hey that's great. But I thought Grant was blocking you?'

Lucy shrugged. 'I had to get tactical.' She scooped Harry into her arms and breathed in his baby scent. 'You reminded me that I know Rob better than most people, I used the same kind of tactics Grant is using.'

'And you're not tempted to just keep your head down and take the easy path?'

'I thought about it,' admitted Lucy.

'For how long?'

'About 30 seconds,' she said with a grin. 'It's just not me.'

Kissing the top of her head Will laughed. 'No, my darling, it certainly isn't.'

Leaving Will in the kitchen, Lucy sat on the settee with a warm body either side of her and read a bedtime story. To think she used to find it so boring reading the same story over and over again. She would groan as she washed and dried and dressed their squirming little bodies every night and long for Will to come home so he could entertain them for an hour while she got on with their evening meal. What she wouldn't give now to return to the tedium of life with her children. She may have won a small victory in the office but it had taken such effort, such determination. Was every day going to be like this, she wondered? Had every day been like this before?

Stories read and children dispatched to bed, Will and Lucy sat down at the kitchen table and wearily picked up a knife and fork. Will had cooked chicken in red wine with onions and mushrooms and peas. There wasn't much on the plate.

'I forgot about any potatoes,' he confessed as they stared at the plate. 'And then when I did remember, there wasn't enough time.'

'It's okay,' Lucy said kindly. 'I'm not that hungry.'

The chicken was a small dried out lump in the middle of the plate, the red wine sauce was a muddy puddle and the onions, cut into huge chunks and still almost raw, sat next to a couple of mushrooms and a spoonful of peas.

Lucy smiled encouragingly and took a mouthful. The wine had been poured over the chicken in the pan and left for a couple of minutes. It was like having a warm glass of rather murky wine rather than the rich red sauce Lucy produced. She chewed the chicken.

'It's okay,' she lied.

'No it's not,' sighed Will throwing down his knife and fork. 'It's awful.'

Lucy winced as she tried to swallow the chicken.

'Toasted teacake?' offered Will.

'Sounds lovely.'

They cleared the table together and Lucy put on the kettle and fished out some teacakes. At least her old clothes would soon fit without any problem. She had barely eaten anything at work over the last few days.

Flopping onto the settee, the TV rolling in the background, they both stared out through the patio doors into the dark garden.

'Any sign of a job?' asked Lucy hopefully.

'No. Well there was one but it was in Edinburgh and it's a long commute,' answered Will.

They both lapsed back into silence.

'You must be pleased you're back on track at work?' he asked

'Yes, I suppose. It's just a case of getting used to it all again.' Lucy decided not to tell Will just what a struggle she was finding the switch. She would rather be at toddler group any day than sitting in the office doing battle with Grant Cassidy. But she didn't want to worry him, he had enough on his plate already. 'It's just a bit intense.'

Will nodded. He would trade intense for a toddler group session. He would trade strategies and tactics and a hard day at the office in place of looking after two children all day. But he decided not to tell Lucy how difficult he was finding it all, she had enough to worry about with her return to work, he didn't want her worrying about him as well.

'You'll soon pick it back up,' he said confidently.

'Of course,' said Lucy.

'In a couple of weeks it will feel like you never left,' Will said. 'You'll be well and truly back in workforce mode,' he added enviously, sending a fervent prayer winging upwards that she wouldn't be the only one.

'I probably will,' trilled Lucy, wondering if a commute to Edinburgh was totally out of the question.

'We just need to keep going a few more weeks,' Will said, trying to sound encouraging.

'Absolutely,' agreed Lucy. 'It won't be long and you'll have a job again and I'll be back at home and everything will be back the way it should be!'

And holding onto that thought, they sat in silence staring out into the darkness.

Chapter 15

It had only taken a few days for Lucy to get used to her new routine and the moment the alarm burst into her dreams she leapt into action. Bleary eyed she dashed downstairs to organise the day, making sandwiches and taking a meal out of the freezer for the children. She checked Emily's school bag and made sure everything was present and laid out shoes and coats before she disappeared into the utility room. Half of the washing from the previous day was dry. Will had obviously put some out on the line. The rest was in the tumble dryer but with several items trailing out onto the floor and with a soaking wet towel thrown in their midst. With a sigh Lucy put all the damp clothes in a basket, shoved in a fresh wash for today and left a big note for Will to put everything on the line.

Hearing the children making their way downstairs she took her opportunity and claimed the bathroom, closing her eyes under the stream of hot water and wishing she could just stay there indefinitely, warm and immune to the noises of the household.

She had found another dress that didn't pull too tightly across her stomach and although her toes gave a little squeal of protest when she forced them into a pair of heels, it didn't seem anywhere near as painful as it had only days before.

Gazing in the mirror she decided she already had new worry lines gathering and she touched her concealer gently over the bruises that were starting to collect under her eyes.

Pulling a brush through her hair she ran back down the stairs and grabbed both children to her chest for a long moment, kissing the tops of each silky head.

'You'll need to go shopping today,' she told Will as she pulled on her coat.

'To the supermarket?' he asked aghast.

'Well unless you can think of anywhere else that sells all the food we need,' answered Lucy looking at her watch.

'But how, I mean when …' he gazed at his to do list in horror.

'Two options,' said Lucy briskly, heading for the door.

'Be ready, the minute you leave Emily at nursery, go straight to the shop. You can be home in time to unpack everything before you go back to collect her. Only problem is Harry will be grumpy because he likes a mid-morning nap. Second option,' she gave her handbag a quick check to make sure she had everything she needed,' pick Emily up and then go.'

'And the problem with that is …?'

'You'll have two children and a trolley to contend with, when you get home you'll have to get straight on with their lunch and they'll both want to help putting everything away,' advised Lucy cheerfully. 'It takes hours!'

She picked up her briefcase, which so far held only the train timetable and a spare pair of tights.

'Right I'm off,' she pressed another kiss onto Emily and Harry's head, tried to ignore the shooting pain of regret as she thought about spending the day at work and opened the door. 'And don't forget to get *all* the washing on the line today. What was the wet towel all about?' and she was gone, not waiting for an answer as Will stood by the kitchen sink and wished with all his heart he was rushing off to work in her place.

Grabbing a couple of coffees on her way in, she deposited one on Rob's desk along with a big grin. She needed to make sure he was still okay with the idea of her taking over Blooming Lovely. He was on the phone but gave her a big wink and a smile as she left the coffee on his desk and she knew that whatever Grant may have tried the day before, it hadn't worked. Leaving her coat in the main office, she squeezed herself behind her desk and flipped open her laptop.

There was no point sitting here regretting that she'd had to come back to work and missing her children. She was here and she needed to make the most of it. She'd managed to emerge from Grant's enforced shadow and grab a client, now she needed to do the very best she could with the case. And somehow get herself out of this ridiculously small office. And get her chair back. And destroy Grant Cassidy in the process. Whoops, maybe that was going a little too far. She probably wouldn't be at work long enough for that anyway, surely Will would find a job in the next few weeks?

Pushing the thought out of her head she carefully arranged all the facts she had about Blooming Lovely around her desk. It was time to turn on the old Lucy Mathers' magic and make this client beg to have Simcock and Bright represent them.

Working flat out, losing herself in her research, Lucy jumped when the door of her office flew open so violently it bounced off the wall and closed again. She stared at Grant's confused face, still on the other side of the door and watched as he tried again, opening the door cautiously and stepping in.

'Good morning Lucy,' he said politely. 'Just wanted to touch bases today and check everything is okay. Where did you say you heard about Blooming Lovely again?'

Lucy sat back and considered him for a moment. There was no doubt in her mind that Grant was doing everything he could to hinder her. She doubted he really cared whether she was struggling with returning to work after having a family. She didn't believe he had any genuine concerns for her wellbeing, any sympathy and murmurs about how she should take things slowly were purely for show. He simply didn't want Lucy in the office.

She put down her pen and met his eyes. 'In your 'spare' office.'

His eyes flashed. 'You went into my office and through my belongings! That's unacceptable behaviour Lucy and I have no option to report this to Rob.'

'No. I didn't go into your office and through your belongings. I went into the room where you are keeping all the current files, which incidentally belong to Simcock and Bright, not Grant Cassidy. And I looked for one I needed.'

He paused and she could see him thinking.

'I wouldn't dream of going into your personal office,' she added. 'I agree that would be quite unacceptable. But those aren't your files Grant, they are business files that we all need to be able to access.'

'I don't agree,' argued Grant. 'I am keeping my files in there and must demand privacy.'

'Your office not big enough for you?' snapped Lucy. 'You can't keep files away from the rest of the staff. It's not … an organic or fluid way to deal with them.'

His lips thinned. 'I need space because I've got so much to do,' he argued. 'I need extra room …'

'Then give me some of your work. Not the silly bits of proof reading you tried to send my way. Let me help. And not by asking me to make coffee,' she glared at him but there was no hint of shame in the look he gave her back. 'If you have too many clients, I'll take some, help you out!'

'No! I don't need help I just need you to stay away …'

'Whatever is going on?' boomed Rob's voice, taking them both by surprise as he appeared in the doorway. There was no way three people could fit in Lucy's office so he stayed in the corridor, his head jutting into the room as he stared at the two flushed figures.

'Having an argument, are we?'

'No,' replied Grant smoothing his tie and wrestling back his composure, 'of course not.'

'No,' agreed Lucy.

'Good. Can't have my two stars at loggerheads, can we?'

Rob laughed, then as no-one laughed with him he stopped, his gaze swivelling from Lucy to Grant and back again.

'A bit of colleague rivalry going on?' he asked intuitively.

Lucy watched him from underneath her lashes. Rob may appear to be slightly confused some of the time, totally disinterested much of the time and very fond of a long, lazy lunch that kept him out of the office, but underneath all that he was as sharp as an arrow and had an instinct she had long since admired.

Neither of them answered and a little smile began to play round his mouth. 'I see,' he said slowly. 'Egos getting in the way are they?'

Both Grant and Lucy looked indignant as they protested.

'Certainly not!'

'Not at all!'

'That's okay,' said Rob waving his hand to calm them down. 'It's perfectly okay, a little healthy competition is good for sales targets. So why don't we make this interesting and see which one of you will be the first one to close their client?'

There was a long moment of silence as Lucy and Grant both stared at Rob.

'Unless you both feel that you can't …'

'That's fine,' answered Lucy quickly. 'I don't mind a challenge. What do you say Grant?'

She stared at him, scowling at the mocking look of disregard he sent back.

'That will be interesting,' he murmured. 'Very interesting. Good idea Rob, count me in,' and with a small, complacent smile he turned his back and walked out of the office, a move which didn't have quite the impact he was hoping for because he had to climb over Rob to get out of the doorway.

Lucy watched him walk back to his office, closing his door firmly behind him.

'You okay with this Lucy?' Rob serious for once and looking slightly concerned as his eyes rested on Lucy.

'Of course!'

'Because you know if you need a little longer to get up to speed, I'll be happy to …'

'I don't need any favours Rob! Or time. I'm quite happy taking the challenge.'

'Okay. Okay. That's good,' and with a satisfied grin Rob went ambling back to his office and left Lucy wide eyed and full of alarm, tapping her fingers nervously against her desk.

It was strenuous enough returning to work, the last thing she needed was pressure to sign up her first client. Why on earth didn't she just keep her mouth shut and with a groan she turned back to her files with a new feverish determination.

When her phone rang and she saw Will's name flash up on her screen she couldn't help the small sigh that erupted.

Putting him on speaker she carried on reading the article she had just found which detailed the rise of Denise Albright, the new CEO of Blooming Lovely and the person behind the idea of a floral superstore.

'Do you realise how many varieties of toilet roll there are?' demanded Will.

'Toilet Roll?'

'Yes. There are literally hundreds of them! Which one do we buy?'

Denise had been part of the sales team only 5 years previously, become area sales manager, national sales manager and then in a move that shocked just about everyone, other than presumably Denise, she had been announced as the new CEO of Blooming Lovely the previous year.

'Lucy? Are you listening to me? Which toilet roll do we get?'

Lucy pulled her eyes from the report reluctantly.

'Blue packaging, quilted, almost at the end of the display.'

'Got it. You disappeared before I had chance to ask you this morning,' said Will accusingly,' what do we need?'

Since her appointment, Denise had overhauled several aspects of the business and although there had been an initial lack of support for her, she had claimed bluntly that was entirely down to the fact that she was female and under 50 and her detractors had eventually been forced to reluctantly admit that she was doing an excellent job.

'Lucy!' demanded Will.

'What?'

'What do I buy?'

Lucy gave an exasperated sigh and stopped reading the report.

'You buy what we need! Didn't you check before you went to see how much bread and milk we had left, if we needed eggs or more juice?'

There was a brief silence.

'Er, no. Should I have?'

'Of course! How else do you know what to buy?'

'I thought you might have a list somewhere.'

Lucy gritted her teeth. 'No, Will. I don't have a magic list anywhere. I just keep a note of what I use during the week and buy more of the same!'

'Okay!' said Will huffily. 'It isn't easy you know! This is my first solo shop.'

'Then perhaps you should have organised it better,' Lucy muttered.

'What?'

'Nothing. I have to go. Bye'

Silencing her phone she turned back to the report on Denise Albright.

10 minutes later her phone rang again and Will's name appeared. Groaning, Lucy answered.

'Yes?'

'Juice. There are so many and …'

'Sugar free orange squash.'

'Ah. Okay. But what about …

'Will, you've been making the children drinks all week, haven't you noticed what bottle it's coming from?'

'Well, sort of but …'

'Then sort of work out which one you need to buy,' and she cancelled the call with a grunt.

It was only 5 minutes before the next call.

'Which yoghurts? I can find the one I know Harry likes but what are Emily's favourites?'

'For God's sake Will! I can't do the shopping by proxy. Just choose some yoghurts!'

'I'm trying my best,' Will responded in a hurt tone. 'I'm just asking for a little support.'

Lucy held onto the edge of the desk tightly, watching her knuckles go white. She should apologise, she decided. Will was right, he was doing his best. But she was doing her best as well; she had returned to work despite a deep seated fear that she was no longer up to the job, she was fighting to get her position back, she had managed to wrestle her first client from the pit bull jaws of Grant Cassidy and she had now agreed to a ridiculous competition to see who could sign their account first. She could do with a little support herself.

'I'm sorry,' she said eventually, a little stiffly. 'I'm just really busy Will and I can't think about yoghurts and this case I'm dealing with at the same time.'

She paused, giving Will an opportunity to apologise in return. Nothing.

'Oh just choose some,' she snapped and cancelled the call with a vicious poke of her finger.

Chapter 16

Will pushed his phone back into his pocket and kicked the wheel of the trolley, much to Harry's amusement.

Forcing a smile for his son, he pushed a hand through his floppy dark hair and muttered to himself as he resumed his search of yoghurts. He bitterly regretted announcing that this would be fun, a change from the daily grind of work and an opportunity to bond with his children. How Lucy must have laughed inside when he'd made such a sweeping statement. He'd had no idea just how arduous it was all going to be! But she could have offered a little more support, he thought as he stared desperately at row upon row of almost identical looking pots of yoghurt. Of course he should have checked before he threw Harry in the car and set off like a maniac to the supermarket. But would it have hurt Lucy to advise him to go through the fridge and cupboards that morning? He felt a little as though he had been thrown to a pack of particularly hungry wolves.

His hand hovered uncertainly over a pack of yoghurts that seemed similar in colour to the ones Emily had been eating during the week. He stared at Harry who was watching him impassively.

'What do you think little man? Are these the ones?'

Harry blinked solemnly and stared at the yoghurts Will was holding.

'Any clue Harry? Smile if you think Emily likes these yoghurts.'

Harry continued staring at his father, no change of expression visible and with a groan Will put the pots next to several others in the trolley. He had bought far too many and he really wasn't sure any of them were the right ones.

Pushing the trolley up the next aisle he felt on slightly safer ground. Bread. Surely even he could work this one out. Letting

Harry hold a long crusty French stick, he piled the trolley with loaves, teacakes, crumpets and anything else that looked vaguely familiar.

'Well at least we'll have sandwiches to fall back on,' he muttered before groaning as the next turn brought him alongside several hundred different cereals.

Will cast a desperate eye over them all before closing his eyes and trying to remember what boxes were currently sitting in the cupboard. Lucy lined up the cereal every morning complete with Post-it notes on each box containing either Harry or Emily's name. Will had cleared them away but he'd never really taken a great deal of notice which child was eating which cereal. He winced a little. Maybe Lucy had a point. A very small point. Maybe he needed to start paying a little more attention and not be quite so reliant on Lucy laying everything out each morning.

'Right Harry,' he said briskly. 'So what do we want eh?'

'Cornflakes,' said Harry happily.

'Cornflakes it is. Ah, just a minute, you don't mean cornflakes, do you? Mummy said you actually mean porridge.'

'Cornflakes,' reiterated Harry with a gummy smile.

Will grabbed a box of porridge and showed them to his son. 'Okay Harry?'

Harry nodded happily. 'Cornflakes!' he shouted in glee.

Will threw the porridge in the trolley. 'Cornflakes it is. Now Emily,' he mused. 'What is it that Emily's been eating?' he asked himself, his eyes running over the shelves.

'Cornflakes.'

'No, she doesn't like cornflakes Harry. Ah!' suddenly Will spied a familiar looking box and grabbed it.

'This is Emily's favourite isn't it?'

Harry nodded. 'Cornflakes,' he agreed.

Will looked at his watch. He really needed to put a move on or he would be late collecting Emily from nursery and that was frowned upon as much as arriving late, something he had been careful not to do since his first morning.

The next aisle was easy. Wine. Without any hesitation, Will grabbed a couple of bottles of their favourite and in the trolley they went. He walked on a few steps then stopped, reversed and added another bottle for good measure. He had a feeling he was going to need it over the coming week. The fresh meat aisle brought him to a standstill. So far his attempts at cooking had been few and unpopular. He realised, somewhat guiltily, that he had been happy to leave all of the cooking to Lucy. In their pre-baby years they had lived off takeaways and anything that was easy to throw in a pan when they both arrived home exhausted. After Emily was born, their meals had become more nourishing and far healthier, but just how Lucy created those recipes was something of a mystery to Will.

He grabbed some chicken and some mince with little idea what it would turn into and then continued to the next aisle where his eyes grew wide and he came to an abrupt stop. Piled high on both sides of him were meals, proper meals, already cooked, already chopped and seasoned, all looking mouth-wateringly delicious and all in a box. He browsed the shelves in awe. He'd had no idea you could buy such an amazing selection of food already prepared for you. Why on earth would anyone make life unnecessarily harder for themselves when all this existed? With an enormous feeling of relief and a much happier look on his face, Will searched through the stacks for the type of meals Lucy regularly produced and soon his trolley held a meal for every night. Feeling much happier, he turned to smile at Harry only to give a yelp that reverberated around the high ceilings of the supermarket.

'Harry!'

The toddler had abandoned the French stick and had instead grabbed one of the packets of yoghurts piled in the trolley. Forcing the foil cover off and his hand in, he was now busy smearing creamy yoghurt over his face, his hair, his clothes and several other items in the trolley.

'Yummy!' he shouted, grinning. 'Yummy daddy!'

'Harry! What on earth, stop!'

Grabbing the yoghurt pot, Will moved it to the end of the trolley and then looked around frantically for something to wipe up the mess that covered Harry's face and was now all over Will's fingers. Lucy always had something to hand. Whatever the emergency she would whip something from her pocket or her bag and take care of things. She would probably have had a pack of baby wipes with her, or some tissues, or both. Or a spare set of clothes – whatever they needed it always seemed to appear from her bag. Why didn't men carry bags, wondered Will looking around for inspiration? Why didn't men have these wonderful contraptions full of items so very necessary to any day spent with a toddler? He fumbled in his empty pockets, not even an old snotty tissue came out. Other than his wallet and phone, he had precisely nothing with him.

He looked around helplessly as an elderly woman walked by, but she just sniffed and carried on walking, probably wondering why he hadn't brought any baby wipes with him, thought Will. Peering up and down the aisle brought him no inspiration whatsoever. There was nothing else for it and gingerly he lifted up the edge of his t-shirt, rolling it upwards slightly so he could use the underneath to wipe Harry's face. If he got the majority of the yoghurt on the inside of his t-shirt, it would go unnoticed, although its cold wetness was already pressing against his skin making Will cringe at the thought of all that yoghurt now smeared over his stomach. With only the bottom half of Harry's face clean, his T-shirt was already soaked. How could so much yoghurt come out of such a little pot he wondered, gamely pulling his shirt out as much as he could to wipe the rest of Harry's face.

'Goodness me! What on earth happened?' asked a familiar voice and turning around, as much as he could with his t-shirt pressed against his son's face, Will saw a surprised Jen standing next to him, watching him contort his body so he could use his clothing as a towel.

'Yoghurt,' grunted Will. 'Banana yoghurt. I put them too close to Harry and …'

They both looked at the Harry who beamed from beneath his yellow mask.

'So I see. Put your t-shirt away, I have some baby wipes somewhere,' and Will sagged in relief as the experienced hand of motherhood took over. Wipes were produced to clean Harry's face and Will's hands, followed by tissues to dry them both and even a little plastic bag to put in all the soiled wipes. In minutes

Harry looked normal and no-one glancing at Will would imagine the state of the inside of his T-shirt.

'Thank you,' said Will fervently. 'Thank you so much.'

Jen laughed, waving away his gratitude as she put everything back in her bag. 'No problem, but if I were you …'

'Yes, I know! Always have baby wipes to hand!'

'How's it going?' she asked sympathetically. 'Getting any better?'

Will shook his head disconsolately. 'Not really,' he admitted. 'I was foolish enough to think it might be fun looking after the children for a few weeks. I never dreamed it would be this exhausting.'

'Poor you. It's a bit of a shock I imagine, working with sensible, business-driven adults one minute and looking after yoghurt mad children the next. It takes some getting used to for anyone and you've been thrown in the deep end.'

Jen's voice was soft, consoling and feeling more than a little sorry for himself, Will couldn't help but soak up the kindness and the sympathy that was flowing his way. He felt that Lucy had shown a definite lack of both when he had phoned her earlier for advice.

'That's it exactly,' he said nodding in relief that someone understood. 'It's so different to my usual day, it's taking some getting used to.'

'You'll get there,' said Jen encouragingly. 'Every day will get a little bit better.'

Will pulled a face, privately thinking that every day seemed to be getting a little bit worse.

'Have you got time for a coffee after you've finished your shopping?' asked Jen. 'Getting your woes off your chest is an important part of child care you know,' she added with a grin.

Will shook his head. 'It's taken me so long I need to shoot off and pick Emily up from nursery.'

Was that a flash of disappointment in Jen's eyes?

'But I would love to another day,' he added impulsively. 'I could do with all the tips you can pass my way!'

'Doesn't Lucy give you tips?' she asked curiously. 'She must be telling you what you need to do?'

'She's very busy at work,' Will defended his wife gallantly. 'It's been quite a change for her as well, one minute looking after the children, the next back into the cut and thrust of it all.'

'I see. Well let's make a point of having a coffee soon then shall we?' Jen pulled out her phone to give Will her number. 'If Lucy's too busy, I'll talk you through a few must and must nots.'

'It's not Lucy's fault …' he began. He wanted to tell Jen that Lucy was struggling to find her feet again after so many years away from the office and of the daily struggle she was having with Grant Cassidy. He wanted to explain how no-one seemed to be taking her seriously now she was a working mother.

'She ….'

Jen stopped him by placing a comforting hand on his arm, carefully avoiding getting too close to his sticky T-shirt.

'It's okay, I understand Will,' she said softly. 'Lucy is probably a little wrapped up in her return to work. It's only to be expected, I suppose. You are doing a wonderful job, but it's difficult without help. You need someone on your side while Lucy is busy at the office.'

There was so much admiration shining from the pale blue eyes that Will couldn't help but feel better.

'I'm trying my best,' he said modestly, forgetting to emphasise how hard Lucy was working.

'Well I'm free as a bird most days,' advised Jen. 'And if you need a guiding hand, I'll be more than happy to offer you any help and advice I can.'

Will couldn't help the wave of gratitude. He had heard the frustration in Lucy's voice when he'd phoned her for the third time that morning. But he had drastically underestimated how difficult this was going to be and if he couldn't phone Lucy up every time he had a question, he needed someone to turn to.

'That's really kind of you Jen,' he said, a great deal of tension leaving his shoulders. 'Really kind.'

Exchanging numbers and promising to catch up soon, Will finished his shopping as quickly as he could feeling a great deal more relaxed about the days ahead.

Chapter 17

When the clock hit 5:00 that evening, Lucy couldn't help the small whimper of relief that escaped her. Snapping shut her laptop, she leaned back in her chair, being careful not to smack her head against the wall which was never far away.

It had been a long demanding week. She had spent a great deal of it missing her children and worrying about how Will was coping, in between fighting against being delegated as Grant Cassidy's personal assistant and proving to anyone who cared that Lucy Mathers may have left to have her beautiful babies but that didn't mean she was now an irrelevant person in the workplace.

She was exhausted. Each morning she had tried to pre-empt what the day may bring and leave Will as organised as possible. But once she was at work, it was impossible to continue to juggle the demands of home in between side stepping Grant and making sure Rob felt she was still up to the job and she had spent the day feeling guilty for snapping at Will about the shopping. She hoped he'd remembered to get some wine. She needed a glass very badly right now. Wondering if she should grab something for tea on the way home, Will's cooking had been barely edible during the week, she decided he may take that as criticism and reluctantly she decided to return empty handed. They could always resort to a takeaway if the meal was as bad as the others he'd produced.

She'd already had to turn down Alice's suggestion that she join her colleagues at the nearest wine bar.

'You're not coming for a Friday drink?' Alice had asked wide eyed.

'No.' Lucy sounded as regretful as she felt. 'I'm afraid that sort of end to the week doesn't sit well with children waiting at home for you.'

Alice had immediately hugged her friend. 'Of course. I keep forgetting how things have changed for you. There was a time our Friday nights were the stuff of legends! But don't worry, I'll bring you up to date with everything on Monday.'

Lucy had watched as Alice walked back into the main office. So much happened on Friday nights. Confidences were shared, gossip was passed around. Situations that had been hanging in the air all week were often resolved over a glass of wine. She wondered if Grant would be there. Another opportunity for him to remind everybody that Lucy couldn't join them because now she was a mother. He would insinuate that Lucy wasn't quite up to speed because she'd had babies. That Lucy wasn't a real member of the team because she had other commitments. For a moment she was tempted to call Alice back and tell her that of course she would be joining them for a drink. She could phone Will and let him know she would be late, he had regularly joined his colleagues for a drink at the end of the week.

But it wasn't just Will she was rushing home to. Her arms longed to hold her children, the days spent apart this week had been a real challenge and all Lucy wanted right now was to slump onto her settee and hug Emily and Harry, relishing the feel of their little bodies next to hers for a short while before they went to bed and she and Will could finally relax. So instead of joining the happy throng, she grabbed her coat and walked briskly to the train station.

Ruthlessly elbowing her way to the last seat on the train, Lucy realised that her feet, far from shouting with pain as they had all week, were now comfortably numb. Perhaps she was already getting used the return to her old life, she thought, she would be back in her red Louboutins in no time!

The children gave her a suitably enthusiastic hug when she arrived at home, although Lucy noticed somewhat sadly that they had already adapted to the idea of their father being the one who spent the day with them. Will already had a glass of wine poured for her and taking her coat, he pushed her gently down onto a seat.

'Dinner will be ready soon,' he advised. 'The kids have had their bath, why don't you relax for a while before we take them up to bed.'

He was walking away with her coat but Lucy reached out and grabbed at his hand. 'Thank you,' she said softly. 'Thank you.'

She read the children a story, averting her eyes from a carpet that clearly hadn't seen a vacuum all week and refusing to look at the dust accumulating on top of every surface in their living room. Will would get his head round it all eventually, she told herself firmly. Hopefully he would soon be back at work and she could stay at home and clean to her heart's content. A delicious smell started to drift from the kitchen and she felt vaguely hopeful that their meal that night might be edible and then she and Will carried the children upstairs and settled them into bed. Tripping over a pile of toys in Harry's bedroom, Lucy willed herself not to mention that they really needed a good tidy and when she went into the bathroom before going back downstairs, she tried to swallow down her gasp at the chaos that had followed bath time with bubbles half way up the wall, wet towels in a heap on the floor, discarded clothes hanging over the edge of the sink and the majority of Harry's bath time toys still littering the bottom of a bath that needed a good scrub.

Unable to stop herself from a having a swift tidy, she went back into the kitchen just in time to see Will take out a tray of pasta bake from the oven

'That smells really good,' she said, trying not to sound too surprised.

Will smiled. He had already emptied the kitchen bin with the incriminating cardboard wrapper that described a delicious pasta bake containing tender pieces of chicken, infused with basil and garlic roast tomatoes with a rich and a creamy cheese topping that was perfect for two people. The rest of the meals were stacked in the spare freezer in the garage that was normally only turned on at Christmas or if they were entertaining.

'Well I hope it tastes as good,' he said, his cheeks flushing slightly. 'And we've got some delicious French bread to go with it.'

He took the stick from the surface and started to cut it into chunky slices. He cut the first slice, which was nothing but a crusty outer ring absent of bread. Looking slightly puzzled, he continued to cut, his surprise growing with each slice until half way through he turned a perplexed face to Lucy.

'I don't understand,' he said. 'Did I choose an empty French stick?'

Grinning, Lucy took it from him and peered inside.

'There's some bread left at the bottom.'

'But I don't … what …?'

'Did you let Harry hold it?'

'Yes. He wanted to.'

'Mm. He wanted to because he bites the end off and then pulls all the bread out of the middle. But his arm doesn't reach all the way up.'

Will took the stick back to inspect the contents and sure enough, about three quarters of the way along, the bread appeared once more, filling the crust.

His mouth hung open. 'Why didn't you tell me?' he demanded.

'Tell you?'

'Not to let Harry hold the bread!'

Lucy stopped smiling and shook her head.

'Will, I can't give you a list of everything that the children might or might not do. It would go on indefinitely! You were the one who said this would give you chance to bond with Emily and Harry. Well that's what's happening. You're getting to know your children and some of their strange little habits and it's a bit of a learning curve but that's what looking after children is like.'

Will stared at the empty French stick. He briefly considered telling Lucy about his traumatic morning at the supermarket. He was certain she would find it hilarious, but she would also worry. She would ask him if he was sure he could cope, if she could do more to help and he had already seen how much returning to work was taking out of her. Will didn't want to give her more to worry about, he didn't want to admit what a struggle he was finding his new role. So he managed a smile instead, shrugging his shoulders as he continued to slice the bread until he reached the part that still had some filling.

'You look tired,' he commented as Lucy sank back into her chair.

'It's been a long week.' It had felt like a month but she kept that part to herself.

'I'll get a job soon,' said Will with a confidence he didn't feel. 'Then you can pack in Simcock and Bright and things will go back to the way they were.'

Lucy smiled and nodded in agreement, although in her experience things rarely went back to the way they were. Once something had happened to break the pattern, whole new patterns emerged. Maybe that was the way it was meant to be. But she pushed her doubts to the back of the many other thoughts laying in an exhausted heap in her head.

Will served up the pasta bake and they sat at the kitchen table with the rest of the bottle of wine.

'This is really good!' exclaimed Lucy in surprise.

Will topped up her glass instead of admitting he hadn't made it.

'You'll have to give me your recipe,' continued Lucy generously. 'Mine are never this tasty.'

Taking a large glug of wine to wash down the guilt, Will knew that he should of course just tell Lucy that his cooking was awful and he didn't think it was fair to inflict inedible meals on her at the end of a busy day. He should explain that he had found a rich vein of ready meals that would make life so much easier and that he could do with all the help he could get. But as Lucy tucked in, the moment seemed to slide by and instead of confessing all, he kept quiet, deciding that he would tell her later but right now he wanted her to simply enjoy her meal and relax. And after they had finished, he insisted Lucy go sit down with a replenished wine glass while he cleared the kitchen before coming to sit next to her on the settee.

Falling onto the settee, Lucy stretched out her toes relishing the feeling of freedom from her shoes. She was exhausted, every day had felt like a lesson in survival. She contemplated telling Will just how difficult she was finding it all but he already felt guilty that she'd had to go back to work. Besides, he seemed to be coping so much better than she was. Who would have thought he would have turned out to be such a good cook? So rather than be the one that complained about how hard life was and how difficult she was finding work, she swallowed the words and sank back into the settee, groaning quietly as she closed her eyes.

Will appeared by her side with more wine. Sinking onto the settee next to her he slid his arm round her shoulders.

'Are you missing being at home?' he asked, hoping that she wasn't about to say that she loved work, couldn't understand why she hadn't gone back sooner and had no intention of becoming a housewife again.

'Yes,' admitted Lucy. 'It's back breaking work but I do miss it all. Are you missing work?'

She held her breath, hoping that Will wasn't about to declare that their change of circumstances should become permanent and she should remain the breadwinner while he became a full time stay at home dad.

'Oh God yes!' Will had started dreaming about being in the office, having deadline after deadline thrown his way, more work than he could cope with and a desk piled high with problems. To some it may have been a nightmare, but he had woken up smiling.

He pulled her closer to his chest so he could drop a soft kiss on her lips before resting his cheek on her hair and yawning widely. 'We just need to get through the next few weeks as best we can until we go back to being who we were,' he murmured sleepily.

'Mm.'

'I'll go back to work and you stay at home.'

'Just how it used to be.'

'Just a little bit longer Lucy darling. We just need to keep it together a little bit longer,' and then the conversation stopped as Will drifted off to sleep holding Lucy close and Lucy continued to stare at her feet with a hundred and one thoughts chasing through her head.

Chapter 18

On Monday morning the alarm sounded, jerking Lucy from a deep, warm sleep that she felt had lasted all of half an hour and with a groan she rolled over. Another week in the office beckoned, she had to get out of bed and start the day.

Bleary eyed she left the children for Will to deal with and went downstairs to organise their day. Shoes and coats by the door, Emily's nursery bag packed and ready. She turned her attention to the fridge. She had been putting notes on yoghurts telling Will who liked what but this morning she opened the door, stared at the contents for a few minutes then closed the door. There was such a strange collection she had no idea which her children might like. She didn't make any lunch either, the breadbin was groaning with new items and she didn't recognise anything in the cupboard. Remembering the wonderful pasta bake he had produced on Friday evening, Lucy stopped in her tracks. Will was obviously finding his way round the kitchen very well without her interference, perhaps she should leave him to it instead of trying to organise his day.

The utility room had been emptied, the washing had been done, dried, ironed and put away. It had taken Lucy most of Sunday and she added to Will's daily list the laundry, which included drying and ironing.

Back upstairs to lay out outfits for both children and then as they all trooped downstairs for breakfast, she leaped into the shower for those precious few minutes when it was just Lucy and the sound of water running over her head. Much to her delight, the skirt she slipped on fastened a great deal easier than she had been expecting. It was still a little tight across her expanded waistline but she could risk tucking her silk blouse inside today rather than leaving it flapping. Even her shoes didn't pinch quite as much as they had the previous week and grinning Lucy decided that her body at least was remembering Lucy Mathers, Account Manager. If only her brain could catch up.

Running downstairs, she grabbed her children, kissed them, breathing in the scent of their hair and threw a kiss in Will's direction.

She was halfway to the door when Will pulled her back and wrapping his arms round her, he gave her such a thorough kiss that her cheeks went slightly pink and Harry who was watching them, chuckled loudly.

'What …?'

'Remember, it's all going to get better. It's not for long, it will soon be over and everything will get back to normal.'

If there was a slight wobble to Lucy's bottom lip she managed to hide it well as sniffing she nodded.

'I know,' she whispered, 'I know.'

Then catching sight of the kitchen clock she squealed and was out of the house, walking briskly to the station.

Walking through the town centre towards her office, Lucy lifted her face to a sun that was trying its best to make an appearance and relished the feel of the slightly warmer air on her face. Will was right, she was making life so much more difficult for herself. She ought to pull back, let Grant have his way. He was the golden boy at Simcock and Bright now. Maybe Lucy should just let him get on with it, keep her head down and wait until Will got another job. She felt a little of the tension leave her shoulders. She could support Will more if she wasn't so entrenched in her work and constantly trying to prove how good she still was. She took a few deep breaths. She would be calmer, she decided. She would not take everything Grant Cassidy said as a challenge. Her heart beat slowed even more as she paused on the doorstep. Lucy Mathers, Account Manager was in the past. Now she was Lucy Mathers, mother and home maker. That's what she needed to cling to.

As she walked into the reception area Alice appeared, her blonde head bobbing in agitation as she grabbed at Lucy's arm.

'He's up to something, she whispered in a low tone pulling Lucy under the shelter of one of the large plants.

'What? Who?'

'Grant. He's up to something.'

Lucy took a deep breath forcing herself to remain calm. It didn't matter what Grant was up to, she wasn't going to join in his silly games anymore.

She smiled. 'It doesn't matter. I'm not …'

'I think it involves Blooming Lovely.'

Lucy's smile disappeared. 'What do you mean?'

'I suspected something on Friday night. He was looking really pleased with himself. And he was being nice to me.'

'Nice? Isn't he normally nice to you?'

Alice shook her head violently. 'Grant Cassidy doesn't even know I exist. He looks through me like I'm a window.'

Lucy felt her heart give a little twitch. She strongly suspected that Alice had a crush on Grant no matter how much she declared to dislike him. It was never easy when the object of your desire had no thoughts about you at all.

'What did he do?'

'He bought me a drink!'

Lucy stared. 'That's it? You think he's up to something because he bought you a drink?'

Alice waved her arms around in exasperation. 'He never buys me a drink! He never speaks to me. In fact, he rarely joins us on a Friday. He's more likely to be somewhere far swankier with Rob.'

Stepping out from the huge palm plant, Lucy headed for the staircase. 'He probably just fancied a change. And maybe he's wanted to buy you a drink before but hadn't been able to find the courage.'

Alice looked at her incredulously. 'Grant Cassidy?'

Lucy had to admit it was a ridiculous thought. That Grant would be tongue tied and bashful round anybody was highly unlikely.

'Well maybe …'

'He was asking questions.'

'About?'

'You! He thought he was being clever,' said Alice furiously, 'he thought I would be too stupid to realise what he was up to.

127

He suddenly wants to buy me a drink, stand and chat to me and I'm supposed to be so overwhelmed I don't realise that he's up to something.'

Lucy was on the bottom step but she paused to listen to her friend.

'He was asking me how you were getting on with Blooming Lovely, who you were speaking to, how far you'd got with the file.'

Lucy tilted her head to one side. 'That's reasonable,' she admitted reluctantly. 'I would like to know how he's getting on with Haydock Sportswear. And if I thought someone would tell me I'd ask them.'

'And then he was asking me about how you were coping with the job.'

'Again, reasonable. He wants me to give in and go home.' Quite a tempting idea, thought Lucy.

'He wanted to know if you carried on working in the evening. Tried to pretend that he was concerned about how it would affect your children.'

Lucy stiffened. Now that was suspicious because she knew full well that Grant gave no thought at all to Lucy's children or the quality of her home life.

'What kind of work?'

'I don't know. He just seemed really interested in whether you were working on emails in the evening, catching up with clients, that sort of thing.'

Lucy thought back to her weekend. It had involved a lot of cleaning and chores that Will hadn't done during the week. She had cooked and cleaned and ironed. She and Will had taken the children to the park and they had sat on the settee with a bottle of wine. It hadn't occurred to her to check her emails.

A small strand of uncertainty started to unfurl in her stomach. In the pre-baby years, her laptop would have been glued to her side. It didn't matter what was planned, meeting friends, going out for drinks, visiting family, she would always find time to check the status of whatever account she was working on. She had never left work at the office.

But she was a very different person now and it hadn't even occurred to her to take her laptop home over the weekend. Life was already full to the brim with her family, work had stopped at 5:00 on Friday evening and she had tried not to think about it again until the alarm had interrupted her sleep on Monday morning. Had she been a naïve to think she could walk away each evening and forget it all, she now wondered?

'I don't trust him,' Alice whispered as a few colleagues arrived in reception, chatting and comparing weekends. 'He looked smug.'

Lucy was suddenly far less sure of herself. 'Have you seen him this morning?'

'Yes, he was in early. Rob as well.'

The uncertainty started to spread and Lucy's stomach began to churn.

'Rob asked me what time I thought you would be in and when I said same time as normal, he did look a bit surprised.

'Surprised?'

'Yeah, then he shrugged and said you knew what you were doing.'

Lucy gazed up the staircase. She had a feeling that something unpleasant was waiting for her up there. Something engineered by Grant Cassidy.

'Well, if I don't get a move on, I'll be late,' she tried to joke, although her mouth was dry and Alice didn't look at all amused.

Taking a deep breath, she walked up the remaining stairs. At the top she gave a cheery 'Good Morning' to the staff already sitting at their desks and she looked into Rob's office where he and Grant were already seated. Deciding to take the bull by the horns she flung open Rob's door.

'Good Morning. Did you both have a good weekend?' she asked pleasantly.

'Lucy! I was beginning to worry, thought you might be in a little earlier today,' shouted Rob in his deep voice.

The small twinges of uncertainty had turned into rampaging dread but with a smile fixed on her face Lucy met Grant's gaze. There was a tiny frown of anxiety knitted between his eyebrows.

'Oh thank goodness Lucy. I was so convinced that you would be in early, I'd started to think maybe you'd been in an accident of some sort.'

There was nothing but concern in his voice and despite the searching look Lucy gave him, the smooth face gave nothing away.

She turned her eyes back to Rob. 'I'm afraid you're going to have to help me out here Rob. Why did you both think I would be in early this morning? Is there something happening that I should know about?'

For a moment Rob stared at her blankly. His gaze swivelled to Grant in horror and then back to Lucy.

'The meeting Lucy,' he said gently. 'You have remembered the meeting?'

His eyebrows rose, disappearing under his bushy grey hair, his lips slightly twisted as though ready to smile when Lucy laughed and said of course she did.

'Meeting? What meeting?'

The half-smile disappeared and the tone lost its softness. 'With Blooming Lovely. They're coming in today for their preparatory discussion. 9:15 as agreed.'

She swallowed her gasp as her eyes swung accusingly to Grant who was looking as perplexed as Rob at Lucy's reaction

'I haven't organised any meeting,' Lucy denied. 'Why would they decide to come for a meeting no-one had organised?'

'Grant organised it for you. Very generous of him under the circumstances. Didn't you read your email?'

'Grant?'

'Yes. He advised them that you were taking over the case and arranged for them to come in this morning.'

'You contacted my client and arranged a meeting without discussing it with me?' Lucy's voice was tremulous, her hands were clenching and unclenching as she glared at Grant. 'How dare you interfere like that! How dare you …'

'Hold on Lucy.' Rob had stood up, one hand held out to stop Lucy's outpouring. 'I think it was very good of Grant to give you an edge like this bearing in mind the competition between the two of you. And he did let you know, I was copied into the email he sent you providing all the details. It's hardly Grant's fault if you didn't read it.'

'Lucy, I'm so sorry! I wouldn't dream of interfering, I was just trying to help.' Grant's voice was solicitous, regretful and Lucy saw him shake his head sadly as though unable to believe the reaction of someone he had tried to aid.

Lucy took a deep trembling breath. 'When?' she demanded. 'When did you send the email?'

'On Friday.' Grant dusted off an already immaculate trouser leg as he met Lucy's eyes. 'Late Friday afternoon.'

Lucy bit her lip. The bastard. The absolute bastard.

'Oh my word,' he continued as though a light had suddenly been turned on. 'Oh Lucy, what time did you leave Friday? Don't tell me you didn't see it!'

Rob looked sharply at Lucy. 'Didn't you see the email?'

Lucy shook her head slowly. 'No, I didn't,' she admitted trying for a calmness that belied the fury in her heart. She had a sudden flash back to Friday evening, how she had watched the clock hit 5:00 and then snapped shut her laptop. She had walked down the corridor saying goodnight to all and sundry and she had caught Grant's eye as she passed his office. He had nodded in her direction tapping away at his keyboard and Lucy had dismissed him from her thoughts. Back in the day her instincts would have told her that he was up to something underhand. There again, back in the day he wouldn't have caught her out because Lucy would have arrived at home and immediately flipped open her computer to see what she may have missed in the 30-minute journey.

'It was a few minutes after 5:00 before I found time to write it,' exclaimed Grant. 'Oh what an idiot! I can't apologise enough, it didn't occur to me that you wouldn't … Sorry Lucy, sorry Rob. This is entirely my fault.'

Rob sat back down. 'Nonsense,' he said briskly. 'It's far from your fault Grant. Don't blame yourself. No-one is to blame,' he added insincerely looking at Lucy. 'Just one of those things.'

Except that Lucy knew he did blame someone. And it wasn't one of those things. It was a disaster brought on them by Lucy.

'It's too late to cancel the meeting, we'll just have to apologise and hope they can reschedule. Hope that they will reschedule and not think we're completely incompetent,' said Rob disconsolately.

'Well maybe not. I did do a lot of research into the group as soon as they showed an interest. And although Lucy has taken it over,' Grant cast a small smile in her direction, 'I think I know enough to have the initial meeting.'

Lucy stared at him. There had been virtually no information attached to the file she had taken from Grant's office. If he knew enough to take this meeting it was because he had spent the weekend working on Blooming Lovely.

She pressed her lips together. 'I've actually already done a great deal of work myself,' she announced. 'In fact, I was ready to phone them today and arrange a meeting.'

The mask slipped ever so slightly from Grant's face. 'You were?'

'Of course. I may not have expected a meeting this morning but that doesn't mean I can't cope with one.'

Lucy turned back to Rob who had a look of disappointment on his face that Lucy had never seen directed at her. 'You know me Rob, prepared for every eventuality,' she said firmly not waiting for him to agree or disagree.

'So you see Grant, I'm perfectly prepared to take this meeting. I just need to gather my things together and I'll be back,' and with a confident smile she walked down the corridor on legs that were shaking.

Chapter 19

When Lucy arrived in her office the phone was ringing and without thinking she answered.

'I can't find Emily's book,' gasped Will. 'She won't go without it and we're going to be late.'

Lucy opened her drawer and pulled out her file on Blooming Lovely. She wondered if Grant had searched for any information she may have after she'd left on Friday night. Perhaps it was time to start locking her door. Or getting a secure filing cabinet in her room. She looked around. If she put anything else in this room then something would have to go and as the only other things in the office were the desk, her chair and Lucy herself it may well have to be Lucy that was relocated.

'I don't know where it is.'

Maybe she could find a smaller desk. But there was only just enough room for herself and Alice who had to squat at the end whenever she came in to help.

'She was reading it this morning but she can't remember where she put it.'

Perhaps she could sit in the corridor. She could leave the desk and the filing cabinet in her room and she could sit in the corridor, her laptop on her knee.'

'Lucy! I need to find Emily's book!'

She stared at the clock on the wall, it was 9:05.

'What makes you think I know where it is?'

She heard Rob's voice boom out a greeting and guessed that Blooming Lovely had arrived, slightly early as all good clients did. Her hands were trembling and she felt nauseous.

'I thought you may have an idea where she may have put it,' snapped Will in exasperation. 'I'm just looking for a little help here Lucy. Has she got a hiding place? Any ideas?'

Alice was at the doorway, her anxious face telling Lucy what she needed to know. The meeting was about to begin.

'I can't help you,' she murmured into the phone. 'Sorry,' and she ended the call and stood up feeling a little like someone who was approaching the hangman's noose.

'Rob said to let you know …'

'It's okay, I'm coming.'

'Is there anything I can do, anything you need?'

Lucy was staring at the doorway. She could turn into the corridor and carry on walking. She was needed at home after all, she could catch the next train and help Will find Emily's book. Then they would forget all this silly nonsense and she would spend the morning tidying Harry's bedroom and making something pleasant for tea. She and Will could laugh about what a ridiculous idea it had been to even consider that Lucy should return to work, even for a few weeks, and she would take up her right and proper role as wife and mother and forget all about how Lucy Mathers used to be an account manager of distinction.

'Lucy?'

Alice was at her shoulder and Lucy shook herself out of her daydream. Or she could walk into the meeting and give Grant Cassidy the fight he clearly wanted.

'Yes,' she said urgently. 'I'm going to leave my laptop here and I need you to open the Blooming Lovely file and print off the report forecasts that I started on Friday. There's also an idea trail I started. There's not a huge amount of information there so print it as large as you can.'

Whipping out her compact Lucy checked her lipstick and ran a hand over her hair. 'Send somebody out to get a bunch of flowers. I need them in the next 10 minutes. The grottier the better.'

Thank God she had put on one of her old power suits this morning and straightening her blouse she looked at her reflection in the glass pane of her door. If she didn't know better she would say she looked just like the Lucy Mathers of old.

'Bring me the file and the flowers. Just smile and put them next to me.'

'Right!' Alice's eyes were enormous but she was already on her toes ready to run into the main office.

'As quick as you can Alice,' and with a last nod of encouragement, Lucy lifted her head up and holding the file that contained everything she knew about Blooming Lovely, she walked into the board room.

'Ah, here she is!' said Grant encouragingly and Lucy sent a warm smile winging round the room as she murmured 'Good Morning'

'Everything okay Lucy?' asked Grant in a concerned voice that was soft enough to appear discreet but loud enough for the room to hear.

Lucy stopped on her way to the chair that had been left for her and turned to give Grant the full benefit of her stare.

'Of course,' she answered calmly. 'Why ever wouldn't it be?'

'Oh you know,' he murmured, turning to the group. 'I'm afraid we had a little problem with communication this morning. Entirely my fault,' he said generously in a way that left everyone in no doubt that it was far from his fault. 'Poor Lucy has been caught somewhat on the hop.'

Lucy watched Rob frown. The motto in the office was always to carry on regardless and never admit that Simcock and Bright were encountering any difficulties of any kind. Maybe Grant still had something to learn about impressing Rob.

Holding his gaze for a moment and forcing a small smile of amusement to touch her lips, Lucy swung back round to face everybody else. There were three strangers at the table, a tall, elderly man and two women. One of them was Denise Albright, the woman Lucy had to impress.

Grant stood up. 'This is Lucy Mathers,' he introduced, giving Lucy an encouraging nod. 'She worked at Simcock and Bright for 10 years and used to be an account manager so with all that experience under her belt we have decided,' he gave a little cough, 'to let her take over the Blooming Lovely account.'

Lucy waited for him to introduce the guests, but seemingly forgetting, Grant sat back down and crossed his legs, leaving Lucy and a deafening silence to reign. Rob opened his mouth but Lucy didn't give him chance and stepping forwards she held a hand out to the younger of the two women.

'And you are Denise Albright, the new CEO of Blooming Lovely, I'm very pleased to meet you.'

She saw Grant's lips thin and Rob's tilt upwards. Almost the first thing Lucy had done is go online and find a picture of Denise Albright along with every scrap of information she had been able to find out about the new CEO. She shook the hand offered, detecting a definite air of sympathy in the direct gaze. She remembered reading that Denise's appointment to CEO had been far from smooth and that the very idea of a woman in charge had left some of the more traditional members of the board in a state of shock.

'I'm Lucy,' she continued. 'And I *am* the Account Manager who will hopefully bring you onboard with Simcock and Bright. Grant is correct,' she looked around, holding everybody's gaze as she slipped into her seat. 'I worked here for 10 years before I left to start my family. Now I've returned I am lucky to have you as my first prospective clients. Just think, four years of ideas all waiting to descend on Blooming Lovely!'

They all grinned, except for Grant who gave a tiny grimace.

'We hope you will be patient as Lucy catches up with the world of business. It's a big difference to the child care she's been devoting herself to over the last four years! But Rob was very keen to have her back in the fold.' He looked appreciatively at Lucy in her suit and silk blouse, her shiny hair sitting on her shoulders and said indulgently, 'I'm sure you'll agree she is a great asset to the business.'

Lucy nodded. 'Oh I am. In my first year as account manager I increased turnover by almost 45%, retention doubled, and we won two awards for business innovation and enterprise.'

'Of course a break from work is ....'

'Exactly what Lucy needed after working so hard,' interrupted Rob giving Grant a firm stare. 'And now, perhaps we can give you a taste of what we had in mind for Blooming Lovely.'

Grant unfastened his suit jacket, flipping open his laptop. 'Maybe I should start, get the ball rolling and give Lucy a little time to catch up seeing as this meeting has come as something of a surprise to her. The main options as I see them …'

The door opened and as they all looked around, in walked Alice, a file under one hand and a bunch of flowers under the other. They were a little dusty, one had a broken stem and the bright head of a marigold drooped at a severe angle. Walking over to Lucy, she smiled, set down both items and without a word left the room.

'No need Grant,' said Lucy. 'I'm quite prepared.' She opened the folder and slid out the work she had already started the previous week. It was far from finished but Lucy was used to thinking on her feet.

She shook out the pages, deliberately making sure everybody could get a glimpse of the ideas she had already recorded together with the spending forecasts and budgets peeping out from the folder. Denise stared at the forlorn bunch of flowers and Lucy could see the alarmed look in Rob's eyes.

'Not quite what we're thinking of in terms of a floral bouquet,' offered Denise dryly.

'No, but this is quite often the public perception,' countered Lucy. 'Flowers are a duty, something bought for mum's on Mother's Day, for a wife on a Friday evening when you haven't made it home before 8:00 any night during the week, girlfriends who you want to woo even though you don't really understand the whole flower thing yourself.'

She saw the interest start to appear in Denise's eyes.

'And before your floral superstore stands a chance of success, the first thing we will need to overcome will be the public's idea of what exactly they will find under its roof. Because if they imagine it to be full of these,' they all looked at the flowers, 'your superstore is destined for failure.'

She watched as Denise stared at the flowers, her eyes thoughtful. 'And how would we alter how the public see us?'

And Lucy grinned. She gave a big, wide, confident smile and looked Denise in the eye.

'Ah well that's where I come in. Because Grant is quite right, I do have years of experience at exactly this sort of thing and I have been working nonstop on your account,' she ignored the white lie and spread out the pages scattered full of facts and ideas. 'I have so many ideas. We are going to turn people's ideas about flowers on their heads. We'll get them to think of flowers as not only something decorative and occasionally essential, but as something desirable. Simcock and Bright will have people flooding to your superstore not because they have a guilty conscience and need to grab a bunch of flowers. But because it's exciting! It's full of things they actually want to buy, items that will cheer up their kitchen and bring a fresh, new scent into their bedroom. Because it's full of choice and beauty. I can make that happen for Blooming Lovely,' she said in a firm voice. 'I can guarantee that failure is not an option.'

When Lucy returned to her office a couple of hours later, she was dizzy with relief. Standing by her desk she took a few deep breaths, her head swimming.

'How did it go?'

Alice had seen her leave the board room and shot into Lucy's office.

Lifting her head, Lucy nodded. 'It was good. In fact, 'she gave a weak grin,' it was better than good, it was fantastic. I really think Denise was on board with everything I said.'

With a squeal, Alice threw her arms around Lucy's neck. 'I knew you could do it. Congratulations! You look all in, shall I get you a coffee? And you look like you could do with something to eat.'

Sinking into her chair Lucy let out a huge breath of air. 'It's not done yet,' she said. 'Blooming Lovely will have to decide whether they want to take the next step and ask for a presentation. But it went as well as it could.'

'They'll choose you,' said Alice without hesitation. 'I know they will. Shall I get you a sandwich or something? You look very pale.'

'I do feel a bit empty.' Lucy looked down at her stomach, she hadn't had anything other than half a cup of coffee during the meeting. 'But I can't cope with any of that green slime you've taken to drinking.' She pulled a face, 'I really think I would be sick.'

'Oh no! I've gone off that myself,' admitted Alice. 'Anyway, no carb month is over now.'

'And what has replaced it?' asked Lucy warily

'High energy. Kathy was reading that it's really important to keep a balance of all food groups in your diet, including carbs but to make sure you fill up on energetic foods.'

Lucy wondered what energetic foods were. Did they go buy themselves from the shop?

'Such as?'

'Er, bananas, eggs, rice, all sorts of things.'

'Bread?' asked Lucy hopefully.

'I suppose wholegrain bread could count.'

'So a bacon butty on brown bread would be high energy?'

'Well, if we walked really quickly to the sandwich shop and back, I think it would be okay.'

Alice was grinning and Lucy hauled herself to her feet. 'Come on then, let's get jogging because not only do I need a bacon butty but I have a hankering for an egg custard.'

'That's a cake!' protested Alice. 'You can't eat cakes.'

'You said the diet included eggs,' said Lucy with a straight face before the two of them dissolved into giggles, hanging onto each other's arms and snorting with laughter. Drying their eyes, they left Lucy's office and made their way down the corridor. At the top of the stairs Lucy stopped and feeling eyes on her she turned to see Grant standing in Rob's office, staring at her, his face grim with no hint of his usual charming, smooth smile. For a moment they stared at each other and then Lucy gave him a big, confident grin and a small wave before following Alice down the stairs.

Chapter 20

Will was late for nursery. He had finally found Emily's book, underneath her bag by the front door and hurling Harry into the buggy, he ran at full pelt to the nursery. He had already learned that taking the car was not a speedier option, parking was a nightmare and the minutes wasted getting the pushchair out of the boot and Harry strapped in usually left him having to run to the door.

Harry was being lurched around, squealing happily and Will had perched Emily on the crossbar at the back where she hung on as Will sped through the streets.

Arriving at the front door, his face red with exertion and unable to speak for the lack of oxygen that was searing his lungs, he doubled over and gasped as he saw the door was closed. That meant trouble. That meant they were late, again, and another black mark would be awarded to the Mathers family. And that meant that he would be in a great deal of trouble with Lucy when she found out.

The door opened and the tall figure of Mrs Worthington appeared to cast a disapproving shadow over Will and his family.

'I'm so sorry.' Will's voice was little more than a croak. 'I couldn't find Emily's book and she wouldn't come without it and – I'm sorry.'

He was still bent over, trying to draw air back into his lungs and Emily stood at his side watching him with interest.

'You're late Mr Mathers. Again.'

'I know.'

Will stood up, pushing back the hair that was clinging to his forehead in sweaty streaks.

'I'm sorry,' he repeated weakly.

'That will be a black mark against Emily's name I'm afraid.'

Closing his eyes Will groaned. How did Lucy get the children out of the house every morning, dressed, ready and on time? It was an impossible task. He wondered if there was a way he could make sure she didn't find out about this latest black mark. It would involve getting Emily to swear to silence and possibly moving her to another nursery school without telling Lucy, but maybe it was possible.

'Are we going to tell Mummy about this?' enquired Emily in a grave little voice.

Mrs Worthington's head swivelled in Emily's direction and then back to Will, whose cheeks flushed even deeper.

'Of course!' he said, as though shocked at the very idea.

'We haven't seen Mrs Mathers for a few days.'

'No. she's er, she's gone back to work.'

Mrs Worthington carried on staring and Will stumbled on.

'Slight change in household circumstances,' he said. 'I'm looking after the children for now. Just for a while. A very short while,' he hoped desperately. 'Until I get another job.'

Emily slipped her hand in her father's, looking up at the severe face staring at them.

'Daddy isn't very good yet,' she lisped charmingly.' He's trying hard but he's not as good as Mummy.'

Was it Will's imagination or was there a minute softening of Mrs Worthington's thin lips? Were her eyes looking at him with a tiny tinge of sympathy?

'It's quite difficult,' he admitted forlornly. 'I really don't know how Lucy managed.'

'Poor Daddy,' said Emily kindly.

He peeped upwards. There was a definite softer edge starting to appear on the face before him.

'Mummy gets very cross with him,' added Emily. 'They had a big row because she said all daddy had to do was get me here on time.' She sighed and a forlorn expression crossed her face. 'She's going to be angry,' she whispered.

'Well, you were only one minute late.'

Will waited, hope spreading across his face.

'Maybe under the circumstances I could overlook today's incident.'

Will held his breath. The last account he had dealt with was leading a team investigating a multi-million-pound fraud. How ridiculous, he thought, that a few weeks later he could feel so much anxiety over arriving at nursery 1 minute late.

'I can understand that you're finding it difficult to adapt. Perhaps planning on leaving a little earlier each morning might help?'

Will nodded, suitably chastened. 'You're right. I will,' he said sincerely.

'Then we'll say no more about today and there will be no black mark.'

'Oh thank you,' breathed Will, the relief coming from his boots. 'Thank you so much.'

Mrs Worthington held the door open and Will passed Emily her bag, dropping a kiss on her head.

'Bye-bye daddy,' she said sweetly and then turned away but not before she sent Will a mischievous grin that made him stop in his tracks. Emily Mathers it appeared, was already turning out to be quite a negotiator, he thought with a chuckle. Just like her mother. And turning the buggy around, he set off for home.

Will had been angry at Lucy's lack of concern about Emily's missing book. She had all but hung up on him and he had glared at the phone in his hand and the silence that was now on the other end. He appreciated she was at work, but her obvious lack of interest rankled. Swearing under his breath as he finally managed to get the children out of the house, he had continued to chew over her attitude as he'd raced to Emily's nursery. And it wasn't just the brief phone call, he'd noticed a distinct lack of the Post-it notes that guided him through his day and there had been no plate of sandwiches made before Lucy left for work and wrapped up and left in the fridge for Emily and Harry at lunchtime.

But his anger had been quick to disappear. If Lucy had phoned him at work and asked him where Emily had put something, he wouldn't have had a clue. And although Lucy hadn't complained, he couldn't fail to notice how much work she'd done over the weekend. Apparently, as well as looking after the children he should also be doing a great deal more around the house. The bathrooms, it appeared, were not self-cleaning, the carpets required regular attacks with the vacuum, neither Emily or Harry were very good at tidying their bedrooms and the mountain of clothes that was shoved into the washing machine on a daily basis then needed ironing and returning to the drawers.

So Will had made yet more additions to his ever-growing spreadsheet and now he was at home and his breathing had returned to normal, he looked at the list of everything he wanted to get done that day.

Putting Harry down for his brief mid-morning nap, he decided to start upstairs and digging out the vac he went into Emily's bedroom. Realising that before he could vac the floor he needed to clear it of toys, it was a good 45 minutes before he had returned everything to the boxes stacked neatly in the corner and vacuumed the carpet. Feeling rather pleased with himself, he went to check on Harry who was no longer in his bedroom.

'Harry,' Will called. 'Where are you?'

In the previous week, Will had come to learn that Harry liked small spaces. He often withdrew to his wardrobe or under the bed or behind the settee. Will had stopped racing round the house in a blind panic whenever his son went missing and he would check each of Harry's favourite spots knowing he would come across him somewhere. But today Harry wasn't in any of the wardrobes. He hadn't gone downstairs because the safety gate was still firmly shut, he wasn't under his bed or Will and Lucy's bed and with a frown Will called him again.

'Harry! Where are you little man? Shall we go downstairs and have some juice and a biscuit?'

Nothing. The panic started to curl in Will's stomach and his voice was louder, a little more demanding.

'Harry! Where are you?'

He checked Emily's room, maybe Harry had slipped in while Will was cleaning and he hadn't noticed him. He checked every bed again, he looked in the bathroom.

'Harry!' he called urgently. 'Harry, where are you?'

He was running from bedroom to bedrooms now, throwing open doors, opening drawers that Harry, small as he may be couldn't possibly be in, searching for the lost 2-year-old. Stiffening, he cocked his head to one side. He'd heard a noise, it was faint but it sounded like someone humming, like a toddler humming a tune he didn't really know.

Hurtling towards the sound, Will threw open the door to the ensuite bathroom his shoulders slumping with relief at the sight of Harry sitting happily on the floor only to yelp in terror.

'Oh my God Harry! What's happened, what's wrong with you?'

His heart was hammering, he couldn't decide what to do first. Should he phone the doctor? That would take time, perhaps he should phone the ambulance straight away. That still took time, perhaps he should just throw Harry in the car and take him straight to the hospital himself.

'Harry, darling,' he dropped to his knees in front of his son. 'Oh Harry, what is it?'

His son was sitting on the floor, singing happily surrounded by toys. His face was purple. Not just a hint of purple, but a deep concentrated purple.

'Can you breathe?' asked Will anxiously. 'Can you breathe okay Harry?'

He grabbed at one of his son's hands. Did he have a rash? Wasn't that dangerous, should he check his back and his chest? His hands were also purple and Will groaned in despair.

'Harry!' he moaned softly. 'Harry.'

He lifted his son off the floor, holding him tight. Harry didn't seem particularly upset. He was still humming tunelessly so his breathing was okay. He wasn't crying or anxious. Perhaps it was some sort of virus, thought Will. Maybe a reaction to something.

'We'll call the ambulance,' he declared. 'We'll phone and they'll tell us what to do while we're waiting. It's going to be okay Harry. It will all be okay,' and he pressed a kiss on one purple cheek.

Turning around he walked towards the door, and then stopped. Turning back slowly, he stared at the reflection he had just caught sight of in the bathroom mirror. There he was, still holding Harry close to his chest, but now the purple rash was spreading across Will's own face. Oh my God, he thought in horror. It was highly contagious. This was serious.

Leaning forward he checked his face in the mirror. The only purple so far was around his lips and on his chin. He lifted a wary finger to touch the rash. He didn't feel any different. His face wasn't tingling or burning, it was just turning purple. Gazing at his fingers, he flinched. They were turning purple as well. Just the tips, where he'd touched his face. Puzzled he moved closer to the mirror and rubbed at his chin a little harder. The purple almost disappeared. He turned to look at Harry more closely and softly wiped a finger against his cheek. Setting his son down on the floor, Will looked at the toys Harry had been playing with, bending down to get a closer look. They weren't toys at all. Closing his eyes in utter relief, Will started to laugh, his shoulders shaking with hysterical relief.

'Oh Harry, you little horror!'

Spread across the floor was the contents of Lucy's make up bag. Pots and tubes of all sorts were scattered across the tiles, many open, some destroyed completely and others tipped upside down as their contents had been shaken and gouged out to make a muddy paste with a deep purple hue.

Will turned on the tap and wet a flannel, wiping Harry's squirming face. His colour improved instantly and Will's knees felt weak with relief. Harry didn't have a highly contagious virus; he'd just had a very pleasant time playing with Lucy's makeup.

'Oh Harry mate, I thought we'd both had it for a minute there,' he said, grabbing his son close and kissing him. 'I really thought it was game over,' and laughing, he sat Harry on the seat by the shower and started cleaning him.

30 minutes later, the laughter had stopped and the anxiety had returned. Most of the purple colour had come off quite easily, but Harry still looked far from normal. There were dark

streaks across his cheeks that simply wouldn't go no matter how much water Will was throwing at them and although the deep purple had disappeared, there was still an unhealthy muddy colour to most of Harrys' face. Will had gone through the bathroom cabinet, looking for whatever Lucy might use to wipe away her make up. He'd tried something called BB cream but that had turned Harry slightly orange which Will had quickly wiped away. He'd found a tube labelled concealer and although it reduced the black smears it still left Harry looking quite an alarming colour. His hopes had been high when he found a fixer spray. He'd sprayed Harry's face gently, waited a moment and then started wiping. It didn't fix the problem, nothing moved and if anything, it was even tougher to shift the strange colour covering his son's cheeks.

Looking at his watch and realising that pretty soon he would have to collect Emily from nursery and that meant taking Harry out into the public domain, Will decided it was time to call for help and taking the toddler downstairs he looked for his phone. He recalled Lucy's stern tone from his earlier phone call. She had obviously been busy and hadn't taken kindly to his interruption. He chewed on his lip for a moment then dialled.

'Hello?'

'Hi Jen, it's Will. I'm in a bit of a dilemma and wondered if you could help me out?'

'Sounds intriguing! What kind of dilemma are we talking about? And what makes you think I might be able to help?'

'It's er, a woman thing you see and I'm not doing a very good job of dealing with it. It concerns makeup.'

Ten minutes later Jen was at the door, a small bag in her hand and a smile on her face.

Pulling her into the kitchen, Will looked at his watch. 'If I take Harry to nursery looking like this, Lucy will find out in seconds. But I can't seem to get it all off!'

'Don't you want Lucy to know?' asked Jen intrigued.

Will shuffled. 'Oh I'll tell her. Probably. At some point. But not necessarily today.'

Jen grinned. 'Took your eyes off him for 10 minutes?'

Will nodded. 'I was trying to be efficient and vac the bedrooms,' he complained. 'I thought I had it all under control and then this happened!'

'Don't worry. It's happened to most of us at some point.'

Will had gathered all the makeup from the bathroom floor and left it in a heap on the kitchen table so Jen could see what had been used. She looked through the messy pile before producing a small bag.

'Your wife is very sensible and is using waterproof makeup and long lasting, smudge free products. Great if you need to keep looking good during the day. Not so good at getting off unless you use the right stuff,' she said as she pulled out a small bottle and some cotton wool.

Will's shoulders sank with relief. 'So it will come off?'

'Of course!'

He checked the time again anxiously.

'Will it take long?'

'I don't think so.' Jen was already wiping Harry's face with soaked cotton wool. 'I don't tend to use a lot of this stuff myself, I'm afraid I haven't got the patience, it's the natural look for me! Lucy obviously wears a lot more make up but it will come off.'

Will looked at the messy pile in bewilderment. 'I don't think she wears half of it,' he said in his wife's defence. 'It's just lying around.'

Jen looked at Will, her blue eyes twinkling as she spoke and the soft pink lips smiling.

'Don't worry!'

Will watched her for a few more minutes, pacing the kitchen floor and looking at his watch.

'Look, I can stay here and get Harry sorted out. You collect Emily and by the time you come back he'll look normal again.'

'Oh I couldn't do that!' Will chewed his lip. 'Could I?'

'Of course you can! Go. Get your daughter. I'm in no hurry. My mum has taken Alfie for the morning so I don't need to rush back.'

Will didn't need any more encouragement and with a grateful smile he gave her an impulsive hug. 'Thank you, Jen. Thank you so much for helping me out,' and he was off, out of the kitchen and on his way to collect Emily.

When he returned, not only was Harry looking completely normal but Jen had washed the breakfast things he had let pile up in the sink, cleaned the kitchen and had brought the vacuum downstairs to attack the living room.

'Jen! You didn't have to do any of this,' exclaimed Will.

'Don't be silly. I remember when Alfie was born, my mum did all my cleaning for the first 6 months because I couldn't seem to co-ordinate getting dressed, looking after Alfie and keeping the house tidy. Something had to give and it was usually the house.'

She was smiling at Will as she unplugged the cord to the vac.

'But Harry is two. I've got no excuse.'

'Of course you have! Harry may not be a new born but you are new to all this so it's practically the same thing.'

Will allowed himself to be convinced.

'But I still feel bad that you've done my cleaning for me.'

'Don't be silly! Lucy is obviously concentrating on work rather than you and the house at the moment. You need help from someone and I've told you, I'm happy to be here for you. You can't be expected to pick up being a stay at home dad overnight.'

Will thought he detected a slight note of censure in Jen's voice.

'Lucy has so much to do,' he said. 'She has to do a lot of things at the weekend because I can't seem to find time to fit them in during the week.' He thought of his multi coloured spreadsheet. He was adding more and more onto the list on a daily basis, but he rarely managed to do half the jobs. 'I really don't know how she used to manage,' he said scratching his head in confusion.

Jen had disappeared into the utility room to put the vac away and when she came back she sat at the table as she considered Will, her blond head tilted to one side and her blue eyes thoughtful.

'It must be nice for Lucy to be back in the office and see all her old friends.'

'I don't think she knows many people in the office any more. Lots of new faces.'

'Even better! Lots of new friends to make.'

Will laughed ruefully. 'I think she's far too busy.'

'I'm sure she is, exciting times for her! Shame though.'

'What?'

'That she's having to put work first. I suppose it's difficult to get the balance right isn't it? With so many demands on her time something has to give. She's very brave, deciding to relinquish all responsibility for the house and the children. Not everyone would be able to do that. It must be quite difficult for both of you.'

Will blinked. He hadn't realised he'd been relinquished. True, Lucy had been a little short with him on the phone that morning, in fact on several occasions and some of the jobs she used to do each morning before she left for work had now stopped. But wasn't that because he should be doing more, not that Lucy had bumped her family down the pecking order in favour of Simcock and Bright? Or was Jen right and were they now taking second place to her more exciting life at work, new challenges, new friends?

'She still does a lot in the house,' he said defensively. 'That's why I was trying to be more helpful today.'

'And that's why I admire you so much!' Jen leant forward, her eyes meeting Will's. 'You are being a wonderful husband and I'm sure when Lucy has more time for you and the children, it will get easier.'

Fidgeting, Will wondered if he should point out more vehemently how much Lucy had to do, how difficult she was finding all this. He should defend his wife, tell Jen how hard she was working. Lucy hadn't abandoned them, she was simply very busy. But the words were suddenly difficult to find, Jen's suggestion had struck a chord. Now that she mentioned it, he was feeling a little abandoned.

'I wouldn't say no to a coffee now we have everything under control,' Jen continued while Will was still thinking what to say. 'And a sandwich wouldn't come amiss either, now you can actually see the kitchen surface!'

And somehow, instead of explaining, Will looked round in appreciation at the spotless kitchen and put the kettle on, grateful that he had someone who understood how difficult he was finding this whole experience and who was happy to provide some much-needed hands on help.

Chapter 21

Lucy didn't have to wait long to find out how Blooming Lovely felt about her presentation. Early afternoon, Rob came bursting into her office to shout that Denise Albright had been on the phone to say they wanted Simcock and Bright to provide an official proposal for their business.

'Don't they want more …'

'No,' yelled Rob in excitement. 'They want you to get on with the presentation. They're in a hurry so we have two weeks to tell them exactly how we will make their superstore fly. We'll be going head to head with Sprackley & Co and they'll choose which company to go with.'

Lucy wanted to weep. She wanted to put her head down on her desk and howl out loud with relief.

'That's fantastic,' she said instead. 'That's really good news.'

'I knew you still had what it takes Lucy. Despite … I knew you still had the magic touch.'

Despite everything Grant Cassidy had said, wondered Lucy? Or despite that she was now a mother of two.

'You can have Alice to help you,' Rob offered generously.

Alice had worked almost exclusively for Lucy before she'd left. But that was when Lucy had signed up the majority of new accounts. Why did it now sound as though Rob was letting her have Alice because Lucy needed help, because she wasn't quite up to the task and would need someone to hold her hand? She opened her mouth to decline his offer, then shut it again quickly. She would take all the help she could get, she decided, nodding her head in agreement.

'Welcome back Lucy,' grinned Rob as he left. 'Welcome back.'

Nodding, she sat calmly at her desk waiting to hear his footsteps travel down the corridor and his door shut and then she put her knuckles in her mouth to stop herself from screaming in delight. She had done it, despite Grant's attempted sabotage. She had the chance of a signing a new account, the first since her return.

Alice came hurtling into her office looking excited and happy.

'I heard Blooming Lovely phoned and want you to present,' she said breathlessly. 'Is it true?'

Lucy grinned. 'It certainly is.'

Alice gave a little squeal, reaching around the table to hug her friend. 'I knew you could do it.'

'It's early days,' cautioned Lucy. 'It's only a presentation, I haven't got their business yet.'

'Well, it's a start. And you've only been back a week!'

Lucy grimaced. 'I'll have to up my game,' she admitted reluctantly. 'I've only got two weeks which will mean working every hour I can. No more leaving on the dot.'

She stared at her laptop. She had checked her emails and Grant had sent one advising of the Monday morning meeting with Blooming Lovely at 5:04 on Friday afternoon. Probably the very moment he saw her walking down the stairs on her way home.

'I can't give Grant any more chances to catch me out. I'll be checking my emails throughout the night from now on!'

A scowl settled on Alice's face. 'I can't believe he did that. And I can't believe he thought I would give him any information about you.'

Lucy stared through the tiny glass pane in her office, across the corridor into the bright empty office opposite with its views of the street and the little patch of green in the centre of the city. She couldn't believe that Rob was prepared to let her be demoted into the old filing room while Grant had two offices. She was an account manager, she should be treated with a certain amount of equality.

She brought her eyes back to her own office.

'Rob said you can work with me,' she said, laughing as Alice clapped her hands in excitement.

'It won't be long before you're back in the big office with me as your official PA.'

'No. No, this is a temporary thing don't forget. Just until Will gets another job. Then I'm leaving. I'm going back to my children.'

'Really? Because if I didn't know any better, I'd say you were starting to enjoy yourself again Lucy Mathers.'

'What? Absolutely not. This is far too hard. I have no idea why I used to enjoy it so much but I certainly don't need the stress of it all now. I'm a stay at home sort of person these days.'

'But you've slipped straight back into it all, it's just like the old days.'

Lucy shook her head. This was nothing like the old days. Back then she'd had nothing to worry about but getting the next deal signed up. Now she had Emily and Harry. All she really wanted at the end of the day was to get home to them. It didn't matter how well she did at Simcock and Bright, once Will was employed again she would relish going back to the mundane tasks of motherhood.

But right now she was still an account manager, with her first new potential account to manage and for the rest of the afternoon she didn't stop for anything as she came up with idea after idea for the launch of Blooming Lovely and its floral superstore.

There was no sign of Grant and it wasn't until Alice poked her head around the door to say goodbye that Lucy realised it was well after 5:00 and she had missed the train she normally caught home. Swearing softly under her breath and gathering together her things, she slipped her laptop into her bag. It would have to go home with her. She still had some work she wanted to finish and she would be checking her emails religiously for the rest of the evening.

Her later arrival at the train station meant she was faced with packed platforms and with a groan she joined the general melee of workers, pushing and shoving to get prime position.

'Lucy?'

Hearing her name she turned around, staring into the crowd before realising that someone familiar was standing right behind her.

'Simon! Sorry, I didn't see you.' She moved an inch to the left so he could elbow his way next to her. 'Do you catch the Horsforth train?'

'Yes, I go through to Pannal. I've seen you a couple of mornings actually but you've always been too far away to speak to.'

He put out his hand to steady her as a large man with an equally large briefcase pushed past almost knocking Lucy over.

'I usually catch the earlier train,' she grumbled. 'It's a lot quieter than this one.'

'Stayed late tonight?'

'I was busy, lost track of time I suppose.'

Simon smiled. 'We heard that Blooming Lovely asked you to pitch. Congratulations.'

'Thank you.'

'It was great news. Not just that you've already potentially got a new client but one in the eye for Grant.'

Lucy gave him a keen look. Other than Alice she hadn't spoken about Grant to anyone else in the office. She had found in the past that sharing one's thoughts and feelings about other members of staff often came back at inopportune moments.

'Oh I don't know,' she murmured. 'I think Grant is too busy with his own cases to worry about what I'm doing.'

'You think so?'

The train appeared down the track and the waiting crowd flexed their collective muscles, eying up the passengers to either side, searching the approaching carriages for space and maybe even the elusive seat. They all shuffled forwards as it slowed down.

Lucy looked at him. 'Of course. Don't you?'

The train shuddered to a halt and the attack started, elbows out, bags and cases used as weapons as everyone tried to get on at exactly the same time, ruthless in their determination to get a decent spot for their journey home.

'No,' said Simon, blocking a very wide man who was trying to slide between Lucy and the door. They both grunted as they surged forward, forcing their way into the nearest carriage which was devoid of free seats and already full of tired, sweaty bodies. They wedged themselves between the end of a seat and the luggage rack which gave some support as the train lurched out of the station.

'No. I think Grant is watching you very carefully. The whole office is watching the pair of you.'

'They are?'

'We all know how highly Rob thinks of you. That's why he asked you back. And we all know how highly Grant thinks of himself. That's why he didn't want you back. Everybody is waiting to see what will happen next.'

Lucy stared at him indignantly. Was she the office entertainment now, her struggles with Grant keeping them all amused?

'We all want you to do well,' added Simon hastily. 'Word got out about the late email he sent you, that's why everybody was so pleased when you pulled it back.'

Lucy sniffed. 'Well I'm not sure I appreciate being the subject of the office gossip,' she said stiffly.

The train shifted to one side and they both hung onto the handrail to stop colliding with each other.

'Maybe I phrased it badly,' Simon said softly. 'Everybody is happy you're back. They're all very interested in how you're going to handle Grant. And so far, you're doing great.'

Lucy felt slightly mollified. 'It did go well today,' she accepted.

'And no doubt Grant isn't too happy about your early break into the lead?'

At Lucy's perplexed look Simon grinned. 'We've also heard about Rob's challenge, the first of you to sign up their client?'

'Ah.' Lucy sighed. 'It seemed like a good idea at the time.'

'It still is. You'll do it, Lucy. And if there's anything I can do to help you at any time, just let me know.'

For some reason, Lucy felt slightly tearful. Simon would have no idea how grateful she was to know there was another person in the office supporting her. She had started to feel that other than Alice, she was quite on her own.

'Thank you,' she said huskily. 'Thank you very much.'

By the time Lucy arrived at her station, it was almost an hour later than usual and there were two anxious texts on her phone from Will demanding to know if she was okay. She answered them as she walked briskly home, hoping the children wouldn't already be in bed. She was just in time for a cuddle and a quick story before they were tucked up, Harry already half asleep.

'Why so late?' Will asked as he served up a lasagne that had Lucy's eyes rolling in surprise.

'Wow, your cooking skills really have improved,' she murmured. 'I just lost track of time and I missed the early train.'

Will put a wine glass in front of her, a slight frown between his eyes. He had taken Lucy's coat and briefcase, as she came in the door and surprised at the weight, had peeped inside to see her laptop in situ.

'I see you've brought work home.'

'I had to because,' Lucy paused, waiting for Will to put the bottle down and give her his full attention, 'Blooming Lovely want to see my proposal.'

There was a small pause, a small but very definite pause before Will leant forward to give her a kiss. 'Well done. Congratulations.'

Lucy waited but sitting back down he picked up his knife and fork and started tucking into the lasagne he had taken out of the cardboard wrapping and thrown into the oven when Lucy had finally sent him a text from the station.

'It was a surprise,' said Lucy watching him, 'because this morning I didn't even know I had a meeting with them. Grant had arranged it to catch me out. But it went well.'

'Apparently.'

'This lasagne is amazing by the way. Something else you make better than I do.'

Will didn't answer. He knew he should, it was the perfect time to explain what he had done, but he kept quiet.

'Rob is delighted of course.'

'He would be.'

'But you don't seem particularly pleased.' Lucy put down her fork. 'What's wrong?'

Will chewed his food slowly, giving him time to decide what *was* the matter and making Lucy wait for his answer.

'I don't think you should be throwing yourself into this job quite as much as you are, bearing in mind you'll only be there a few more weeks?'

'I don't know how long I'll be there. And I know you said I should take it easy but you know that's not really my style.'

'I'll have a job soon and …'

'But will you? You haven't even got an interview yet so I can't start planning my leaving announcement just yet.'

Scowling Will threw down his fork. 'I'm looking! There just hasn't been the right job…'

'I know! I'm sorry.' Holding up her hand Lucy felt a stab of contrition. Will was desperate for a job, he was scouring every available source and speaking to anybody who might be able to help on a daily basis.

'What I mean,' she said in a much gentler tone, 'is that we don't know how long it will take for you to find the right job and in the meantime, we need the money so I have to stay at work. And I can't turn up and not do my very best.'

'And that means bringing work home? demanded Will truculently.

Lucy lost her sympathy. 'Only when I need to,' she snapped. 'Just like you did when you were working.'

'But this is temporary Lucy. Remember? You work for a few weeks and fill the hole while I get a job.'

'It still counts! I'm the one working at the moment and if that means I have to bring work home then I will!'

'What about the children?'

Lucy stared at him, the lasagne on her fork falling back onto the plate.

'What on earth do you mean? You're looking after the children now, that's the whole point!'

'I know.' Will couldn't help but recall Jen's words, about Lucy's exciting new life, about the balance that was needed and how that all seemed to be in favour of work.

'It seems work is starting to come first. What about everything else?'

He immediately regretted the words, they sounded whiny and selfish. He wished he could swallow them, make them disappear.

Lucy looked down at the delicious lasagne. She'd already noticed that the living room and Emily's room had been cleaned. In fact, she had felt a slight twinge of something she couldn't quite put her finger on but she suspected was a less than commendable sense of resentment that Will seemed to have gotten to grips with the whole dad at home thing so easily, whilst she was struggling every day, doing battle with Grant Cassidy and trying to regain all the ground she had lost over the last four years.

'Are you saying you can't cope?'

Will took a deep drink of wine instead of answering. He wasn't actually coping very well at all. Without Jen, Harry would have sported a purple face when his mother finally arrived home and the living room would still have been wearing an inch of dust on every surface and a carpet that could have hidden a family of mice amongst the debris and general clutter. He could tell Lucy what had happened to Harry, she would find it funny he was sure. Maybe he should confess about the ready-made meals at the same time, that Jen had taken on the cleaning and that their daughter had been forced to negotiate with Mrs Worthington to stop another black mark being registered against her name.

He could tell her that this was the hardest job he'd ever had to do in his life and that he was barely managing, that the spreadsheet of tasks was now so long he often didn't have time to read it and that he had a small crack on the screen of his phone after throwing it across the room when it continued to send out alarm after alarm one tense morning. He could explain that he was exhausted, worn out with the constant attention two small children required.

And Lucy may grumble about Grant Cassidy, her tiny office and Rob's reluctance to treat her equally, but he had seen the glow start to appear in her eyes. He felt his wife was beginning to enjoy her return to work and the one thing that kept him awake at night, despite his extreme exhaustion, was the thought that he may not find another job and that Lucy would stay at Simcock and Bright and their change of roles would become a permanent thing. She would once again become Lucy Mathers, Account Manager and he would be just Will, stay at home dad.

He could tell her how he was feeling.

'Of course I can cope,' he snapped instead. 'With the children and the house.'

'Good!' Lucy snapped back. 'Because I had to!'

They ate the rest of their meal in silence, before Will made a great deal of noise clearing the kitchen and the debris of their meal and after a second of hesitation, Lucy left him to it and sat in a corner of the living room to carry on working on her pitch. Neither of them apologised and for the first time in their married life, they went to bed with their backs turned firmly against each other.

Chapter 22

When Lucy's alarm broke into her sleep the following morning, she couldn't understand why she felt so down. She struggled out of bed and grabbed her dressing gown before remembering the argument from the previous night. Her eyes flew to Will. He was sitting up in bed yawning and rubbing his eyes. Turning away, she set off for the bathroom.

'Lucy!'

Pausing, she looked round. He was out of bed and standing behind her.

'I'm sorry,' he whispered, pulling her into his arms. 'I'm sorry I snapped, I'm sorry we argued. I'm sorry I didn't give you more support.' He scratched his chin. 'I'm sorry I wasn't more excited about your potential new client. I'm sorry …'

He screwed up his eyes in thought. 'I'm sorry ….'

'Okay! I get it. You're sorry.'

'I am.' He peeped at her from between his eyelashes. 'Very sorry.'

Lucy smiled and for a moment she leant her head against Will's broad chest and let her body relax into his.

'I'm sorry too,' she murmured, not really wanting to move. 'I think we both over reacted.'

'I appreciate everything you're doing Lucy. I really do. But it's important to remember we've changed places for a short time. I'll soon be back at work and you'll be at home with the children. I suppose I don't want you to get too overwhelmed with work when it's not going to be permanent.'

Lucy nodded, reluctantly leaving Will's chest.

'You're right. But I have the chance of a new client and I owe it to Rob to work as hard as I can on the proposal, even if it's the only one I do.'

For a moment Lucy thought the argument was going to start again but instead Will pulled her back into his arms and kissed her, a long lingering kiss which was ruined by Harry erupting into their room and Emily's voice demanding breakfast and with the moment broken, Lucy began her morning dash to organise everything before she left for the office. But this morning her mind couldn't help but wander in the direction of Blooming Lovely and the campaign she must now put in place and she spent a little more time than she'd intended in the shower, thinking over a couple of ideas that came to her. Wondering why her makeup case seemed so messy, she had spent a moment or two more than usual on her makeup. Then she spent several minutes staring at her shoes as she wondered if she could really pull this off, all of which had made her late and it wasn't until she was already halfway to the station that she realised she hadn't laid out any clothes for the children to wear or left Will a note detailing their activities for the day.

Running up the stairs to work, she dropped a coffee in front of Rob and perched herself on the corner of his desk.

'I need a bigger office,' she said without preamble.

'Bigger? Well I suppose yours is a little on the snug side.'

'Snug? I don't actually fit in it, that's more than a little snug.'

Rob screwed up his face. 'We just don't have anywhere at the moment Lucy.' He looked a little puzzled. 'Although I'm not sure why,' he added, 'we always used to have enough offices.'

'It's because Grant has three! That's why we've run out!'

'Three? No, he's got a spare one for …'

'No-one with an office the size of Grant's needs a spare one. And the other office is being used as a filing room, under his instruction. Why can't we go back to having it as an office? My office.'

Rob was fiddling with his paperwork, a sure sign that he had lost interest in the conversation.

'Apparently the files had outgrown the filing room,' he said looking at his watch.

'And if I can get the files back in the filing room?'

The phone rang and with a look of relief Rob reached out his hand to take the receiver.

'Lucy darling, you know I don't care. As long as everything is working as it should. If you can find a bigger office, have it by all means.' And then he was shouting 'Hello!' into the receiver and Lucy was dismissed.

It was the best she would get from Rob and as far as Lucy was concerned, he had just agreed that she could have the office which Grant had appropriated as a filing room.

Walking out of Rob's room, she glanced into her old office where Grant sat, in her chair, flicking through some papers. He was leaning back, which he could do because of all the space behind him and his feet were stretched out, which he could do because of all the space in front of him. Lucy's tiny office would probably fit in the footprint of his desk she thought, glaring at all the empty space surrounding him. Suddenly Grant looked up, catching her stare and refusing to be embarrassed, Lucy sent him a large smile before moving causally on to her own tiny office. He would no doubt spend the next hour trying to find out what she had on her agenda.

It actually didn't take an hour. Within 30 minutes a breathless Alice appeared in the doorway, her cheeks flushed and her eyes bright.

'Grant has just asked me out for a drink!' she announced in a squeaky voice.

Lucy sat up. 'Really?'

'Yes! He said that he'd enjoyed chatting to me on Friday night and did I want to grab a glass of wine with him tonight.'

Lucy didn't answer. She looked at Alice's excited face and cursed Grant Cassidy. There was no doubt in her mind that her friend had something of a crush on the man she declared she hated. And there was also no doubt in Lucy's mind that Grant had decided to use this to his advantage and Lucy couldn't bear the thought of Alice being hurt. She bit her lip wondering how to broach the subject.

'Of course he's on a fishing expedition,' said Alice in a matter of fact voice.

'Fishing?'

'Definitely. He hasn't given me a second glance since he arrived.' Alice's cheeks went a slightly darker shade of pink and

Lucy had the impression that Alice had been rather hoping Grant's cool gaze would swivel in her direction. 'It's a bit of a coincidence that he suddenly wants us to have a little chat. He'll want to know all about you and how you're doing with Blooming Lovely.'

Relieved that she didn't have to be the one to suggest Grant was asking Alice out for some very underhanded motive, she leaned back cautiously, resting her head against the wall.

'Pretty devious really,' she said. 'But no more than I would expect of him.'

Alice didn't seem to be listening, her thoughts clearly not in the room with Lucy.

'Have you told him you're not going?'

Alice looked surprised. 'Of course I'm going.'

'What? But Alice you've just said …'

'Oh I know what he's up to but I'm still going.'

There was a slightly dreamy look on her friend's face that worried Lucy. 'Alice! He's using you. Why would you want to join him for a drink?'

'Because he's handsome. He's got beautiful eyes. And sometimes when he smiles it's very gentle.'

Lucy's was doubtful. 'Grant, gentle? Really?'

'Absolutely!'

'But if you think he's just asking you out because he wants information, why …?'

'Why not? Don't worry, I won't tell him anything I shouldn't but why not let a good-looking man take me out for a drink. I can still enjoy myself.'

Lucy stared. How could anyone enjoy themselves on a night out with Grant Cassidy, regardless of his motives.

'Are you sure this is a good idea Alice? Not because of me or the account, but how awful spending an evening with a man who … who, well who …'

'Who wouldn't ask me out without an ulterior motive?'

'I didn't mean that …' began Lucy hastily.

'Because I get to spend a few hours with someone who I,' Alice ducked her head down shyly, 'who I quite fancy. It will probably be the only date we ever have and as long as I go into it with my eyes wide open, it's not a problem.'

'No!' gasped Lucy. 'You really think you would enjoy an evening under those circumstances?'

'I'll soon find out,' said Alice cheerfully.

Lucy shook her head. She really didn't think this was a very good idea.

'Please be careful,' she begged. 'Don't get hurt.'

'I won't,' Alice said happily. 'But I am going to the hairdressers at lunchtime. And I may see if I can find a nice top for tonight,' and she was gone, humming happily as she disappeared down the corridor.'

Lucy spent a good hour fretting about Alice and her potential date with Grant. She considered confronting him and telling him that she was aware of his game and that he must leave Alice out of his manipulations. But her mind recalled the excitement in Alice's eyes and she had a feeling her friend wouldn't appreciate her interference. She thought about sitting down and telling him everything she was doing so he wouldn't have to use Alice, but she knew that he would find a way of scuppering her efforts. In the end she reluctantly concluded that Alice had made her decision knowing the facts and it wasn't up to Lucy to intervene. But she glared darkly down the corridor in the direction of Grant's office. If he upset Alice, he would have Lucy to deal with.

Eventually her thoughts came back to the office and she mused over the situation for a while before walking into the main office and sitting herself next to Hannah's desk.

'Hi! I'm sorry I haven't had much time to chat to you since I came back.' Lucy pulled a face. 'There's been so much to catch up on!'

Hannah gave her a warm smile but Lucy couldn't help but notice the deep shadows under her eyes and the lines of exhaustion settling between her eyebrows. All she wanted from Hannah was an agreement to relocate the filing room, but looking at the woman in front of her Lucy stretched out her hand in concern.

'Hannah, you look shattered. Is everything okay?'

'Yes. Actually, not really. It's been a tough couple of months and I'm just feeling the strain.'

'Anything you want to talk about?'

Hannah shook her head. 'Oh it's nothing dreadful. My mum has been ill, Jared and I haven't,' she glanced down at the table, 'haven't been getting on too well. Arguing, that sort of thing. We're trying to work through it but it's quite exhausting.'

Lucy screwed her face in sympathy. She and Will had been incredibly lucky. They had arguments but they usually ended in the bedroom and they both still felt incredibly happy in each other's company. Well, they had until the last few weeks when an element of tetchiness had suddenly appeared in the Mathers household. She pushed that thought aside.

'I'll be frank,' she gave Hannah what she hoped was a winning smile, 'I came to talk to you because I wanted something.'

Hannah laughed. 'Well at least you're honest! What can I do for you?'

'Well, it could benefit both of us. I want a bigger office …'

'I can't say I'm surprised! It's difficult to believe that Rob thought it was okay to put you in that cupboard!'

'I know! I think Grant was behind that. Well, I know Grant was behind that. A little manipulation to make me feel inferior.'

Hannah was watching her closely. 'And?'

'And I need to move. Because I need more space and also to show Grant Cassidy that he can't have everything his own way.'

'Have you got a plan?'

'I want to put the files back where they were, in my office.'

Lucy held up a hand to ward off Hannah's protests. 'I know Rob agreed to a new system and more space for the files but I've just spoken to him and he's happy for us to move things around so I can have a bigger office, as long as I sort out the filing system.'

'And how do I benefit from this plan?'

Lucy grinned. 'Because it's a job you can remove from your to do list. I'll get the files back, sorted, alphabetised, whatever you need them to be. This new scheme of Grant's is pie in the sky, we both know that. And in the meantime the files are a mess, which is probably causing you more work?'

'I suppose,' said Hannah slowly. 'It is a bit of a mess and I can't get a straight answer out of Grant as to what he wants me to do with them. Are you sure Rob is okay with this?'

'Absolutely!' said Lucy, hoping her voice was full of confidence. 'I've just spoken to him and he said I could do whatever I need to.' Not quite what Rob had said thought Lucy, but a close approximation.

She watched Hannah hopefully.

'Okay. It is one job I could do without right now. As long as the files are accessible again, I don't care where they are. Go for it Lucy.' She gave her friend an encouraging smile. 'It's good to have you back, especially if you take Grant down a peg or two. I've had enough of him interfering in office management!'

Chapter 23

Will had taken Emily to nursery, arriving on time under the watchful gaze of Mrs Worthington and was back in the house, his sleeves rolled up as he stood in the utility room. He had spent the morning regretting the argument he'd had with Lucy. Jen had been mistaken, Lucy hadn't relegated her family in favour of Simcock and Bright, she was simply doing her best to make sure the mortgage was paid until he found another job. Of course she was busy, hadn't he been busy when he had been the one leaving the house with a cheery good bye every morning? He should have been more supportive, encouraging about her efforts. And he needed to step up his contribution and make sure that she didn't have a thousand and one tasks to catch up on every weekend.

Lucy had been loading the washing machine every morning before she left the house and Will's job had been to get it dried during the day. He had failed significantly and Lucy had spent a great deal of her weekend catching up with the piles of laundry, some half dry, a lot still soaking wet that had taken over the utility room. It had also transpired that everything that went in the washing machine needed even more attention when it came back out and Lucy had spent several hours ironing and putting everything neatly back in drawers on Sunday afternoon.

So the spreadsheet had been tweaked and several entries for laundry management had been added, although Will was still confused as to just how many tasks could realistically be addressed during the course of each day. His timesheet was now a rainbow of colours and growing to a frightening length. He was beginning to think that maybe it wasn't the way to run a house and look after children but at the moment it was the only thing keeping him sane.

'We can do this Harry,' he declared, examining the piles of washing he had brought downstairs. 'It needs organisation, that's all. We need to get as much in the washing machine as we can to start off with.'

Harry watched him from his position on the floor, surrounded by towels, socks and slightly muddy trousers from their weekend walk in the park.

'That's what mummy would do, isn't it?'

Harry dribbled, and looked around for something more interesting to play with as Will started piling everything into the washer.

'That's why we bought this washer,' grunted Will as he forced in a few more towels with his foot. 'I remember Mummy saying she wanted a large capacity drum, or something like that.'

Having pushed in as much as he could and closed the door, he peered at the buttons and knobs.

'She said it was because you two created so much washing. Although I have to say little man, I hadn't realised just how much gear you went through!'

He watched as Harry dribbled a little bit more, the jumper he was wearing was already wet through and would need to join the dirty laundry soon. He needed to find a way of keeping Harry cleaner during the day, that might cut down on the task in hand. Perhaps he should turn up the heating and take off Harry's jumper, leave him to wander around in a vest during the day. That should help. Choosing a button that seemed to promise a hot, clean wash, Will set the programme and scooped Harry into his arms just as an alarm sounded on his phone.

'Come on Harry, a quick nap for you and time for me to wash the breakfast things and tidy the kitchen,' and off they went to examine Will's spreadsheet and get on with the next task.

Checking on the washing an hour later, Will was surprised to find it still in action. Another hour and he began to scratch his head in amazement. 'Why is it taking so long do you think Harry? I'm sure when Mummy does the washing it's in and out in an hour.'

Abandoning the still swirling clothes, he collected Emily from nursery and several hours after he had closed the door on dirty clothes, Will discovered the cycle had finally finished. 'No wonder this all takes so long,' he muttered to himself, grabbing a basket for the newly washed clothes. 'That's a ridiculously long time for a wash to take.'

He pulled out a few towels, staring at them as they fell into the basket. He didn't remember any of their towels being a streaky grey. Shrugging he pulled out more items and a pile of underwear hit the basket along with one of Will's shirts and a pair of Harry's dungarees, all looking like the results of a tie dye experiment. One of Lucy's jumpers burst out next. It was one of her favourites, a soft cream jumper that she loved because it covered her bottom and she said was perfect for hiding her worst excesses. Except that it would no longer cover her bottom. In fact, it would barely cover her midriff and with a whimper of horror Will held up a severely shrunken jumper that looked as though it would be a tight fit on Emily and was no longer a pretty cream colour.

He carried on pulling out more and more washing, all the same unappealing muddy colour, several jumpers that were now much smaller except for one which seemed to have gone the opposite way and had sleeves that were several feet long and had lost its shape entirely.

'What's that?' asked Emily who had appeared in the doorway and was pointing to the jumper Will was examining.

Will pushed the jumper into the basket. 'Oh, nothing. Have you finished your lunch? Do you want to watch TV for a bit?'

'Mummy doesn't let us watch TV until later,' Emily advised, watching her father as he threw a towel over the clothes piled in the basket. 'Was that Mummy's jumper?'

'Mummy's? Er, no, not Mummy's.'

'It looked like Mummy's jumper, but the wrong colour.'

Will's mind was racing. Lucy had done this before, he was sure. She once told him that a red sock had slipped in with the whites and turned everything pink. He closed his eyes. Did she say what she'd done about it? He couldn't remember, in fact he had a feeling he hadn't really listened. A rugby match was about to start and pink washing had seemed a little unimportant at the time. But she had done something, he was sure. There was a solution.

'Have you broken all the clothes?'

Will's eyes flew to his daughter's face. She was examining the basket with interest.

'No! Not at all!'

'It looks like you have. Are those Harry's trousers?'

Will grabbed at the leg of a murky pair of trousers hanging from the basket. 'It's because they're wet,' he improvised. 'Clothes look a different colour when they're wet.'

'Mummy's don't.'

'You watch, as soon as they dry they'll look just like they should.' Standing up Will ushered Emily away from the scene of the crime. 'And I thought TV could be a treat today, because you've both been so good.'

Emily stared at him, her little nose wrinkled in thought. 'What have we done?'

'Done? Well, you've just been good,' said Will vaguely, moving her towards the living room.

'I don't feel as though I've been good,' Emily told him gravely. 'Have I done something extra special?'

'No, yes. It's just that …. you've just been good, that's all.' Should it be this challenging, wondered Will, negotiating with a four-year-old.

'But if I've done something really good I want to know what it is so I can do it again.'

Emily was standing in front of the TV, her hands on her chubby hips, watching her father flick through the TV channels to find something appropriate.

Will groaned. 'It's not that you've been particularly good,' he admitted. 'I just thought you might like a treat.'

'Are we telling Mummy?'

Will's eyes flew to the shrewd blue eyes that were watching him. He grappled with his conscience.

172

'Of course, you should always tell Mummy everything that happens,' he said slowly. 'But she might tell me not to let you watch TV in the afternoon.'

Emily nodded. 'She would.'

'So you can tell her but …'

'Are we telling her about the clothes as well?'

'Clothes?'

'How they've come out dirty?'

Will shoulders slumped, was there nothing that his daughter didn't notice?

'I've told you, they'll be clean when they dry. They just look a funny colour at the moment.'

Emily stared at him. 'Mummy will notice that her jumper has long arms,' she advised him. 'Even if you get it clean.'

Will nodded dejectedly. 'I know,' he whispered.

'Me and Harry will watch TV while you try and get them all the right colour,' Emily told him soothingly. 'And maybe you can chop of the bottom of the sleeves?'

It may well come to that, thought Will darkly. Or perhaps there was a label on the jumpers and he could buy some new ones before Lucy noticed.

'Thank you,' he said to Emily who looked pointedly at the clock. 'I think you better start drying them daddy,' and then she pulled Harry onto the settee next to her and they sank in the cushions to chuckle over the cartoons Will had selected.

Back in the kitchen, Will pulled out his mobile phone.

'Jen!' he said urgently as his call was answered. 'Oh God Jen, I'm so sorry but I need your help again!'

An hour later Harry and Emily were still watching TV and Jen, who had dropped off her son at her mother's house, was going through the ruined clothes.

'How much washing did you put in?' she asked in amazement.

'As much as I could fit.'

'And you didn't sort them out first?'

'They were all dirty. How much more sorted do they need to be?'

Jen was putting the sodden clothes into piles.

'Well for a start off, you don't fill the drum to capacity every time you use the washing machine.'

Will looked doubtful. 'Well then it would take twice as long to get it all clean!'

'Longer than this?' asked Jen giving him an admonishing look.

'Ah, yes. Sorry.'

'And you sort out the colours, you don't just ram everything in together.'

Will's head drooped even lower. 'Sorry. But can you do anything?'

Putting some of the clothes back in the washer, Jen shook her head. 'The colour we can sort out with a little of this,' she showed him the sachet of colour run rescue she had brought with her. 'But these jumpers are ruined I'm afraid. What setting did you have it on?'

Will pointed and Jen gasped in horror. 'That's the hottest temperature you can choose, with a soak and a pre wash thrown in with a couple of extra rinses! No wonder it took so long!' She was holding up Lucy's once pretty cream jumper. 'Nothing I can do to rescue this I'm afraid.'

Will groaned. 'I was just trying to save Lucy some work. She doesn't need to spend the weekend doing laundry.'

Jen put the washer on, leaving another sachet on the surface for the next pile of ruined clothes.

'You're very sweet you know,' she said softly. 'Lots of men wouldn't try this hard. My ex certainly wouldn't.'

There was a slightly bitter note and Will wondered if he should ask her more. Was it the done thing to ask where her ex had gone? Should they have that kind of conversation in his utility room?

'I try,' he said instead.

'And I'm sure Lucy really appreciates it. Well, I hope she does.'

They wandered back to the kitchen and Will put on the kettle.

'My husband found it impossible to be faithful,' Jen announced, making Will wince at her candour. 'I kicked him out before Alfie was even born. I decided I would be better off without him altogether. Fortunately mum lives really close by so I've had plenty of help.'

'Right.' Will's cheeks were a little pink, he wasn't used to this kind of conversation. His friends wouldn't dream of opening their heart to him about their relationships. Not unless it involved a rugby ball or a cricket bat.

'But he would never have helped out like you are,' continued Jen. 'He thought everything to do with children, cooking, housekeeping, was all a woman's work. He would go out and buy new clothes before he would wash any!'

Will handed her a cup of coffee. 'Well I might be doing that,' he confessed ruefully. 'Lucy loved that cream jumper.'

'I bet she doesn't mind too much though. At least you're trying.'

Shrugging his shoulders Will pulled a face. 'I may be trying but as you've seen first-hand, it's not always a success!'

'I think you're doing an amazing job,' Jen put out a hand to cover his. It felt good, a warm touch of encouragement in a long day. And although Will wondered if he should be more vocal about how hard Lucy was working, he decided to allow himself the luxury of someone telling him how wonderful he was. It seemed an awfully long time since anyone had said "Well done" to him.

'And I've brought you a present,' Jen added with a grin.

She left the table and returned with a small black bag which she placed almost shyly in front of Will. 'I figured you might need a little bit of help when you're out and about and bearing in mind I might not always be there,' her eyes twinkled as Will blushed, 'I thought this might help.'

Will put down his cup and opened it to peer inside.

'Oh Jen,' he said laughing as he pulled out a selection of baby wipes, tissues, small bags and a handful of other emergency items. 'You didn't have to but thank you! Thank you so much.'

'I thought it might be something Lucy had already done for you?' said Jen in a questioning tone. As Will shook his head she continued. 'Well it's the sort of thing that us mums always have with us. I'm sure Lucy meant to put one together to help you out. She was probably just too busy to remember,' she said generously. 'But I decided if Lucy didn't have time, I'd do one for you.'

There was a twinge of guilt as Will thought about how Lucy raced around every morning trying to do as much as she could for Will before leaving for work.

'She does so much every morning,' he began.

And of course, Lucy had no idea about the yoghurt incident at the supermarket because he'd never told her. Or about Harry covering himself with her make up. And it was unlikely that he would regale her with the funny story of his epic fail with the washing machine and how he had ruined two of her jumpers. So it was quite understandable that Lucy hadn't provided him with a little bag of emergency solutions.

'She does try to help me,' he said weakly. 'Maybe she hasn't realised just how bad I am at the whole housework thing!'

Jen was watching the emotions chase across his face. 'If she doesn't appreciate what you're doing she certainly should,' said Jen in a gentle, admiring tone. 'Because I think you're pretty special Will Mathers. And Lucy should feel the same way.'

Chapter 24

Lucy waited. Despite Rob's agreement that she could relocate the files, she waited until both Rob and Grant were on appointments and out of the office for a few hours before she set to work. Watching them both walk towards the staircase, she grabbed Alice and two volunteers from the main office.

'Now!' she hissed and within 30 minutes her office was cleared and the cabinets and boxes of files moved back to their original home.

Walking into the bigger office, Lucy felt her heart soar. She could now have a desk, a chair and a filing cabinet without having to climb over the furniture to reach the door. She had a window, a real window that gave her a view of the sky, which despite being rather dismal and grey had never looked better. And she even had a narrow view of the patch of green that was Park Square, an inspiration after the claustrophobic office she had just escaped.

But she didn't spend long admiring the view. This was only the beginning and she couldn't afford to give Grant any excuse to move the files again. The cabinets were lining the wall waiting to be filled once more from the overflowing boxes and she made a start by grabbing a handful of files.

'Alphabetical?' she asked her small group.

'Current and historical?' offered one of them.

'Date of sign up?' hazarded another.

'Alphabetical, then colour coded whether current or historical,' suggested Alice. 'And a note of the sign up date on the corner of each folder.

They all looked at each other.

'That's the one. Go!'

They worked silently other than the occasional demand for a particular colour folder or a grunt at a particularly strange spelling.

Lucy glanced at her watch, it was time consuming work and they were barely a quarter of the way through. She needed it finished before Rob or Grant returned. She wanted to be sitting in her executive chair in her appropriately sized office before either of them could throw a spanner in the works. She knew Rob would never evict her if she was already settled, he didn't care enough about the filing system. But Grant could demand things were put back, unless it was a fait accompli.

'Reorganising?' asked a voice and Lucy looked up to see Simon in the doorway.

'Sort of,' grunted Lucy. 'Putting the filing system back together.'

'Ah. And then of course with the files back in here you can …?'

He looked across the corridor to where Lucy's desk and chair were now sitting in the centre of the room.

'Exactly.'

'Rob know?'

'Yes.'

Lucy didn't have time for niceties, she was working as quickly as she could, her hands flying through the files.

'Grant …?'

'No.'

'And you're in a hurry because he would try and stop you.'

It was a statement not a question and Lucy just looked at her watch and carried on working.

Simon watched them for a moment. 'So, alphabetical, colour coded folders and a date?'

'Date of sign up,' advised Alice, gathering a pile of completed folders and sliding them into one of the cabinets.

'Hmm. Very fluid and organic.'

Lucy stopped and looked up at him as he leant in the doorway, smiling.

'Oh we've all heard about Grant's plans for the filing system,' he told her. 'And how it left no office for you when you came back. Need a hand?'

He was pulled into the group, a pile of files taken from the box and placed in front of him and a marker pen put in his hand.

They worked quickly and when Hannah passed the office 20 minutes later and saw what was happening, she put down her empty coffee cup and joined them, nodding at Lucy's grateful look.

It was done. Even as Rob's voice drifted up the staircase, the last file was placed in a cabinet and the door slid shut.

Lucy felt weak kneed with relief as her group all took a deep breath looking pleased with their intensive few hours of work.

'It's actually a good system,' nodded Hannah.

'Very fluid,' added Simon.

'And possibly orgasmic,' chuckled Alice and they all doubled over in fits of silent giggles.

'Thank you,' whispered Lucy as Hannah retrieved her cup and left the room. 'Thank you all,' she added as Alice swept away the other two and they scuttled back into the main office.

'Thank you so much,' she said to Simon as they stood in the corridor. 'I really appreciate your help.'

His blue eyes were twinkling. 'No problem. I'll come and visit you in your new office,' he promised, 'now that you have room for an extra body,' and he was gone, leaving Lucy to slip across the corridor and behind her desk to catch her breath.

It was 10 minutes later that she heard Grant's voice in the doorway of his office. He was talking to Rob about the client he had just met, advising Rob what an excellent opportunity it seemed to be.

'Wonderful! Wonderful!' boomed Rob. 'With you and Lucy both on top form, we'll be unbeatable.'

Grant's voice suddenly sounded a little less enthusiastic. 'Well once Lucy has had time to catch up I'm sure that will be the case,' he said. 'But we mustn't rush her.'

'Don't be silly,' shouted Rob. 'Lucy's already back on her game. Aren't you Lucy?' he shouted down the corridor in the direction of her old office. 'You'll have to keep your eye on her Grant,' he chuckled, 'or it might be you that's playing catch up,' and his voice faded as he escaped back to his own office.

Sitting at her desk, Lucy watched as Grant walked down the corridor to peer into the glass pane of the door before his head swivelled around to stare angrily into her new office.

'What is the meaning of this?' he asked icily, appearing in her doorway, his back stiff and set, his eyes flashing with anger.

'Hello Grant. Did you have a good meeting? What's the meaning of ….? Oh the change of office?'

Lucy relished the feeling of being able to push her chair away from her desk without giving herself concussion on the wall behind her. She smiled and crossed her legs, swinging her foot clad in a pair of grey high heeled shoes. She suddenly realised that she hadn't had to take them off during the day. Normally about now her feet would be screaming for release and she would slide them off under the desk and wriggle her toes luxuriously.

'Rob said it was a little silly me being in that tiny office when we could move the files back in there.'

That wasn't exactly what Rob had said but it was close. Well, not really close but she knew Rob didn't care. And now that it was already done and dusted, he wouldn't like Grant arguing or dragging out a conversation about files.

'I had plans for the files.'

'Oh? What were those exactly? I did check with Hannah before I moved anything and she told me you hadn't instructed her what you wanted to happen to them. And in the meantime,' she mused as she watched him straighten his tie, 'they were in a bit of a state. Not very …fluid.'

For a moment she wondered if she had gone too far as Grant took a step towards her. But he stopped, clearly bringing himself back under control as he managed a small tight smile. 'Well if Rob would rather postpone the new filing system …' he murmured.

'He would,' reiterated Lucy.

'If he wants to postpone it then of course I'm in agreement. Rob and I agree about most things.'

Lucy smiled. 'That's good to know. Rob and I used to disagree about lots of things. But he did always listen to me.'

'So it would appear. Well, I have work to be doing so, enjoy your new office Lucy,' and with another tight smile he left her laying her head onto her new desk and stretching her arms out in relief.

Lucy left work late. She had been engrossed in her work on Blooming Lovely and luxuriating in the space she now had. As the clock ticked its way past 5:00 she dragged Alice into her office.

'Are you sure about tonight?' she demanded even as she admired the shine on her friend's newly trimmed and washed hair.

'Absolutely! I'm looking forward to it.'

Alice had also bought a new top which matched her eyes and clung to her tiny waist. Her cheeks were flushed and her eyes were shining.

'But Alice …'

'Stop worrying! I know what I'm doing. Grant wants to buy me a drink and I'm going to let him.'

'But …'

'And I won't tell him anything about Blooming Lovely, so don't worry.'

But …'

'I'll simply have a pleasant evening out with a good-looking man.'

Lucy was silenced. 'Please don't go,' she beseeched. 'I don't trust him at all.'

'I know. I don't either.'

'Then why on earth are you …'

'Stop worrying! I know what I'm doing.'

Lucy shook her head. Why anybody would willingly spend any time with Grant Cassidy was beyond her comprehension.

'Well be careful,' she reiterated.

'I will,' said Alice and with a little giggle she left the office.

Lucy looked at her watch and gave a little squeal. She had missed the early train and the next one was always so crowded.

She walked quickly towards the stairs but not before she caught sight of Grant in Rob's office. Rob was looking disgruntled and Lucy suspected that Grant had brought up the subject of the files. She gave a little smile. He was wasting his time. As far as Rob was concerned that particular subject was already dealt with and closed and with a little skip she set off as quickly as she could towards the station.

She arrived to a scene of chaos. Several trains had been delayed due to signal failure and the platforms were a mass of angry commuters all consulting their phones and complaining loudly. She groaned, realising that there was no way she would get on the next train, there were simply too many bodies between her and the edge of the platform. She looked at the timetable. There was another train in 45 minutes, if it turned up. She may be able to get on that one.

She jumped as she felt a hand at her elbow and turned to find Simon standing behind her.

'We'll never make it through for the next train,' he said confirming her thoughts. 'No point standing here being bashed about.' Lucy winced as someone's briefcase caught her sharply in the back. 'Shall we grab a coffee?'

Looking around her at scenes of near riot, Lucy nodded, resigning herself to the idea of being late home and followed Simon as he pushed his way back into the main station. They were soon settled at a tiny table for two with a couple of coffees in front of them watching as dozens of other commuters made the same decision only to find all the tables taken.

'Travel strategies,' advised Simon with a grin. 'Sometimes it's best to give up on the train and then the next struggle is over a seat for a coffee.'

They watched as a small fight broke out over the last remaining chair and Lucy warmed her hands on her coffee mug

'I'm already late,' she grumbled. 'Will is going to think I'm not coming home at all tonight.'

She ought to call him and let him know. She would once she was on a train but right now she didn't want to get into an argument about why she was late and why she was putting so much effort into her work.

'You're lucky having him at home. Using childminders must be a nightmare when you get delayed like this.'

Simon was watching her over the rim of his cup and Lucy shrugged. 'I wouldn't know. I didn't exactly plan to come back to work,' she blurted out. 'I came back because Will was at home and could look after the children.'

And then for some reason she found herself explaining that Will was unemployed and she had come back to fill the empty coffers of their bank account, facts she hadn't given to anyone other than Alice.

She gazed at the kind blue eyes anxiously. 'Obviously, Rob doesn't realise I'm only back temporarily,' she said warily. 'I mean, he could probably work it out but it's not something that we've discussed …'

'Your secret is safe with me,' interrupted Simon. 'Really, don't worry, I won't be telling anyone.'

Lucy nodded gratefully. 'Who knows, I may stay on at work,' she said brightly. Which she could if she wanted to, she thought. She could get a childminder, one who was patient and understood the vagaries of the train service. She could spend her weekends enjoying her children as much as possible in between washing and cleaning and shopping. She could make the most of the last few hours of the evening before they went to bed, provided she managed to get home in time. She could book holidays to see their nativity plays and sports days and make sure it was clearly understood that if one of them was ill she needed to go home, no discussion.

Or she could forget about Simcock and Bright and go back to the job she had once complained about constantly but now missed dreadfully, being a full-time mother.

She realised she'd fallen silent and Simon was watching her sympathetically. 'Maybe there's a job just around the corner for Will, then you'll have a choice.'

Lucy nodded. It was something she had told herself virtually every day since Will had broken the news about his redundancy. Although she was beginning to believe it less and less.

'Maybe.'

'But we'll all miss you if you go,' said Simon with a grin, 'And who will keep Mr Cassidy in line if you disappear!'

Lucy laughed. 'I think it might take more than I've got to beat him,' she said regretfully.

'Oh I don't know.'

Simon leant forward and she suddenly noticed what nice eyes he had, very clear, very grey and very nice.

'I think you're doing a pretty good job Lucy.' He reached out a hand to cover hers gently. 'And I think you're doing an amazing job for your family. Will is a lucky guy, having a wife like you, I hope he appreciates it.'

Lucy stared down at his fingers touching her own, softly, not at all intrusively and wondered if Will did appreciate what she was doing. She had been trying to help him as much as she could with looking after the house and the children but when she'd needed his support the previous evening, when she needed him to say how well she'd done getting her first potential new client, all he had done was complain. And even though a little voice in her head was telling her to move her hand and tell Simon that her husband did appreciate her very much, she left her hand where it was, relishing the warm support she could feel flowing from his fingers and wondered if Will was aware of just how hard this was for her.

Chapter 25

The next day Lucy spent the journey into work deep in disorganised thought. She had started to prepare for Will's day as she normally did, then she had stopped. When she'd arrived home the previous night there had been another superb meal waiting for her. She had peeped in the utility room to see how much washing there was to do only to find it all done, dried and folded neatly in a basket waiting to be ironed. Her husband seemed to have everything pretty much under control. There was no need for Lucy to spend a frantic half hour every morning organising his day, she could do with spending that time organising her own.

There was a rather large ball of anxiety starting to gather momentum deep inside her stomach. Will was coping far better than she had ever believed possible. What if he suggested that their new roles become permanent? Will, stay at home dad. Lucy, working mum. The thought made her squirm, she wasn't finding the return to work as easy as Will seemed to be finding his new role. She wasn't at all sure how she would feel about this being a long-term solution.

Without reaching any conclusions she made her way to the Simcock and Bright offices. At least there was one good thing on the horizon. With the bigger office she had appropriated, at least she could stretch her legs and lean back without fear of bodily injury and feeling slightly more cheerful she made her way upstairs.

Alice was already sitting at her desk in the main office, her blonde head bent over some paperwork. Lucy could see Grant sitting in Rob's office, where he was usually to be found first thing each morning but instead of looking at Rob, who was reading something from his laptop, his eyes seemed to be on Alice.

Catching Alice's eye, Lucy rolled her own in the direction of her office and it was only a matter of minutes before Alice arrived.

'How did it go?' demanded Lucy. 'Did he try to find out about Blooming Lovely?'

Alice sat down. She couldn't stop smiling and her eyes were shining.

'No. I told him I wasn't going to talk about you or anything that you were working on and that was the end of it.'

'Really?' Lucy's voice was disbelieving. 'Really? But I thought ....'

'We actually had quite a pleasant evening.'

Lucy's mouth hung open. 'You had a nice time with Grant Cassidy?'

'Yes.' Alice looked happy. Her cheeks were flushed and there was a definite air of complacency on her face.

'But didn't he ...'

'He behaved perfectly. I told him straight away that I knew he was trying to use me, manipulate me into giving him information and that it wouldn't happen.'

'So what did happen?' asked Lucy, intrigued by the thought of her lovely natured, slightly dizzy friend taking Grant Cassidy to task.'

'Well,' mused Alice. 'He was surprised. He went very quiet and stared at me for a while.'

Lucy leant forward. 'And?' she breathed, caught up in the moment.

'Then he smiled and said I was refreshingly honest.'

'Did he admit that's why he asked you out?'

'Not exactly. I thought he might decide to leave but we started chatting and then we had another drink.'

Lucy tried and failed to visualise a relaxed Grant chatting away to Alice over a glass of wine.

'And you enjoyed it?'

'Of course. As I suspected, when he's not trying to take over the office, he can be a charming person. He's very amusing and we had a lot in common.'

'Like what?'

'Music, books, things in general.'

'You and Grant like the same books?'

'Yes, isn't it strange! Who would have thought we were so similar?'

Well certainly not Lucy and she couldn't help the frown that creased her forehead.

'Alice, please tell me you haven't fallen for him! He may have said all the right things but I'm fairly sure that he is still trying to manipulate you and I couldn't bear if you got hurt by Grant because of me.'

Alice stared back, her eyes serious.

'And it couldn't be that we had a good time because he liked me?'

'Er …. of course. But you know what he's like! In the office he's …'

'But that's in the office Lucy. You're different in the office. You used to be manipulative and ruthless, that's why you were good at your job.'

Lucy stared open mouthed at her friend. 'I wasn't! I never …'

'Yes you were,' interrupted Alice calmly. 'It wasn't necessarily a bad thing, it's how you were. But I knew the real Lucy, the one that was funny and kind and generous. The one that made me giggle and would always be there to help me. So maybe there's a nicer side to Grant.'

'If it exists it's very well hidden,' grumbled Lucy.

'I'm sure it's there.'

'And you want to find it?'

Alice grinned suddenly. 'He is very good looking.'

'But he's not a nice person Alice. Whatever you say, he's not a nice person!'

'He was nice to me last night.'

Bewildered Lucy gave up. 'Are you going to see him again?'

'Depends if he asks,' answered Alice in a matter of fact tone. 'This isn't about you Lucy,' she added in a firm tone, 'this is about me going on a date with Grant. He knows I won't tell him anything so he probably won't ask again but if he does, I'll be going.'

'Right,' said Lucy faintly. 'Well if you're sure.'

'I am. Stop worrying.'

Lucy sat back in her chair, rubbing her forehead. There did seem to be a lot to worry about at the moment and despite what Alice said, she was concerned that her friend was being used by Grant.

'Are you okay Lucy?'

Alice's eyes were solicitous and for a moment Lucy felt close to tears. No, she wasn't alright. This was all proving far harder than she had ever imagined.

'Is everything okay at home? Is Will coping? It's a major ask for him to suddenly take over sole care of two children.'

Lucy snorted. 'Apparently not!'

'But I thought he was struggling with getting them to nursery on time, making meals.'

'Not at all,' said Lucy in a tight voice. 'Turns out he's an amazing cook, he can look after the kids and clean the house and yesterday he even did all the washing.'

There was a slight pause as Alice watched her friend drumming her fingers against the desk.

'And that's bad because…?

'It's not bad, it's all good.' Lucy stared out of the window. 'It's all really good,' she insisted.

'And yet you don't seem very pleased,' probed Alice in a gentle tone. 'In fact, I'd say that you seem quite put out by Will's success.'

Lucy's eyes flew back to Alice. 'No! Of course not! I'm pleased for Will, really I am.'

Wasn't she? She didn't have to worry about Will and the children during the day, she could devote her time to her job and Blooming Lovely. That was wonderful.

Alice remained silent, her eyes sympathetic as she watched Lucy struggle.

'I am pleased,' Lucy insisted. 'It's just that it makes me feel, I feel …'

What on earth did she feel she wondered. Miserable because her husband and children clearly didn't need her on a day to day basis? Resentful because Will had turned out to be a superb cook and excellent at keeping on top of the household tasks?

'Inadequate,' she answered in a small voice. 'It makes me feel inadequate.'

'Because he's managing so well?'

'Because I found it so hard and maybe that's because I wasn't very good at it.'

Alice tutted loudly. 'Don't be ridiculous! You are a wonderful mother. You were from the very first day. And don't forget Will is only doing this for a short time. If he thought this was it, this was his job for the next 10 years he'd probably already have checked himself into counselling!'

Lucy tried to smile but her heart wasn't really in it. She felt so bad resenting Will's success.

'Lucy!' boomed Rob's voice and shaking herself out of her gloom, she painted a bright smile on her face and turned towards the door where Rob and Grant both stood.

Alice stood up to leave but Lucy waved her back into her seat. There was plenty of room for them all in her new office.

'Good Morning Rob,' she said, her eyes pinned on Grant. He was looking at Alice with what could only be described as a somewhat baffled expression and Lucy felt her heart skip a beat.

'Excellent news,' shouted Rob, his face wobbling slightly with good humour. He seemed oblivious of the secretive glances flying round the room, his eyes on Lucy even as hers were on Grant and Grant's were on Alice who sat, composed and calm, waiting for Rob's news.

'McCarthy and McCarthy.'

That caught the attention of both Lucy and Grant and their eyes swivelled to Rob as he beamed at them. 'They're coming into the office tomorrow, to discuss their issues and a potential renewal of their contract.'

Grant nodded, his hand checking his already immaculately knotted tie.

'That's excellent news,' he murmured. 'I'm sure we can get to the bottom of any problems.'

'We need to! I don't want to lose them as clients which is why you and Lucy will be doing everything you can to keep them.'

'Of course. Lucy will be able to give me all the background details so when I meet them I can …'

'No! I want to be part of it.'

Lucy stood up, wishing she had put on slightly higher shoes. Grant was quite tall and she hated having to look up to meet his eyes. 'I brought them on board, I should be part of this meeting.'

'That was several years ago Lucy and I'm sure you'd be the first to agree that a lot has changed since then.'

'No. Nothing has changed. I might have been out of the office for a while but I'm still me, the person who signed them up in the first place.'

'Yes but in the last four years …'

'I've become a mother. So what? Are you saying once you have children you can't do the same job anymore?' challenged Lucy, ignoring that she had felt exactly that way only a few weeks earlier.

'Of course that's not what I'm saying.' Grant's voice had an edge of irritation not normally heard in the smooth tone. 'But you have to admit …'

'Rob, I want to be part of this, with Grant of course. I need to be part of the team, not someone checking facts in the background.'

'You're not ready yet, you need more time.' Grant turned to Rob to emphasise his point. 'She needs more …'

'No I do not! Rob let me help.'

Rob held up both arms, calling for silence and reluctantly both Lucy and Grant stopped talking.

'I quite agree,' he began and Lucy held her breath waiting to see who he was agreeing with.

'Lucy should be part of this, she knows the McCarthy team better than anyone else.'

Resisting the temptation to punch the air and hoot with joy, Lucy restricted herself to an exultant smile, unable to stop herself from sending a look of triumph in Grant's direction.

She had to concede that he hid his feelings well, only the smallest tightening of his lips indicating his disappointment.

'Of course,' he said calmly.

'Lucy, read over the file, remind yourself of the original terms of the contract. Then update Grant and the two of you need to come up with a strategy.

Lucy nodded happily.

'Right, I'll leave you to get on with it,' and he was gone, Grant following him, his shoulders stiff with disapproval.

'Well,' said Alice happily,' it looks like you're going to get to know Grant a whole lot better over the next few days,' and with a cheeky grin she disappeared, leaving Lucy standing in her office wondering if she had just scored a victory or shot herself in the foot.

Chapter 26

Will was determined that today would be without incident. He went back to the remnants of his spreadsheet, organising his day to the last second. He delivered Emily to nursery a full 5 minutes ahead of schedule and kept an eagle eye on Harry.

The ruined jumpers were still hidden away in the utility room. He'd fully intended to confess all but when Lucy had arrived home with dark shadows under her eyes after another day in the office trying to keep up with Grant Cassidy, his heart had constricted and he'd slid the jumpers amongst a pile of boxes in the corner. When he had a little more free time perhaps he would be able to replace them and she would be none the wiser.

Rather than piling the breakfast things in the sink, he put them in the dishwasher straight away and then dashed around the living room gathering together Harry's toys, plumping the cushions and shutting the door so when Lucy came home it would still be tidy. He spent the morning working flat out to complete everything on his spreadsheet. After putting some more clothes in the washer, being very careful about the setting he chose, he looked at the clock in amazement. He was on track, for the first time since he had taken over Lucy's role, he was actually on time with everything. He slumped onto one of the kitchen chairs. Okay the kitchen didn't have the sparkle Lucy left behind and even Will could see the dust beginning to layer up on every surface in the house. There were piles of clothes folded and waiting to be ironed and toys were gathering in every corner, but he felt as though he was finally making real progress.

For once he wouldn't have to phone Jen and beg for her help with another household emergency. He felt quite pleased with himself. His hand hovered over his phone. He wanted to phone

Lucy and tell her that he was managing, that she had no need to worry about her children that day because her husband was coping with the job in hand. But she didn't know he hadn't been coping because the truth was something he had shared only with Jen. Plus the last few times he'd phoned Lucy at work she had seemed far too busy to talk to him.

His fingers drummed on the table then he picked up the phone and dialled.

'Hello, Jen.'

'Good Morning. Oh dear, what's happened now?' she asked with a giggle.

Will couldn't help smiling back. 'Absolutely nothing! No makeup emergencies or washing disasters, I've kept control of everything today,' he told her, feeling a little smug.

'I told you it would happen. You just needed a little time to get into the swing,' said Jen warmly. 'It's a lot to ask but I knew you'd get the hang of it.'

Will felt a little glow, the sort of glow he hadn't felt for some time.

'I am feeling very positive about everything today,' he admitted. 'And it is partly down to you. I don't know where I would have been these last few days without you bailing me out.'

He could tell Jen was smiling.

'I'm just glad I could help.'

'Look, no problems today, nothing I need help with so why don't we have that coffee we promised ourselves? Come around, bring Alfie and we can sit down and chat.'

'That sounds lovely! It's a date.'

'A date? Oh Jen, I didn't mean …'

'A play date you idiot!'

'A play date?'

It was a phrase he vaguely remembered Lucy using.

'A play date. We let our children play happily together while we have a coffee and a catch-up.'

Will relaxed. 'A play date. Exactly, let's have one of those.'

Later that day he collected Emily and fed both children a mishmash of food. Since Lucy had stopped organising their lunch, mealtimes had become erratic, although he had noticed with the lack of choice now available, Emily's insistence on colour coded foods seemed to have disappeared. She was wise enough to understand that when her dad was in charge, whatever was on her plate was all that was on offer and she had tucked in quite happily to bright orange carrots and very green peas with her fish fingers the evening before. Clearing away the remains of lunch, he answered the door to Jen and Alfie and ushered them into the kitchen.

Harry and Alfie were soon knee-deep in Lego and toy cars while Emily, considering herself far too grown up to play with them but not wanting to be left out, joined them under the kitchen table with her colouring book.

'Well this is a change,' Jen said with twinkling eyes. 'Are you sure you don't need me to rescue anything? I've got a bag full of baby wipes, tissues, colour restorer, makeup remover – everything I thought we might need.'

Will pulled a face. 'I have needed a lot of help, haven't I?' he sighed. 'Who would have thought it could be so hard!'

'Any mother will tell you it's not an easy job. But you've done so well Will, so very well. I really admire the way you've stuck at it.'

The glow came back and Will couldn't help the grin that spread across his face. At least someone thought he was doing a good job.

'So,' he said putting a coffee and a plate of biscuits on the table. Since Lucy had gone back to work the biscuits had been relocated from the top shelf to somewhere far more accessible. 'What exactly do the adults do on this play date?'

'Oh, we vent. We complain about our husbands and the amount of washing we have to do. We talk about clothes and hair and the latest gossip. We tell each other how well we're all doing, even if we don't really believe it, we support each other and provide company and a shoulder to cry on if necessary.'

Will's eyebrows raised.

'Well, I suppose the husband bit is off the table.'

'For both of us. My husband hasn't been around for a long time. I could complain about how he behaved when we were still married but to be honest, I get quite bored of remembering those days.'

Will watched as Jen took a sip of coffee. Her eyes had lost their twinkle.

'What happened?' he asked gently.

'I realised very early in our marriage that I had made a huge mistake and he was a serial philanderer. But he was always sorry, it was always the last time and he always insisted he loved me.'

Will was at a slight loss. He really wasn't used to this kind of conversation so he remained silent and let Jen speak, hoping he was providing the support and the necessary shoulder to cry on required on a play date.

'I found out I was pregnant at the same time I found out he was having yet another affair. I decided it was no way to bring up a child so I said it was over. The divorce finalised a few days after Alfie was born and I've been on my own since.'

'It must have been very difficult,' said Will quietly, remembering back to the early days after Emily had been born. There had been two of them and they had still found it exhausting and frightening. 'At least you had your mum.'

Jen nodded. 'It made all the difference. That's why I admire you so much Will, you're trying so hard to look after your children.'

Will's conscience gave him a little poke. 'Well Lucy is still doing a lot of the work in the background,' he said generously. 'I'm just doing what I can.'

Jen was staring at him, her eyes wide with admiration. 'But she couldn't have gone back to work if you weren't the kind of person you are. She must be very grateful to have a husband like you.'

Embarrassed, Will shrugged. He didn't think Lucy was particularly grateful at the moment. She seemed to be more concerned about Grant Cassidy and her potential new client.

'And you're even managing this well!' laughed Jen, intruding on his thoughts.

'This?'

'Our play date! For a novice, you're doing a fine job.'

'Well,' he cocked his head on one side. 'We could spend more time talking about inadequate husbands. Let's face it, you've seen all my faults first hand! Clothes? Mm, I've managed to ruin a lot of Lucy's with my washing skills so perhaps we'll leave that one for now! Hair,' he ran a hand through the untidy locks that fell onto his forehead, 'as you can see, not my strong point. That only leaves the gossip and I'm afraid I have none to offer!'

Jen chuckled. 'Actually, the main topic of conversation at the moment is you,' she confessed.

'Me?'

'The fact that you're a stay at home dad, how you're coping, how the children appear.'

Will stared at her. 'You mean everybody is watching me?'

'Absolutely! The first time Emily shows up at nursery without her hair brushed or Harry is seen wearing a pair of dirty trousers, everyone will immediately decide you're not coping.'

'That seems a bit harsh!' said Will indignantly. He remembered the first morning he had sent Emily to nursery with her hair sticking out at all angles and he grimaced.

'It is. But that's gossip for you.'

Will blinked. 'So Lucy and I are the hot gossip of the day?'

'You are,' said Jen gravely. 'And if anyone were to find out that you had ruined Lucy's clothes in the wash or allowed Harry to play with her makeup, the phones would be ringing off the hook.'

'Are you going to tell them?'

'Of course not silly.'

As Will's shoulders dropped in relief Jen leant forward to give him a reassuring smile. 'You don't gossip about your friends Will. I'm on your side.'

'As long as we keep dating?' asked Will with a grin.

'As long as we keep dating,' Jen repeated and they both sat chuckling as they watched the children play happily under the table.

Chapter 27

Lucy was wearing the highest shoes she could cope with. She had managed to squeeze into one of her old suits, although breathing was a challenge and as she strode along the pavement to Simcock and Bright she thought she detected a little glimmer of the old Lucy Mathers in the reflection of the windows she passed.

She had worked until late last night, much to Will's disapproval. She knew Grant would be doing the same, she knew he would be determined to take over today's meeting and she had to be ready. They had spent a lot of time over the last 2 days discussing every aspect of the McCarthy contract and he probably knew as much about them now as she did. Lucy needed to be able to match him point for point and she had spent the previous evening with her eyes glued to her laptop to ensure she didn't miss anything.

She hadn't laid out any clothes for the children this morning, she hadn't prepared any lunches or taken any washing into the utility room. She had no idea where Emily's school bag was or if both of Harry's shoes were in the cupboard or under his bed. She had focused on the meeting and left Will to deal with the children and the house. And if there had been a tiny prickle of guilt as she closed the kitchen door, she quickly reminded herself that when Will had been working, he never did any of these things before he left for the office shouting goodbye, his mind already on other things.

She had scoured the McCarthy files and come to the realisation that nothing had gone wrong, it was simply that not much had happened. There had been few proactive suggestions coming from Simcock and Bright, in fact very little of anything. The McCarthy account had been neglected. She had feverishly penned a list of suggestions, hoping that the main question of why they had been overlooked would be directed at Grant and not herself.

'Morning Lucy!'

It was Alice, pink cheeked from a brisk walk to the office.

'Did you get a lot done last night? Are you ready? What do you think Grant will do?'

The questions were fired at Lucy as they both presented their passes at the door.

'I worked all night but I'm sure Grant did too,' Lucy answered as they made their way up the stairs. 'I think I'm ready,' she added nervously.

'You'll be wonderful,' said Alice with confidence. 'I know you will.'

'And Grant?' asked Lucy, peeping at her friend.

'I'm pretty sure he'll be ready and full of confidence,' agreed Alice calmly. 'But he's not the one I care about.'

'No?'

'No. I may think he's a hunk,' her cheeks went a shade pinker,' but that's outside of work. In work, it's all about you,' and she gave Lucy a dazzling smile that couldn't fail to warm her heart.

'Then wish me luck,' whispered Lucy and set off down the corridor to her office.

She was almost there when the world suddenly lurched sideways and Lucy had to grab onto the wall to stop herself hitting the floor with her face. Bewildered, she looked around, not sure what had caused her to lose her balance like that and cautiously she took a small step forward only to keel sideways again.

Looking down, she saw that the heel of one shoe was listing at a 45-degree angle, bent over and unable to take Lucy's weight.

Giving a small yelp, Lucy hobbled into her office, keeping the weight off one foot by walking on her toes. She looked as though she were doing a very bad impression of John Wayne and with a grunt she threw herself into her chair and pulled off her shoe. One heel had snapped, not completely but enough to make it unusable and Lucy stared in despair. She didn't have time to buy another pair and she couldn't turn up at the meeting in her stocking feet. She looked at the clock, the visitors would be here in 10 minutes and Lucy had no shoes.

'Alice,' she screeched down the phone. 'Alice, I need help.'

She had barely put the phone down when Alice came barrelling into the room, her face a picture of concern.

'What's wrong,' she gasped. 'What's happened, are you okay?'

'No,' yelped Lucy. 'My shoe. My heel. Look at it!'

They both stared at the broken heel. After a few seconds their eyes moved to Alice's sensible black shoes but Lucy shook her head, she knew that Alice had ridiculously tiny feet and there was no way Lucy would be able to squash her toes into her friend's shoes.

Alice was looking round wildly for inspiration.

'Er, Sellotape? Staples? Glue!'

Lucy tilted her head. 'Glue? Super glue might do the trick. Do we have any?'

But she was talking to air, Alice had already dashed out of the office, returning a few minutes later with her hands full of everything she thought might help.

Carefully, Lucy allowed a few drops of super glue to touch each side of the heel and then pushed them together. She held them tight for a moment then placed the shoe on the desk while she looked at everything else Alice had brought in with her.

'What's that?'

'Insulation tape. It's black, I thought it might help.'

Lucy grabbed the reel of shiny black tape. It was a ridiculous notion but she needed all the help she could get. Maybe the glue and the tape might just get her through the meeting. She examined the shoe. The glue seemed to have set although there was now part of an invoice stuck to the broken heel which she tried to peel away gently. The heel was now more or less straight but with fragments of paper stuck along one side.

Between them, they managed to wrap black tape over the crack, reinforcing the break and covering the stubborn bits of paper. The tape was a little wrinkled but it was the best they were likely to manage in such a short time. Lucy slipped the shoe back on and stood up cautiously. She could feel how tenuous the repair was and she practised walking around the office. If she leant onto her toes, knees bent and all her weight thrown forward, she could take a step without putting any weight on the heel. She looked very odd, as though she were straining against something as she walked, swinging her foot around in an odd movement to stop the heel coming into contact with the floor.

'It will have to do,' she said almost sobbing with frustration. 'At least it looks okay.'

To the untrained eye Lucy was wearing a pair of plain black shoes. A closer inspection would have revealed that one heel was very shiny and wrapped in wrinkled plastic tape but Lucy couldn't envisage why her shoes would come under such scrutiny during a business meeting. Anyone watching her move would have wondered what sort of accident she'd had to be left walking with such an odd gait but as far as Lucy was concerned, she just had to make it to the office.

'I need to get in there before everybody else,' she declared. 'I can be sat down when they arrive. Help me,' and they set off for the door.

Leaning heavily on Alice and only allowing one foot to make full contact with the floor, Lucy made it to the end of the corridor and then stopped in horror. The McCarthy visitors had arrived. They were standing at the top of the stairs being greeted by Rob and Grant before moving into the meeting room and every one of them had turned to look at Lucy.

'Good Morning Lucy,' said Mr McCarthy senior. 'Rob told me you were back at Simcock and Bright. How lovely to see you again.'

They were all watching, every eye on her as she stood, slightly lopsided with Alice behind her, hands pressed against Lucy's back, taking her weight and trying to keep her upright. She smiled, not moving as she nodded.

'Yes. Yes, how lovely to meet you again,' she shouted enthusiastically.

Rob frowned. 'Mr McCarthy has been looking forward to meeting you Lucy,' he said encouragingly, holding his hand out in her direction. 'Why don't you come and join us?'

They all turned to look at her again and Lucy nodded even more, her head bouncing up and down.

'Yes,' she said, fervently. 'I will.'

They all waited. Lucy remained very still, nibbling slightly on her bottom lip.

'Er, are you coming now?' asked Rob, worried eyes swivelling in Grant's direction. 'Or would you rather not …?'

'Yes, of course I want to come. In fact, I am coming, right now,' and trying not to look at all concerned, Lucy began walking towards the meeting room.

Alice followed, crouching down with one hand firmly pushed against the small of Lucy's back to provide balance as Lucy made sure not to put any weight on the shattered heel. Swaying dramatically from side to side, swinging her leg to avoid putting any weight on her heel, she arrived in front of the gathered group, sweat beginning to form on her upper lip with the effort.

'Here I am, 'she said gaily, praying they would all move inside the room and let her bring up the rear. No-one moved, all watching Lucy's approach as though slightly hypnotised by the sway of her movement.

'Shall we go in?' she asked desperately, waving her arms towards the door until Rob, who was staring at her with concern, finally moved forward.

'Er, yes, come on everyone, let's get started.'

In the melee of movement in the door, Lucy took a few rapid shuffling steps and launched herself into the nearest chair, almost being sat on by Mr McCarthy senior who was slowly easing himself into the seat.

Putting her papers on the desk and trying to compose herself, she saw Grant watching her in fascination. She sent him a wide smile, encompassing the whole room as though trying to put them all at ease.

'Right. Er, let's get started shall we?' asked Rob, still watching Lucy warily out of the corner of his eye. 'Can we get anyone a coffee?'

Grant stood up, unbuttoning his jacket. 'I'm going to get Lucy a drink,' he said solicitously, moving towards the pots of coffee already set up on the side table. 'I'm sure you remember

Mr McCarthy, that Lucy left Simcock and Bright to start a family.'

Several startled glances flew her way, no doubt wondering if she had been left in such a sorry state by the production of her children.

Lucy glowered at him. Unable to stand up, she allowed him to set a coffee by her elbow and under the eyes of the rest of the group she managed a reluctant thank you.

'But now,' she said addressing Mr McCarthy, 'I'm back and I think it's time we got to the bottom of any problems. I'm sure you'll tell us why you're unhappy and I hope that you'll take some comfort from knowing I'm able to pick up your account again.'

It was a bold statement and she saw Grant's eyebrows wing upwards in surprise. He hadn't expected her to go on the offensive quite so quickly.

'I'm sure Mr McCarthy will be aware that everyone at Simcock and Bright will be working hard to answer any concerns he may have,' he murmured admonishingly. 'We're all here to help.'

'But we clearly haven't managed,' snapped Lucy, 'that's why Mr McCarthy is here. Because Simcock and Bright have let him down somehow and maybe a good starting point is finding out how.'

'Let's not forget that you've been away from the office for four years Lucy. You're not exactly up to date with the case.'

'And let's not forget Grant, that I was the one who signed up McCarthy's in the first place and I think I have a better idea than anyone else at Simcock and Bright exactly what they wanted from us.'

Forgetting everyone else in the room the two of them glared angrily at each other, Grant losing his smooth smile and Lucy's cheeks pink with emotion as Rob stared in disbelief at them both.

'Well,' drawled a clearly entertained Mr McCarthy. 'I have to say Lucy my dear, I've certainly missed you. There's no doubt, Simcock and Bright hasn't been the same without you over the last four years,' and with a delighted chuckle, he opened his briefcase and took out his list of complaints.

Chapter 28

Lucy had been sitting in her office staring out of the window for the past half an hour. Her head ached, her foot ached and her heart felt quite achy as she cringed at the thought of the meeting.

It had ended well, both she and Grant had come up with several suggestions, many of them appealing to Mr McCarthy. He had visibly relaxed as the meeting had progressed and he seemed happy with the solutions offered. But every time Lucy thought of her broken shoe, her strange walk, and the way she and Grant had virtually attacked each other in the meeting room, she wanted to open the window and jump.

Rob had given them both a very hard look as they had said goodbye to their visitors, but he had left the office almost immediately for another appointment. Lucy and Grant had exchanged a rather shamefaced look, for once almost on the same side and Lucy had limped back to her office, taking off her shoes and throwing them in the bin.

Alice had been busy and Lucy had begged June from the main office to pop out and buy her a pair of replacement shoes so she could at least walk home. Maybe it would be her last walk. Rob might well say that she needn't come back after today. That far from being the Lucy Mathers of old, she had become something of a liability at Simcock and Bright and she just wasn't cut out for this anymore.

'Here you are.'

A shoe box appeared in front of her and Lucy pulled out a pair of black shoes, squat and clumpy with a total absence of any heel. She stared at them. They really were quite ugly and she looked up at June who was holding out the receipt.

'There wasn't much to choose from,' she said with a shrug.

There had to be at least 30 shoe shops in Leeds, thought Lucy. And whilst she didn't expect June to visit every one searching for the perfect pair of shoes, she was fairly certain that June could have found a better pair with very little effort.

She looked down at the shoes again. She vaguely remembered making an unkind comment many years earlier about June's tendency to wear rather ugly, flat shoes. She had a feeling that June also remembered the conversation and she couldn't help thinking back to Alice's comments earlier about Lucy's ruthlessness in the office. Maybe this was karma. Do as you would be done by. If that were the case, then Grant, the shoes - they could all be part of a great big lesson in humility for Lucy.

'Thank you, June,' said Lucy with a smile, 'I really appreciate you doing that for me.'

She slipped on the ugly shoes, holding out her feet so June could admire them.

'I certainly won't be breaking the heel!'

Was that a small glint of shame on June's eyes? Probably not. Karma didn't tend to work quite so quickly, it was more likely to be a gleam of satisfaction.

'It's okay,' mumbled June and then she was gone, leaving Lucy to stare out of the window again, her mind wandering far and wide.

A little while later she looked up to see Grant and Rob both entering her room. Grant had his eyes cast down towards the carpet, his shoulders not quite as high and straight as usual and Lucy almost felt sorry for him. He had probably been enjoying his job until she entered the building.

'I know I said competition was good for business,' began Rob without any preamble. 'But your little display this morning was less about healthy competition and more like a bare-knuckle fight!'

Lucy hung her head.

'I don't know what possessed you both! And Lucy, are you okay? Why on earth were you walking around like that?'

'Broken heel,' muttered Lucy, still staring at the floor.

'Heel!' shouted Rob. 'Broken heel, then why on earth didn't you just say so instead of doing an impression of Quasimodo?'

Because it was a lack of control. It was like Grant turning up without a tie, which wouldn't happen. Or with a button missing from his jacket, another scenario that simply wouldn't happen. Sighing Lucy looked up.

'Sorry,' she offered.

Grant was watching her with a suspiciously sympathetic look and Lucy suspected that he actually understood.

'Well, I don't want either of you behaving like that again. Understood?'

They both nodded.

'Fortunately, McCarthy was very impressed with your ideas. Your joint ideas. And he has decided to give us another chance. He wants all your proposals in writing complete with projection forecasts and growth patterns and he will consider staying with Simcock and Bright, for the time being at least.'

He couldn't help the smile that broke out. 'You can both count yourselves very fortunate. And you are now working, *together*, on the McCarthy file. Do not let me down.'

Lucy couldn't decide whether she was delirious with relief that it had all worked out or desperately unhappy at the thought of having to work even more closely with Grant.

Rob walked out leaving Lucy and Grant staring at each other assessing the other's reaction.

'You should have told us about your heel.'

'I know.'

'Although, it was quite funny, watching you walk down the corridor like that.'

Lucy gave him a sharp look.

'For a while I really wasn't sure what you were doing,' Grant was struggling not to laugh but for once there was no mockery in his eyes as he carried on. 'No-one knew what to say.'

Unwillingly, Lucy's shoulders relaxed and she couldn't help smiling. 'I looked stupid.'

'Not stupid! A little possessed maybe?'

And then the laughter broke out and without saying anything more they both clutched their sides with tears rolling down their cheeks.

After a few minutes of manic chuckling, they brought themselves back under control and Grant buttoned his jacket and checked his tie in Lucy's window taking a deep breath to dispel the last remnants of humour.

'Well, I must get on,' he said his face back to its normal blank expression and with a small nod in her direction he left, leaving Lucy wondering if the moment had actually happened and whether it was a breakthrough of some kind or simple hysteria.

She walked to the train station in her flat shoes. Despite the news that McCarthy were staying, she felt dispirited, tired. She had made a fool of herself because she'd been so determined to beat Grant Cassidy and show that she was still a force to be reckoned with. But in truth, in her ugly new shoes and with the memory of Rob's disappointed face, she doubted that she was.

She had left late again and she walked into a Leeds station that was packed with bad tempered commuters and people desperate to get home. She hadn't caught the early train all week and wearily she started to push her way through the crowds to the platform.

'Lucy!'

A hand brushed her elbow and she turned to see Simon standing behind her.

'Wow. You look shattered,' he said sympathetically.

'Busy day,' shrugged Lucy.

'The train is running late again,' he told her apologetically.

'Of course it is.'

'Fancy a coffee?'

Lucy stared down the platform at the crowds and the general atmosphere of despair.

'No. But I could really do with a glass of wine,' and turning her back on the chaos she followed Simon to the pub in the entrance of the station.

They grabbed a small dirty table and Simon went to the bar to collect a couple of glasses of chilled white wine which was surprisingly good. Lucy took a deep drink and sighed in pleasure.

'You have had a bad day!' said Simon watching in amusement.

'It actually turned out okay. We saved the McCarthy account.'

'That's great! So why the long face?'

'Oh, you know.'

Simon didn't say anything. Clearly he didn't know.

'I made a complete fool of myself in the meeting. Grant too. We were so determined to outshine each other we forgot we had clients present and almost started fighting.'

Simon nodded seriously, although Lucy could see the amusement on his face.

'I see. Did you hit him?'

'No! Well. Not quite.'

Lucy broke into a grin. 'I came pretty close. Rob was not amused.'

'What did Grant do this time?'

Lucy heaved a large sigh. 'Actually, not that much really. It was my fault. I'm trying so hard to get back to where I was when I left work, I think I over reacted a little.'

Simon sat back, sipping at his wine. 'I think Grant probably provoked you,' he said kindly.

'It doesn't seem to take much these days. I'm like a bear with a sore head at home, I start fights in the office, I can't say that returning to work has been particularly easy!'

'But Will must understand how hard it is for you?'

Lucy stared into what was left of her drink. She was beginning to wonder if Will did understand. He should, he'd been the one working until recently. He knew what it was like to come home, tired, a little tetchy and still with so much to do to get a start on the day ahead.

'Maybe,' she said in a non-comital tone.

'I imagine it's hard for you both, switching roles like this.'

Lucy nodded, suddenly unable to speak. It was hard, so much harder than she had imagined.

'Getting the right balance is difficult,' said Simon, looking thoughtful. 'It's what ended my marriage.'

Lucy looked up. She had noticed Simon wasn't wearing a wedding ring but other than that she actually knew very little about him, other than the fact that he was often there for her, a little rock of support amongst the drama of the office.

'What happened?' she asked quietly.

Simon looked down at the table. 'My fault,' he said ruefully. 'I thought it was all about work. If I worked harder, I would get more money. If we had more money, we could buy a bigger house. But when we had a bigger house, I needed more money, and then I wanted to take Susie on a wonderful holiday so that meant more money which equated to more work. One day I came home and Susie said she hardly knew me anymore, she hardly even saw me anymore. I went into work early, left late. I'd forgotten my wife somewhere along the line. She left, met someone else, moved into a tiny flat and she was happy. Which was a lesson for me rattling around in the great big house I thought we both wanted.'

Lucy's heart constricted. She and Will had been on the same path, until his loss of job brought it all crashing down. But they still had each other. She remembered the fight they'd had the previous night, and the night before that. At least, she hoped they were still on the journey together, it was getting a little hard to tell these days.

Simon looked up and tried to smile. 'It taught me a valuable lesson about life work balance,' he said, trying to sound positive. 'Don't put too much of yourself into work Lucy, not when you've got someone waiting at home for you.'

A wonderful idea, thought Lucy. Unfortunately, it didn't pay the mortgage or the credit card.

'And make sure you tell Will how difficult you're finding all this. You don't have to pretend you're coping. This is a big change for you, I've no doubt Will appreciates what you're doing for the family and if he doesn't…'

Lucy waited.

'Well if he doesn't, he's a fool,' grunted Simon, his cheeks a little pink. 'He should be very thankful that he has a wife like you at his side.'

She watched the emotion flick across Simon's face. He was as tall as Will although a much slighter build. His eyes were grey and his hair was fair and neat, not wild and falling onto his forehead like Will's constantly did. He looked up to catch her staring and she blushed, caught in the act.

'Maybe we should check the trains,' she suggested putting her empty glass on the table.

Simon held her eyes for a moment then nodding in agreement, they left the bar and joined the throng all equally determined to get on the next train that appeared.

Lucy thought about Simon as she walked home from Horsforth station. Maybe he was right, a life work balance was important. Will had begged her to take things slower at work, just do what she needed until he had a new job. But she'd been so determined to show everybody that she was as good as she'd always been, that she was the old Lucy Mathers. Perhaps she needed to adopt Simon's example and restore some order to their life work balance. Her bag bounced against her hip and she thought of the laptop inside and the files she had brought home to work on. They could stay in her bag she decided and she would sit on the settee with Will instead. They could share a bottle of wine and talk about things, like they used to. She would thank him for working so hard in the house, for doing such an amazing job with the children. She may even admit how very difficult she was finding things at work, how overwhelmed she felt, how much she was pushing herself for reasons she didn't really understand. Picking up the pace she was at home in minutes and walked into a kitchen which was warm, full of delicious smells and so welcoming that she wanted to burst into tears.

The children were on the settee with their books and not giving Will's disapproving look time to develop, Lucy apologised for being late.

'The trains are so unreliable,' she said. Not mentioning that part of the delay had been a glass of wine with Simon. 'I'll try and catch the earlier one tomorrow, I promise.'

Will didn't complain, instead he took her coat and hung it up and then wrapped his arms around her to bury his face in her neck. 'Good,' he said simply before pressing a warm kiss on her lips.

'Mummy!' protested Emily and laughing, Lucy slipped out of Will's arms and sat down to read them a story.

She could hear Will in the kitchen and she held both children close to her side. This was all she needed, to come home to Will and her babies. She was so lucky.

'We had a play date today Mummy,' lisped Emily.

'Did you darling? With Zach?'

'No, with Alfie.'

Lucy frowned, trying to think who Alfie was.'

'Is Alfie's mummy Jen?'

'Yes.'

It was Will, standing in the doorway.

'She and Alfie came around for an hour or so this afternoon.'

'Really? What on earth for?'

Lucy turned over the page for an impatient Harry and looked back at Will.

'Because I invited her.'

Lucy stopped reading again. 'But I don't really have much to do with Jen. I don't think Harry and Alfie really play together at toddler group.'

'I didn't invite her because she was your friend Lucy. Jen and I get on really well, she's been very helpful to me and I invited her round for a coffee and a catch up.'

Ignoring Harry's mumbles for her to continue reading, Lucy sat, still and silent on the settee. She was trying to recall what Jen looked like, all she could remember was well groomed golden hair and a slender figure. And perfect pink lipstick.

'Helpful? How?'

'She gives me advice, when I ring …'

'You ring her?'

Will bit his lip. 'Yes. Sometimes. When I need help.'

'What kind of help do you need from Jen? Why don't you ring me?'

'Because,' snapped Will in exasperation, 'you've made it quite clear that you don't want disturbing at work!'

'That's ridiculous.' Lucy was on her feet now, her eyes flashing as she stood in front of Will.

'Is it?'

'Yes!' Okay there may have been a couple of occasions when Will had phoned at completely inappropriate times but how would he feel if she phoned him constantly during the day to ask him questions about what vegetables she should make for tea.

'Yes,' she reiterated firmly. 'Of course it is. And what on earth have you needed to ask her?'

Will didn't answer straight away. He didn't want to discuss the details. He would have to confess to Harry covering his face with Lucy's makeup, that he had made a mess of the washing, that he'd allowed Jen to vacuum the living room because he hadn't had time. He might end up confessing that he was buying ready meals and failing at his new role.

'Just things!' he said vaguely. 'She's been very supportive.'

'And I haven't?'

'Not always.'

Their voices had risen, the exchange becoming more heated and both children had stopped looking at their book and were now gazing at their parents.

Lucy looked at their anxious faces and brought her voice down to an aggrieved whisper.

'I am as supportive as I can be,' she said angrily, 'but I have a job to do now.'

'But you're not always here for me Lucy and Jen is.'

At Lucy's shocked gasp Will ran a hand through his untidy hair. 'I'm sorry, I didn't mean it quite like that.'

Lucy had turned away and Will reached out, grabbing her arm. 'Lucy don't, I'm sorry, really.'

'What I meant,' he said gently, keeping hold of Lucy's arm so she had to listen, 'is that when you're at work and I need to speak to someone, get some advice, I've been asking Jen. We've become friends and she has been a real help to me over the last few weeks. Would it make you feel better if I'd invited Fran round instead?'

Yes, thought Lucy. A hundred times better, although she had no idea why.

'You can have anyone you want for a play date,' she said stiffly.

'I didn't mean to upset you Lucy, I'm sorry, it all came out quite badly.'

Lucy pulled her arm away gently, smiling down at the children who were still watching their parents argue.

'I understand,' she said quietly. 'You think I'm putting work first?'

'No!' insisted Will. 'Not exactly. I know you are having to work hard and …'

'But you think I should give you more support? Be there for you, whatever the time of day, no matter what I'm involved in at the office, like your new friend Jen,' she snapped bitterly.

She wondered what Will would say if she told him she'd had a glass of wine with Simon in the station. Would he say that he understood, that she needed support and that he couldn't always be there for her?

'I'm sorry,' said Will in a tired voice. Briefly he considered telling Lucy just how much he was struggling, the hundred and one things he had done wrong. Maybe she would understand his dependency on Jen. Instead he turned his face away, frustration evident in his eyes.

'I'll put the children to bed,' said Lucy calmly. 'Then I have some work to finish,' and without looking at Will she scooped Harry into her arms and took Emily by the hand before leaving the room.

Chapter 29

Will watched Lucy leave the house the next day with an uneasy feeling beginning to grow in his stomach. They had barely spoken last night and although they had been polite and courteous to each other since waking, he had a growing suspicion that their marriage was suffering at the hands of their temporary change in roles. Lucy had said goodbye and kissed him on the cheek and Will had said 'have a good day' and kissed her back but there had been no warmth, just an unsettled look in both their eyes.

Lucy spent the time on the train staring out of the window, trying to analyse the squirming feeling of anxiety in her gut. She and Will rarely argued and this new feeling of tension that sat between them was both new and unnerving.

Rob was sitting at his desk as usual but for once Lucy scuttled past, not yet ready for an encounter after her performance the previous day and with her head down she sought the sanctuary of her own office. Alice was already there, laying some papers on Lucy's desk.

'Guess what!' she demanded of Lucy.

'What?' asked Lucy with little interest as she slipped behind the bigger desk in the bigger office that she had fought for with such determination, now feeling quite unimpressed by both.

'Grant has asked me out again. He wants me to go for a meal with him.'

Alice was dancing on the spot.

'Probably wants to know where I'm at with my plans for Blooming Lovely,' said Lucy dismissively.

'What?'

'You know what he's like! He'll want to know what I'm doing …'

'Or maybe he enjoyed having a drink with me and wants to take me out again?'

Alice's face was hurt, and Lucy closed her eyes briefly in regret.

'Oh Alice I'm sorry! I didn't mean …'

'Yes you did. That's exactly what you meant. I've told you before, this isn't about you. Grant knows he won't get any information from me but he's still asked me out,' said Alice quietly. 'I would have thought you could be happy for me Lucy, without thinking that his only motive could be you and your job.'

'I'm sorry,' insisted Lucy, 'really I'm sorry. I spoke without thinking.'

Alice gave her a long cool look then turned towards the door. 'Let me know if you need any help today,' she said. 'Unless you think I might tell Grant all about it later.'

Lucy wanted to cry. Will was angry, she had insulted Alice and it wasn't even 9:00 yet. What on earth was going so tragically wrong with her life, she wondered. She seemed incapable of keeping the balance Simon had spoken of the previous evening.

She pulled out her files without enthusiasm and then gave an inward groan as Rob appeared in her doorway. One of the few things that irked him was a bad meeting with a client. A potential fight between two of his account managers in the meeting room would be fairly high on his list. He watched her for a moment.

'Are you okay Lucy?' he asked in a tone that was remarkably quiet for Rob.

'Yes. I am,' nodded Lucy fervently.

'No issues today, nothing broken?'

The colour flooded into her cheeks. 'No. Everything is good.'

'I'm glad to hear it.' Was it her imagination or was there a slight twitch to Rob's lips?

She gave him a searching look but he kept his face impassive.

'Let's hope it remains that way. I've got another account for you by the way.'

Lucy forced her lips to smile, despite the surge of anxiety in her stomach. That would make three accounts. Pre-baby she would have thought nothing of that, she often had multiple accounts spread across her desk all at a different stage in the proceedings, all needing different levels of attention. But right now, three accounts seemed an unfeasibly large number.

Great!' She said, trying to look enthusiastic. 'What is it?'

'Some organic mother knows best baby food account,' replied Rob dismissively throwing a file on the desk. 'It's small and it's the same old stuff everybody's doing right now but every account helps.'

Lucy ran an experienced eye over the basics, it would be a lot of work for little reward, the sort of account she would have passed over to someone else without hesitation four years previously.

'And Grant doesn't want this one?' she asked hopefully.

'He said he's at his limit at the moment and we both thought this would be more your thing.'

'My thing? Why? Because I've had a baby?'

Lucy's eyes flashed as she challenged Rob but he simply nodded his head. 'Exactly. You'll probably understand all this stuff and you'll have something to discuss with the owners.'

Lucy's mouth gaped in outrage. 'I'm going to be given all the accounts that have anything to do with babies, good or bad, simply because I've had one myself?'

Rob gave her a hard look. 'If you don't want it,' he said, reaching out his hand, 'I can pass it on to Lewis, I've promised to start slipping him some of the smaller accounts.'

'No!' Lucy's hand snatched the file back. Any account was better than no account. She swallowed her pride with difficulty. 'I'll take it. Thank you,' and then glared at Rob's back as he retreated from the office.

What a wonderful morning, she thought, staring out at the grey sky. Her new role now seemed to be anything baby related because she would understand it better than a high-flying executive like Grant who had never spent several hours in the delivery ward and sobbed for no apparent reason for two weeks afterwards.

She would apologise again to Alice, and she would have to work with twice as much energy to make Rob forget about the McCarthy meeting, but she would soon have him smiling again. And that just left Will and if Lucy was very honest with herself, she couldn't fix that quite as easily because she wasn't entirely sure what the issue was. She had always prided herself on her problem-solving skills, perhaps she should pop Will in a folder and see what she could do with him.

'Hi, you look deep in thought.'

Simon sat himself opposite her desk and Lucy couldn't help but give him a big smile. He was one of the few people who seemed to be on her side at the moment.

'Oh, difficult day,' she sighed.

'Already? That's tough. Anything I can do to help?

Press the restart button on her day, thought Lucy. Give her a chance to be more understanding with Will, to be a better friend to Alice and maybe a little more honest with Rob.

'Thank you but it will all be okay. I just need to work a little harder on the whole life balance thing.'

'It must be tough,' said Simon sympathetically, 'everybody all wanting their piece of your time. But there does need to be some allowances made,' he continued firmly. 'It will take you time to adjust.'

'I haven't exactly helped myself,' admitted Lucy. 'I've insisted from the moment I walked back in the door that I was the same person as before and that I could manage everything just as well as I ever did. Will told me to take it easy and I ignored him and now he thinks I'm putting work first.'

She had needed to prove a point, thought Lucy. The trouble was she was proving to herself that she wasn't the Lucy Mathers of old.

'Well I still think a little leeway is called for,' said Simon. 'Achieving a work life balance isn't easy, you've only been back at work a couple of weeks!'

Tears pricked at Lucy's eyes. 'It is harder than I thought it would be,' she whispered, blinking furiously.

'Then be kind to yourself. Even if no-one else is, at least be kind to yourself.'

She lost the battle and a single tear rolled down one cheek.

'Thank you,' she sniffled. 'At least I know you're on my side. And Alice,' she added generously because she was under no doubt that her friend remained loyal even if Lucy had insulted and upset her.

'I'm sure there's more than us. Will is in your corner, he must understand how difficult this is.'

Lucy was doubtful but she nodded.

'And part of getting used to a day in the office is looking after yourself so how about I take you out for a sandwich at lunch time? Unless you're into those awful green protein things the rest of the office has been drinking?' he added with a look of horror.

'God no! A sandwich sounds lovely.'

And it did, thought Lucy with a slightly more positive attitude on the day. She would apologise to Alice, smile at Rob, have a sandwich with Simon and when she got home she would sit down and have a chat with Will and all would be okay. She would tell him that she was finding her return to work unbelievably stressful. She may even admit that she was a little jealous of how easily he seemed to be coping with his role reversal. It wouldn't be easy, but maybe it was time for some straight talking in the Mathers household.

With her work home balance in mind, Lucy made sure she caught the earlier train home, something she hadn't managed in quite some time and when she arrived in the kitchen to hug her children and give Will a determinedly pleasant smile, she found him in the middle of decanting one of his pre-prepared meals from the box onto a baking tray.

'What's that? Something yummy for tea?' asked Lucy innocently as she held Harry up high and listened to him chuckling.

She put him back down, dropping a kiss on Emily's head.

'Are you making something special?' she asked intrigued, moving nearer to the oven and watching what Will was doing.

Will stood very still. The box was still by his elbow and try as he might he couldn't help his eyes fly towards it.

Lucy leant round him and picked it up. 'A delicious chilli con carne meal for two, all ready for you to pop in the oven and simply bake,' she read slowly.

She looked at the carton, about to go in the oven and she looked at Will and the guilt written all over his face.

The box was still in her hands and excruciatingly slowly, she put one and one together and came up with a very large number.

'You've been buying meals,' she stated. 'That's why your cooking has improved so much. You've been buying meals and pretending you've cooked them?'

Will nodded. He took the box out of Lucy's hands and fiddled with it aimlessly without speaking.

'And when I've been complimenting you on the wonderful meals you've been serving, that was all out of a box? You haven't been cooking at all?'

A shake of the head.

'But you didn't tell me? You let me think you were putting all this time and effort into making something lovely. You let me think you had become an amazing cook in a few short days but it was a lie.'

Lucy's voice was getting higher as she spoke and there was a wary look creeping across Will's face.

'And there I was, thinking how easily you've taken to being a stay at home dad when in reality you've been cheating! You've been cheating and letting me believe that I was inadequate!'

A frown crossed Will's face. He had certainly cheated and lied by omission, he was very unclear where the inadequacy came into play.

'I'm sorry Lucy,' he started. 'I should have told you …

'But you didn't. You kept quiet, all the time I was eating your meals and saying how wonderful it all was, you didn't say anything.'

'I know and I should …'

'What else,' demanded Lucy, looking round the kitchen with angry eyes.

'What?'

'What else. You've been lying about cooking, what else have you been lying about? Have you had someone in to help you with the cleaning, the washing? Is someone else taking Emily to nursery, Harry to toddler group?

'Don't be silly! Of course not, I wouldn't do that …'

'But you already have. You've cheated and lied about one thing so why not something else?'

Will stared back, riled by the suggestion and conveniently ignoring the fact that Jen had in fact sorted out all the washing this week. And every time she came around, which was frequently of late, she would run the vacuum over the living room or some other household task which she laughingly told him was perfectly acceptable under the flag of providing support to a friend.

'I said I'm sorry!' he yelled. 'I saw them in the supermarket and thought it would be okay, for a while, until I got better at handling everything. What's wrong with buying meals already made for you anyway.'

'The price for one thing! I bet the shopping is costing twice as much as it did.'

Ah, Will thought. He'd wondered why the weekly bill had shot up so suddenly.

'But the deceit Will, why didn't you just tell me?'

'Because I wanted you to come home to a lovely meal and I'm rubbish at cooking. Even I was fed up of eating my food and because it was one less thing to for you to worry about!'

Lucy shook her head sadly. 'I would have preferred the truth, every time I would have preferred an inedible meal and the truth,' she said sadly.

She looked down at the children, watching their parents have yet another row and wondered where all this had come from. They had been such a happy couple before she'd tried to help by going back to work. And the strange thing was that part of her was relieved to find that Will's skills in the kitchen hadn't improved magically overnight. She felt so much better knowing that he wasn't finding it all so easy while she struggled with her new role. But for some reason she couldn't bring herself to say that.

'Anything else?' she demanded instead. 'Any more secrets, anything else you've been hiding?'

'No, of course not,' said Will not entirely truthfully.

And then they got on with the task of putting the children to bed and eating the chilli, which didn't exact fulsome praise from Lucy. They sat on the settee in silence for the rest of the evening and yet again they went to bed with an atmosphere of resentfulness and unhappiness wedged firmly between them.

Chapter 30

Walking to work, Lucy collected coffees and pastries. She stood one in front of Rob as he talked loudly on the phone and gave him a big smile which he responded to automatically. Then she took a latte with an extra shot and a topping of chocolate sprinkles together with a white chocolate and raspberry muffin and placed them both in front of Alice with an apologetic expression on her face.

'Thank you for all the help you give me,' Lucy said softly. 'Thank you for being an amazing friend. I'm not at all surprised that Grant asked you out to dinner. You're a lovely person and anyone with any sense would want to see more of you.'

Alice's hand fluttered to her mouth and she jumped to her feet to wrap her arms around Lucy. 'I understand,' she said generously. 'You've got a lot on your plate right now and some of it is directly down to Grant. I was suspicious of him at first.'

'And now?'

Alice giggled, her cheeks flushing a delicate shade of pink. 'Well not so much now,' she said breathlessly.

Grabbing her friend's arm and scooping up the coffee and cake, Lucy marched her away from the main office and into Lucy's office, closing the door firmly behind them.

'Tell me all!'

Alice looked shy. And happy. In fact, decided Lucy, she had that certain glow about her that came only from the first flush of romance.

'There's not much to tell really,' began Alice dreamily.

'Rubbish! You can't stop smiling. What happened?'

Another soft giggle from Alice as she tucked a stray wisp of blonde hair behind her ear. 'We went to an Italian, turns out Grant loves pasta almost as much as I do. He eats it almost every day!'

Lucy smiled encouragingly. She suspected that Grant did not eat pasta every day. She had seen him taking a sneaky look at his washboard flat stomach as he walked down the corridor. It was not a pasta lover's stomach.

'And we shared a bottle of wine. He even likes rosé which is amazing because nobody else ever does, they always want white or red and look at me funny when I ask for rosé, like I can't make my mind up. But Grant said it was a perfect choice and he loves rosé with pasta.'

Lucy carried on smiling even though she wanted to snort with derision. She could tell just from looking at Grant Cassidy that he had never entertained a glass of rosé in his life! He was a definite dry white and rich red person. No doubt dictated by what he was eating and not just because it was the cheapest bottle on the menu.

'And we talked and talked.'

'About?'

'Oh everything! He wanted to know all about me, where I grew up, what I liked, what I wanted to do with my life.'

Lucy's fixed smile was starting to give her a headache. It must have been a huge effort for Grant to listen to someone else for several hours. To let someone else take centre stage.

'And?'

'And that was it,' insisted Alice, her cheeks changing to a deeper pink.

Lucy looked at her consideringly. 'Did he kiss you?'

'No!'

'Liar.'

'He didn't, well not properly.'

Lucy gave her friend a disbelieving look. 'Are you telling me Grant Cassidy doesn't know how to kiss someone?'

'I didn't mean it like that! He called me a taxi and when it came, he looked at me and said what a lovely evening he'd had.'

'And he tried to kiss you but you wouldn't let him?'

'No, he kissed me on the cheek and then,' Alice's cheeks were almost magenta as she twisted her fingers together and grinned manically, 'he gave me the softest kiss on the lips and said he hoped we could do it again.'

223

Silently, Lucy congratulated him. Perfectly played, she thought, for a lovely, kind-hearted creature such as Alice, perfectly played.

'And do you want to see him again?'

'Oh yes! I had a wonderful evening.'

'Really?'

'Really. You don't understand Lucy, he is actually a nice person away from the office.'

Lucy was highly doubtful.

'He's charming and considerate and wonderful company and I am seeing him again, definitely.'

Lucy nodded, trying to look pleased for her friend whilst silently thinking that if Grant broke Alice's heart she would personally pull his own from his body and rip it apart in front of him.

'Well if you're sure …'

'I am. And he didn't ask about you once if you're worried.'

'Not even a …'

'Nothing. He told me you'd both lost it a little in the McCarthy meeting and you were both in Rob's bad books. He really regretted that, said it was a bit of a wakeup call and that maybe he'd let things get out of hand.'

That, Lucy really didn't believe but other than raising her eyebrows as far as they could reach, she kept silent and let Alice continue.

'I think he's starting to see how good you are at your job, he seems to quite admire you.'

This time Lucy couldn't help the snort of disbelief that erupted, turning it into a cough at Alice's hurt look.

'Mm, let's see,' she murmured and let an ecstatic Alice return to her desk, a beaming smile still sitting on her face.

Lucy had a busy morning. Despite her anger at being given the baby food account just because she'd had a baby, she would still do her best and she had arranged a call with Erin Goodfellow, the creator of Bountiful Baby Foods.

It was a long tortuous conversation as Erin spent half an hour telling Lucy how her philosophy of organic goodness had been the starting point for her business.

'But it's not an original idea,' interrupted Lucy trying to get the conversation back on the track of marketing strategy.

'What do you mean?' Erin's voice had become distinctly cooler.

'There are several other baby food brands that follow the same ethos, organic produce, handmade, all very similar.'

'Are you saying that I've copied my idea?'

'No! Not at all. What I'm saying is that any marketing must be carefully handled to differentiate you from anyone else offering a similar product.'

Lucy leant back in her chair, rolling her eyes at the ceiling. She really hoped Erin would decide to go to another company. Lucy had enough on her plate without throwing a fragile ego into the mix.

'Mm. I see what you're trying to say. But my brand is quite different.'

'Really. How?' asked Lucy dutifully.

'Because I believe in my product. I believe that by giving our children only goodness from an early age, we'll get only goodness back.'

Lucy pulled a face. Maybe that's where she had gone wrong, perhaps if she had filled Harry with organic goodness instead of fish fingers, he wouldn't be the ball of mischief he was now.

'I see,' she said, not seeing at all.

Alice appeared in the doorway and Lucy motioned to her to sit down.

'Did you follow the route of goodness?' Erin demanded.

Lucy paused. Which route where they talking, she wondered? Lucy's own route in life which had been less about goodness and more about wine, take away meals and snacks. Or were they still talking about stuffing children full of goodness, the benefits of which parents would reap at a later stage?

'I er …'

'With your children? Did you use organic only products?'

Grant was now at Lucy's door and she waved him in to take a seat next to Alice, who she noticed blushed sweetly as he smiled in her direction.

'Well, not really. I mean not absolutely …'

'Then you don't really understand my thinking at all!' accused Erin sounding disappointed.

'Oh I do understand,' insisted Lucy as Alice opened a file and started making notes and Grant watched Alice, a strange expression on his face.

'I didn't go down the organic route with my children but I do understand your philosophy.'

Alice peeped upwards and saw Grant watching her, which made her giggle and return to her notes whilst unconsciously leaning a little closer to Grant.

'Why?'

'Sorry?' Lucy was losing track of the conversation; she was far more interested in watching the expressions chase across Grant's face. She really couldn't pin it down, he looked intrigued.

'Why didn't you use organic products?'

Or maybe less intrigued and more fascinated.

'Well, the price for one,' answered Lucy.

He was watching Alice as though he'd never seen anyone quite like her before and his face was …

'You put a price on your children's wellbeing?'

'Oh er, well yes,' admitted Lucy. 'Some people have to you know.'

His face was soft and …

Lucy gasped, causing both Alice and Grant to look up at her.

'It doesn't have to be expensive. You can source everything locally and make your own food, that's what I did.'

His face was tender. Grant Cassidy was looking at Alice with a tender expression!

'That's how I started my business.'

'But you wouldn't want everybody else doing the same. It would put you out of business, which would be a shame having only just started.'

Lucy's mind was racing. Could she have misjudged this man? Was he indeed a different person out of the office and the charming and thoughtful person Alice declared him to be?

'Yes, well,' sniffed Erin. 'That's why I need a good marketing company.'

He seemed genuinely smitten by the soft, beautiful nature of Alice. Maybe he hadn't encountered anyone so loyal and good and sweet before.

'You need a good marketing company and a big budget,' said Lucy firmly, really wishing Erin would go away. 'As I said, there are lots of baby foods out there that are organic, full of goodness, best for baby. It doesn't really matter about your philosophy, that won't sell jars. The bottom line is that you need someone to persuade the public to buy your jar of food rather than another jar of food.'

Grant stopped looking at Alice and turned his eyes on Lucy.

'And that takes a big budget,' continued Lucy. 'If you don't have the budget, you won't get the results. Simcock and Bright would do an amazing job for you, but you need to understand now that it won't be cheap.'

Grant was smiling, not at Alice but at Lucy. And if she didn't know it was impossible, she would say that there was a glimpse of something very closely resembling respect coming her way.

'I see,' said Erin stiffly. 'Well, you certainly don't beat about the bush.'

Lucy shifted in her seat, she needed Erin to finish the conversation, she needed Alice and Grant to leave her office, she needed to sit at her lovely big desk and do some hard thinking, because nothing seemed to be happening as it should at the moment.

'But I appreciate a little honesty. I think Simcock and Bright may be the agency for me. I would like to arrange a meeting and we can discuss the possibility in more detail. If I like what you say, I may ask you for a proposal.'

'You would?'

'I would. I'll send over all the details you'll need, Goodbye.'

Putting the phone down, Lucy stared at the two people sitting opposite her.

'Bountiful Baby Food is interested?' asked Grant curiously.

'It would seem so.'

'Well done. That was an excellent pitch, Lucy. I can see why Rob thinks so highly of you,' and seemingly forgetting why they had both come to speak to Lucy in the first place, Grant and Alice both stood up and wandered to the door, shoulders almost rubbing as they looked into each other's eyes and grinned happily.

Chapter 31

Lucy had dropped the Bountiful Baby Food deal on Rob's desk and basked in the smile he sent her way.

'Excellent! I knew you could do it Lucy.'

Did he, wondered Lucy? Because the previous day he'd implied she needed to up her game.

'I think there was another baby food account up for grabs,' he said shuffling through some papers, 'or was it baby clothes?'

Lucy frowned. 'Rob, I don't just want accounts to do with babies.'

'But it's what you're good at, why not exploit it?'

'It's the first one I've ever done!'

'Yes but you're a mother now. You've got all that,' he waved his arm around expressively, a slightly bemused look on his face. 'Baby knowledge.'

Lucy put her hands on her hip, glaring at him across the table. 'Are you telling me Grant will never be asked to take on a baby related account because he hasn't had any children?'

'Well there would be no point would there. Not when you can do it,' said Rob with a perplexed look on his face at Lucy's apparent lack of understanding.

'And the sports account he's trying to pitch, does he play all the sports they cover? McCarthy produces outdoor wear, are you telling me Grant is a keen rambler in his spare time?'

Rob looked unsure. 'I don't think Grant goes rambling,' he said slowly. 'He's never mentioned it.'

'Because it's unimportant! We're account managers. We have the same title and I refuse to be the one dealing with anything remotely connected with babies just because I'm a mother.'

'I'm only trying to help,' said Rob indignantly. 'Stick to your strengths, that's what I always say.'

'Not when it comes to pitching for accounts,' snapped Lucy. 'Then you always say go get 'em!'

Rob sniffed and gave her a disapproving look. 'I just think that now you're back we need to make sure you have accounts you can deal with.'

'No! I will not be treated like a sub species who can only do baby related things. Grant and I will deal with a variety of accounts, at all times.'

She stopped, remembering that this was a temporary return, that what happened in the future wouldn't affect her because she would no longer be an account manager. But that made her feel even angrier and her good mood at signing up a new client destroyed, Lucy stomped back to her office and spent the day on Blooming Lovely and McCarthy and watching the clock until it moved past 5:00 and the time she needed to leave to catch the early train.

She walked down to the station keeping a keen eye open for Simon and it was as she was standing shivering at the final set of lights that she saw him, a few people ahead. Skipping across the road she grabbed his arm.

'Fancy a drink?' she asked, hoping the desperation didn't show in her voice.

'Of course.'

If Simon was surprised, he kept it well hidden and linking arms against a sea of commuters, they made their way to the uninspiring but very convenient station pub.

Insisting on paying for the drinks, Lucy placed two glasses of wine on the table and slid into a seat opposite Simon.

'Everything okay?' asked Simon, watching her take off her coat and unwind her scarf.'

'Not really,' confessed Lucy. 'And I'm sorry for using you like this, as my permanent shoulder to cry on. You must be positively soggy by now!'

Simon's voice was soft as he reached out to pat her hand. 'I don't mind Lucy. You know that. I think you've got an awful lot going on and if I can help in any way then I'm glad.

Lucy tried to smile, even though she really wanted to sob. Simon was such a nice person, she bet he had never lied to his wife about cooking.

'Will lied to me!' she burst out, her hand flying to her mouth even as she spoke, regretting both her honesty and her disloyalty instantly.

'Lied! About what?'

'Nothing important I suppose.'

If it wasn't important why had she spent the night tossing and turning and the day reliving the conversation in her head, wondered Lucy.

'I mean, what he was lying about wasn't anything major, something silly. It's just the fact that he was pretending, letting me believe he was coping so well.'

At Simon's slightly nonplussed look Lucy started at the beginning.

'Will has been buying ready meals instead of cooking. I thought he'd become an amazing cook overnight; his lasagne was far better than mine.'

Was that what had upset her so much, she thought? That Will not only seemed to be coping so well but had also turned into a much better cook than Lucy herself?

'Anyway, it turns out the freezer is stacked with all these meals he only has to warm up.'

'And that upset you?'

Yes! Oh not the meals, if he'd told me that he couldn't cook and he was buying it all in I probably wouldn't have cared. In fact,' Lucy added, the truth causing her to squirm slightly in her chair, 'I would probably have been a little bit relieved that he wasn't finding it all plain sailing.'

'But he didn't tell you?'

'No. And he had the chance, I kept saying how lovely it all was and how well he was doing and all he said was thank you, he was trying!'

Simon sipped his wine, watching Lucy struggle with her emotions.

'I was so angry,' she admitted. 'Maybe more than the occasion warranted but I've been finding it a real challenge adjusting to work and it's been worse thinking that Will was finding it a doddle.'

'It's probably exactly what I'd have done,' said Simon with a nod. 'Why cook when you can buy something that someone's already cooked for you! It's probably a man approach.'

'But would you have lied about it?'

Lucy looked him in the eye.

'Would you have pretended you made it yourself, let your wife think that you'd spent the afternoon making Beef Stroganoff when all you'd actually done was open the packet?'

Simon pulled a face. 'I never had to look after two children like Will is doing …'

'Would you have lied?'

She knew the answer. Simon was a kind, considerate person. Lucy couldn't imagine him lying about something like this, he would have let his wife eat the meal then shown her the packet and they would have laughed over the whole thing. There again, if anyone had asked her a few weeks ago, she would have said the same thing about Will.

'I probably wouldn't have lied,' agreed Simon reluctantly. 'But don't forget …'

'Stop defending him Simon. It's lovely of you to try and stick up for him but there's no excuse really.'

They fell into a short silence. Lucy hadn't mentioned anything about Will's play dates with Jen. She had wanted to tell Simon, see the expression on his face, decide whether it was okay that her husband was having dates of any kind with another woman. But bearing in mind she was sitting in a pub with a work colleague, on what some could construe as a work date, she decided that this particular situation was more complicated and maybe she needed to keep it to herself for a little longer. Simon had proved himself to be a source of support at the end of the day and something she was starting to become more reliant on. And wasn't that exactly what Will had claimed Jen was, his daytime support, nothing more, nothing less. So why did she feel so comfortable sitting here with Simon and so dreadfully uncomfortable about Will and Jen sitting in Lucy's kitchen sharing a coffee.

'Lucy,' his hand slid over the table and rested on Lucy's own. It was warm and comforting. 'Have you spoken to Will about all this? Does he know how you're feeling?'

'It's complicated,' she muttered.

'Of course it is, but you could start by telling him how you feel, how difficult you've found it coming back to work, how you feel he's let you down. Get it off your chest.'

'Why are you so nice to me?' whispered Lucy.

'My marriage fell apart because we didn't talk about how we felt, I don't want yours to do the same.'

Lucy smiled tremulously and Simon moved his hand with a sigh.

'Will is a very lucky man. If you were my wife, I would be moving heaven and earth to make sure I didn't lose you.'

'Oh.' she said in a rather squeaky little voice.

'He's made a few mistakes but give him a chance Lucy.' He emptied his wine glass and set it carefully down on the table before looking up to meet Lucy's eyes. 'But remember that I'm always here for you, whenever you need to talk, I'll be here.'

Walking home, her mind weary with thoughts, she breathed a sigh of relief as she walked into the kitchen, snatching at Emily who was waiting for her and kissing the soft velvety cheek.

'Hello my darling. Have you had a lovely day?

Her daughter nodded solemnly, then tipped her head to one side as she watched her mother take off her coat and lay it over a kitchen chair.

'We didn't have anyone to play today mummy,' she offered. 'Was daddy in trouble for letting Alfie come to visit before?'

Lucy's heart constricted. 'Of course not! You can have friends around to play anytime you want.'

And of course they could, she thought, so why had she made such an almighty fuss?

'Was daddy in trouble for making you a nice meal then?'

'No of course not,' denied Lucy, wondering how a four-year-old could be quite so perceptive. 'It wasn't the meal, it was something at work,' she lied, 'something had upset mummy, nothing to worry about.'

She turned around to find Will watching her, his hair falling on his forehead, his clothes smeared with the remains of Harry's tea, his eyes wary as they rested on his wife.

Taking a deep breath, Lucy covered the short distance between them and slid her arms around his neck. 'Work is hard,' she said in to his hair, 'and sometimes Mummy comes home a little bit frazzled.'

There was a moment of tension then she felt Will's shoulders relax and his hands warm and firm at her waist. 'I remember it well,' he murmured ruefully. 'And I should be more considerate and …'

'No.' Lucy pressed her fingers against his lips. 'We're both finding this a struggle Will, we both need to be a little more understanding.'

He smiled and ignoring Emily's interested gaze, he pressed Lucy against the kitchen wall and kissed her, his lips sliding across hers, his tongue teasing the corners of her mouth until she felt her stomach tugging with a familiar sensation that had been significantly absent over the last few weeks.

'Perhaps we need an early night, remind ourselves of how we feel about each other,' he whispered in her ear. 'Let's spend the night being very supportive!' And with a delighted grin, Lucy decided that her emails could wait, she could deal with her new account in the morning and who cared if the bathroom needed cleaning, an early night with the husband she loved was an excellent idea.

Chapter 32

Lucy was late. She had woken up in Will's arms and it had been such a relief after the coldness they had been showing each other of late that she didn't want to get out of bed and end the moment. She poked a foot from under the duvet and groaned as Will gave her a helpful shove from behind. Hearing Harry's squeals as Will threw him over his shoulder, she left him to get the day started and concentrated on getting herself ready. She no longer set out clothes for the children, left meals in the fridge or put in any washing before she left for work and these days her morning routine consisted of her getting herself what Will referred to as 'office ready' and going over her growing to do list for the coming day.

Running downstairs, she grabbed her bag and walked into the kitchen to find Will with her coat in his hand, ready to slide it onto her shoulders. At that moment Harry shot out from under the kitchen table tripping over the trailing hem of the coat and causing Will to let go of it as he shot out a hand to rescue Harry.

Kissing her son on top of his head and scolding him gently for being so clumsy, Lucy was relieved they had avoided a potential trip to the hospital and turned to Will to congratulate him on his catch. Her words died in her throat and standing up she faced her husband who was staring at a receipt in his hand, one which had fallen out of Lucy's coat pocket.

'You went for a drink last night before coming home?'

Lucy bit her lip. She had shoved the receipt in her pocket as she carried the two glasses of wine back to the table.

'Yes.'

'With Alice?'

How Lucy wanted to say yes. How much she wanted to look Will in the eye and tell him that she had been a little down after the Bountiful Baby food discussion and had a quick glass of wine with Alice before coming home. But that would be a lie and Lucy, even in her hour of need, had to accept that a lie would be a big mistake with their relationship so fraught.

'No.'

'Who did you go with?'

Lucy swallowed. 'Simon. I don't think you've met him,' she added, knowing full well that Will and Simon had never been in the same room together. 'He's in the accounts office.'

She wondered if it had sounded as casual as she tried to make it appear, a quick drink with a colleague before coming home. Nothing more.

'Simon?'

'Yes.'

The tension in the room was palpable and she looked anxiously down at Emily and Harry. They were becoming quite adept at recognising that their parents were on the verge of another disagreement.

'Was that the first time?'

'No.'

Will placed the receipt carefully on the table.

'I see. Is that why you've started catching the later train?'

'No!'

Lucy felt on safer ground here. She caught the later train because she was working hard and often missed the first one. Okay, maybe yesterday she had deliberately missed the early one so she could see Simon but that was only because she needed to talk to him, tell him about Will's lie and get a male perspective on the situation.

'There was a delay,' she decided a small white lie was acceptable. 'A train had been cancelled and we went for a drink. For goodness sake Will, its exactly the sort of thing you used to do when you were working.'

She reached out for her coat and slipped it on, gathering her bags.

'How many times?'

Lucy wanted to ignore him, walk out of the door, go to work and pretend this conversation had never happened.

'Why does it matter how many ….'

'How many times,' roared Will, making Emily jump and Harry's eyes open wide with alarm.

'I don't know! Twice, three times. I don't see what difference it makes, you have Jen around to talk to. According to you she gives you the support I don't. Well it's the same for me too. I need someone to listen to me and that someone is Simon.'

How she wished she could take those words back as they hung in the air between them.

'I have to go, I'll be late,' she said into the silent room.

'And are you coming straight home tonight, or will you be having a drink with Simon?'

'It's not like that!' insisted Lucy. 'Simon is nice and thoughtful and occasionally we have a coffee and I moan to him about everything that's happened that day. That's all it is Will. That's all.'

He picked up the receipt reading it carefully.

'This says two glasses of wine. Two large glasses of wine.'

'Well last night it was wine,' she agreed weakly. 'But normally it's coffee.'

Will put the receipt back down, staring at her as though he'd never seen her before and Lucy glanced desperately at the kitchen clock.

'Will, please. This is silly. You've made friends with Jen, you told me it helped to have someone to talk to about your day.'

And how Lucy had hated to hear him say that Jen was the friend he was turning to for help.

'Well Simon is exactly the same for me. A friend, who happens to catch the same train, who listens when I moan, who helps me cope with my day.'

Will was still staring at her and shaking her head Lucy kissed the children and walked to the door.

'Don't make any more than there is to this situation, it's nothing,' she said firmly. 'Absolutely nothing,' and then she left closing the door firmly behind her.

Will stood perfectly still for several minutes after Lucy had left. Eventually, feeling Emily's hand tug on his he shook himself out of his reverie and looked down at his daughter.

'Are you unhappy Daddy?' demanded Emily.

'Of course not pumpkin. Of course not.'

With a determined smile he picked both children up at the same time and smothered them in kisses until their serious faces broke into giggles and then he put them back down as he continued to get ready for the day ahead, his actions automated as his heart reeled from the conversation he had just had with Lucy.

He'd wanted to tell her to forget about work, grab her by the shoulders and make her talk to him, honestly, like they used to. He wanted to know about Simon, why he was the perfect candidate for Lucy's outpourings. He wanted to demand that she never see him again, that she walk through the station with her eyes cast downwards so they wouldn't encounter each other on the platform and feel obliged to speak. His heart was racing as he helped Emily pull on her shoes and get ready for nursery.

He remembered how upset Lucy had been the night she found out that Jen had been round for a play date and how he'd accused her of being unreasonable. He'd insisted Jen was his toddler group buddy, that they chatted just like Lucy used to with Fran. He had accused Lucy of being difficult, not understanding that Jen was simply a friend who helped him out occasionally. He felt his stomach shift uncomfortably as he wondered how important Simon had become in Lucy's work life, how much help he was providing. And why did it leave Will feeling so anxious? Over the years Lucy had known dozens of work colleagues, both male and female that she would regularly grab a drink with, analyse the day's events, discuss strategies. Why was this different, why did he feel slightly threatened at the thought of his beautiful wife sitting opposite Simon at a bar as they discussed their day and sipped chilled white wine?

It had seemed the ideal solution when Lucy had proposed going back to work, how on earth had it all come tumbling down so quickly, he wondered, the cold morning air stinging his cheeks as he took Emily to nursery.

When Jen called by that afternoon, she found Will sitting morosely at the kitchen table, lost in his thoughts.

'Anything wrong?' she asked in concern putting Alfie on the floor and sitting opposite Will. 'Has something happened, are you okay?'

'I'm fine. Lucy and I … we had a bit of a row. This morning. And the day before actually. In fact we've been having a few.'

'Oh Will, what a shame.' Said Jen, her eyes full of concern. 'I always got the impression you and Lucy got on really well, hardly any arguing.'

'We do. We did,' said Will sadly. 'But since she's gone back to work, we seem to have done nothing but fall out about silly things.'

'Well they're not silly if it's making you fall out.'

Jen stood up and filled the kettle. 'What kind of things?'

Will struggled with himself. He had been devastated this morning when he found out Lucy was talking to Simon about how difficult she was finding life at work. It should have been Will she was talking to. And yet here he was, about to do the same with Jen. He didn't speak straight away but everything was whirling round his head. Maybe he needed a female perspective on this whole thing. And Jen was always so patient, so reassuring. She would tell him where he had gone wrong, make sure he understood what was going through Lucy's head.

'I've not been cooking, not properly. I've been buying meals in boxes and warming them up,' he blurted out. 'Lucy found out and she was really mad.'

'What on earth for?'

'Because she thought I was cooking, well I let her think I was cooking.'

Jen poured two cups of coffee and put them down on the table.

'But you didn't argue about it?'

'Yes. We had a huge fight.'

'I see.'

Will looked at her anxiously. 'I know I lied but I was trying to make things simpler. Why was she so angry?'

Jen peered at him over the rim of her cup, her face in a thoughtful expression.

'I must admit I have no idea Will. I wouldn't care less if you were making them yourself or getting the next-door neighbour to help. What does it matter? I have to admit that Lucy was being a tad unreasonable there and I can't believe you had a row over something so insignificant.'

Will looked into the pale blue eyes.

'Really? Because I thought I must have done something really bad, broken an unwritten kitchen rule of some sort.'

'Believe me Will, that was definitely not your fault. Maybe Lucy was a little tense about something else. I think she was being unfair to you, it seems a little selfish of her to insist you cook a meal every night when you've found a better alternative.'

Will's face darkened slightly.

'Is there something else?'

'She's been having a drink with a bloke called Simon, after work.'

Jen gasped, putting down her coffee to stare at Will.

'She's seeing someone else?'

'No! Not like that. She's had a drink with him once or twice, after work.'

Will sincerely hoped it was only once or twice.

'Just like I have a coffee with you,' he said trying to convince himself that it was indeed exactly the same thing.

'But that's not the same at all.'

Will groaned.

'I mean come on Will, it's one thing us having a play date and a quick coffee every now and then but going for a drink with a colleague after work, that's something else entirely.'

'Is it?' pleaded Will. 'She just talks to this guy about work and what's happened, like I talk to you about washing and shopping. Couldn't it be the same thing?'

Jen shook her head firmly. 'Sorry. I know you want to make excuses for her, because that's the sort of person you are, sweet and caring and thoughtful. But this is serious Will, very serious.'

His shoulders slumped as he stared at his tea. He'd been desperately hoping that Jen would laugh at his worries, tell him he was being silly and say that Lucy was entitled to a friend, just like Will himself.

'It's not serious,' he said suddenly.' I would know if it were.'

He remembered the previous evening and how he had taken Lucy in his arms and told her how much he loved her and the look in her eyes as she kissed him and said they would get through this nightmare.

'Lucy needed a shoulder to cry on and it should have been my shoulder. I need to make sure she knows I'm here for her and always will be.'

The worried expression disappeared, replaced by determination.

'I've made mistakes, I should have told her about the meals …'

'But you were doing what you thought was best. You can't blame yourself for that.'

'Doesn't matter,' said Will stubbornly. 'I should have been honest with her right from the start, how hard I was finding it all, how much I needed help. If I'd been honest with her, she might have told me about Simon.'

'You think so?' asked Jen doubtfully. 'Because I don't think …'

'I have to believe that. I can't lose Lucy!'

Will pushed a shaking hand through his hair. How had this all gone so terribly wrong? He looked round to check on Harry who was sitting on the floor with an ice lolly he had given all the children when Jen arrived.

'Oh Harry mate, what have you done now?'

The lolly had broken and most of it had melted inside Harry's top which was now stained blue to match his lips.

'Sorry Jen, I'll have to get him changed and put his clothes in the washer.'

'Do you want me to …'

'No! Sorry, I meant no thanks. Maybe it's time I started doing all this for myself,' Will said ruefully. 'I can't keep relying on you to bail me out.'

Jen stepped forward and put a gentle hand on Will's arm as he scooped a soaking wet Harry from the floor.

'You know I don't mind helping Will. I admire you tremendously for how determined you've been to do a good job of all this and I want to help any way I can.'

The pale blue eyes were full of concern and Will nearly handed Harry to her.

'I know and I'm grateful but I've got this Jen, thanks.'

Will stripped Harry and put on a new vest and top, putting the wet clothes straight into the washer. He couldn't help grinning, maybe he was learning after all. If this had happened a few weeks ago he would have been telephoning someone for advice.

Expecting Jen to have taken Alfie home, he went into the living room and to his surprise found that not only was she still there but had taken the vac to the floor and was now attacking every surface with the Mr Sheen.'

'Jen, stop! You don't have to do all this for me you know, you're making me feel guilty!'

Polishing the TV stand, Jen beamed. 'No need, I've told you before Will, I love being able to help you. To be honest it can get a little bit lonely at home sometimes. Being here, with you and Emily and Harry … well I'm far happier here than being at home by myself.'

Will smiled but he held out his hand to take the polish and duster away from Jen.

'But I can't have you cleaning my house,' he said gently. 'These are jobs I'm meant to be doing. I need to be able to do them on my own, be more independent. I can't let you come here every day to help me out. Especially when I'm unhappy that Lucy is spending time with Simon.'

Jen's face darkened. 'But I've told you, that's very different. Do you think that's why she's only interested in work? Maybe it's because of this Simon person?'

Will shrugged his shoulder, his face pale and anxious. 'Then I'll have to make sure nothing happens,' he said simply. 'I have to.'

When Jen finally left Will gave her an impulsive kiss on the cheek.

'Goodbye Jen.'

'What's this for? Don't say goodbye, we'll probably see each other tomorrow,' she said gaily.

'Maybe. But thank you for everything Jen, I can't tell you how much help you've been to me,' and he closed the door, silently promising himself that this was the start of a new regime where Will stood on his own two feet.

Chapter 33

As the train rattled and rolled its way into Leeds. Lucy decided that she was going to hand in her resignation. The money she was earning simply wasn't enough to warrant putting her marriage in jeopardy. She couldn't be Lucy Mathers Account Manager, Lucy Mathers mother of two and Lucy Mathers, wife. She had been foolish to think that she could combine a career with everything else and she had been even more foolish to allow her relationship with the man she loved to become tainted by resentment and worry. The change in roles had been too much for them, her husband had been forced to turn to someone else for support and there was no way Lucy was going to sit in her office and watch her marriage crumble whilst he leaned ever more heavily on the shoulder of his new friend.

She would tell Rob that she had returned too soon, that she wasn't the person she used to be. The past tense was an apt description for her, she used to be the best, she used to be an amazing account manager, she used to be number one in the office. But now, today, she was none of those things.

The tears started rolling down her cheeks as she saw the door of Simcock and Bright and by the time she had climbed the stairs they were in full flow. For once Rob wasn't seated at his desk, which Lucy decided was probably a good thing. She needed to explain clearly and calmly that she couldn't continue, not drown her boss in tears as she sobbed her way through an explanation of how difficult things were at home, culminating in her husband being convinced she was having an affair.

She stumbled down the corridor into her office and sitting down with her coat still on she sobbed into a tissue.

'Anything I can do?' asked a concerned voice and looking up she saw Grant Cassidy, standing in front of her desk having discreetly closed the door behind him.

Too tired to give him her usual glare, Lucy shook her head, her sobs calming as she blew her nose.

'No thank you.'

He sat down and she sighed and wiped her eyes.

'I'm okay,' she said dismissively.

'Clearly you are not,' he disagreed crossing his legs and watching her mop her face.

'I am! In fact I'm more than okay. I've come to my senses and you'll no doubt be very pleased to hear that I'm leaving Simcock and Bright.'

She looked at him defiantly, her chin up even as she worried about whether her mascara was now forming black circles under her eyes.

'Leaving? Why?'

'Because you were right. I wasn't ready to come back, certainly not in this role. Congratulations!'

Lucy sniffed again but refused to let any more tears escape as she took off her coat and flipped open her laptop.

'Now if you'll excuse me, I have a letter or resignation to write and I'm sure, like me, you'll want it on Rob's desk as soon as possible.'

Grant didn't move and with a shrug, Lucy started typing.

'I think that would be a mistake,' he said calmly as Lucy frowned at the keyboard and tried to find the correct words.

'Really.'

'Yes, really.'

Lucy deleted everything she had written and started again. Rob didn't really need to know about ready meals in boxes and play dates with a woman called Jen.

'Well I don't and I'm leaving, 'she insisted stiffly. 'And quite frankly, I thought you would be very happy at the thought.'

'I agree that a few weeks ago I would have been delighted,' said Grant, sneaking a peek at his profile in the window and straightening his tie.

Lucy stopped typing, Rob didn't need to know about Simon and receipts for wine either. She just needed to say she was leaving and save the explanations for another day.

Sighing she looked up at Grant, she would find it easier to concentrate if he wasn't there.

'You didn't want me here, now I'm leaving. Be happy.'

'But I'm not. You see Lucy my dear, I was very miffed when I heard you were coming back because all Rob had done for the entire time that I've been working here was tell me how good you were.'

Lucy stopped typing.

'He did?'

'He did. And it did become very tiresome after a while. Then he announced you were coming back and how I'd have to look to my laurels and I was even more annoyed.'

Lucy nodded. 'That would be annoying,' she said with feeling, remembering the occasions when Rob had pointed out to her how Grant was now the most important person at Simcock and Bright.

'And I decided before you even arrived that you would be an irritating person who I wouldn't like.'

'I see. And was I … am I?'

'Well, you are a little bit irritating,' Grant held up his hand to ward away Lucy's indignant reply, 'but actually quite likeable.'

'I found you annoying,' retorted Lucy. 'I still do actually.'

Grant smiled. 'You've made no effort to hide that.'

Lucy wondered where this was going. Was Grant about to ask for her email address so they could keep in touch, new best office friends.

'Well I'm going now so you should be pleased.'

'It's in my interests for Simcock and Bright to be the best they can be. I happen to think that you are very good at your job, and that's actually good for both of us.'

Lucy stared. 'You think I'm good?'

'Not as good as I am obviously,' he said smoothly, 'but good.'

Lucy closed her laptop and concentrated on the man in front of her.

'And?

'And I think it would be a shame if you left. At least give it a little longer to see if you can achieve the balance.'

'What balance?'

'The work home balance.'

Lucy wondered if he'd been talking to Simon. Had they all discussed whether she would be able to cope, whether she needed someone to provide support at the end of the day? Maybe Rob had asked Simon to be Lucy's end of day train buddy.

'I do actually have a sister who recently returned to work after having a baby.'

Lucy blushed.

'I could tell you didn't believe me but she did tell me the hardest part was finding the balance. Apparently, it's not an easy task, one that takes a lot of work together with a great deal of co-operation from your partner. But it can be done.'

Lucy tapped her fingers on the desk, staring out of the window for a moment.

'And has she found it? Her balance.'

'Indeed. She is very strict about priorities, work is work, home is home. But she is much happier.'

'And you think that's what I need, a balance?'

Simon had said as much a few days before but it had been on a much more personal level. When suggested by Grant it became a much more realistic option, a more business-like approach.

'I do. And I think that now we've overcome some of our initial - antagonism towards each other it would be a shame if you were to leave.'

Had they overcome their feelings, wondered Lucy. Or did Grant have an ulterior motive.

'Are you trying to be nice to me?'

'I don't believe the office is the place for niceness,' Grant said with a shrug of his shoulders. 'I simply think that from a business point of view together we can make Simcock and Bright a force to be reckoned with.'

Staring at him, Lucy could find no hint of mockery in his smooth features.

'What about Alice?' she demanded suddenly.

It was one of the few occasions she had seen Grant caught unawares. His cheeks flushed slightly and he went through the usual process of straightening his tie and checking his trousers for non-existent fluff.

'Alice?'

'Yes Alice. What's going on? Do you really like her, are you trying to get information from her?'

Grant looked shocked. 'I would never do such a thing!'

'Yes you would.'

He tried to look indignant before giving a little shrug.

'Well maybe if the circumstances warranted it,' he admitted.

Lucy's lips thinned with anger. 'So you are …'

'Stop! Alice made it quite clear from the beginning that she would never divulge any information about you. And quite frankly, it was unnecessary because you kept telling me everything I needed to know.'

'I did not!'

'Actually you did. You were so insistent that you could do the job as well as I could you are forever telling me what you are going to do next.'

Lucy sniffed. 'So why are you seeing Alice?'

Grant looked uncomfortable, his shoulders twitching underneath his jacket and his foot bouncing slightly.

'I fail to see what that's got to do with the conversation we were having.'

'It's important to me.'

Lucy wondered if he was about to walk out, she had never seen him so reluctant to give his opinion or look so ill at ease. She started to smile.

'You've got the hots for her!'

'What a ridiculous expression. I do not have …'

'You fancy her, don't you?'

'If you mean am I fond of Alice then the answer is yes,' he said with reluctance. 'But I still don't see that's any of your business …'

'If you hurt her, I'll come after you,' Lucy said in a friendly tone. 'I will make your life hell.'

Grant looked slightly alarmed.' What on earth …'

'Alice is lovely, she's gentle and sweet and adorable and we both know you could break her heart. I'm just suggesting that you don't.'

'She certainly inspires loyalty in you.'

Lucy didn't reply, she watched Grant fidget beneath her gaze.

'Okay, she is very different to anyone I've dated before but I find her interesting.'

'Interesting?' A smile broke out as Lucy watched him blush deeper. 'That's the best you can do? Interesting!'

'It's all I'm prepared to say on the subject!'

Standing up, Grant turned towards the door.

'I do not have ulterior motives regarding your friend,' he said in a stiff tone, 'and please, reconsider your position. I think that both of us working here can only be good for Simcock and Bright,' and he disappeared, striding down the corridor to the sanctuary of his own office.

As 5:00 came around, Lucy still hadn't written her resignation letter and she gathered together her things to make sure she caught the earlier train. It would stop her bumping into Simon, which she decided was a good thing. It also meant that she would soon be home, which she decided may not be a good thing if Will wanted to continue the conversation, they'd started that morning. Lucy's heart still stung when she remembered the look on Will's face as he'd asked her about Simon. She knew how he felt, she'd experienced a strange rush of emotions when he'd told her about Jen and their play dates. For some reason the thought of her husband sitting opposite the golden-haired Jen chatting about his day and their children had brought a thudding anxiety across her chest.

She had been prepared to hand in her notice this morning to save her marriage. After speaking to Grant, she was now wondering if she could maintain a life at the office and at home, at least until Will had another job. But their relationship undoubtedly needed some work and the least Lucy could do was stop her little tête-à-têtes with Simon each evening. Perhaps both she and Will needed to be a little more honest about the strain this was having on them and the support they needed.

'Drink?'

It was Simon, not waiting for a chance meeting at the station but standing in Lucy's doorway, a smile on his face and his eyebrows raised in query.

'Oh, er, no, not tonight.'

Lucy pulled on her coat, she really wanted to catch the early train, she couldn't afford to have Will thinking she was late home because she had wanted to spend some time with Simon.

'Sorry Simon,' she didn't have time to tell him that her husband thought she might be having a clandestine affair in Leeds station every evening. In fact, she wasn't sure whether that was an appropriate conversation to have with Simon full stop. 'I need to get home tonight.'

'Okay. Well maybe tomorrow.'

And maybe not, thought Lucy but she smiled and dashed past him, determined to catch her train.

When she arrived home, Will was in the kitchen. They stood for a moment, looking at each other without speaking and then Will walked towards her, helping her off with her coat. For a brief moment Lucy wondered if he was going to check the pockets and frisk her for evidence, but instead he smiled and kissed her gently.

'Hello. Had a good day?' he asked as he hung up her coat and took her bags so she could slip of her shoes.

The heels had been getting steadily higher over the last few weeks but Lucy was still relieved to throw them off and climb into her rabbit slippers each evening.

Should she tell him she had been prepared to hand in her resignation, she wondered? Would he be happy that she was prepared to put home and family first? Or would he see it as a guilty gesture, putting space between her and Simon?

'It was okay,' she shrugged.

'Chicken casserole for tea,' he announced checking the oven and then standing up to look her in the eye. 'I didn't make it, I've got dozens of those boxes still in the freezer. It seemed silly to waste them.'

Lucy nodded, she looked down at the floor and then back up at Will's eyes watching her.

'Sensible,' she murmured.

'I'm a rubbish cook,' Will declared in his new spirit of absolute honesty. 'So you'll soon be coming home to rubbish meals, but I'll try.'

Lucy felt her lips begin to twitch. She remembered the awful meals Will had produced the first few days he had been at home.

'It will help the diet,' she offered, peeping at him from under her eyelashes.

Will grinned. He stepped forward and wrapped his arms around her with a relieved sigh, pressing his face into her scented neck. 'I love you Lucy Mathers,' he whispered. 'I love you so much.'

It was going to be alright, thought Lucy thankfully as she clung to him. It was going to be alright because at the end of the day she loved Will and he loved her and that meant they could cope with anything.

'I love you too,' she murmured and kissed him before sliding out of his arms and turning to cuddle Harry who had erupted into the kitchen.

The relief she felt was enormous. She watched Will as he cleaned and tidied in the kitchen, she hugged her children and she felt a great spurt of optimism engulf her. They would get through this, she decided happily. They would survive this strange switch in their roles and come out even stronger at the other end.

She went into the living room to read the children a story, sinking onto the settee with a child at each side.

'Goodness me daddy has been working hard today,' she said to Emily. 'This room is positively shining.'

She looked up to share a big smile with Will who was standing in the doorway. He didn't smile back, looking at her with a stricken look on his face instead.

'Oh daddy didn't do it all,' sang Emily, busy looking for her favourite book amongst the collection on her lap. 'His friend Jen came around to visit and she does all the cleaning for him.'

Chapter 34

Lucy sat at her desk, staring out of the window. It was a struggle to concentrate on anything, despite the growing pile in front of her. Blooming Lovely were almost due for their proposal, McCarthy wanted a progress report meeting and Erin from Bountiful Baby Foods had already phoned twice that morning demanding to know how Lucy would go about launching her new business.

The previous night had resulted in a row that had left Lucy shaken to her core. Her overwhelming anger at finding out Jen had been cleaning their house had resulted in a screaming match between Lucy and Will during which they both said things which were definitely not conducive to saving an already rocky relationship.

Emily and Harry had started crying which had led to a temporary halt as the children were comforted and reassured and put to bed. But the moment Will and Lucy were back in the living room, rage had erupted again.

Lucy had accused Will of lying yet again, not only had he been buying ready meals but he was leaving the cleaning of the house to his new friend. When Will retaliated that Jen was a kind and caring person who was simply trying to help him out in difficult times, Lucy had told him he was hypocritical, suggesting that Lucy may be having an inappropriate relationship with Simon when he was entertaining Jen every day. Will had insisted that having a drink with someone after work was an entirely different and more dangerous activity than arranging a play date for their children.

Neither had been prepared to listen to the other and Will had ended up storming out of the house, returning in the early hours of the morning and sleeping on the settee. Lucy was eaten up by the thought that he had spent the evening at Jen's, bewailing his unfaithful and unreasonable wife. Even when Will informed Lucy that he'd spent the night at the pub, she had been unwilling to believe him and sniffed the clothes he had dropped in the laundry basket trying to detect any unfamiliar scent.

She had left the house without speaking to him, her heart contracting at the worried expression on the face of her daughter, who may only be four years old but who was far too intelligent not to notice a deterioration in the behaviour of her previously loving and devoted parents. Arriving at work, Lucy had attempted to throw herself into her many tasks but nothing could occupy her mind for longer than a few minutes before her thoughts returned to the sorry state that was her marriage.

Alice had poked her head around the door several times and brought her countless cups of coffee. The dark smudges under Lucy's eyes were obvious and Alice had waited patiently for an explanation. But Lucy couldn't bring herself to admit that the reason for her damp eyes was her suspicions about her husband and his new best friend, so she insisted all was well and wiped her tears away discreetly at regular intervals.

Grant appeared during the morning, fidgeting slightly as he handed her a file.

'I think perhaps you might want to look at this again Lucy. You seem to have suggested that McCarthy & McCarthy concentrate on fresh flowers rather than hiking boots for their first quarter.'

Lucy looked at the file in front of her.

'Did I?' she asked blankly.

Grant nodded and turned to leave before coming back to stand in front of her desk.

'I can't help getting the feeling that there's something more than a return to work bothering you. I don't suppose I can help in any way, but I hope you manage to sort things out,' he said in a quiet voice and then left, closing Lucy's door gently behind him.

The tears started again. Not tears of rage that she had made a mistake, or anger that Grant had been the one to point it out. She cried because Grant had been nice to her for the first time since she'd arrived back at Simcock and Bright and it was simply too much for her shattered emotions to deal with right now.

When Simon appeared to give her a warm smile and ask how she was, all vestige of control disappeared and sobs began to shake her shoulders as she bit her lip, quite unable to tell him just how truly dreadful everything actually was.

'What is it?' asked Simon urgently. 'Is it the children, is everything okay at home?'

'The children are fine,' Lucy had managed in between badly controlled sobs.

'But something has happened at home?' hazarded Simon.

Lucy could only nod.

'Well this isn't the time or the place,' he declared. 'I'm taking you out for lunch, you can tell me what's happening then, away from the eyes in the office.'

At 12:30 he appeared again and without asking, he gathered Lucy's coat, pushing her arms inside as one would with a child and leading her towards the door.

'Just going for lunch,' he told a surprised Alice who was walking down the corridor in the direction of Lucy's office. 'Don't know how long we'll be,' he continued cheerfully. 'Hold the fort would you?'

They didn't go far, a few streets away from the office and down some steps into a dimly lit Bistro where Simon, still without speaking to Lucy, pushed her into a chair with her back to the room so her tears could run unchecked and unnoticed and then called the waiter over and asked for two glasses of wine.

As Lucy started to protest Simon sat down opposite. 'Medicinal,' he said.

The waiter brought the drinks over and Simon immediately ordered a couple of lasagnas and then sat back, waiting for Lucy to explain.

'Will and I had a huge row last night,' she obliged tearfully. 'I found out that Jen has been helping Will with the cleaning. I thought he was coping and it turns out Jen is doing it all!'

'And who is Jen?'

'A mother from the toddler group. Apparently, she's been a wonderful friend,' said Lucy bitterly. 'Will said she is always happy to help him when he needs it.'

The tears rolled down her face. Will had demanded to know what was so very wrong with letting someone help him with the house. What did it matter who did it as long as Lucy came home to a clean house at the end of a long, working day? It had been a difficult question to answer because it involved Lucy admitting that she had been slightly jealous that Will had found adapting to his new role so easy whilst Lucy had struggled with her return to work. And when he had shouted that he had needed extra help because Lucy has started putting work before everything else, she had exploded, telling him that the only reason she had stopped doing so much to help was because he seemed to be coping. And now she had found out it was all a lie and it was Jen that was coping.

'She seems to have taken Will under her wing. She cleaned my living room yesterday! And she gave him a bag of baby wipes!'

'Baby wipes?'

'She's been helping with the washing and cleaning and anything else that he's needed.'

'And is that …'

'And they have coffee and chats and according to Will, she is the support he's needed because I only think about work!'

'Have you …'

'No! I thought Will had it all under control so I stopped helping so much. I didn't know it was Jen who was in control.'

The sobs were back, shaking Lucy's shoulders.

'He's lucky to have found a good friend,' suggested Simon tentatively. 'It must have made life easier for him.'

'All he had to do was tell me the truth. I wouldn't have minded.'

'Wouldn't you?'

Lucy sniffed, picking up her fork and then putting it back down. The thought of food made her feel positively sick.

'What if there's more to it, what if something else is going on,' she said, twisting at the napkin in restless fingers. 'Will has been lying to me, he has never lied to me before. Suddenly Jen is in his life and he doesn't tell me the truth anymore.'

Another sob escaped her as she looked at Simon in despair. 'What if they're having an affair?' she asked in a whisper. 'What if she goes to visit him every day because they're having an affair?'

'They probably don't have time for an affair if she's doing all the cleaning and washing,' suggested Simon with a glimpse of humour.

The tears rolled down Lucy's face.

'Oh Lucy, I'm sure it's not the case. He would be stupid to risk losing you.'

Peering at him between the tears, Lucy saw his cheeks go slightly pink.

'He would be a fool to put his marriage at risk,' Simon said firmly. 'I don't care how wonderful Jen has been. I'm sure it's nothing more than friendship.'

'Like us.'

'Like us,' he agreed.

Lucy remembered the look on Will's face when he had found the receipt in her pocket. He had been unhappy when he found out about her friendship with Simon, why didn't he understand how she felt about Jen.

'Will said he will do everything in the house himself from now on.'

As the argument had raged backwards and forwards, Will had declared that if it made Lucy feel any better, he would refuse any help from anyone from now on. He wouldn't even let the till assistant help him pack the shopping. Lucy had shouted that it wasn't everyone else she was worried about, just his best friend Jen who was cleaning the house while Lucy was at work. When Will had told her she sounded petty and jealous of his new friend, Lucy had screamed that she didn't care how she sounded, he didn't want her having a drink with Simon, well she didn't want Jen dusting her ornaments.

And yet here she was, having lunch with Simon, unburdening her marital issues onto his broad shoulders. She wondered if Will and Jen were sitting in the kitchen, sharing a coffee as Will groaned about his wife's lack of understanding and her insistence that he stop letting Jen help him.

'I was going to leave Simcock and Bright.'

Simon's eyebrows shot upwards. 'You were?'

'It's not worth losing Will, nothing is worth losing him. I was going to hand in my notice.'

'But you didn't.'

'Grant said I needed to work harder at the whole balance thing.'

Simon's eyebrows couldn't go any higher.

'Grant said that?'

His surprise brought the first smile of the day to Lucy's face.

'Maybe there is a more pleasant Grant Cassidy underneath the immaculate suit.'

'I wouldn't go quite that far,' said Simon hastily. 'But he is right. It is all about balance. You and Will just haven't found yours yet.'

Lucy's tears had stopped. Her head ached, her eyes stung and her heart was heavy. This balance that everybody spoke of seemed quite elusive. Whenever things became difficult, she seemed to find herself turning to Simon. Maybe that's what Will had found with Jen, in which case, would he be able to suddenly evict her from his life?

Chapter 35

Will read the email twice before the words sank in. He had a job interview. Shaking his head in disbelief he read it again, to make absolutely sure but it was definitely an interview. They were very much looking forward to meeting with him, he had been recommended by several people and they were fairly sure he was exactly what they needed. The role was in Leeds, the salary was amazing and the start date was immediate.

Trying to stand up and realising that his legs were shaking too much, Will closed the laptop and dropped his head in his hands. At last. He had begun to wonder if it would happen at all and whether he was now an indefinite stay at home dad with a busy working wife who regularly had a drink with someone called Simon after a hectic day in the office. But here it was, the chance he needed and in a surge of relief he gave a loud whoop, followed by an agonised yelp!

They wanted to see him that afternoon, if possible. Of course, Will could phone and advise that it wasn't at all possible, he had two small children to look after and needed a great deal more notice than they had provided. But after waiting so long for what seemed like the perfect opportunity, the last thing Will wanted was to delay the interview. He sent back an email saying the afternoon was perfect and then he pulled his mobile towards him, staring at the blank screen for a long time.

He and Lucy had embarked on a blazing row the previous evening. He had tried to explain that Jen was being helpful, that he had gone to change Harry and, unasked, Jen had given the living room a quick clean. But Lucy had demanded to know how many other times he had allowed Jen to tidy and clean and help in the house and in line with Will's new approach he had confessed that she had helped him out on several occasions. In fact, it had become an almost daily occurrence that Jen would pop in for a coffee and invariably at some point he would find her cleaning, dusting or vacuuming.

He hadn't been ready for the wave of rage that came from his wife but it had made him equally cross and as Lucy had thrown accusation after accusation in his direction, he had started to hurl a few of his own across the net, mainly Lucy's unacceptable behaviour with Simon. When Lucy demanded to know what was so terrible about going for a quick drink after work with a colleague, Will decided not to tell her it was Jen who had pointed out this meant Lucy had started to put work and her new colleagues before her own family. Instead he shouted that Lucy was behaving badly and that she should be getting home as quickly as she possibly could every night to see her children. The suggestion that Lucy was behaving irresponsibly towards Emily and Harry had taken the disagreement to a whole new level and both had spent the next few hours saying things they would probably regret in the cold light of day.

Will had woken with a headache, a tight pain across a head which was full of confusion. He knew he should have told Lucy of his failures, his accidents and his reliance on Jen but he had genuinely been trying to keep any additional worry at bay while Lucy tried to adapt to her old working life. And he couldn't understand why she was so against Jen in the first place. If Fran had come around and offered to run the vac over the carpets while Lucy dealt with an emergency, would that have been a bad thing, he'd shouted at her? Lucy had been unable to answer and Will had accused her of being jealous because he had made his own friends at the mother and toddler group, which exacerbated things further as Lucy pointed out that he was the one going through her pockets and insisting she was behaving inappropriately.

Only the day before Will had reached the conclusion that for many reasons, he would rely less on Jen and reduce the amount of time they spent together in the house. But that was yesterday, the day before he had been invited for an interview and was in desperate need of a babysitter.

He picked up his phone, sighing as he gazed at the list of contacts. He could phone Lucy herself, but after last night he wondered if she would even answer his call. Jen was the answer.

Having spent the morning in a complete daze, alternatively excited at the thought of the upcoming interview and desperately unhappy at the state of his marriage, Will collected Emily from nursery, gave the children some lunch and then nervously pulled a suit from the wardrobe. He had begun to wonder if he should sell his collection of slim line suits and expensive shirts to raise some money while he sat at home. It felt good to be back in his uniform and he couldn't help smiling as he checked his appearance in the mirror.

'Wow! You look fantastic.'

Will knew that Lucy would have said the same thing. She would have told him he was amazing, that he would sail through the interview, that they would be lucky to have him and that she loved him. But Lucy wasn't there and instead he allowed Jen to walk slowly round him as he stood in the centre of the kitchen.

'Not too much?' he asked anxiously.

'Oh no, not at all. You look great. I love a man in a suit, very sexy Mr Mathers.'

'Thanks. I must admit I'm a bit nervous.'

'No need.' Jen stood in front of him smoothing his already smooth lapels. 'You'll get the job, I'm absolutely certain. You look the part and I'm sure you're fantastic at your job. They would be mad not to be impressed. I believe in you Will, I know you'll do well.'

It was what Will needed to hear and impulsively he gave Jen a hug.

'Thank you so much for doing this for me,' he said. 'I did promise myself I would stop depending on you so much but I needed someone today and you've always been there for me.'

He moved his arms but Jen caught hold of one hand, holding it tightly.

'I'll always be here for you Will. Stop trying to manage without me, there's no need.'

Will smiled and tugged his hand away gently.

'I need to get going. Can't be late for my interview!'

The children, not having a clue what was happening but recognising their father in what had been his everyday wear until recently, gave him a kiss and prompted by Jen said good luck and straightening his shoulders Will left.

At 4:00 he phoned Jen. His voice was excited, full of enthusiasm.

'I'm so sorry I've been so long. The interview has been great and we just kept talking and talking!'

'Wonderful! But don't worry, I'm in no hurry at all. Take whatever time you need.'

'Well,' Will began reluctantly, 'They want me to stay for a coffee and a sandwich and discuss a few more points.'

'Then stay,' said Jen happily. 'Please, stay as long as you need. The children are fine and I'll feed them if necessary.'

'I can never thank you enough for this Jen, you've been a lifesaver today,' and then he was gone.

As Lucy walked home, her head full of thoughts of her husband, Jen and how hard life suddenly seemed to be, she didn't notice the car missing from the drive and she walked into the kitchen warily, wondering if there would be a rerun of last night. The kitchen was empty and hanging up her coat and slipping off her shoes, Lucy stood for a moment welcoming the peace. She could hear Emily's voice giving some sort of instruction in the living room, she could hear Harry's chuckles and what seemed to be another child's voice. Frowning she opened the door. Her children were sitting on the settee along with another toddler who she vaguely recognised and sitting amongst them was Jen. Her arms were around Lucy's children and Harry's head was resting on her shoulder as she read them a story.

'Mummy!' said Emily happily and slid off the settee to give Lucy a hug.

Lucy stared. She looked around for Will but there was no-one else in the room and her eyes came back to Jen, nestled deep in Lucy's settee with her arm around Lucy's son.

'Where's Will?'

'He had to go out. Didn't he tell you?' Jen frowned. 'How strange, I thought he would have let you know.'

'Know what?' For some reason Lucy was finding it hard to breath and her voice was high and wispy. 'Where has he gone?'

Jen closed the book she'd been reading and smiled, allowing Harry to climb over her knee to join Alfie on the other side.

'He had an interview. Isn't that marvellous? Although as I said, strange that he didn't tell you.' The frown was back, exaggerated, as though she couldn't understand why a man might not tell his wife his good news.

'He's very excited of course,' continued Jen. 'It's exactly what he's been looking for. And he looked so handsome in his suit, I can't see how they'd be able to resist him. It's been going well, he's kept me updated throughout the afternoon, he's late home because they couldn't stop talking to him.' She gave a happy little laugh. 'Such good news, don't you think?'

Lucy wondered if this was in fact a dream. Maybe she had fallen asleep on the train and she was still in the overcrowded carriage, her head leaning on Simon's shoulder for support. The rhythm of the train had lulled her to sleep and she was simply dreaming that she had arrived home to find Jen ensconced in her living room looking for all the world like Lucy's replacement and full of news about Will. News that Lucy wasn't part of.

'I'm sure he'll be home soon. Would you like a cup of tea while you wait?'

She was definitely dreaming, decided Lucy. Had Jen just offered her a cup of tea in her own house?

'No.' What Lucy needed was a large glass of the cold white wine she knew was sitting in the back of the fridge.

She watched Jen who was still nestled against the cushions Lucy had painstakingly chosen over the last few years. The apparition didn't seem to be disappearing, maybe she wasn't dreaming after all.

'You can go now,' said Lucy bluntly. 'Thank you for looking after the children but you can go now.'

'But I want to stay and talk to Will about the interview.'

'No. I will talk to him about the interview. You can leave.'

The dreamy state was fast disappearing.

'I see.'

Slowly Jen stood up, not hurrying at all as she stretched out her petite frame and looked around for her shoes.

'I suppose Will can update me tomorrow,' she said pleasantly as she located them at the side of the settee and then leaned down to pick up Alfie.

Maybe Will would update Lucy as well, about the potential job which he had discussed with Jen and not with his wife. About how handsome he looked in his suit.

Lucy followed Jen into the kitchen and watched her put Alfie in his coat. She wanted to wrench it from Jen's hands and throw it out of the door, along with Jen.

'You don't seem very happy about Will's interview,' suggested Jen as she tucked Alfie inside the warm coat and began to put on her own, equally slowly. 'But then I suppose you don't know much about it yet.'

Lucy knew nothing about it, because Will hadn't told her anything. He seemed to be keeping his sharing moments for Jen.

You know Lucy,' both their coats were now on and Lucy had flung open the kitchen door as a hint that their departure was needed. 'You can't blame Will.'

'Blame him for what?' Lucy's heart was beating so loudly the words were echoing in her ears like a bad phone signal. Why shouldn't she blame Will, what had he done that would result in a rebuke from his wife?

Jen's pale blue eyes stared into Lucy's soul. 'He's been trying so hard and he's a wonderful father. But he needed help Lucy, and you weren't there. You haven't been there for him since you started your new job and Will knows that. You haven't been there but I have, so you can't really blame him.'

'Blame him for what?' repeated Lucy in a loud, strident voice. 'What shouldn't I blame him for?'

But Jen just smiled, a sweet, knowing smile and lifting Alfie into her arms she walked out of the door Lucy was holding open.

'Poor Lucy,' she whispered softly as she passed Lucy's rigid figure in the doorway, 'poor little Lucy,' and humming happily to herself she held Alfie close and left.

Chapter 36

Will pulled into the driveway to see Lucy standing in the open doorway, her slim figure caught in the light from the kitchen as she stood, quite still and watching Jen who was loading Alfie into his car seat.

He groaned. The plan had been that he would be home long before Lucy. There would be a bottle of wine on the table and he would tell her that at long last he'd been offered an interview. He would confess that he'd asked Jen to help him out minding the children but Lucy wouldn't mind because they would be too excited at the prospect of a new job on the horizon. The constant burden of a huge mortgage and equally huge credit card bill would at last start to recede and they could sit and talk to each other honestly about how they were feeling and how to resolve the issues that were suddenly plaguing them.

But the company hadn't seemed to want him to leave. They had been complimentary and enthusiastic and Will would be amazed if they didn't follow up with an offer of a job. The downside being that Lucy had come home to find Jen in charge of the children, and Lucy seemed to have a problem with Will leaning on his new friend.

He climbed out of the car, his eyes pinned on Lucy's rigid figure.

'You're back at last,' trilled Jen. She closed the car door on an already sleeping Alfie and walked the last few steps to meet Will on the driveway.

'How did it go?' she asked placing a hand on his arm. 'Did they offer you the job?'

Will tore his eyes away from his wife and gave Jen a rather strained smile.

'It went really well,' he said, 'thank you again for looking after the children.'

'No problem. Do you think you've got the job?'

Will wanted her to go away. He needed her to leave so he could take Lucy in his arms and explain the position he had been in and how it could prove to be the answer to all their woes.

'Who knows?' he said casually. 'I need to speak to Lucy actually so if you don't mind ...'

'Of course not,' and reaching up, Jen gave him a kiss on the cheek and a sympathetic squeeze of his arm. 'Good luck,' she whispered and then with a last wiggle of her fingers she climbed in her car and drove off.

Will looked up and saw that Lucy had disappeared and with a long stride he ran into the house.

'Lucy! Lucy. I've got some wonderful news.'

He found her in the living room, holding the book Jen had been reading.

'I know,' she said. 'Jen told me all about it, the interview, how you've been keeping her updated all afternoon with how well it was going.'

'I wanted to tell you myself, I was hoping I would be here before you got back so I could tell you all about it.'

'You didn't even tell me you had an interview.'

Lucy put the book with the others and brushed past Will to go into the kitchen. She needed that glass of wine.

'I didn't want to bother you at work. I ...'

'Not bother me?' asked Lucy incredulously. 'You think I would have been angry if you'd phoned me up to say you had an interview? I would have come home straight away, I would have looked after our children.'

Will pushed a desperate hand through his hair. Jen was right, he did look handsome in his suit, she'd forgotten just how good looking her husband was.

'I know how busy you are, I know how difficult it's been settling back in. And I didn't want anyone to see it as a problem that you had to leave early to look after your children.'

'My children will always come first,' said Lucy pointedly. 'Always. And if Simcock and Bright can't handle that then I don't fit in there.'

'I know, I know. I'm sorry.'

'But it's okay because Jen was here to help you. And you have told me how helpful she is, how you've had to rely on her because I don't have any time for you anymore.'

Will was certain he hadn't used those words, but their argument last night had been vicious and there were many things said by both of them that would take time to forget.

'I know I said I would stop asking Jen to help but I needed someone to look after the children today. I needed someone at short notice and Jen stepped in which meant I could go for an interview.

Lucy glared at him as she filled her glass to the top.'

'An interview that went really well …' began Will.

'Yes, please tell me about the interview. Although Jen has already given me a summary.'

Lucy's tone was hard and resentful and Will stopped trying to explain.

'You don't seem particularly excited that I may have a new job,' he suggested quietly.

Taking a deep breath, Lucy tried to get the green-eyed monster that was running rampant through her thoughts back under control.

'Sorry. It was just a bit if a shock arriving home to find - someone else looking after the children and telling me all about your job interview.'

Will didn't answer. He filled his own glass with wine and waited.

Lucy took a deep breath. This was the news they had been waiting for. It was more important than Jen.

'Please, tell me all about it.'

They sat at the kitchen table and relaxing a little, Will explained how he had received an email that morning inviting him to a meeting with the board.

'I could have rearranged it to a more convenient time,' he pointed out, 'but I thought it was best to strike while the iron was hot.'

He grinned and Lucy thought he looked happier than she had seen him appear in several weeks. It was such good news, the news they had both been waiting for. She wondered if the pay would be the same, whether they could finally relax.'

'And so you asked Jen to babysit?'

'Er, yes. It seemed the most sensible thing to do. The meeting was really good. They seemed very positive from the start.'

'That's wonderful!'

'It went so well. They were talking as though I already had the job!'

'And didn't Jen mind giving up her afternoon to look after our children?'

'Er, no. The CEO in particular seemed impressed, said he'd had a personal recommendation from my old boss and he thought I was ideal.'

'I'm so pleased. Has Jen looked after the children before?'

'What? No.'

'She just looked so comfortable, I thought she must have spent a lot of time with them before today.'

'I've told you, we've had a couple of play dates. Well, we haven't, I mean Alfie and Harry have. Anyway, the interview,' he said pointedly. 'It went well, I'm very optimistic.'

Lucy sipped her wine struggling for control. Will finally had a chance at another job. Order would be restored; they could go back to the life they had been enjoying. She wouldn't have to leave her babies each morning, think about their sweet faces and soft little bodies throughout the day when she was inundated with work and clients like Erin Goodfellow. This is what they had been waiting for and it was finally here.

She thought back to the moment Will had arrived home, Jen's touch on his arm, the soft kiss she'd placed on his cheek. What had Jen meant, it wasn't Will's fault? What exactly wasn't Will's fault?

Lucy realised Will was watching her, waiting for her to respond.

She smiled, raising her glass in his direction. 'It sounds very promising,' she said, pushing the picture of a smiling Jen kissing his cheek from her mind. 'Congratulations.'

She knew it sounded stiff, that he was expecting a whoop of joy, arms thrown round his neck and maybe even tears of relief.

'Well I can see how pleased you are for me,' snapped Will pushing back his chair with a loud grating noise. He pulled at his tie and unfastened the top button of his shirt. He looked so handsome, a slight shadow on his chin, his dark hair flopping onto his head. 'I thought you'd be ecstatic at the thought of being able to leave work.'

'I am. I'm just … a surprise…'

'Daddy are you going back to work?' asked an interested Emily as she came into the kitchen and slipped her hand into her father's.

'Hopefully poppet. We'll just have to see what happens.'

'But who will look after us?'

Will exchanged a look with Lucy who was clutching her wine glass like a lifebelt.

'Well, mummy will probably stop working.'

He looked at Lucy with his eyebrows raised, giving her chance to answer but her thoughts were still racing round her head in a disorganised jumble and she simply stared back, silent.

'Will Jen look after us?'

Lucy held her glass so tightly she wondered that the stem didn't snap in two.

'No sweetheart. That was just because daddy had to go somewhere urgently and she said she would help.' He stared at Lucy. 'Like Fran sometimes helps, comes and looks after you when mummy has to go somewhere.'

But it wasn't Fran he'd turned to. It was Jen, with the golden blonde hair and the pretty pink lips who had gazed at him with such adoration and told Lucy that it was her own fault that Will had felt abandoned.

'Then who will look after us?' demanded Emily, a cross expression settling on her face.

Lucy put her wine down on the table and reached out to pull Emily onto her lap. 'Stop worrying sweetheart. I'll probably stop working when daddy starts his new job, then it will be like old times, me, you and Harry in the house and daddy at work.'

Emily nodded, satisfied with an explanation she could understand and sliding off Lucy's knee she skipped back into the living room.

Returning to the old times would mean Lucy no longer had to jump out of bed and make herself office ready. She wouldn't have to spend her journey into work wondering if Grant Cassidy would have some devious ploy up his sleeve. She wouldn't have to smile brightly throughout the day to convince Rob that she was enjoying her return to work and was coping admirably. She wouldn't have to worry about McCarthy & McCarthy or Blooming Lovely. And she wouldn't have to speak to Erin about her Bountiful Baby line. It would be wonderful. Just her and the children again. Spending her days cleaning and washing, taking Emily to nursery, on time, and joining her friends at mother and toddlers. Hadn't she sat at her desk over the last few weeks praying that she could do just that, go back to being Lucy Mathers, housewife and mother. She wondered why the thought lay a little flat in her chest. She should be hopping up and down with excitement.

Will was watching her and the emotions that were playing across her face.

'And will you?'

Lucy looked blank.

'Will you stop work?'

She grabbed her glass from the table and took a sip. 'Probably.'

'Probably? I thought you were desperate to pack it all in and get back to normal?'

She was, wasn't she? She couldn't wait to tell Rob that she had tried her best but she really wasn't that person any more.

'I am.'

'Then why only probably. What's at Simcock and Bright that makes you want to carry on working?'

'Nothing. I mean I will stop working. But you haven't been offered the job yet and we have lots of bills to pay and there's no point rushing anything …' Her voice tailed off.

'I see. It's obviously grown on you, going back to work?'

'No. Not really.'

'But you're not in any hurry to leave.'

'Let's just wait and see what happens shall we?' suggested Lucy trying to smile. 'Let's see if you get the job and then we can make decisions.'

She started to walk towards the door but stopped at Will's side. She caught his hand and squeezed it gently. 'I'm so proud of you darling, so very proud,' she said.

'Really? Because you don't seem overly pleased Luce.'

Lucy shook her head frantically. 'Just tired. Long day,' she muttered. 'It's wonderful news, absolutely wonderful,' and she went in search of a place where she could curl up and cry, although she had no idea exactly why or what was making her feel so very lost and unsure, but it had a lot to do with the way Jen had squeezed Will's arm and the rather triumphant look she had cast in Lucy's direction behind Will's back.

Chapter 37

Both Lucy and Will tried to act as normal the following morning. Lucy smiled a great deal and said again how pleased she was that Will seemed to be back on track. Will smiled even more and declared himself happy that he had at least an opportunity of work. But when Lucy finally kissed them all goodbye and closed the kitchen door behind her, Will realised how tense his shoulders were and how stiffly he had been holding himself. Clearing the breakfast things from the table, he scooped them straight into the dishwasher and turned it on so he could empty it before lunch Then he collected shoes and coats and placed them next to the door, ready for their departure.

He had spent the night tossing and turning. Excitement at a potential job mixed with puzzlement over Lucy's reaction had kept him awake until the small hours. Although Lucy had lain still and silent next to him, he had felt that she too had spent much of the night awake. At one point he had whispered her name softly to see if she reacted but there was no response so he continued to stare at the ceiling.

Hoisting Harry into his arms, he ran up the stairs and kept a firm hold on his son until he was dressed and ready for the day. Will had learned the hard way that as soon as Harry was free he would disappear into some murky corner leaving Will to scour the house for him. He pulled out Emily's clothes and started to help her get dressed.

'Can I wear my flower socks today daddy?'

'No, they're in the wash. You can wear them tomorrow.'

'Mummy said I could wear them today.'

'Well mummy probably didn't know they needed washing. You can have pink or yellow ones today, which do you want.'

'I want my flower socks.'

'Not today Emily. Pink or yellow, Choose.'

He looked down at her stubborn little face and folded his arms. 'Quickly Emily. Or you'll be late for nursery and you'll get a black mark.'

Emily looked upwards.

'And we will be telling mummy, and we'll tell her that it was because you wouldn't put on your socks.'

Emily stared at him, her small chubby face considering the options. 'I'll wear my pink ones,' she decided, giving him a sweet smile. 'And the flower ones tomorrow,' she added wagging her finger in warning.

Will couldn't help grinning. His daughter would no doubt grow up to be every bit as feisty as her mother at the board table.

Dressed and ready with time to spare, they walked to nursery where they joined the throngs arriving at the door. It was the earliest they had ever arrived and Emily slipped her hand into her father's and pulled him down for a kiss.

'Well done daddy, she lisped. 'You're getting as good as mummy,' and with a smile she skipped indoors, leaving Will scratching his head and wondering which one of them was actually in charge.

As soon as they arrived back home he gave the kitchen a quick clean and sat Harry down with some chubby Lego bricks while he flipped open his laptop to check his emails. Nothing. He glanced at his watch. It was still only a little after 9:30, it wasn't necessarily bad news, Yet.

He glanced at the clock and tucking Harry under his arm they went upstairs where Will gathered all the clothes scattered on the children's floor and moved them to the laundry basket and gave both rooms a quick tidy. Back downstairs he looked in the freezer to decide what to feed the family tonight. There were still a handful of ready meals left but next week he would have to start cooking again. Maybe he should look up some recipes, go online and see what he could manage with limited cooking skills and even less time. Perhaps Lucy would give him a genuine smile if she came home to a mediocre meal of undercooked chicken and overcooked potatoes. They would get through an evening without an argument about Lucy bringing work home and Will leaning on Jen too much. He pulled out a mini shepherd's pie from the freezer for Emily and Harry and left it to defrost as he heard a knock at the door.

'Jen!'

'I hope you don't mind me popping round, I had to catch up with you and see how it all went yesterday.'

For a moment Will wondered about saying he was busy. That he really didn't have time and he would see Jen at the next mother and toddler group. He didn't know why Lucy became so agitated whenever Jen's name came up in the conversation or why she seemed so against the idea of Jen helping him out occasionally. But if last night was anything to go by, their friendship was causing Lucy problems and the last thing they needed right now, in their suddenly strained marriage, was yet another problem.

But the moment was brief. At least Jen would be happy for him. She would tell him how clever he was and how well he had done and if he were honest, he needed that right now.

'Come in.'

He held the door open wide to let her in, only slightly surprised when she leant forward to kiss him on the cheek.

'So tell me all about it,' she said in excitement as she shrugged off her coat and sat down at the kitchen table.

Will grinned happily and recounted the previous day, who had said what to who, how he had been received, how they had reacted.

'Oh Will, it sounds so promising! I think you really impressed them, I'm sure they'll follow it up with an offer.'

His smile dropped. This was the sort of reaction he had expected from Lucy, not an interrogation into why he had asked Jen to help him out.'

'What's wrong?' Jen's voice was gentle, concerned. 'You look worried. Is it because you haven't heard from them yet? I'm sure you will, it sounds like you had an amazing interview.'

'Well I haven't heard anything yet so maybe it wasn't quite as good as I thought,' answered Will trying to sound light hearted.

'You will.'

Silence fell for a moment.

'There's something wrong isn't there. Is it anything I can help with?'

Jen's hand snaked across the table to rest, feather light on the back of Will's own and he stared down at it for a few seconds, lost in his thoughts.

'Remember, that's what our dates are all about,' said Jen with a soft laugh. 'We unburden, share our problems. If I can't help at least I can listen.'

Will chewed on his lip.

'It's Lucy,' he admitted, feeling slightly guilty. Maybe this is a conversation that should remain between himself and Lucy.

'She just didn't seem as excited as I thought she would.'

'She's unhappy that you may have a new job?'

'No! Not unhappy. She's pleased, very pleased.' Lucy had said she was pleased, several times. It just hadn't seemed to be coming from her soul. 'I just thought she would be more relieved, happy that she could stop work and stay at home again.'

'I thought she wanted to leave work?'

'Yes. She said that she will. Probably. Once I've actually got the job and settled in.'

Will ran a hand through his already tousled hair. 'I just thought she would jump at the chance of going back to how things were. You know, me at work and her at home.'

Jen pulled a face, sympathy filling her eyes. 'Oh Will, how heart-breaking for you.'

'What? No, it's not that. If Lucy wants to carry on at Simcock and Bright then she can. I just had the impression she was finding it very demanding and didn't want to carry on any longer than she absolutely had to.'

'And instead it looks as though she has loved going back to work, despite everything that she told you.' Jen gave a sigh, her eyebrows drawing together in concern. 'Why would she lie about that I wonder?'

'Lie?' Will looked startled. 'Lucy's not lying. I must have got the wrong impression, that's all.' He shifted uncomfortably in his seat. This was not the conversation he had imagined. He had expected Jen to give his some perfectly logical explanation why Lucy had been reserved in her reaction. He had imagined her nodding sagely and saying that of course that's how Lucy had behaved, because that's how any women in her position would react and Will was simply being insensitive.

Jen's concerned face was watching him.

'Forget I said anything,' said Will, standing up. 'Actually, I need to get a few things done before I pick Emily up from nursery so …'

'Will, I didn't want to be the one to say this. But I think I need to. I can't bear the thought of you being deceived in this way.'

Will wondered where the thundering noise he could hear was coming from before he realised it was his heart.

'Deceived?'

Jen stood up and came to stand next to him, her hand reaching out to hold his hand as she spoke, her face a mask of concern and worry.

'I think there's another reason why Lucy doesn't want to leave work.'

Will looked down at their joined hands before pulling his gently away and taking a step backwards.

'What kind of reason?'

'I really didn't want to say this Will. I know how hurt you're going to be and I didn't want to be the one to hurt you.'

'What kind of reason?' Will repeated, staring at Jen. 'What are you talking about?'

She took a step forward to bring herself close to him again but Will held up a hand, warding her off, keeping some distance between them.

'What are you trying to say?' he demanded.

Jen shook her head in distress then stepped back and sat heavily back into her chair.

'Lucy is having an affair. With Simon. That's why she doesn't want to stop work, because it will mean she will have to stop seeing him.'

'No.' Will's response was instant. 'No. No.'

'I've suspected for a while. I recognised the signs you see. All the times my husband was unfaithful, I've become quite the expert at knowing when it's happening.'

'No. Lucy wouldn't. She would never have an affair.'

'Oh I'm sure she didn't mean it to happen. People rarely do. But I'm afraid that it's true Will.'

Will's face was grey. 'No. I don't believe you.'

'I know you don't want it to be true …'

'It's not true.' Will shook his head. 'It's not true.'

'I'm sorry Will. But she told me, last night.'

'An affair? She said she was having an affair?'

'She said that Simon …'

'Did she say she was having an affair? Did she use the words?'

Will's voice was rising, his face contorted in anguish.

'Not exactly ...'

'Then she isn't.' Will turned away, his voice flat and definite.

'Will, she is …'

'No. Lucy wouldn't do that, not to me, not to the children. She wouldn't.'

'I'm so sorry Will. She said that she started leaning on Simon for support, just like you and I did, but that it became more, so much more.'

'No! She wouldn't.'

'Yes …'

'NO!' Will's voice resonated round the kitchen causing Harry to freeze and look at his father, his bottom lip wobbling alarmingly.

Will felt sick. He scooped Harry into his arms and held him close for a second.

'I think you should go Jen.'

'Oh Will, please don't blame me for telling you …'

'I don't. But you're wrong. You've made a mistake.'

'Will …'

'No. I don't want to talk about this anymore. You've made a mistake. And I really do have some things I need to do so I'll see you later.'

He walked towards the door, holding it open as Jen collected her coat and bag.

'Will you be okay?'

'Of course. You're wrong. Lucy isn't having an affair.'

'But …'

'Please Jen. Please go. We'll speak later.'

'You understand I'm only saying this because I can't stand you being hurt. Like I was.'

'I understand.'

He was standing straight and unbending at the door as Jen walked towards him.

'If you want to talk, I'm always here for you.'

'Thank you.'

'And you'll let me know as soon as you hear about the job?'

'Of course.'

Will forced a smile. 'Thank you Jen, but you are wrong.'

Jen was outside now and stepping forward Will started to close the door.

'I think we both know that I'm not wrong,' whispered Jen, her words covering Will like a toxic mist. 'I'm so sorry Will, but I am still here for you, remember that.'

Chapter 38

The journey to work seemed long and tedious as Lucy sat on the train and thought back to the previous evening. She felt guilty for being so unenthusiastic about Will's opportunity. She should have cheered and hugged him close, telling him how wonderful it all was. Instead, she had spent the evening fretting over what may have happened between her husband and Jen. Whatever it was, Jen clearly thought that Lucy was the one to blame. She turned her head to gaze out of the window at the landscape whipping by. Will wouldn't betray her. Would he? Oh why was life so complicated? It hadn't been this hard when Lucy had been at home looking after her children and Will had been the one to go to work each morning. She scowled. Or maybe it had been and she just hadn't noticed.

Arriving at the office she trudged up the stairs, contemplating that she may be close to the end of her time at Simcock and Bright. She tried to feel happy. It's what she had wanted. She ought to feel relieved but instead, she was feeling slightly let down. It all felt somehow unfinished.

Alice was already in Lucy's office, watering the plant she had brought in the day before and humming happily as she placed some post on the corner of the desk.

'Good Morning. Oh, you look tired. Bad night with the children?' she asked sympathetically. There was already a coffee in place, still steaming gently, and Lucy sank into her seat to grasp it thankfully.

'Just a bad night in general,' she sighed, flipping through the post.

'Oh dear,' trilled Alice. 'Well, no meetings today so nothing too strenuous.'

'You sound disgustingly cheerful,' complained Lucy, watching her friend as she drifted around the office, straightening a file here and a chair there.

Alice smiled dreamily. 'Well, the sun is shining and it's such a lovely day.'

Lucy glanced out of the window. There was the tiniest of gaps in the overcast sky letting a weak ray of sunlight force its way outwards, which was doing nothing to dispel the chill March air or the blustery northern winds.

'No, it's not. Oh my God!'

Alice swung round.

'What?'

'You're in love!'

She watched the blush shimmer upwards until Alice's entire face had taken on a rosy glow.

'No, I'm not!'

'Yes, you are. Look at you.'

Lucy jumped out of her chair and frogmarched Alice to the mirror that hung on the wall next to the coat rail.

'Dreamy eyes. Check. Can't stop smiling. Check. Seeing the best in everything and everyone. Check. Rosy cheeks. Check. You, Alice, are in love.'

Their reflections stared back and Lucy couldn't help notice that next to her friend's luminous glow she looked far from fresh and dewy. There were shadows beneath her tired eyes, her mouth was turned down and her skin looked blotchy and red.

Alice giggled, pulling herself out of Lucy's grip. 'Don't be silly, she said in a breathy voice. 'I am no such thing!'

Lucy watched her enviously. She remembered when she had first started dating Will and she would find herself sitting in the office, smiling for absolutely no reason. Or she would suddenly recall his smile or the feel of his lips on hers and she would blush deeply and shuffle in her seat, wondering if everyone could tell how smitten she was. She would stand in the doorway of the pub where they were meeting and as her eyes fell on him her stomach would skip with delight and a shiver would run down her spine. She wondered what Jen meant when she said it wasn't Will's fault.

'Although, I did see Grant again last night,' offered Alice, unable to hold back her smile.

Lucy sighed. 'Please don't fall in love with him Alice. I know you think he's wonderful and charming and all those things but I still worry about him breaking your heart.'

Alice grinned. 'Stop worrying. He can only break my heart if I give it to him and I haven't.'

'Haven't you?' It seemed to Lucy that Alice had placed it gently on a plate and handed it to him reverently.

'No.'

'But …'

'No! Don't spoil it Lucy. You don't know him as I do and I'm telling you there's nothing to worry about. Anyway, I thought you two were getting on better?'

'Well,' said Lucy dryly, 'he hasn't tried to stitch me up in the last few days if that equates to us getting on better.'

'Did he tell Rob about the mistake you made on the McCarthy account?'

'No but …'

'Did he encourage you to hand in your notice?'

'Well no but …'

'Then maybe you need to meet him halfway and accept that he was just doing what you would have done in days gone by and protecting his position.'

Lucy's mouth hung open. 'But you were the one who told me how despicable he was and how nobody liked him! You wanted me to bring him down a peg or two and then kick him while he was on the floor!'

Alice looked a little startled and then grinned. 'Did I? That must have been before he kissed me!'

Lucy shook her head. She wasn't sure she could cope with a loved-up Alice when her own heart was feeling so fragile.

'Well please be careful,' she muttered darkly. 'They all let you down in the end.'

Alice stopped her tidying and gave Lucy a quizzical look.

'Will's never let you down.'

'Hasn't he?'

'Lucy! Is there something going on?'

'I'm just saying. They can't be relied on. Men, I mean.'

Alice watched her friend for a moment and then dropped into a chair as Lucy stared despondently at her desk

'You don't seem very happy Lucy. Is there something wrong? I mean apart from Grant and work.'

Lucy shook her head but didn't speak.

'Are you sure? Because you look like someone with a lot on their mind.'

Lucy gazed out of the window. The stray sunbeam had disappeared, forced out by grey clouds that had united to cast a steel grey umbrella over the sky.

She thought about telling Alice that she suspected her husband had crossed a line in his friendship with Jen. That something had happened and that it was Lucy's fault. She could tell Alice how Jen had gazed at Will, touching his arm, kissing him, knowing that Lucy was watching them both. But the words stuck in her throat. Telling Alice made it more real.

'I'm okay,' she managed, hoping the tears would remain at bay. 'Just a lot going on at the moment.'

Alice stood up to leave, but not before she came around the desk to give Lucy's shoulders a gently squeeze. 'It will all work out Lucy darling, whatever it is I'm sure it will all work out.'

Oh for her strength and conviction, thought Lucy longingly. If only she could be as certain that everything would indeed work out.

As Alice left, Grant arrived and Lucy watched as they paused in the doorway to share a small intimate smile. She glared at him as he took a seat, unbuttoning his jacket as he sat down and straightening his tie.

'What do you want?'

'Good morning Lucy. I hope you're well,' he said pointedly.

Lucy grunted, watching him warily. They may have resolved some of their differences and he may be, as Alice constantly insisted, a much nicer person than she had originally given him credit for but Lucy was still a long way from trusting him.

'I see.' Grant smiled, and Lucy thought she could detect an air of triumph about him. Calm but definitely smug.

She waited.

'I thought it was only fair to let you know that I've finally resolved the issues with Haydock Sportswear.'

Lucy clenched her fist under the table. She knew Grant had been working tirelessly on the account and with the added incentive of their little bet as to who would be the first to sign up their client, she imagined that he was pulling out all the stops in an effort to reach the winning post before she did. She had been tempted to ask Alice if she knew how he was doing but her conscience had stepped in.

'I see.'

'We had a meeting yesterday,' he shot out his cuffs and then angled his head slightly, looking straight into Lucy's eyes. 'They agreed to engage Simcock and Bright. We'll be signing the contract in three days.'

Lucy refused to show any reaction as he waited, a small smile still curving his lips.

'Well,' she said casually, 'that gives me a target to aim for.'

'Three days? You think you can pitch Blooming Lovely and get them to sign in three days?' asked Grant in amusement.

Lucy thought it was highly unlikely. There again, it was also very possible that she wouldn't be here in three days. Will had made it clear that if he phoned to tell her he had been offered the job, he expected her to run for the door and catch the next train home. It was a tempting thought.

'I don't see why not,' she answered with a slight toss of her head. 'I've done it before.'

For a moment their eyes did battle across the desk before Grant stood, straightening his jacket and grinning.

'But can you do it again Lucy Mathers? Do you still have what it takes?'

'We'll soon find out won't we,' snapped Lucy and gritted her teeth as Grant left, chuckling in amusement.

Lucy worked like a demon for the rest of the day. She kept her phone by her side and scanned it constantly for any sign of an update from Will about his interview. Shouldn't they have been back to him by now, she wondered. They had been so keen to see him at such short notice, wouldn't they be equally quick to come back with an answer? She called Alice into her office and told her that Grant was on the verge of signing Haydock Sportswear.

'Did you know?' she asked Alice casually.

'You mean did Grant tell me and I kept it to myself instead of passing on the information?'

It sounded dreadful when said out loud and Lucy slumped in her chair groaning.

'God I'm sorry Alice. I'm being a real cow about this. My head is all over the place.'

'It's okay. I can tell you're not yourself. But I've told you, Grant and I have an unspoken agreement not to discuss anything about work and then neither of us says anything we shouldn't.'

Lucy was still having trouble believing that Grant would be so ethical.

'Of course,' she murmured doubtfully.

'Really! He's competitive at work but outside the office he's … lovely.'

A blush filled Alice's cheek and Lucy forced herself to stop being so cynical.

'How lovely?' she queried watching Alice blush even more.

'Very.'

'Mm, I can tell,' teased Lucy. 'But please …'

'Stop! I am being careful. Grant and I are just enjoying each other's company, it's not serious and you don't have to worry.'

And she was gone, leaving Lucy to work feverishly on her proposal for Blooming Lovely. For her to stand a chance of beating Grant she needed them to decide she had done such a good job presenting her ideas that they wanted to sign up with Simcock and Bright on the spot. It was a big ask, even for the Lucy Mathers of old.

At 5:00 Lucy decided that although she had enough work to keep her occupied throughout the night, she wanted to catch the early train home. She needed to see Will, she needed to find out if he'd heard anything about the job and she really needed to ask him about his friendship with Jen. He would groan and tell her she was being ridiculous but this wasn't about helping a friend with the cleaning or the washing. She wanted to look into Will's eyes and ask him how he felt about his new friend, whether she made his heart race as she walked in through the door, whether he became breathless at the thought of seeing her again. She wanted him to tell her, truthfully, what had happened between them and how exactly he felt about the new woman in his life.

So despite the mountain of work she still had to do, she left in time for the early train, her heels clicking down the pavement as she walked to the station. She was surprised when she caught sight of Simon on the platform pushing his way through the crowd of weary workers, all desperate to get home.

'You don't normally catch the early train,' she said as he reached her side.

'I hadn't managed to speak to you today. I thought it would be nice to have a catch up on the way home. You've looked a little frazzled. Everything okay?'

Okay? Lucy was beginning to think nothing would ever be okay again. She had expected her return to work to be difficult because she was leaving her children and her comfort zone. She had not imagined that she would need to worry about her husband striking up a friendship with a blonde seductress at the local mother and toddler group.

She smiled weakly. 'It's been a bit full-on today.'

The crowd around them moved forwards slightly, a sure sign someone had spotted the train rolling into the station and Lucy and Simon both stepped nearer to the platform.

'Grant? Work? Or Will?'

Lucy considered for a moment.

'All of them! Grant is on the cusp of signing his new customer, I have three days to pitch and sign Blooming Lovely or I lose the bet and Will …'

A gust of wind heralded the train's arrival and the crowd surged forwards, pushing and shoving as they fought for a seat. Too far back to stand a hope of sitting down, Lucy and Simon found themselves wedged in a corner, pressed against each other.

'Will?'

What could she say? That she had arrived home the previous evening to find Jen looking far too comfortable on Lucy's settee. That she had been visiting regularly to vacuum Lucy's living room, and maybe her bedroom too for all Lucy knew. That she had been offering Will the support that Lucy had apparently failed to provide. That she had touched Will gently on the arm, kissed him on the cheek and sent a secretive smile winging Lucy's way behind Will's back.

'He had an interview,' she said instead.

'Oh.'

'He thinks it went well. He's expecting them to offer him a job.'

'Right.'

The train surged forward and Simon put a steadying hand at Lucy's waist.

'And will you stop work?'

'I suppose so.'

Another lurch sent them swaying sideways and this time Simon left his hand wrapped lightly around Lucy to keep her upright.

'Do you want to?'

'Of course.'

Of course she did. Returning to work had been demanding and difficult. She preferred staying at home. She was worried about Grant making a fool of her. She was worried about Will drifting into Jen's outstretched arms. She was worried that their marriage was straining under the change of roles. She was worried that deep down she had actually started to enjoy being back in the office.

'I see. And when will you leave?'

'He hasn't got the job yet! Let's wait and see.'

They fell into silence, swaying in rhythm with the train. The Horsforth sign appeared through the window and the train started to slow down.

'I'll miss you.'

Lucy smiled, the first genuine smile that had touched her face all day.

'And I'll miss you, Simon. It's been wonderful having someone to vent to at the end of the day.'

She clutched her bag a little tighter as the brakes were applied and the train began to lurch into the station.

'Maybe I'll have to phone you each evening,' she joked. 'Let you know the trials and tribulations of a day spent looking after two children! See what advice you can offer me.'

She was laughing but as she looked into Simon's face, he was staring back, his face serious.

'Lucy,' he began.

The passengers began to shuffle around. Some heading for the doors, others leaping into empty seats.

'Lucy …'

Lucy tried to take a step backwards, heading for the door but couldn't move as Simon's hand suddenly tightened around her waist.

'Simon I need …'

And then she had to stop speaking because Simon was kissing her. Sliding a finger under her chin, he tilted her head upwards so he could kiss her softly on her lips.

Lucy could hear movement all around her. The train stopped with a shudder people shoved towards the exit. She could feel Simon's lips on hers, soft and very gentle. They were exactly how she would have imagined them to feel, if she had ever imagined Simon kissing her.

He lifted his head, his eyes burning into hers.

'Lucy …'

'I have to go!'

Pushing him away, Lucy stepped into the corridor and joined the throng discharging onto the platform. Her hands were trembling as she hung onto her handbag. What had just happened? Turning, she saw Simon through the window, watching her and for a moment she wondered how they looked to onlookers. Did they appear to be in love? Did they seem engrossed in each other, reluctant to part? A scene from an old film started to play in Lucy's head. Something about two star crossed lovers who met on a platform, whose affair existed only during the brief time they spent together on a train.

The train began to pull away and Lucy turned away, her body shaking as she tried to gather her chaotic thoughts.

Chapter 39

Lucy's cheeks were burning as she walked home. The scene kept replaying in her head as she hurried along the street. What on earth had possessed Simon to kiss her? She hadn't encouraged him. She certainly hadn't led him to believe she wanted to be kissed? Didn't you, asked a voice deep inside. She hadn't pulled away. She hadn't gasped and slapped his face. There had been a moment, the tiniest, tiniest moment when she had realised what he was about to do. As his head dropped closer to hers and his eyes were gazing into her own, she had known what was going to happen. She could have moved her head, kept her lips away from his. She could have said no.

If she were honest, and honesty she decided was becoming quite painful, she had to admit that in those brief moment she had wondered what it would be like to be kissed by another man. As her heart fretted about Will's relationship with Jen, she had defiantly wondered how it would feel if someone other than Will kissed her.

It hadn't been unpleasant. Simon's lips had been soft and warm. The kiss had been gentle and almost comforting. But she had also known the very second Simon's lips rested on hers that this was not for her. The only lips she ever wanted were Will's. It had proved, if any proof was needed, that she had no desire to have a relationship with anyone but her husband and it had also put a fire in her stomach. She wasn't prepared to let Jen take him away. Will was hers and she would make sure it stayed that way.

Marching up the driveway, she could see Will's reflection through the glass door. He was standing in the kitchen, his back to the door as he faced the sink. She didn't know where they had gone so wrong over the last few weeks, but one thing she did know was that she loved her husband and she would not let him think any differently. Jen had to go, Lucy would leave work if necessary and they would pick up the strands of their old life, even if it was a little knotty in places.

She threw open the door ready to confront him. They needed to clear the air.

'Will …'

'Lucy – are you having an affair with Simon?'

Lucy stopped. Her mouth fell open as she stared at her husband. His hands were covered in suds from the sink and his face was ash grey. He was watching her with a mixture of anger and dread in his eyes as she stood in the kitchen, her coat still on, her bag hanging from her shoulder, shock in her eyes.

'What?'

She blinked several times. She had wanted to confront Will about Jen. She had wanted to challenge his dependence on her. She had wanted to know why Jen said that Will shouldn't be blamed for the way he had behaved. Her mind raced back to the train, the moment when Simon's lips had touched hers and her cheeks filled with colour.

'Of course not,' she squeaked, racked with guilt for not stopping Simon. 'What an incredible thing to say.'

Even to Lucy, her voice sounded weak. She should have been outraged. This wasn't meant to happen. She was meant to accuse Will and listen to him defend himself. But she thought about the moment Simon had kissed her and her blush deepened.

'Oh Lucy.'

Will's shoulders dropped and he pushed his soapy hand through his hair, leaving it wet and covered in suds.

'Stop this! Will I am not having an affair, I would never do that.'

Taking off her coat, Lucy threw it angrily at a chair.

'How could you even suggest such a thing.' Kiss or no kiss she shook her head in confusion. 'Where has this come from Will, what on earth are you saying?'

Will was watching her carefully, his face uncertain.

'You have drinks with him after work.'

'A drink! Once or twice.'

'You don't want to give up work.'

'What? What on earth has that got to do with Simon?'

'You don't want to stop seeing him.'

'No! Will stop this.'

Shaking Lucy stepped forward but Will retreated, his back against the sink.

'Are you Lucy? Are you having an affair with him?' he whispered.

Lucy's hand went to her mouth, covering its trembling. '

'What are you saying Will. How could you believe I would do that?'

He was shaking his head, his eyes suddenly unsure. 'I just thought …'

'You thought what? That I leave here every morning and somehow conduct a passionate affair with a man I hardly know in a busy office or on a public train?' said Lucy angrily.

'I thought …'

'And what about you,' she demanded. 'What about you and Jen?'

'Me and Jen? What do you mean?'

'Your special friend Jen,' goaded Lucy, her voice full of anger. 'Always here, cleaning, washing, helping. What else has she been doing for you Will?'

Her voice was high, almost a scream and Will gave her a disgusted look.

'Don't be ridiculous. There's nothing between me and Jen.'

'Isn't there? You spend enough time with her. She was the first person you spoke to when you found out about the interview…'

'I told you why! I didn't want to disturb you at work.'

'Because I wouldn't have cared? Because I wouldn't have come home instantly if you'd told me what was happening. Because I neglect you?' shouted Lucy.

'Neglect? What on earth are you talking about?'

'Jen told me how much you needed her. How you've had to turn to her.'

Will's face creased with disbelief. 'That's ridiculous. Jen would never say that …'

'Wouldn't she?'

Lucy was shaking, her anger flooding her brain. 'What have you done?' she yelled. 'What did you do with her?'

'What …'

'She said it wasn't your fault. That it was my fault. What was my fault, what did you do?'

'You're being ridiculous,' said Will firmly, looking anxiously towards the living room where the sound of the TV could be heard. 'Stop shouting, you'll upset the children.'

'I bet she's been here today hasn't she?'

It was Will's turn to blush, the colour staining his cheeks.

'She … er, popped round for a coffee and to see how the interview went.'

'She can't stay away. I bet you don't want to go back to work because it will spoil your afternoon get-togethers with Jen!'

'No! You know how much I want to get another job. I can't wait to get back to work.' His voice rose, matching Lucy's for anger and volume and Emily's head peered round the door. Her lip was trembling and her eyes were filling with tears.

'Mummy?' she said hesitantly.

Lucy swallowed hard. She swallowed the accusations and the anger and brushed away the tears as she turned to face her daughter.

'Hello sweetheart.'

'Why are you shouting,' demanded their daughter. 'Why are you shouting at each other?'

Will closed his eyes briefly then stepped forward to pick her up and hold her high in his arms.

'We're sorry darling. Mummy and daddy were having a disagreement. It's like when you and Harry argue, except that we're a lot bigger so it's so much noisier when we argue.'

Lucy tried to join in, laughing at herself.

'Was mummy screeching? I was just a bit cross, that's all.'

Emily looked at the two of them, her face was serious and her eyes wide.

'You are always cross with each other. I don't think you should go to work anymore mummy. It's making you and daddy very angry,' and she wriggled out of Will's arms and went back into the living room where they could hear her telling Harry that mummy and daddy were sorry for shouting.

'Well she has a point doesn't she,' bit out Will in a low voice. 'Even our daughter can tell this isn't working.'

'You make it sound like I went back to work because I was missing it! Let's not forget I was trying to stop us losing everything while you looked for another job!' said Lucy in an outraged whisper.

'But you don't want to stop.'

Lucy turned away. Her hands were still trembling and she told herself that she was finding it difficult to think clearly because she was so angry. It should have been an easy question to answer. Of course she wanted to stop work, hadn't she said so many times over the last few weeks. So why were the words refusing to come out?

'I see.'

Will's voice was hard, angry. 'You hate work so much yet you don't want to stop. But it's nothing to do with your relationship with Simon.'

'I don't have a relationship with Simon!'

But he had kissed her and again Lucy felt the colour fill her cheeks.

They stood in the kitchen, glaring at each other, both full of anger and suspicion.

Will remembered Jen's words earlier that day. That Lucy had all but admitted having an affair and she wouldn't want to stop work because it would mean not seeing Simon again. That she hadn't meant to do anything wrong but Simon had been there for her, a shoulder to lean on.

'Did I let you down Lucy?'

'Let me down?'

'I know it wasn't easy for you to go back to work, did I let you down? Did I leave you with nowhere to turn but Simon?'

Tears started to roll down Lucy's cheeks because that was the very question she had wanted to ask Will. Had she deserted her wifely duties to the point where he'd had to look around for someone to lean on. Had the softly spoken Jen appeared in their lives because Lucy had left the door wide open for her.

'Do you really believe I could have an affair Will?'

Their eyes met, hers full of tears and his full of anguish.

'No,' he whispered. 'But you thought …'

'I thought you were getting too close to Jen. I still think she is too close to you. I've seen the look on her face ...'

Will groaned. 'You've got it all wrong Lucy…'

'No, she said stubbornly. 'I haven't. You may not feel like that about Jen but I think she feels that way about you.'

Will shook his head impatiently. 'Rubbish. Jen is a friend,' he said firmly. 'Nothing more. Nothing less. She's been a good friend and I've needed her help a lot.'

'Because I …'

'Because I wasn't very good at the whole father at home thing,' interrupted Will. 'Because I foolishly thought it would be a doddle.'

'And I found going back to work so very hard,' admitted Lucy. 'It was nice to have someone to unburden myself to at the end of the day without worrying you. But that's all it is, I am not having an affair. I would never do that to you Will.'

They were facing each other, only a foot apart but it seemed to Lucy like an insurmountable distance. They both nodded, accepting the other's explanation. But neither of them were satisfied. She believed Will but she knew that there was something wrong with his relationship with Jen, even if he himself wasn't aware of it. And every time she thought of the kiss she had allowed Simon to give her she wanted to curl up and cry. She had no desire for a relationship with him, but how would Will feel if she admitted that they had kissed. She didn't think they would ever recover.

After a long moment Will, stood up straight.

'I'd better get on with something to eat,' he said.

He smiled, but Lucy could tell it didn't come from his heart. Did he believe her, she wondered? Or could he simply not cope with the thought that she would betray him.

'I think I'll go get changed.' Lucy wanted to take off the clothes she had worn that day, she had to remove the smell of her journey home, the feel of Simon's hand on her back.

Will nodded and as Lucy walked towards the stairs he half turned.

'By the way, I got a call this afternoon. The company I spoke to have offered me a job. They want me to start as soon as possible.'

Lucy stopped, her eyes flying to Will's face.

'So there's nothing to stop you leaving work. If that's what you want to do of course,' and he turned his back and started peeling potatoes as Lucy stood in silent shock at the bottom of the staircase.

Chapter 40

Will kissed Lucy goodbye the following morning and although she leant into his tall frame and kissed him back, both pairs of eyes were uncertain and full of doubt. As Will began the relentless morning schedule his mind returned again and again to Lucy's accusations. How on earth could she believe that there was anything between Jen and himself? Jen had been a wonderful friend and he would have floundered without her support on several occasions. But then Will himself had accused Lucy of having an affair, another ridiculous idea. He thought back to how her face had flooded with colour when he'd mentioned Simon's name and he groaned. His mind churned, uncertain which way to turn.

Emily was delivered to nursery, the kitchen cleaned, the washing in and lunch prepared and Will stood for a moment in the kitchen and grinned. He had finally found his way round the hundred and one tasks that filled his day.

He watched Harry playing happily under the table and for a moment his eyes became glassy with emotion. He would actually miss spending the day with his children. Harry threw one of his cars across the kitchen floor where it came to a skidding halt next to Will's foot. He wouldn't miss it enough to not take the job though, he decided with a chuckle. In fact, he couldn't wait to climb out of bed at some ridiculously early hour on a Monday morning and spend hours stuck in the traffic before facing the relentless grind of a day in the office.

The previous evening had passed quietly after Will and Lucy's argument. They had crept around each other, both overly polite, both at pains to state that they believed each other and neither really daring to give vent to their true feelings. Lucy hadn't mentioned leaving work and Will had refused to push her. He had wanted her to throw her arms in the air and shout

Hallelujah as she wrote her resignation letter. He had wanted to twirl her round the kitchen and say thank you for making the sacrifice of returning to work but now the crisis was over and she could revert to Lucy Mathers, wife and mother. But neither had happened and Will was still waiting patiently for Lucy to speak to him about work. She had mentioned casually as she left the house that she had her proposal for Blooming Lovely the following day and both had tensed, avoiding the other's eyes. She left, Will's heart aching with frustration at the vision in his head of Lucy and Simon, sitting side by side on the train, Lucy telling Simon tearfully that she had to leave work. That they wouldn't be able to see each other anymore.

He picked Emily up in plenty of time, allowed the children the allotted 10 minutes at the playground and returned home to dry the washing from the morning. He'd half expected to hear a knocking at the door and when it arrived, he threw it open and welcomed Jen into the kitchen.

'I thought you might phone,' she began breathlessly as she unzipped Alfie's coat and let him totter into the living room to find Harry, 'to tell me if the company had come back to you.'

Will was finding it a struggle to contain his grin as she hung up her coat and turned to face him, her face expectant.

'Actually they did,' he said his smile splitting his face in two. 'They want me to start on Monday.'

A loud whoop filled the kitchen and Jen threw her arms around Will's neck.

'That's fantastic! Oh Will, I'm so pleased for you.'

Hugging her back, Will thought that this was the reaction he had expected from Lucy. Not the strained silence that had filled the house.

He pulled back slightly to look at Jen's exultant face and was taken by surprise when she reached up to press a kiss on his lips.

'I'm so proud of you. You're amazing.'

Will flinched and dropped his arms but Jen was busy clapping and didn't seem to notice his discomfort.

'You must be so pleased?'

'Yeah.' Will scratched his head. 'It is a relief.'

Sitting down at the table, Jen leant forward so she was a little nearer to him and suddenly Will was a little unsure of himself. The kiss had been unexpected. There again if Fran had grabbed hold of him and given him a kiss he wouldn't have thought twice about it. Maybe Lucy's paranoia was beginning to rub off on him but he refused to let it spoil a friendship that had come to mean a lot to him.

Jen was grinning happily and Will couldn't help but join in.

'And what about Lucy?'

His smile slipped.

'What about Lucy?'

'Did you speak to her about the affair?'

Jen's tone was sympathetic, conciliatory.

'I did. There is no affair,' he said firmly.

A frown joined Jen's eyebrows. 'But I told you Will, she's definitely having an affair. She …'

'No. She's not. We spoke last night and there is no affair.'

Will pushed his chair back and began to pace the kitchen.

'I shouldn't have believed you in the first place Jen. Oh I know your heart was in the right place but you're wrong. I don't want to talk about it anymore, thank you for your concerns but Lucy is not having an affair.'

Jen's lips thinned. 'Is she leaving work?'

Will struggled for an answer.

'When she's ready. Maybe not straight away.'

'Why? If she isn't having an affair why would she stay at work?'

Will didn't have an answer. It was a question he had been asking himself all morning. He didn't have an answer and he didn't want Jen to give him one.

'Jen, please stop. I don't want to discuss this. Lucy is not having an affair,' he said firmly. For the first time he felt quite irritated by Jen's presence. She had been concerned and had let him know of her worries. That he could forgive, she had been in the same position herself with her husband and wanted to protect Will from the same experience. But her insistence was going too far and he just needed her to stop. He and Lucy would work out their problems without Jen's interference.

Jen looked almost angry for a moment and Will could tell that she was holding herself back.

'Anyway, I am going back to work on Monday,' he said with forced joviality. 'So I'm afraid our play dates will be coming to an end. I have to say I don't think I could have managed without them, or you. Thank you for being such an amazing friend Jen.'

'It's almost a shame,' murmured Jen. 'You are so good at being a father, I'm sorry you have to stop.'

'Good! Hardly,' snorted Will. 'All the times I've had to call you for help. I would think the children will be glad to see me walk out of the door on a morning.'

'But it's going to make life much more difficult for us isn't it?' asked Jen her eyes wide and a little distressed. 'How are we going to manage?'

Will stared. 'What?'

'How will we be able to see each other once you're back at work?' fretted Jen. 'I suppose it might actually be easier if Lucy does continue to work, it might give us a little bit more freedom. And you'll soon see I'm right,' she sniffed. 'She won't be able to hide her affair for long!'

Will's heart was beating painfully hard. It was thudding inside his chest and for a moment he felt quite nauseous.

'What do you mean?' he asked faintly. 'What are you talking about?'

'I'm talking about us silly,' said Jen leaning forwards on the table and giving him a coy look. 'I'm talking about how we keep seeing each other when you go back to work.'

Will's eyes filled with horror. He stared at the woman in front of him and remembered what Lucy had said, that Jen wanted more out of their friendship, that Jen was smitten with him, that Jen was manipulating him. He had laughed at her, rebuffing all her accusations and accusing her of being unreasonable and jealous.

'When I go back to work, we won't be seeing much of each other,' he said slowly. 'In fact, we may never see each other again. I'm sorry, but that's the way it's likely to be.'

Jen stopped smiling and gave Will a startled glance. 'But Will …'

'Jen, I hope you don't think there was anything more than friendship between us over the last few weeks,' he said, his voice shaking slightly. 'Because I have to say that's all it was as far as I was concerned, friendship.'

Jen was on her feet, moving closer to Will as she held out her hands.

'But it was so much more than that Will. I could see it in your eyes. I know you feel the same way I do.'

'No! No really Jen. Please believe me, I appreciate your friendship but there's nothing more to it.'

'But Lucy was so mean. She refused to help you and left you to cope on your own. If I hadn't been there …'

'Lucy wasn't mean!' shouted Will in horror. 'She was struggling with a new job. Every morning she spent time getting everything ready for me, she spent her weekends catching up on all the things I didn't get around to doing. That's why I didn't tell her about all the stupid things I'd done. I didn't want her to worry about home as well as work.'

Jen shook her head, her face screwed up in resentment.

'I wouldn't have let you down like that. I didn't. I was always here for you…'

'I think you should leave.'

Will grabbed her coat from the back of the chair. He couldn't believe what was happening. He couldn't believe he hadn't seen it coming. He couldn't believe that he had accused Lucy …

'Why did you tell me Lucy was having an affair?' he asked.

'Because she was and you just couldn't see you were better off without her!' spat Jen. Her face an unpleasant mask of dislike. 'She was making a fool of you and you couldn't see through her.'

'You made it all up, didn't you?' Will groaned, putting his hands over his face as he thought back to the moment when Jen had put her hand on his and told him in a soft voice full of regret and sympathy that Lucy was having an affair. And he had let her get inside his head. He had believed in Lucy but he had allowed those nagging doubts to crawl through his brain, leaving suspicion and doubt in their wake.

'You said it deliberately to make me doubt her. She never said anything to make you suspicious, you made it all up,' he whispered in anguish.

'She'll leave you and then you'll come running back to me …'

'I will never come running to you Jen.' Will's tone was cold and angry, his face dark and terse. He couldn't get this woman out of his house quickly enough. How could he have believed for a moment that Lucy would betray him?

He walked into the living room and gently guided Alfie back to his mother, handing her their coats.

'Please leave Jen. I never want to see you again.'

For a moment panic filled Jen's face. 'I'm sorry,' she whimpered. 'I'm sorry. I didn't mean to make you angry. We can still be friends Will, we can …'

But Will was closing the door and slowly her face was disappearing even as he could hear her voice begging for one more chance.

'We're right for each other Will, I know we are,' she pleaded from outside. 'Will! Will!'

But Will wasn't listening and with a heart overflowing with regret he turned away and walked into the living room to take his children into his arms and bury his head deep into their soft silky hair.

Chapter 41

The office was buzzing when Lucy arrived. A couple of people were laughing heartily, there was a good-natured argument about the previous night's football results being carried out at the top of the staircase and Rob's voice was booming out of his office as he related a story from his glory days as a hotshot account manager.

Lucy looked around. It had been a mammoth task returning to work. The office which Alice insisted hadn't changed at all, had in fact changed in a hundred and one tiny ways. It had taken Lucy time to get to grips with the new computer system, the phones, the filing system - even where to find a pen. And almost every day she had bewailed the fact that she wasn't at home, with her children. She had longed to stand in the kitchen and wash countless cups and plates. She envied a day spent catching up with the washing and ironing and missed the chaos of the morning and getting two children dressed and out of the house.

Walking to her office, Lucy sat behind her desk and gazed out of the window. Grant Cassidy had not made her return easy. He was still a rather prickly thorn in Lucy's rear but she had to admit she had started to enjoy some of their exchanges. In fact, Lucy admitted to herself ruefully, she had started to enjoy a great deal about being at work. It was exhausting juggling motherhood and a job. She was convinced that both Rob and Grant felt she was slightly less than she had once been simply because she'd left to start a family. But the cut and thrust of the office suited her. She had missed the atmosphere, she'd missed the work and most of all she had missed the Lucy Mathers she had once been. What a shame she'd realised all this just as she'd also realised that if she wanted to save her marriage she would have to leave.

Because there was no doubt in Lucy's head that Jen wanted Will. He may not have seen it himself, he may be unaware of the strength of Jen's feelings but Lucy knew without a shadow of a doubt that Jen would do everything she could to get Will for herself and there was no way Lucy was going to let that happen. Will said he believed she wasn't having an affair with Simon but she had seen the uncertainty in his eyes and if he needed her to leave work to prove she didn't care if she never saw Simon again, then that's what she would do because Lucy was not going to lose Will. He was worth any sacrifice.

With a sigh, she spread her files across her desk. Her presentation for Blooming Lovely was the following morning at the same time Grant had his meeting with Haydock Sportswear to sign their contract. Unless Blooming Lovely decided at the meeting that they wanted representation by Lucy, which despite her boast to Grant the previous day, was an unlikely scenario, she would lose the bet. Grant would sign his client first. Maybe that in itself was a good enough reason for Lucy to leave, she wasn't sure she could cope with his smug look and the triumphant smile he would send her way. He would probably splash out on a new silk tie which he could admire in the window even as he reminded her that he was now the most successful account manager at Simcock and Bright and that Lucy's days were sadly behind her.

Only a few more days and she would be gone, back to the relentless grind of life with two small children, back to the life she had loved and been reluctant to leave. There was a strange sense of calm about Lucy as she worked. She took her time and enjoyed each moment looking out of the window, admiring the view even though it was of a grey sky, countless rooftops and a minute square of grass she could see from the very corner of her office. She even smiled as she looked over at the filing room that Grant had manipulated her into during her first week back in the office. Now that it was over, she almost relished those confrontations and her insistence that she was every bit as good as Grant Cassidy and would prove it.

'Lucy?

Looking up she found Simon standing in her doorway and the calmness took a slight detour. Her face blank, she watched him come in and close the door behind him, taking the seat opposite Lucy.

'I wanted to talk to you about …'

'I think we need to talk about …'

They both stopped and Lucy took a deep breath.

'Simon, what happened last night must never happen again,' she began.

His face fell and a frown settled between his brows.

'I'm sorry Lucy I don't …'

'No, please hear me out. If I did anything to make you think you should kiss me, then I apologise.'

'It was entirely my fault. I …'

'The fact is,' continued Lucy, 'I love my husband. We may be experiencing some problems, our changed circumstances have made life complicated, to say the least. But I love him. You have been a friend, a good friend. I've been grateful for the encouragement you've provided me with over the last few weeks but that's all it has been. A friendship.'

'Lucy I …'

'And if you can't accept that then maybe we need to stop …'

Stop what thought Lucy. She had insisted to Will that there was nothing to stop between herself and Simon.

'I'm leaving,' she said. 'I think it's the best thing to do in the circumstances.' She hoped he wouldn't ask what the circumstances were because it was still disorganised chaos in her head.

'Will has been offered the job and I don't need to work anymore so I'm leaving.'

It sounded very simple when said out loud. Maybe it was that simple and Lucy was making it a great deal more complicated.

'I'm leaving but in the meantime, I think we should stop …'

She was going around in circles. What exactly did they need to stop? Stop catching the same train? That seemed a little extreme, would they make a declaration each morning to say which train they intended to catch each day to avoid accidental meetings on the platform? Stop seeing each other? That implied that there had been a relationship in the first place. And that meant that maybe Lucy was just as culpable for the kiss as Simon.

'Maybe we need to avoid each other,' Lucy said carefully.

'I won't kiss you again.' Simon looked stressed, uneasy. His normal calm exterior was decidedly fraught. 'If that's what you want I …'

'Of course it's what I want! I love my husband, I need to make sure our marriage gets back on track. That's not going to happen if I spend my evenings kissing you on trains!' exploded Lucy.

'What I mean is, we can still be friends. You need someone you can talk to and I want to be that person…'

'No. Really Simon. It's best that we don't have anything to do with each other. Not after … well, you know.'

Lucy moved uncomfortably in her chair. She hadn't exactly pushed him off. She had stood there and let it happen.

'Maybe we became a little too close,' she continued a little more gently. 'But I think the best thing is if we …'

'I'm sorry about the kiss, I thought it was something you wanted as well but we can carry on being friends. I want to be there for you.'

Lucy looked a little alarmed. 'Will is there for me. He's the one I should have been talking to. I was trying to keep it all away from him because I didn't want him to be worried but he's the one I should be leaning on. And from now on I will.'

Simon's head drooped. 'Of course,' he said disconsolately. 'Of course.'

Lucy looked towards the door praying she would see Alice heading down the corridor towards Lucy's door. She wanted this conversation to be over.

'I'm sorry Simon. I didn't mean to give you any false …'

'Really, it's okay.'

She heard footsteps and looked up hopefully but it was Grant heading her way. He stopped when he saw she had someone in her office but catching sight of Lucy's wide, rather alarmed eyes, he pushed open the door.

Lucy smiled encouragingly, a rare occurrence when Grant entered a room and she saw his eyebrows fly upwards.

'Sorry to interrupt,' he said smoothly. 'I needed a quick word but if you're busy …?'

He smiled in Simon's direction and looked quizzically at Lucy.

'No, no. Simon was just leaving.'

For a moment nobody moved and Grant watched as Simon remained at Lucy's desk, clearly struggling with something. Then slowly he stood up.

'Yes. I was leaving. Goodbye Lucy,' he added and with another long look in her direction, he walked out and disappeared down the corridor.

Lucy couldn't help the release of the breath she hadn't realised she was holding, noticing that the hand resting on top of her desk was shaking slightly.

'Everything okay?'

Grant was standing in front of her desk, for once not preening or admiring himself in the window as he watched Lucy regain control.

'We er, I needed to speak to … we needed to clear …'

'None of my business Lucy dear,' Grant interrupted. 'Offices are the sort of places where people often get the wrong idea about things. Best to let everyone know where they stand.'

Lucy nodded, her calm air returning.

She stared out of the window as she had for much of the morning.

'Indeed,' she murmured.

'And nothing else is wrong?'

'No. Everything is actually very well.'

He watched her for a moment.

'You're leaving, aren't you?'

Lucy's head swung away from the grey sky to meet Grant's blue eyes.

'How on earth …?'

He sat down, straightening his tie in what was now a very familiar gesture.

'I'm good at reading people. That's what makes me good at my job. You're different today. It occurred to me it's because you've decided to leave.'

Lucy considered denying it but instead nodded her head.
'Yes.'

'And nothing I can say will change your mind?'

'No?'

'Any particular reason?'

'Home, work, life. You were right, it's a tricky act to balance and I haven't done a very good job of it. It's time to stop trying.'

'I see.'

Silence fell and they both gazed out of the window for a while.

'Of course, some might say it's because you can't take the competition.'

Lucy stiffened. 'Competition? You mean, you?'

'I can understand it,' Grant continued with his smooth smile back in place. 'You used to be number one in this office and now you're not, it's hard to take.'

Lucy's mouth opened and her eyes flashed as she prepared to tell Grant Cassidy what she thought of his theory. And then she caught the tiniest flash of humour in his eyes.

She grinned instead.

'Desperate for me not to leave eh?'

'I would prefer if you stayed,' he admitted.

'You don't mind the competition?'

'Better the devil you know.'

'Sorry Grant. Not even the prospect of showing you how good I really am can change my mind. I'm afraid my time here is ended.'

'Oh well,' Grant sighed as he stood up and tugged his jacket into place. 'The place will certainly be quieter without you. And of course, I will still have the pleasure of seeing you admit failure tomorrow when I sign Haydock Sportswear.'

'How do you know I won't sign Blooming Lovely?' challenged Lucy.

'It's not going to happen. We both know that. Although you came close,' he added in a condescending tone. 'You did better than I expected.'

'Because I'm good at my job,' flashed Lucy. 'I could give you a run for your money.'

'But you're not staying so that won't happen.'

Lucy's shoulders drooped a little.

'No,' she said reluctantly. 'No, it won't happen.'

'Then good luck with your life Lucy and prepare yourself for defeat tomorrow,' and he was gone leaving her almost regretting her decision to leave the office and Grant Cassidy behind.

Lucy didn't let anything distract her for the rest of the afternoon as she worked on her presentation, leaving it on her desk, completed and ready for delivery, before she gathered her bag and coat and walked into Rob's office.

He was pouring over some paperwork and barely looked up as she sat on the corner of his desk. Taking a white envelope from her bag, she laid it carefully in front of his computer. Rob stopped reading and stared at the envelope.

'Is that what I think it is?'

'It's my resignation. Were you expecting it?'

Rob leant back in his chair and met Lucy's eyes.

'Sort of,' he admitted. 'Although I was hoping you would enjoy being back at work enough to stay.'

Lucy nibbled on her lip. 'I'm afraid it was only ever going to be temporary Rob.' In the beginning, she had consoled herself with the thought that it wouldn't be for long and then she could walk away. It was only recently she'd accepted that she had come to love being back at Simcock and Bright. 'I'm sorry to have been a little untruthful with you, I just needed a job while Will found work.'

'I know but I was hoping …'

'You know?' Lucy's eyes opened wide. 'You know?'

'Yes. I'd heard on the grapevine that his company had gone under. I must admit I'd resigned myself to the idea that you were never coming back but I thought I'd give it one last go, bearing in mind you probably needed the money.'

Lucy's mouth was hanging open in astonishment. 'You knew all along that I was just coming back for a few weeks? You knew about Will?'

'Of course. Lucy darling, I may be getting old and a little senile but I was as sharp as you are once upon a time. There's

308

very little that happens in this office or,' his voice turning slightly gruff, 'to the people I care about, that I'm not aware of.'

'You let me come back. Even though you knew I wouldn't stay?'

'Of course. You were very good at your job.'

Lucy could feel her eyes filling with tears.

'I've let you down.'

'Nonsense! You are doing what you need to do. I heard about Will's new job and I wondered if this was on its way,' he said pointing to the white envelope.

Lucy couldn't answer. Her throat was tight with tears as she looked at Rob's slightly ruddy face.

'I take it Will approves of you leaving work?'

'He doesn't actually know yet. But I have to do it … for all sorts of reasons and one of those is Will.'

'Not having problems I hope? If there's one thing I would have put my money on it would be you two lasting the course.'

'Nothing that can't be resolved by me leaving.'

Rob picked up the envelope, twirling it in his fingers.

'I'll tell you what. Why don't we put this in here?' he opened a drawer and dropped the envelope inside. 'Just for now. The one thing I have learned about problems is that sometimes they change from day to day. And the solution changes with them. If you still want me to accept this next week, I will. But until then, it stays here.'

Lucy smiled a rather watery smile. 'I don't think that this ….'

'Humour me.'

She nodded. 'Okay.'

Sliding off the desk she set off towards the door before stopping and dashing back to press a kiss on Rob's cheek.

'You're a pretty amazing man you know,' she whispered as he blushed furiously. 'Thank you, for everything,' and then she left, feeling her way down the staircase amid the tears that were falling unchecked down her face.

Chapter 42

Lucy walked swiftly home. She wanted to get there as quickly as possible and tell Will her decision. He had to understand that all she wanted was him, not Simon, not her office, not a bigger desk or a better chair, just Will. Hopefully they could get back to where they had been and pick up some of the pieces.

Opening the kitchen door, the first thing that she noticed was the silence. There was no TV playing, no sounds of chatting, no washing machine whirring or children launching themselves at her knees.

'Will?' she said uncertainly. 'Will?'

The kitchen table was empty, except for two wine glasses and for a moment fear gripped Lucy's heart. Had Jen been here? Had Jen been sitting at the table drinking and chatting to Will just like Lucy used to. Had they been discussing what a bad wife Lucy had been and how Jen could do so much better?

'Will?' she shouted.

Her voice echoed around the empty kitchen and Lucy clutched her heart in panic. Had Jen taken them? Was Lucy too late to stop Jen taking over her life, taking her husband and her children?

'Will, where are you? Where are the children?'

She heard footsteps come hurrying down the stairs and looked over to see her husband skidding into the kitchen in his sock feet, his hair flopping everywhere, his blue eyes cautious.

'Sorry, I was just tidying Harry's toys.'

Lucy looked around. 'Where are the children?' she asked tremulously. Please don't say they're with Jen, she prayed. Please don't say that woman is looking after them.

'They're at Fran's. I explained that we had something to do and could she take them for a couple of hours.'

'Something to do?' echoed Lucy. 'What do we need to do?' she asked fearing for the answer.

'We need to talk.'

Sliding her coat from her arms, Will took her bags and pushed her gently down into a seat before grabbing a bottle of wine from the fridge and filling the two glasses on the table.

'We need to talk Lucy. We need to be honest with each other and talk about what is going wrong because,' his voice broke slightly and he put the bottle down on the table. 'Because I feel as though I'm losing you somehow and I don't want that to happen, I can't let that happen, I love you darling, with all my heart and soul and I will not let you slip away from me so we are going to sit here and talk, just the two of us until we know how each other is feeling, really feeling.'

Lucy held her breath. She looked into the blue eyes she knew so very well and held her breath.

'And I am going to start by saying how very sorry I am and that you were right. About Jen.'

The breath came out, in a big gush and she grabbed at her glass and took a gulp.'

'I truly believed Jen was a friend, someone to rely on. I thought she was great, always ready to jump in and encouraging me to talk about my worries and problems.'

Lucy stayed silent. That could have described how she felt about Simon.

'You told me she wanted more and I thought you were being jealous and unreasonable. I deliberately refused to back away from Jen because she was my friend, not one of yours I'd inherited with the children and the house, but my own friend and I thought you were being ridiculous.'

Will grabbed his own glass and took a restorative drink. 'But you were right, she thought our friendship was so much more than that.'

He wouldn't go into too many details he decided. It was bad enough that Jen had deceived him without making Lucy live through it all. 'She wanted us to be … more. She told me that you were having an affair with Simon and it's my fault that I let that idea stay in my brain.' He shook his head. He should never have listened; how could he ever believe that of Lucy? 'And you didn't seem to want to stop work despite telling me how difficult you were finding it and how much you wanted to stop so I started to think that it was because of Simon.'

Lucy looked down at the table. She could understand exactly how Will had been led unwittingly into a friendship that was so more than it seemed on the surface.

'But I understand now how stupid I was, how insane the thought was. I'm so sorry Lucy. I love you. I will always love you. I hope you can understand and I ....'

Lucy pressed her hand onto the back of Will's, stopping him mid-sentence.

Should she tell him what happened? That she too had relished a friendship with someone who it turned out had wanted more. At least Will had seen sense before it went any further. Well, she presumed he had. Or maybe he had kissed Jen one afternoon, between the cleaning and the washing, he may have pressed his lips on hers wondering what it would be like to kiss someone else.

She could ask him but did she want to know the answer? And if she asked, she would have to tell him about Simon and the kiss they had shared on the train, and would that help either of them?

'I understand,' she said. 'I really do understand. Simon ...'

She bit her lip. What she said next could help heal the wounds or stir up a hornet's nest.

'It turns out that Simon wanted to be more than friends,' she offered huskily. 'I told him today that I loved you and that I didn't think we should share our train journey home anymore.'

She could see in Will's eyes that he wanted to ask questions, that he wanted more information about Simon and his need for more. Lucy saw him struggling to accept what she had said and leave it where it belonged, in the past.

'And I also handed in my notice,' she added, providing a distraction. 'I told Rob I was leaving.'

Will's eyes flew to hers.

'Do you want to leave?'

And that was the tricky question. Lucy had spent the day wondering that very same thing and had come to the surprising conclusion that despite her complaints and her worries, she didn't actually want to leave Simcock and Bright. She had hated the thought of leaving her children each morning to spend the day consumed with office matters. But it hadn't taken her long to remember the thrill it gave her, the sense of accomplishment she felt at the end of the day. She would never be the Lucy Mathers of years gone by; her life was different now. The most important thing in the world were her children and no deal, however much effort she had put into it, would ever equal that. She would never be the person who was prepared to work until midnight, who never really stopped thinking about work, who woke up each morning raring to get back to the office. But she could still be good at her job, she could still be fantastic at her job. She just needed to find the balance.

'I am happy to leave, I don't want you to think …'

'Do you want to leave?'

Lucy swirled the wine in her glass and thought deeply.

'Not really.'

'Then don't.'

Panic erupted in Lucy's stomach.

'But I said once you got a job that I would leave and …'

'You said that once I got a job we could decide what to do for the best.'

'But you want me to …'

'I want you to do what makes you happy. And if that's working at Simcock and Bright, then that's fine by me.'

'But the children ….'

'We'll sort something out. The children will have two happy parents and that's worth a great deal.'

Will was leaning back in his chair. The anxious look had disappeared from his eyes and he looked more relaxed than Lucy had seen him appear in a long time.

'Maybe we both made mistakes, maybe we were both a little naïve. But the fact is that we want to make this work.' He leant forward to take Lucy's hand in his, his eyes blazing. 'And we can make it work. As long as we know we love each other, that's all that matters.'

Lucy looked into the blue eyes she adored. 'I love you,' she said in a clear loud tone.

Will grinned. 'And I love you.'

'And we're going to be alright.'

It was a statement not a question and Will nodded.

'We certainly are.'

'And work?'

'You decide what you want to do. We'll sort out childcare, I'll help.'

Lucy felt as though a dam had been released, letting free all the tension and worry of the last few weeks.

'Rob put my resignation letter in a drawer. He said we'd think about it later.'

'Clever man,' twinkled Will.

'Grant said I was only leaving because he won the bet.'

'Foolish man. He should know that will only make you work even harder.'

'I think Alice is in love with him.'

'God help her.'

'I'm beginning to suspect he may be in love with her.'

'So he may have a heart after all?'

Lucy giggled. 'Let's not get too carried away. But I would like to keep an eye on them.'

'Of course. True love isn't always the smoothest of paths.'

'Ours has been a little bumpy lately,' admitted Lucy.

'Nothing we can't cope with. Not as long as we've got each other.'

Peeping up at Will from beneath her lashes, Lucy had a suggestion. 'Maybe Jen would baby sit for us?'

Will choked, spraying the wine he was drinking over the table.

'I think not. All contact with Jen has stopped forthwith.'

Lucy wondered what had happened. Maybe she would ask one day, when some time had passed and she felt a little stronger. Maybe Will would ask what happened between her and Simon. Maybe she would tell him.

'What time is Fran expecting us?'

'Oh not for a while,' grinned Will. 'I thought we might appreciate some time together. Just the two of us.'

Lucy sighed with happiness. She emptied her glass and stood up, taking Will by the hand.

'Then why don't we continue this conversation upstairs,' she whispered.

'That's a good idea,' said Will solemnly. 'I need a hand changing the sheets and emptying the laundry basket ... ow!'

Wincing from the blow Lucy aimed at his back he swung her round in his arms. 'Have I told you I love you today?'

'I think you have,' murmured Lucy. 'But you can always tell me again,' and with a little squeal she found herself hoisted up in Will's arms as he flicked off the kitchen light, grabbed the bottle of wine and carried his wife upstairs.

Chapter 43

'Harry, eat your breakfast and stop messing around. Emily, you can read that later, find your shoes. And both of you .... wow.'

Will stopped his efforts to organise the children and whistled at his wife as she stood in the doorway.

It was the morning of the Blooming Lovely launch and she had pulled out all the stops. Her favourite power suit from the pre-baby wardrobe had been rescued and was not only on, but fastened and with room for Lucy to breath. Her chestnut hair shone in perfect waves on her shoulders, her face was bright and full of confidence and on her feet were her Christian Louboutin shoes, adding four inches to her height and making her look every inch the successful business woman.

'You look amazing,' said Will with an appreciative smile. 'I'd sign with you in an instant.'

'You don't want to open a floral superstore in the middle of Leeds.'

'But I would if you told me it was a good idea.'

Lucy chuckled. 'Let's hope they appreciate me as much as you do,' she said giving herself a final check in the mirror.

'Right I'm off, be good for daddy please,' she said dropping kisses on two small heads. 'and ...oh.'

Will swept her into his arms and ignoring her bright red lipstick and the carefully brushed hair, he kissed her firmly, wrapping his arms around her slim figure.

'Goodness me,' said Lucy looking quite flustered. She looked down at Emily and Harry who were watching the exchange with interest as they spooned cereal into their mouths.

'Well, I'm going to have to check my makeup on the train but what a send-off!'

'Good luck my darling. I know you can do it.'

Lucy certainly hoped so and she spent most of the journey into work going over her pitch in her head, her stomach a swirling mass of nerves.

Will wasn't the only one impressed with her appearance and she saw several heads swivel as she walked through the office and into Rob's, sliding herself onto the corner of his desk as she had a million times before.

'Good Morning,' she said brightly as she placed a coffee for Rob in front of him and openly admired Grant.

'Looking very sharp today,' she said innocently. 'Got anything special happening?'

She heard a chuckle from Rob as Grant smoothed his already smooth silk tie and checked his jacket.

'Actually, I'm signing my new client,' he said calmly. 'Pity you didn't manage to sign yours but there again I did tell you I would win.'

'You haven't won,' answered Lucy, equally calmly. 'I have a meeting with Blooming Lovely this morning.'

'You are giving them a presentation. Nobody says yes at a presentation,' dismissed Grant.

'Of course they do, if the presentation is good enough.'

'And you think yours is?'

'Absolutely!'

Grant allowed a small laugh to escape and he stood up. 'Perhaps it's for the best that you're leaving,' he taunted. 'You appear to have lost your grip on the realities of the business.'

'Or maybe it's just you that's never managed to sign a client up at a proposal meeting,' suggested Lucy in a mocking voice as she slid from the desk and took a step forward. 'Perhaps it's a good that I'm leaving so you don't feel quite so pressured.'

They were standing with only a few inches between them, Lucy an inch or two taller than normal courtesy of her heels, staring each other in the face like prize fighters about to enter the ring.

Laughing Rob stood up and walked round the desk, placing a hand in between them both.

'I have to say I'm disappointed you're not staying Lucy. You two have made the office a far more interesting place recently.'

They stepped back allowing Rob to force a little more space between them.

'Well if you will excuse me,' said Grant, 'I need to collect the contract for my client to sign. I should have it on your desk before lunchtime Rob,' and with a victorious grin he walked out.

'And I need to prepare for Blooming Lovely,' said Lucy happily and with a grin in Rob's direction, she left and made her way to her office and an anxious Alice who was going to assist her.

Lucy had the larger of the meeting rooms. Denise Albright was being accompanied by four members of her team and as Lucy was giving a full presentation, she needed the projector and the whiteboard.

She was standing in the room, anxiously looking round to make sure everything was perfect when she heard voices and saw Alice stepping forward to welcome the Blooming Lovely delegation and lead them in the direction of the meeting room. Looking across she could see into the smaller meeting room where Grant was laying several folders on the desk and preparing for his meeting with Haydock Sportswear. He looked up and they stared at each other through the glass until the door opened and Lucy turned to greet Denise Albright.

The meeting was long and gruelling. Lucy went through every stage of her proposal. She had answers to every question, forecasts for every eventuality, diagrams, facts, figures, examples and every point they brought up she covered smoothly. Halfway through she took off her jacket, hanging it carefully over the back of a chair and looked up to see that Grant was meeting his guests. Hands were shaken and greetings made as Grant led them into his meeting room, catching Lucy's eyes as he did so. Lucy saw him reach for the blinds that would obscure any view of the office but then his hand paused. He held Lucy's gaze for a moment and then with a smug smile he turned his back, leaving the blinds up and the view clear. Lucy grimaced. He wanted her to see him beat her. She would be able to tell when the meeting had finished and the documents had been signed and as he walked triumphantly out of the door and into Rob's office, he would walk right past her window leaving her in no doubt that he had crossed the finishing line.

Turning around to her gathered group, Lucy launched herself back into the task in hand with even more vigour and positivity and continued to convince Denise Albright that Simcock and Bright were the only agency who could meet her needs.

As the morning wore on, Lucy became aware of a great deal of activity from the other meeting room. Papers were being passed around, frowns had settled on a few faces and someone from the main office had been called on to dash between the meeting room and the printer as more and more paper was being produced. Having been there herself on many occasions, Lucy deduced that some term or other had been disputed last minute which would result in the contract being amended. The contract would still be signed, she had no doubt, but it looked as though it wasn't quite as straightforward as Grant had hoped.

Concentrating on her own meeting, Lucy pushed, cajoled and explained until it was done. All questions had been answered, every point covered and finally could sit back in her chair, her feet glad of the rest as she looked round the room. It had gone as well as she could have dared hope and the vibe she had from the room was supremely positive.

'And all I can say now,' she sent a smile round every person in the room, 'is that I hope you agree that Simcock and Bright are the best people to represent you in this very exciting step in the growth and development of Blooming Lovely.'

She received a small round of applause which she took graciously even as she cast a glance over to Grant's room to see how the signing was progressing. The frowns had gone and every head was now bent over the small pile of paper set in front of each one of them. It looked as though they had reached the final stage. Grant would shortly be prancing past her window, holding up his contract so she could see it clearly.

'Thank you so much for a truly excellent presentation,' said Denise Albright. Lucy tried to look humble although she did, in fact, feel very pleased with herself.

'It's not a difficult decision because I had already decided that you would be the ideal person to help us through this very important stage for our company.'

Lucy stopped thinking about Grant Cassidy and gave Denise her full attention, a little shiver travelling down her spine.

'I've asked a few people about you and heard nothing but good things.'

'People?' asked Lucy blankly.

'Well, Mr McCarthy for one. Mr McCarthy senior.'

'Mr McCarthy?' repeated Lucy. 'Mr McCarthy of McCarthy and McCarthy?'

'Yes. He's my father in law, well he will be shortly.'

Lucy's mouth gaped open. She had read everything there was to know about Denise Albright, how had she not known this fact.

'He is?' she asked faintly.

'Yes. A recent event,' added Denise looking down at the large diamond ring on her hand in the manner of someone who was still getting used to its presence. 'He has nothing but good things to say about you.'

'I see.'

'There's no point beating about the bush,' began Denise. 'We like the proposal, we like you. I don't think there's anything to be gained by us saying we'll think about it. We want to engage Simcock and Bright. Let's get the contract signed so we can get moving on this.'

Lucy heard Alice give a little gasp from the opposite end of the table and Lucy's eyes swung back over the corridor to Grant's office. He was looking relieved and the Haydock team were nodding at each other in satisfaction. They were about to sign.

'I don't suppose you have a contract ready but as soon as ...'

'I do actually.' Lucy hoped her voice sounded normal because she was having trouble breathing and the whole room had taken on the echoey atmosphere of a swimming pool.

'I have a contract drawn up and ready.'

'Ah, confident eh? I like it.'

No, thought Lucy. Desperate. It had made her feel better continuing to believe that she could sign Blooming Lovely up today, even as her head had agreed with Grant and told her there was no chance.

She glanced over to Grant's meeting, unable to help the small smile of victory from curving her lips. They still hadn't signed. Pens had appeared on the table but yet again someone was pointing to something on the contract and the rest were all looking at their own copies.

'Absolutely,' agreed Lucy. 'I believed we were the best choice for you.'

She stood up, her legs trembling as she grabbed the pile of documentation she had laid out in readiness for the meeting. Pulling out the contract, she risked a quick glance at Grant. He was leaning over and explaining something, a hint of exasperation on his face. Her hand shook as she returned to the table. She glanced at her watch, at Denise Albright pen in hand, smiling and back over at Grant who was running a hand through his normally immaculate hair. They still hadn't signed.

'The contract is exactly as we've just discussed,' said Lucy, trying to keep her voice under control. 'Obviously you'll want to read it through.' She saw Ollie from the main office dash over to the printer yet again and then head towards Grant's room.

She pulled out her pen, the one Will had bought her many birthdays before, and sat down rather heavily in her chair.

'So let me get the ball rolling,' she opened the folder and flipped straight to the back page where at the bottom sat her name and that of Denise Albright. She signed in the empty space and glancing at her watch again she filled in the date and next to it the time before pushing the contract over to Denise.

She was finding breathing difficult, and swallowing, and moving. She could hear the beat of her heart and she could hear small anxious noises coming from Alice as they both watched Denise take the contract and start to read it through. Lucy stood up and walked to the window. Grant was distributing new sheets around the room but he saw Lucy staring and he stopped to look past her at the team from Blooming Lovely, sitting around the table reading their contract.

His eyes swivelled to Lucy in disbelief and then with a surge of energy he almost threw the rest of the paperwork across the table and grabbed a pen. Lucy could see his shoulders moving as he spoke, his arms were waving and the energy he was giving out could be felt across the office. The Haydock Sports team adopted a slightly bemused expression but as Grant continued to gesticulate, it seemed they all sat up straighter and began to read a little faster.

Lucy turned back to her own group who were racing through the contract as Denise nodded and continued to turn the pages. Lucy wondered if she were going to be sick. Alice certainly looked as though she were about to throw up in the waste basket next to her. Lucy willed herself to remain calm although she had an overwhelming urge to grab Denise by the neck and scream at her to stop reading and just sign.

She looked over her shoulder. Grant was standing stock still in the middle of the room. Even from here she could tell he had stopped breathing and they both watched one of the Haydock directors reach out and take hold of a pen and as though in slow motion, lift it nearer to him before settling it on the paper and signing.

Grant's eyes flew to hers and he grinned, throwing back his head and laughing in exultation. They had signed.

Behind her Denise had reached the final page. 'All looks exactly as we discussed. That's great.'

With no more ado she signed, her hand moving easily over the paper before she pushed it back across the desk to Lucy.

Blooming Lovely had signed and lifting the contract, Lucy looked through the glass to see Grant watch her in disbelief as she held it up high so he could see what she was holding.

There was a general hub as the Blooming Lovely team walked out and almost into the arms of the Haydock group and for a few minutes the office was full of noise as they all made their goodbyes and departed. As the last person turned to walk down the stairs only Grant and Lucy were left facing each other and both dropped their eyes to the contract the other was holding. Without uttering a word, they both turned in the direction of Rob's office and set off walking briskly, Lucy almost sprinting trying to keep up with Grant's long stride.

Looking out of the corner of her eye, Lucy could see that Grant was ahead of her, his naturally long stride eating up the distance between himself and Rob's office and with a small grunt she went up a gear almost skipping in an effort to keep pace with him. She saw the filing cabinet move across their path a second before Grant did and she swerved to the right even as he made contact, hitting his shin on the hard metal and yelping with pain. The poor unfortunate person who had decided to relocate his files gave an alarmed shout and ducked as Grant vaulted over the cabinet and staggered leaving him a few steps behind Lucy as she aimed for Rob's door. She saw Rob look up, no doubt alerted by the thundering footsteps and the yelling and she was close enough to see his eyes grow wide as he took in the approaching figures. Lucy was breathing hard, forging ahead before she gasped and lost her balance, tottering wildly along the floor. Something was holding her back, hanging onto her legs and with an outraged shout she pushed on, waving her arms around as she tried to regain her balance. Looking down she saw that her heel had caught in the strap of a handbag peeping out from behind a desk. She didn't have time to stop and pick it up and with an enormous effort she lifted her foot high, mid run and kicked it free, watching the bag sail through the air, disgorging its contents across the office. Grant had the lead again but as the door approached with a few more steps all that was needed to reach the office and Rob's amazed face, an unwitting pair of workers wandered right across their path. Noticing Grant and Lucy hurtling towards them at speed their conversation halted and they froze mid-sentence, grabbing each other's arms. Grant lurched sideways, taking a few steps to the left to swerve around them and skidding back on track. If Lucy went around them she would have to navigate a desk and a pot plant. With a loud yell worthy of any rugby forward dismissed a sideways step and instead ploughed through the centre, sending both workers flying in opposite directions.

'What the …'

Rob leapt to his feet and took an involuntary step back as both Grant and Lucy reached the doorway at the same time. Both tried to storm through, their shoulders wedged together as they refused to give way.

Lucy brought her elbows up and landed one sharply in Grant's side but instead of delaying him, it gave him the impetus he needed and he catapulted through the door and in two strides he was at Rob's desk'

'I've signed up Haydock Sports,' he shouted.

With a howl Lucy jumped forwards aiming herself at the corner of Rob's desk as she had a hundred times before. But her speed was her undoing and as her bottom landed on the polished surface she skidded across until rather than sitting on the corner she was laid almost full length across his computer.

'I've signed up Blooming Lovely,' she gasped.

Rob was looking at them incredulously. Struggling to sit up, Lucy saw that the outer office had come to a standstill as everyone stared into Rob's office in amazed silence.

Grant pushed Lucy's contract out of the way.

'I signed my client first,' he insisted. 'I signed them at, 'he glanced down at the contract in his hand, 'at 11:08.'

Lucy was still trying to pull herself upright but the papers underneath here were sliding around and she couldn't get any grip. She held her contract up so she could show Rob the time as she lay across his desk

'I signed them up at,' she looked at her contract, '11:08.'

'No! I signed first. I was watching, Denise hadn't signed when Haydock did,' said Grant in outrage.

'But I signed. And that's part of the contract,' argued Lucy, realising her skirt was starting to ride up with all the wriggling she was doing.

'You signed first! You put in the time and then got them to sign? That's unfair!'

'Why? At least I didn't have to get it reprinted half a dozen times before they'd put their pen to it.'

'You cheated,' yelled Grant. 'You cheated so you could win.'

'And you wouldn't' shouted Lucy back, rolling round on the desk looking for a way off. 'You wouldn't move heaven and earth to win?'

They glared at each other, Lucy noticing for the first time ever that Grant's tie wasn't straight as he stared down at her laying across the desk, waving her arms around as she tried to stand up.

He started to grin, his lips stretching and his smile becoming wider and wider until it broke out into a laugh and once he started laughing he just couldn't stop. For a moment Lucy gave him an indignant scowl. Then she looked down at herself languishing across Rob's desk, legs flailing, determined to be number one again. A giggle erupted, followed by another and another until uproarious laughter left her struggling to breathe.

She was aware that an astonished Rob had sat back down, watching as Grant held out his hand and helped Lucy get off the desk, as gracefully as she could under the circumstances.

Laughing until they were exhausted, holding each other up as their sides began to ache, they eventually stopped, both sitting down and placing their contracts in front of an amazed but chuckling Rob.

'I think I have to declare that one a draw,' he said wiping his eyes on his tie.

Lucy pulled down her skirt to a more respectable level and Grant straightened his crooked tie.

'Agreed,' they both chorused.

'And now, do you mind if I have a word with Lucy alone?' said Rob with a slightly more serious face. 'There are a few things we need to discuss.'

Grant nodded, taking a moment to compose himself before giving Lucy a slight nod and leaving the office. Lucy, still recovering, sat back in the chair, wondering how many times she had sat here in front of Rob as they discussed business in particular and the world in general.

Rob opened his drawer and took out the envelope. He held it between two fingers and raised an eyebrow at Lucy.

She shook her head. 'Change of plan,' she said cheerfully.

'Good.' Rob dropped it into the bin.

'Not so quickly, you might not like what's coming,' warned Lucy.

'Try me.'

'I want to start later, after I've taken the children to nursery,' she began.

Rob nodded.

'And I will be finishing at 5:00. Exactly at 5:00, without any admonishing looks because I'm going home on time or insinuations that I'm not putting in a full day.'

Rob nodded.

'And I'm not taking all the baby accounts. It will do you and Grant good to deal with some of them,' she added darkly. 'I prefer dealing with the likes of McCarthy to Erin and her Bountiful Baby Foods.'

Rob pulled a face but nodded.

'And I want to be recognised as an account manager, not Grant's assistant or some sort of second class being because I took time off to start my family.'

Rob opened his mouth to argue but Lucy leapt in. 'Oh you may not realise you're doing it but believe me there's a definite attitude towards mothers returning to work and I won't feel grateful that I've got a job when I've also got babies. I've got a job because I'm good!'

Rob smiled and nodded.

'Although I am actually grateful Rob, very grateful, because I realise you tried to help me and you did offer me my job back when you thought I needed it and I can never thank you enough.'

Lucy's voice trembled a little and both their eyes were suspiciously bright.

'So, if you're happy with my terms, I would like to stay at Simcock and Bright please.'

Lucy left early. She announced to Rob that it had been a tiring day and she was leaving and with the account she had signed up, Rob just shrugged his shoulders and said okay.

She knew that there may always be a little part of her that worried whenever she arrived at the train station, just in case she caught sight of Simon on the platform. But she could cope with that. She felt as though she could cope with anything at the moment.

When she arrived home, Will was up to his armpits in fish fingers and mushy banana and for a moment she stood in the kitchen doorway and watched her family. The house was a tip but Lucy didn't care. She would have to get used to it when both she and Will were working and who cared anyway. As long as they were all happy.

'Early? Goodness me, first day as a permanent worker at Simcock & Bright and you've sloped off early.'

'New start! New me!'

'Rob didn't mind.'

Lucy sat at the table and nibbled at a little bit of left-over fish finger.

'You know Rob,' she said happily. 'He doesn't sweat the small stuff. As long as I keep signing up the clients, he's happy.'

'Right – just a minute. Blooming Lovely signed up?'

Lucy tried to look casual and failed.

'They did,' she giggled. 'What else did you expect.'

'Of course they did,' said Will with a grin. 'I'd expect nothing less from Lucy Mathers Accounts Manager. Absolutely nothing less.'

Chapter 44

'Where are Harry's shoes?' shouted Will, looking frantically through the pile on the floor.

'Have you looked in the utility room? He's started putting them away when he comes home.'

'Got them!'

Will lined up both children's shoes and coats by the door. He had thrown in a pile of washing and taken out some mince to defrost. 'I thought we could have lasagne for tea,' he yelled up the stairs.

'Good idea.'

Lucy appeared, dressed in a slim fitted blue dress that gathered across her waist in soft folds and emphasised the narrow waistline that had re-emerged. She slipped on a pair of stilettoes and grew a few inches.

'You look nice,' murmured Will.

'Got a potential new client coming in this morning. Have you checked Emily's bag?'

'Yep, all present and correct.'

Will picked up his briefcase. He left before Lucy who always took the children to nursery before jumping on the train into Leeds. The traffic was diabolical as it always was and he had no doubt he would spend the next hour in a bad-tempered gridlock with horns blaring and motorists shouting. He loved every minute of it.

'See you tonight,' he said grabbing his wife and pulling her close for a kiss. 'Have a good day.'

Lucy gave the kitchen a quick tidy before hurrying the children out of the house. Harry had joined Emily at nursery and a childminder called Annie picked them up at lunch and took them to her house where they stayed until Lucy collected them on her way home, having always caught the early train. The children loved Annie and came home every day with stories of the adventures they'd had and a collection of paintings and artwork they'd done. Sometimes Lucy wanted to be the one to take them to feed the ducks and make spaghetti pictures. But never enough to decide to leave Simcock & Bright and she was just grateful that Emily and Harry were happy and settled.

Walking briskly through the centre of Leeds, she held up her face to the sun, high and bright above the streets. She loved this walk, a few minutes to get herself ready for the day ahead. And today she had a very important job to do before the real work of the day began.

She had been keeping a careful eye on Grant's diary, waiting patiently for the right moment and this morning she and Alice had the opportunity Lucy had been waiting for. Catching Alice's eye, they both walked down the corridor and stopped outside Grant's office.

'Ready?' asked Lucy.

Alice giggled. 'Ready.'

Alice continued down to Lucy's office while Lucy opened the door to Grant's. She still regretted not having her old room back, but she understood that Rob couldn't turf Grant out simply because Lucy was emotionally attached to the space that had been hers for so long. But there was something she could reclaim. Sliding behind Grant's desk she pulled the chair out, pushing it towards the door. She peered down the corridor to make sure Grant hadn't arrived earlier than expected and then back up the corridor to check Alice was in place.

'Go!' she giggled and like a red arrows manoeuvre, they slid the chairs out of one door, passing each other smoothly in the corridor and then back into the next door.

'Welcome home,' whispered Lucy as she slipped into the black leather seat.

Grant would never spot the difference. To him the chairs were identical. Maybe to everyone else they were identical, but Lucy knew this was the chair she had been sitting in when her waters had broken, her first day as a mother. If she'd just asked, Grant would probably have swapped chairs without the need for an early morning drama. But he would have smirked and made her feel as though she were being silly thought Lucy as she leant back. She could swear this chair was more comfortable. This way was much more fun.

She looked out at the blue sky and grey rooftops, a view so very familiar. She was back, Lucy Mathers, Account Manager. Back in her chair where she belonged. Now, she thought with a little smile, she just had to work out a way of getting her old office back!

The End

Printed in Great Britain
by Amazon

80134278R00192